D0917659

Murder on Mount Desert

Murder
on
Mount Desert

DAVID RAWSON

Down East Books

To Gail

Copyright © 1995 by David Rawson
Jacket illustration © 1995 by Chris Van Dusen
Cover design by Tim Seymour Designs
Color Separations: High Resolution, Camden, Maine
Printed and bound at Capital City Press, Inc., Montpelier, Vt.

2   4   5   3   1

Down East Books
P.O. Box 679, Camden, Maine
BOOK ORDERS: 1-800 766-1670

This is a work of fiction. Names, characters, places, and incidents either are the
product of the author's imagination or are used fictitiously. Any resemblance to
actual events or persons, living or dead, is entirely coincidental.

Library of Congress Cataloging-in-Publication Data

Rawson, David, 1963-
    Murder on Mount Desert / David Rawson.
        p.   cm.
    ISBN 0-89272-373-4 (hardcover)
    ISBN 0-89272-363-7 (paperback)
    I. Title.
PS3568 . A86M87   1995
813'.54—dc20   95-34706
                                                        CIP

1

Thursday Evening
Patrol Area: Mount Desert Island
Temps mild; wind 5–8 knots, SW;
calm seas and clear skies

A compelling satisfaction consumed me as I completed a pair of citations. Don't misunderstand me: I perform my duties for the Hancock County Sheriff's Department with utmost sincerity and not a trace of vindictiveness. Job satisfaction followed a job well done, not another notch on my gun. I felt the self-fulfillment that comes from a quarry stalked, a trap well-laid, and the prey's fate inevitable. This target I had tracked for weeks. The eventual capture transcended satisfaction: it felt wonderful.

That night I chased neither bank robbers nor jewel thieves, only a speeder. Many people laugh at the posted speed limits; most occasionally "bend" them to their interpretations. When you've seen a gory, needless death caused by speed, as I have, you don't laugh so loudly. Speed limits exist for a reason; they are serious business. I'm not claiming I never bend the laws myself. I keep up with traffic like everyone else. Yet for any set of traffic, road, and weather conditions, there's a finite limit to how fast I'll go, no matter how many cars may pass. Even with my training in high-speed driving, I find that the posted limits are usually a good idea.

The scofflaw in this case: a summer racer. Many people acquire new cars during the long Maine winter. Kids often acquire powerful machines that can't be put to the test on snowy, ice-shrouded roads. When summer comes, it's time to pop the T-tops, roll down the windows, crank up the stereo, and race for the coast. It happens every year, just as reliably as every year around graduation there occurs a rash of fatal accidents.

This quarry perfectly fit the profile. As the summer flocks returned to their nesting grounds, reports about a black car flooded the sheriff's department. It would materialize behind another car, close rapidly behind blinding headlights, then charge past to roar into the night. One county patrolman came close enough to identify the car as a late-model Corvette, satin black. Witnesses described the occupants as a gaunt, dark-haired male about eighteen years old and alongside him, a girl the same age, generally wearing an indiscreet halter top, her long blonde hair fluttering like a flag out of the roof. Mud and road dust obscured the license plate; witnesses could not even verify a Maine registration. He evaded every speed trap as if he knew where it would be. So far he'd been lucky: no collisions, no pedestrians wounded lurching out of his way. But time must eventually prevail.

To catch him demanded brain power, not horsepower. I plotted my trap, looking for a weakness, waiting. When the rotation put me on nights, I had deduced enough of a pattern to catch him. While he avoided a regular route, he confined himself to the same handful of roads. Once reaching the island he would travel down one side, up the other, on no particular route. The geography of Mount Desert Island meant the roads on the east side met those from the west at a single choke point at the top of Somes Sound. There was his weakness. I had found a mile-long chink in his armor.

Luck helped. Only one bridge links MDI with the mainland, at Thompson's Point on the north side. The road forks immediately after the bridge, forming the two major arteries down the east and west sides of the island. Anyone coming onto the island has to use that bridge, then take one of the branches. Thus my plan. The fork is guarded by a convenience store, where one of the night crew knows me. I needed her to tell me which way the Corvette went. Armed with that, I could take him.

Around eight, I patrolled the north end of the island. From the reports I knew he appeared just after sunset. I planned to stay close to the fork until dark. If he hadn't showed up, I'd continue the patrol elsewhere. I didn't expect success the first night; I certainly didn't expect the car to flash by as I strolled out of the store. Naturally, he obeyed the posted limits: a green-and-white Caprice with light bar and five antennas is not easily hidden. He took the east fork, toward Bar Harbor. I looked closely. There could be no mistaking the drawn figure of the driver, or the blonde hair streaming out of the roof. The dark machine gleamed under the streetlights as it growled southward. The road crested a small rise, turning sharply left. There I lost sight of the car. It didn't take hearing as acute as mine to detect the change in pitch as he hit the gas.

A charge of adrenaline energized me as I calmly opened the door. I did not need to hurry: I had done my homework. I started the engine, backed clear of the pumps, and nosed down the west branch of the fork.

I had to fight to keep the excitement from usurping control. Though I had done little more than catch a glimpse of my quarry, I could feel the jaws of the trap closing. I knew my feelings were woefully premature; such thoughts could blow the whole plan. Nevertheless, the pursuit thrilled me. I intently watched the road, concentrating on driving. I prayed the radio did not call me away to some menial task. Every belch of static jabbed at me, twisting my stomach until I heard someone else's code called.

It would take time for the Corvette to complete the circuit of the east side before zipping over the sound. I did not rush, cruising to the turnoff a quarter hour after leaving the store. I headed across the top of the sound and took up position just beneath the crest of a hill, near a phone company shack. I parked, killed the lights, flipped up the switch on my radar to READY, but not ON. It was ready for immediate acquisition but no radar detector could defeat it.

I waited as the dusk melted into a clear night. It was unusually clear for early summer in Maine. I found the constellation of Virgo in the southern sky, Spica a spot of blue luminescence just off the horizon. The sky progressed from the pale blue of sunset to a deeper blue, then to the cold indigo of night. I hadn't watched the stars in some time. With little light pollution, the sky passed from day to night with amazing speed.

Utility lines overhead glowed, betraying a car coming over the hill. I put my finger on the radar switch, flipping it to ON as the car broached the hill. Forty-five in a thirty-five zone—a clear violation. The quiet approach told me this was not my target. I snapped on my parking lights. As the driver approached and saw my cruiser, I saw the reflected glow of his brake lights. On another night I would have taken him; tonight he was small fry. I let him pass, dousing the lights after him.

I reset the radar and returned to the stars. Trees behind me obscured the northern stars. Without the big dipper, I had trouble identifying the constellations. So many stars made it difficult. I stared heavenward and started creating my own constellations.

A distant rumble cut through the still night. Seemingly unremarkable at first, it rapidly evolved into something interesting. As it grew closer I realized I listened to the throaty snarl of those chromed exhaust pipes. The volume surprised me. The calm night and the open waters of Somes Sound between us amplified the noise. The intensity increased, the pitch altering slightly as he worked the accelerator. I heard the squeal of rubber as he negotiated a corner, then the sound abruptly muffled as he dropped below the hill.

I fired the engine in preparation. My plans and a little luck had conspired perfectly. Nervous, I drummed my left fingers against the steering wheel, close to the radar switch, while my right hand poised near the toggle that would activate the blue lights. My hands were slimy, clammy with sweat. I dried my left palm on my trousers. A nervous contraction of muscles tensed my right index finger; it jumped and activated the lights. Suddenly all my attention refocused as I fumbled to snap down the switch. I looked around nervously, hoping that I had not betrayed myself. The Corvette did not yet show, though the headlights played on the lines overhead. The growl kept coming.

Then he appeared. Four white headlights peeked over the rim of the hill, first aiming at the stars before the car bounced over the peak. I snapped on the radar, immediately triggering the alarm. I glanced at the indicator only long enough to verify a violation. The first digit was a six. After that it didn't matter.

Only one decision remained to be made, but it was not mine. I knew my radar technique denied him sufficient warning, but it would tell him he'd been tagged. Once he knew, what would he do? Flip around in the middle of the road and try to retreat? Or punch it and hope to outrun me? On a long straight run his car could beat mine without trying, but on the twisting island roads it would be a match. What would he do?

I wanted to deny him any advantage. I checked the road quickly, flipped on all my lights, and pulled onto the roadway, the engine gasping for more air as I rammed the pedal into the floorboards. I hoped the sight of a county cruiser in his path would stop him. At my advance he swung the wheel hard: he was trying to retreat. Once perpendicular to the road he was committed. I turned toward him and hoped to cut him off before he could accelerate away. If he made it over the hill with enough open road ahead of him he might escape. I dared not risk the innocent drivers ahead by engaging him in a nighttime high-speed pursuit. *My* chance would come again. The race was only to the top of the hill.

The race ended before it began. Maybe I overestimated his driving prowess, perhaps I had rattled him, or maybe he just hit something on the road. Whatever the cause, with his broadside to me he punched it. At first it looked like he might beat me. We were still five hundred feet apart, and my engine had only begun to crank out speed. Then he lost it. Instead of straightening, he fishtailed, pointing the Corvette toward the shoulder. The kid did a masterful job of avoiding the trees, but I did a better job of closing the distance. He got his wheels out of the sand only to confront my car blocking his escape. Gravel flew as he hit the brakes, skidding to a stop.

I relished the victory. I did everything in slow motion, letting him stew as I called the dispatcher. I slowly squared my flat-brimmed hat on my head, picked up my clipboard, and got out. I strode over to his door and began the process of issuing the tickets he had earned.

Half an hour later, after a full search of their records and the car, I signed my name to the bottom of the summons with a flourish. I double-checked the information, replaced my hat on my head, and returned to the Corvette. I had somehow neglected to tell the kid he could get back inside while he waited. I soberly handed him the summons, his registration, and license. "Sign here, sir."

He turned toward me, eyes glaring hotly. As the flashing lights alternately washed his face in blue or white, he transformed from savage to pitiful. He reached out to the clipboard, signing quickly, snapping down the pen with a loud click.

I tore off the copies, handing them to him. "Your court date is the thirteenth of next month." That the court date happened to fall on a Friday the thirteenth delighted me. "I'd advise you to read the back very carefully before you take any action. Understand?"

"Yeah." He whipped open his wallet and replaced his license, threw the registration into the car, then stuffed the summons into his back pocket. "I got it."

"I sincerely hope you do."

He nodded, turning toward the car. He mumbled something under his breath. While it didn't sound complimentary, I elected to ignore it anyway. I reached in front of him, blocking his path. "Uh-uh. You can't drive home. Your girlfriend will have to drive."

"Come on, man!" he pleaded. "I don't live that far, just up in Dedham! Let me drive it home. I'll leave it there. I promise, man. You can follow me, to make sure."

"Afraid not." I gestured for the girl to come around. I noticed she had put on a sweatshirt over the halter. I handed back her license.

"I'm going to broadcast your status, so don't try to change drivers. I may follow you to make sure, so be careful. I've been known to be in several places at once. Don't do anything stupid."

"Look, it's a new car!" He was begging now. I almost felt sorry for him. The thought of going home in the *passenger* seat of his new Corvette while his *girlfriend* drove would be something he wouldn't soon forget. "She's never driven it before, she doesn't know—"

Begging quickly wears thin. "Her license is relatively clean." I made sure she noted my disdain at her speeding citation. I backed up a little. "I could call a tow truck." I ran my hand over the fiberglass nose. It felt smooth, as if it had been waxed that morning. "I'd hate to see it damaged, though. Towing can be rough."

"Come on, Sean." The blonde had also had enough. "Give me the damn keys. Let's go home."

Two against one, he had lost. He handed over the keys. He pointed threateningly at my chest. "You'll hear from my father's lawyers by Monday morning."

I smiled. "I'll be up all night, waiting."

Defeat overtook him. I could see it in his sunken shoulders. He climbed in the passenger door, flopped into the seat, and slammed the door. The girl took the driver's seat, started the car carefully, and backed onto the road. She put it into gear (very smoothly, I thought), and started away. I watched them go, a grin stuck on my face. Whatever happened the rest of the night, no matter how dull or routine, my shift had been made. I tipped off my hat and climbed into the cruiser. I killed the blues, called the dispatcher to report I had cleared the scene, and headed over the hill.

Somes Sound is a rarity in North America: geologically speaking, it is a fjord, a deep, water-filled canyon with characteristic U-shaped sides. A magnificent view of the sound can be had by driving its eastern shore. Later that evening I did just that. A fringe benefit of being a patrolman in Maine is the opportunity to spend a clear night enjoying some of the most beautiful scenery in the world. A bright first-quarter moon danced on the calm water, a long shaft of silvery moonlight paralleling my northward course.

Unfortunately, some of the visitors choose to enjoy the area in bizarre ways. As I rounded a blind corner, my headlights caught a man walking down the middle of the road. "Walking" did the man a disservice: his unstable method of locomotion hardly justified that term. A stained T-shirt hung off his narrow shoulders, almost reaching the tops of his perforated jeans. Looking more closely, I noticed that bare feet propelled him along.

At first I thought him alone, then, about fifty feet ahead of him, a woman came into view. Clad in darker clothes, walking with a determined, firm stride, she did a good job of staying ahead of him. I heard the man pleading with her to stop, to wait for him. She went on. He stopped a moment, bent over as if catching his breath, then he lumbered ahead in a staggering run, finally catching up with her. She whipped around, her arms tightly folded across her chest. The volume and tenacity of their dialogue carried back to me clearly. If either of them had any idea of my presence, they kept it hidden.

The woman halted the debate by turning her back and stalking off. The man refused to let her go, and stumbled after her until they faced off for another round. I had no idea how long it had gone on, but decided they would only continue if not stopped. I sighed, reached under the dash, toggled the blues, and approached. They abruptly ceased arguing and turned toward me, the woman bearing an indignant face, the man befuddled. I parked to keep them in the lights, then stepped out. I switched on my Mag-Lite as I walked around the hood. A steel case and five D-cell batteries made it a good, yet very subtle, defense. "Can I help you?"

"Great," cried the woman. "Just great. See what you've done, you moron?"

The man turned to her, pleading. I noticed his words weren't exactly slurred, but they were hardly distinctly spoken. "Come on, Jan, it's not my fault. I said I was sorry, didn't I?"

He reached out to touch her hand, but she slapped it away. "Don't touch me."

"Okay," I said, intervening. "Sir, would you please step back?"

He reluctantly complied. He looked up at me, his eyes fluttering with alcohol in the beam of the light. "Yes, sir. I don't mean no trouble, sir."

"Good. What's your name, sir?"

He straightened up. "Paul Charrette."

"Do you have a license, Mr. Charrette?"

He patted his pockets, then shrugged. "I must have left it."

"Have you been drinking, sir?"

He smiled crookedly. "Just beer."

"Do you have any idea how many you've had tonight?"

He shrugged. "Eight or nine, I guess."

"I hope you're not planning to drive tonight, Mr. Charrette."

"Hell, no. I can barely walk."

"Good." I turned to the woman. "And you are?"

"Janice Patrick." She slid a hand into her back pocket and came out with a dog-eared Massachusetts license. I should have known. It seemed most of the summer problems were caused by the summer people, who brought their unusual ways and manners to Maine. "That really is his name, officer."

I handed back her license. "Are you two friends?"

She stole a glance at Charrette before answering. "Most of the time."

"What's going on?"

"I'm stayin' at a friend's house for the week," she explained. "Paulie rents out the house next door. Some friends came up tonight, so we had a little party. He came over, which was fine, but he kept drinkin' and drinkin', and well. . . ." She looked at him again, and shook her head. "He gets amorous when he's drunk, you know what I mean? Not dangerous—just amorous."

"Was anybody hurt?"

"No, nothing like that," she replied quickly. "I can usually handle him, but tonight he just kept at it. So I walked out. He followed me, and now he won't leave me alone."

"Thank you." By then, Charrette had found a tree to lean against while he tried to light a cigarette. "Mr. Charrette, have you been bothering Miss Patrick?"

"I didn't mean anything by it," he said after a moment. "I really didn't."

"She'd like you to leave her alone."

Charrette spoke to me, but he kept his eyes fixed on her. "Well, I'll try. But you know how women get."

"No, I don't. Why don't you tell me?"

"Oh, come on." His head bobbed up and down as he spoke. A glaze over his eyes told me he would likely pass out soon. "You know."

"Mr. Charrette, she has expressed a desire for you to stop. We have two choices. You can either leave her be, or I'll have to arrest you."

"Arrest me?" he said, a sudden flash of energy helping him to his feet. The flash quickly evaporated and he fell against the tree. "You can't do that."

"I can, sir. I would rather not."

He considered his options. Then he threw up his arms. "Okay, okay. I promise I'll leave her alone."

"All right." I turned to Patrick. "Where do you live?"

She pointed south. "About a mile and a half back that way."

"I'll take you both back home, if that's all right with you. I'll give you a number to reach me if he puts up any more trouble tonight."

"Okay."

I opened the passenger door for Patrick, then quickly frisked down Charrette before helping him into the back seat. I did a three-point U-turn in the middle of the road, hoping to get Charrette back home before he slipped into unconsciousness or threw up on my back seat.

After attending to a brawl at Blackwoods Campground in Acadia National Park, then taking the report of a Bar Harbor businessman who returned to his store to find the front window shattered, I pointed the cruiser into the driveway leading to the high school. Lights still burned in the lobby and cars dotted the lot. I drove past the door, turned around in the open lot beyond, parking close to the door. I picked up my portable radio from the charger, told the dispatcher I'd be out of the cruiser, and went inside. I went left, up a short staircase, down a darkened hallway. Tall windows looking out on the surrounding marsh covered one wall, oak-veneer doors with heavy brass latches the other. I pulled gently on the first door, hoping to open it quietly. My right hand dropped to the top of the radio to turn down the volume. The hinges creaked, making my entrance louder than I had hoped. I closed the door behind me and stood still while my eyes adapted to the darkness.

The only light in the big room came from the wash cascading down from the stage lights, seeping into the seats like fog over rocks. At first I could see nothing except actors on stage. Slowly shapes eased out of the dark shadows. It took a while for my eyes to adjust enough to discern people from seats. During that time I dimly noted the production being staged before me. I knew the name of it; at least, I knew that I had once been told.

Amid the scattered observers I focused on the shape I recognized, seated front and center—as befitted a director. I made my way down the aisle, slipped into the second row, and sidled along until I came behind her. "Hello," I said softly. "How's it going?"

The director waited until a particularly charged exchange of dialogue finished, then turned around. Even in the near-dark, backlit by the stagelights, her features were unmistakable. Shoulder-length sandy hair, disarrayed after a long day, framed her face with wavy borders. She had virtually no eyebrows, so pale were they against her freckled skin. Widely separated eyes perched on either side of the crooked nose—many years ago it had been broken by an overzealous brother and never did set just right. The dim lighting could not bring out the color of her eyes, but I knew they sparkled with the fire of emeralds. The lights did reveal the trademark teeth, large white incisors turned slightly inward, victims of the same accident that had broken her nose.

I've known Robyn Cole a long time. We grew up together in the village of Eagle Harbor, attended the same elementary and high schools, even belonged to the same church. Yet in spite of the proximity, we never knew each other until coincidence placed us in the same American Short Fiction class at the University. It didn't take long for two good students in the back row to realize we had something in common besides Faulkner. Things developed from there, through another two years of college, then back to the island. Our relationship had progressed to a comfortable plateau. Sometimes I wondered whether we were bound to climb to the summit or fall into the valley, but mostly I was glad to have made it so far.

She set her reading glasses on a small end table. "Hi, Jimmy. Slow night?"

"Average."

"Did you bag the Corvette?"

I couldn't help but smile; she couldn't help but notice. "I got him."

"Keeping the streets safe."

"It's my job." I leaned forward. "How're things going?"

She twisted around to check the production. "Okay. This scene took a lot of work. It still needs attention."

"I'm looking forward to the premiere."

"You managed to get it off?"

"Yuh. Barring too many sick-calls, anyhow. I wouldn't abandon you to face the critics alone."

"Screw the critics. The day these short-sighted, pompous old fools rate a show on its merits rather than how many times they laughed or how offended they are, I'm outta here."

I started to reply, but Robyn held up a hand. She checked her notes, watching the show. She saw something that eluded me. I saw four people trying to convince me the empty stage around them was the inside of their house as they planned the future and reminisced about the past. It looked fine to me: smooth, natural, well-timed. Robyn must have seen something else, because a flurry of scribbles went down on her legal pad.

She looked up. "We're getting there."

"Looks real good."

She nodded slowly. "A little rough around the edges. But the base is solid."

"You're the boss."

"I know." She turned back to the stage. As the dialogue ran on, the older male on stage grew more exasperated, his voice louder, shorter, more clipped. He hesitated a second, then stormed off the stage as the lights dimmed.

Robyn applauded loudly. "Very good, very good. You guys have come a long way." A set of red lights bathed the stage in fire. Robyn picked up her clipboard and squinted slightly. She resists glasses. "Skip the next scene, and the next, and set up for scene five. Maria, change the table props. Start in five minutes. This'll be the last one tonight."

From unseen quarters I heard people moving and talking as they carried out their orders. Robyn wrote down more notes before turning back to me. "You working 'til three?"

"Yuh."

"Still going to take me to the beach and lunch?"

"Yup."

"Pick me up by eleven?"

"Around ten, I think."

"What's the weather like?"

"The clouds disappeared. The stars are out, bright and clear."

She sighed. "I wish we could go down to the beach now."

So did I. "Not this weekend."

"Next?"

"Have to wait and see. Can never tell what the weather's going to be like tomorrow, let alone next week."

"That's the story of my life. Maybe we—"

I cut her off; I thought I'd heard my call number on the radio. I pulled it closer to my face and opened the volume. "County nineteen to dispatch, go."

"County nineteen," cackled the dispatcher sitting at the radio console miles away. "Jamie, are you still at the high school?"

An undesirable side effect of returning to your hometown as a law officer is that all the ladies who knew you as a kid continue to address you as they always have done. My mother had tried to create a nickname for me. It took until second grade to get rid of it. Still, a few who knew me when I was small persisted with the annoying appellation. At first you cringe: nothing's harder than acting in an offi-

cial capacity while being addressed as a kid. "Affirmative, dispatch."
"Ten-four, county nineteen, stand by." She paused only a few
seconds. "We have a report of a traffic accident on Route 102 South,
just north of Echo Lake. EMTs are responding."
    At the words "traffic accident" I moved, sliding out to the aisle.
"County nineteen. Ten-four. ETA five minutes." I didn't have time
to say good-bye to Robyn: I cleared the door, dashed through the
lobby and into the cruiser. I flicked on the lights and siren as the tires
churned up the gravel and spun it backward on the way out.
    I raced toward the scene, balancing on the tightrope between
driving faster than I could handle and reaching the scene in time to
help someone who might not have five seconds to waste. At such
times my concentration acutely focuses on the task of driving. The
scene of my earlier operation with the Corvette made only a fleeting
impression before I cleared the hill, passed the telephone shack, and
turned left onto 102.
    Echo Lake is about as far south of the intersection as the high
school is to the north. I covered the distance in good time. There
was no mistaking the scene of the accident. Two cars, their emergency flashers illuminating the area with amber light, parked alongside the road. One man walked along the roadway, setting up flares.
I saw no damage to either car. I parked the cruiser beyond the second car, leaving all the lights on. I picked up my radio and put it into
the leather holder, replaced my hat, grabbed my flashlight, and
opened the door. At first I saw nothing. I heard voices; two people
hovered on the other side of the cruiser, but I had to step beyond
the trunk before the grim sight struck me.
    Among the things a police officer must accept with his job are:
the prospect of imminent lethal danger; informing someone who
thinks their brother, spouse, or child is still alive that they are wrong;
and viewing the grisly remains of abrupt, violent death. The pink-
and-gray wreckage splattered over the asphalt before me had once
been a human being. The victim's back faced upward, the head
twisted at a grotesque angle over the shoulder. Legs and arms bent
at impossible angles, signifying shattered bones inside that would
have been excruciating had the victim been able to feel them. A long
path of blood, interspersed with shreds of clothing and larger pieces
of what I reluctantly realized were flesh, trailed away from the body.
A puddle of blood seeped downhill from the body. I did not need to
conduct a closer observation to know that the ambulance, its wailing
siren approaching, would be unable to offer any aid.
    I bit my lip, then took a deep breath and knelt alongside the

body. I detected no life signs, no movement that might signal breathing, no sounds, no blood pulsing from any of the dozens of open wounds. A tall, bearded man in his early thirties knelt opposite me, carefully examining what should have been a face. He looked up at me, shaking his head. "I tried to administer mouth-to-mouth, but he doesn't have a mouth anymore."

Not a single part of me doubted this stranger's word; not one neuron of the billions inside my head gave me any indication that I should. Yet my training demanded that I do what I could, and that meant checking for myself. I crossed to the other side, inadvertently placing my foot into the growing puddle. I had a firm footing, so I ignored it, but kept my knee off the ground. I gently reached out and touched the side of the head, not wanting to cause further harm. Nevertheless I had to move it slightly. I set my teeth and did so with gentle caution. The stiffness mutely shouted volumes. The bearded man had not lied. The man's mouth had disappeared amid broken facial and jaw bones, shattered teeth, dangling shreds of muscle that looked uncomfortably like fresh meat. Glassy, empty eyes confirmed all I didn't want to know.

The ambulance siren stopped and the vehicle slid to a halt. Only the bearded man spoke up. "I'm an EMT. I'll deal with the ambulance crew," he said. "I'll tell you about it later." The attendants moved quickly. I could see as they approached the body the same initial revulsion and horror I had felt, followed by the overpowering sense of duty and training. They were far more capable than I, even if nothing could be done. I left them to their job, as I returned to mine. I stood up and surveyed the people, a varied group of the curious. They would have to be questioned.

First, I had to make a preliminary report. I withdrew my radio. "County nineteen to dispatch."

Ruth, the night dispatcher who had been working the county radio longer than I'd been alive, responded somberly. How did she know? "County dispatch. Go, nineteen."

"County nineteen off at the scene. Ambulance has arrived. Fatal hit-and-run. Request another officer for traffic control, over."

"Ten-four, county nineteen. County seventeen is en route. Sergeant Dickinson is also responding."

"I'll be standing by."

"Ten-four, county nineteen."

I retrieved my notebook and pen from the cruiser and returned to the crowd. None of them looked to have any more information than any of the others; in fact none of them looked like they would be able to provide me with anything useful at all. "Did anybody see anything?"

As expected, I met with unanimous head shakes. Some of them looked from one to each other, as if they all tried to keep a secret from me. I knew they simply hungered to see if the guilty party stood among them. "See anything unusual? A car driving too fast, a car without any headlights?"

One man, older than the others, nodded slowly. He jerked his thumb over his shoulder. "I came down from that way. 'Bout fifteen minutes ago, I guess. Maybe less."

I made a note in the book. "Route 102?"

He looked up as if remembering. "Yuh, 102. When I drove by the fire station back in Somesville, I saw a car parked in the driveway."

An overactive imagination at work. I took notes anyway; often a tale might contain a shred of valuable evidence. "Why did you notice it?"

He cleared his throat. "Well, I might have been going a little fast through town. I thought it might be a cruiser, so I slowed down. But as I passed, I saw two people inside and no front plate."

"What kind of car?"

"Big American job. Maybe a Chrysler, I didn't get a good look at the grille but I thought I saw the pentagon. Didn't look new. Black, or maybe real dark blue."

"The people inside—did you see them?"

"Afraid not."

"Two men? Two women?"

"Sorry. Can't help you. Just a couple of people, lurking in the driveway."

"Lurking," I repeated.

"Yes, officer. Lurking."

"What's the difference between lurking and parking?"

"I don't know," he said nervously. "It just seemed suspicious— a dark car, two people in it. They were waiting for something."

"Sounds like parking to me."

"It's what I saw, officer."

"May I have your name, please?" He provided it, then his address. "Thank you. That may be a big help." More likely a dead end, I thought. There were so many legitimate reasons for it to be there. "Did anyone else see that car? Or anything else?"

"I didn't see the car," said someone else. I turned around to face a middle-aged woman, holding tightly to the arm of the man next to her. "I think I saw that man," she said, indicating the body on the road. "He was jogging along the side of the road."

"Where exactly did you see him? And when?"

"About half a mile up the road. We drove past him as we headed north, then turned around and ran into him—," she paled as she realized what she had said. "I mean, saw him again, with all the people here."

"We missed a turn and had to turn around," explained her companion. "It couldn't have been more than five minutes between when we first saw him until we came back."

"Which side of the road was he running on?"

She thought a moment. "On my left."

"He ran with the traffic, not against it?"

She looked at her friend before replying. "Yes. He seemed to be well off the road surface."

"Off the road surface? Was he on the dirt? Maybe on the grass?"

"Oh, he wasn't on the pavement. That's all I saw."

"How about a car like the one this man just described? Did you see that?"

"I don't remember."

"Several cars passed, perhaps five or six before we turned around," said the man. "I'm afraid I didn't look at other cars very carefully."

"Anything else you'd like to add?" They had nothing. I took down their names as well, and thanked them. Flashing blue lights approached. "Please wait a moment," I said to them all.

County twenty-three, patrolman Ed King, pulled up. "What's up?"

"Looks like a jogger, hit-and-run."

"What do you need?"

"I've got to ask a few more questions before I can clear these cars. Try to keep traffic moving, will you?"

"No problem." He pulled ahead and parked beyond the ambulance, and immediately started directing traffic around the accident. I returned to the witness pool.

The bearded man who had knelt beside the body met me. "My name's Levasseur. I'm an EMT, that's why I stopped."

"You were the first one here?"

"Yes. Just after it happened, I guess. I was headed south. I remember one car ahead of me; it looked big, it could have been black, but I really can't say. Suddenly it swerved to the side of the road. Right onto the shoulder, you could see a cloud of dust come up. It swerved over, then zigzagged a little, then tore off up the road. I didn't see the body until I was closer." He shrugged. "I can't say if he hit the guy, or just didn't choose to stop. That's about all I can tell you."

"About the car. Could you get a make?"

"It was big. Probably American."

"Chrysler? Ford? Chevrolet?"

He shrugged. "Pick one. They all look alike."

"Four-door? Wagon?"

"Four-door, I guess. No—wait. It was a two-door."

"A two-door. You sure?"

"No. But I think so."

"Could you see how many people were inside?"

"I wasn't looking. I'm sure there was a driver; I doubt that's very helpful."

"I had expected a driver. Did you see the jogger?"

"I might have seen him out of the corner of my eye. He seemed to be jogging along the dirt. I could be wrong; I'm not even sure it was this man."

"You never know what may be important, Mr. Levasseur. Anything else?"

"Nothing. I was too far behind the car to see any details. By the time I got to the man in the road—well, he hasn't changed much since then."

"I understand." Another set of lights came up the road. Traffic moved better already. "You said you saw dust as the car hit the shoulder. Are you sure?"

"Absolutely. It raised quite a cloud."

"Any idea where?"

"I think it was near that phone pole," he pointed. "But I can't be sure."

"It's a start." I wrote his name and address, and looked up one more time. "Does anyone else have anything to add?"

Nothing came forth. Before I could start asking more general questions, one of the ambulance attendants approached me. "Can I talk to you?"

"Excuse me." We stepped back from the crowd. I noticed that the body on the ground had been covered by a white sheet, already stained. "Well?"

"Well, nothing. I'm sure you know he was dead before you got here. It doesn't look like he lived for more than a few seconds after the impact. Massive head trauma killed him right out. He never suffered from the internal injuries and bleeding."

"I'm not surprised."

"You have a knack for understatement. We've called for the coroner. He'll be here in a few minutes. We'll just leave him be until then."

"Okay."

Sergeant Dickinson, an enormous, muscular man who had been an officer for more than twenty years, joined us. I had no doubt that in those years he had witnessed scenes like this one before. Nor did I doubt it had the same gut-wrenching effect on him as it had on the ambulance attendant and me. He nodded as he recognized me. "Hoitt. What's the story?"

"Sketchy, sir. Looks like a hit-and-run. Some reports from these people make it sound as if it wasn't an accident, but there's not much to follow."

"What kind of reports?"

"One witness told me he saw a car 'lurking' at the fire station. Lights out, just waiting. Another claims he saw the impact, said he saw the car—," I checked my notes, "—swerve to the side of the road, onto the shoulder. Then it zigzagged around and headed quickly up the road."

"Sounds imaginative."

"It's worth checking out, sir."

"Of course, of course." Dickinson knelt beside the sheet and lifted it up. His face remained impassive as he gently replaced the sheet. "Guess he didn't have much of a chance."

The attendant shook his head. "No pulse, no breath, no nothing when we got here. We called Gibbs."

Dr. Gibbs served as local medical examiner. In spite of the overwhelming evidence, a qualified person had to sign the death certificate. Dickinson nodded. "We'll leave it to him, then."

"Whoever hit him didn't do it halfway," said the attendant.

"Right." Dickinson gazed down at the sheet a long moment, then looked up abruptly. "Any ID?"

The attendant shook his head. "He had a key pinned to his shorts. Dave's got it with him," he added, pointing to the ambulance. "Other than that, nothing."

"A quick identification of the corpse is out of the question." Dickinson crossed his arms. "Chances are someone is waiting for him back home. Someone who will eventually realize he's missing. I'd hate to be the one who answers the phone when that person calls the station."

"Can't help you, Sergeant," said the attendant. "Precious little of anything left to analyze. We could make a few guesses about his appearance."

Dickinson thought a moment. "We'll have to go door-to-door. I'll call down a couple more men. Maybe this guy jogged a regular route. Someone may recognize his description."

A red-and-white Chevy Suburban pulled up in front of my cruiser, a red light flashing on the dash. The door opened and out stepped a man of average height, dressed in denim jeans under a plaid cotton shirt. He walked right up to us, without any regard for the grisly scene before him, without asking anyone permission. Thick black-rimmed glasses hung on his nose, slipping lower as he walked. On his belt hung a compact gray box marked EHVAC. As much as anything else, the beeper identified Mike Twitchell, head of the Eagle Harbor Volunteer Ambulance Corps.

He approached Dickinson first. They shook hands. "Hi, Gene."

Dickinson nodded. "Mike."

"Jimmy," said Twitchell, nodding toward me.

"Mike."

"I heard the call go out," said Twitchell. "What happened?"

"Hit-and-run," I replied.

"Great," said Twitchell with a grimace. He performed our ritual once again, kneeling beside the sheet, lifting a corner, having a good look. "I heard the call. I didn't expect this. I've seen a few fatalities, but each one still hits you hard. Jesus, what a mess."

He put down the sheet to survey the scene. "Anything turn up on a car?"

"Only generalities. Possibly a large, dark, Chrysler coupe." I heaved up my shoulders. "Can't be more than a few hundred of them on the island."

"Probably not a local. The summer crowds outnumber us already." Twitchell stared down the road, then shook it off as if trying to exorcise a winter chill. "I'm going to check in with the EMTs. Didn't mean to interrupt your investigation."

"Good to see you, Mike." Dickinson waved before he turned back to me. "Have you questioned these people?"

"They told me what they saw," I said. "Which wasn't much."

"Ask one more time. Listen for any unusual details, anything. Especially ask if anyone saw this guy before the accident."

"One couple did."

"Try to get a description. Then get anyone without a personal stake out of here."

"Yes, sir." I returned to the crowd. None had left; they'd hardly moved, like mute statues. They stared as if I were an actor stepping off the stage and out into the audience. I headed first for the couple who had seen the victim before the accident.

It took more than an hour for the medical examiner to arrive, certify the obvious, and permit the body to be taken to Dixon's funeral home. Two patrolmen had arrived and had begun pounding on doors. The crowd had thinned considerably; only Levasseur remained with Dickinson. King kept the traffic flowing. As it grew later, his job grew easier.

Dickinson and I walked off the roadside, looking for evidence. The first indication of the accident came about a hundred yards north of the body. We measured the exact distance, as we did with all the marks we found. We discovered deep, fresh ruts in the sandy shoulder. There was no misinterpreting the darker color of the freshly turned gravel. A large vehicle, moving rapidly, had left the pavement at a sharp angle, straightened out, then traveled the shoulder parallel to the road.

The marks validated Levasseur's statement: someone had left the pavement and run along the shoulder at high speed. That indicated something sinister which I did not want to accept. Dickinson must have realized the same fact. He ordered me to go over the area adjacent to the marks several times. An honest accident should have left brake skids where the car veered for the shoulder. We found none.

"Where the hell are the brake skids?" asked Dickinson. "Hoitt, have you seen any?"

"Not yet."

He smoothed the hair at the back of his head. "That's strange."

I continued searching. I found a pair of J-strips near the yellow line, but they were too old. I detected no sign of anything to force the car off the road. With the lack of brake marks on the shoulder, there appeared to be only one conclusion: this was no accident. The road offered damning but inconclusive evidence. After all, many things could have pushed the car off the surface without leaving a trace. Possible, certainly, but not likely.

Twenty yards beyond the body Sergeant Dickinson discovered the first evidence of impact. The tire marks revealed no change. The path stayed straight and true, with no change of texture to mark brake application. Ground into the gravel we found a shredded piece of elastic-backed terry cloth, the kind used for athletic sweat bands. Just beyond lay crystalline shards of a shattered headlight. A few yards farther a narrow, deep groove marked where something had been dragged through the dirt. The trail shifted sideways, then disappeared as the tire tracks returned to the pavement.

A little farther, traces of blood stained the asphalt. Along with them came scraps of T-shirt and shorts, terry cloth, and a single mangled sneaker. This trail ran along the edge of the road, then veered toward the center before ceasing near the chalk outline. It appeared that, after the first hit, the victim had been pinned to the car, dragged along in its headlong rush. A continued lack of brake skids indicated the driver had no intention of letting the victim escape.

I continued walking while Dickinson and Levasseur minutely examined the last few feet of the trail. Not much farther along I noticed a set of dark marks on the asphalt. Kneeling down I touched them. They had the sticky, slick feel of rubber. "Sergeant Dickinson, could you come here?"

He came immediately, Levasseur right behind. "What is it?"

"These, sir." I pointed to the ground. "Parallel marks."

"Skid marks?" He turned to Levasseur. "Did you see any sign of braking after the accident? Brake lights, tires squealing, anything?"

Levasseur shook his head. "No brake lights, that I'm sure. I was busy driving, but I couldn't hear anything."

On closer inspection the tracks looked peculiar. "Sergeant, I don't think these are brake skids."

Dickinson knelt beside me and ran his fingers along the tracks. "I think you're right, Jimmy." He pulled a pocket knife from his belt, scraping off a sample of the black-coated asphalt. He rolled it between his fingers. "Seems fresh. It rained yesterday morning." He stood up to face Levasseur. "You said the vehicle left very quickly afterwards?"

"I thought so," he replied.

"Makes sense." He rubbed his hands together. "I think we have a very serious case here."

"Too much for us?" I asked.

"Too much for us," he echoed. "I'll call the state police. They may want to send someone down tonight."

Dickinson wouldn't have called in the state police for a simple hit-and-run. If all those years of experience told him something was wrong, I had to respect that. "What now?"

"You've been here a while, Jimmy. Escort Mr. Levasseur back to his car. Then go to the station and write your report immediately. I'll be there in a little while. I'll check on the door-to-door, call the troopers, and see what's next." He reached out and touched my shoulder. "You've done a good job here. Make sure all the details go into your report."

"I'll do my best. Mr. Levasseur, if you'll come with me."

Levasseur followed me back to his car. I thanked him again for his assistance and his keen observations, then ushered him into the flow of traffic—it seemed heavy for so early on a Friday morning. I had to wonder how many people drove by because they had heard already. I returned to my cruiser, backed around to head north, then started up route 102.

It had been a long night. A lot of paperwork, follow-up questions, then more paperwork were bound to follow. When the state police detectives arrived, there would be more questions, more reports. The one thing that stuck with me was the piece of data I did not have: the identity of the victim. I had spent the last hours searching for clues about his death, talking to people about the last moments of his life, yet I had no name for him. After all that work it seemed strange not to know his name. He remained as much of a mystery as if I had never seen him at all.

A monotonous forty-minute drive took me back to the station. I used the time to collect my thoughts, and prepare to put them down in triplicate on the requisite forms. Other departments and other men would take over the job of apprehending the killer. Whoever the victim was, once I signed off my last round of reports I expected not to deal with the dead man in the road again.

I was wrong.

2

Friday Morning
Patrol Area: Mount Desert Island
Temps warm; wind 12–18 knots, SW;
seas calm, skies clear

Robyn lives on the northwest side of the island, at a cove just south of Indian Point. As I live near the south end, it's necessary to use some of the more heavily trafficked roads. I had to battle the early summer traffic, but, as a veteran of many such encounters with the annual invaders, it didn't take me long to find the alternate route best suited to my impatience and my truck's off-road capability. True to my word, I arrived at Robyn's just after ten o'clock.

I drove up the long drive she shared with her landlord, bouncing along the cratered drive, wondering yet again how her little Volkswagen could make that journey day after day and remain in one piece. The jarring bumps sent my head up to the roof, despite a heavy-duty suspension. Of course I drove three times faster than she did; that might have had something to do with it. I pulled up next to her car, killed the engine, and jumped onto the grass.

Robyn rents a beautiful cottage on a sloping meadow, a view of Bartlett Island and Blue Hill Bay just out her back door. The previous owner had felled all trees within a hundred feet, leaving nothing but grass and granite ledge for a lawn. While it lent the place a barren, isolated outlook, it yielded a breathtaking view. At one time it had been a summer home: white clapboards and big windows, a fieldstone-faced chimney climbing the shore wall, a wooden deck reaching off the back. Robyn had been fortunate to rent the little house; I envied her.

The steps creaked beneath my feet. I pressed the doorbell once, paused, then hit it again. This time a voice cried, "Is that you?"

"It's me."

The curtain beside the door rolled back, unveiling a familiar face. I heard the old brass latch snap back, and the door opened. "Come on in. I'm almost done fixing lunch."

Robyn's one year younger and two inches shorter than I. Her hair falls just past her shoulders, kinking in response to the increasing humidity. It forms a delicate, insubstantial frame around high, arched cheekbones already darkened by the sun. Deep smile lines extend back from the corners of her eyes. Today, she wore only sandals and her one-piece swimsuit, black with a diagonal purple stripe crossing her chest. It pulled more tightly than I remembered. There are many reasons I feel the way I do about Robyn Cole. The most important is not how well she fills out her swimwear, but I must confess it's a definite plus. "Okay. I'll just collapse on the couch."

She headed toward the kitchen. "Hungry? Thirsty?"

"I just had breakfast."

Inside, the house has three rooms. The large, central living room spans the full width, front door to back porch. At one end opens the kitchen and dining area; opposite are the bedroom and bathroom. It may be small, but the craftsmanship of the paneled walls and hardwood floors cannot be ignored. Neither can Robyn's taste and touch in furnishing. A tiny place, that could easily have been a confining apartment, instead exudes cozy comfort.

I left the front door open and dropped into the deep couch. Robyn's cat, named Binkley but more frequently (and aptly) called Stupid, stretched his front claws, arched his back, flipped around, then resettled onto the couch back. I rubbed my eyes. Constant practice enables me to exist on a few hours of sleep, but, without the pressure, it takes a while to reach full wakefulness. Robyn said something, but I didn't catch it. "What?"

"I said, what happened last night? The call that came in while you were at school."

"A hit-and-run. Some jogger got nailed near the lake. A real mess."

"Sorry I missed it."

"I can show you the pictures when they come back."

"I'll pass."

I readjusted my position. Tired of my disturbances, Binkley leapt off the couch and skidded around the corner, his declawed paws digging for traction on the polished wood, as he aimed for the bedroom. "What are you making?"

"What?" I could hear the chime of the silverware drawer opening and closing, and shuffling as Robyn walked across the tiled floor.

"I said, what are you making for lunch?"

"Sliced ham, potato salad." The drawer opened and closed again. "Pickles, and cookies. Leftovers. Okay?"

"Fine."

"It'll be just a minute."

"Take your time." If she said just a minute, it would probably be closer to five. I closed my eyes and drifted away.

I didn't drift far. Robyn came out of the kitchen, depositing the wicker picnic basket beside the door. "Let me get my shorts." She disappeared into the bedroom, returning with a light cotton shirt over her shoulders, tied in the middle, the trailing end of the knot tucked into white Nike shorts. "I'm ready."

I rolled off the couch. "Let's go."

She opened the screen. "Can we take my car? It looks like such a nice day and I've been dying to put the top down."

I nodded. "Let me get my stuff. I'll help you with the top."

I retrieved my canvas bag and tossed it toward her car. It took only a minute to push down and secure the top. I hopped behind the wheel and we were off. Robyn's hair flowed back from her head, wind straightening the kinks while it knotted the ends. Now and then I stole a glance in her direction. The night before, I had entered a darkened hall and found a director at work, her mind busy on the stage, concentration focused not on the visiting patrolman but on blocking, lighting, and lines. The director was gone now, replaced by a beautiful and clearly tired young woman with a precious day off.

I swerved to avoid slamming dead center into a pothole that would have caused the VW to bottom out. The abrupt motion apparently caught Robyn by surprise. Her eyes opened wide, one hand clamped onto the suicide strap while the other clutched the windshield.

"Having trouble driving?"

"No. I forget your car can't take the bumps like my truck. Sometimes I don't remember until I'm in them."

"I see." She let go of the windshield but not the strap. "If you'd use the highways now and then you wouldn't have to worry."

I shook my head. "I hate traffic."

I did my best to avoid the larger pits, weaving back and forth as the road wound down the side of the ridge. At the bottom I turned right onto the main road for a few hundred yards, then left onto another set of ruts that led down to the water. The beach and the water hid behind a thinning stand of pine trees. As we drew closer, the stench of drying seaweed, the musty dead smell of the salt marsh, and the unmistakable perfume of the ocean drifted through the trees, mixing with road dust in a familiar, marvelous way.

The beach was crowded, for that particular beach, at least. Only a hundred feet long, it doesn't take much to fill up. Strictly locals know about this beach. The ocean intrudes into a cove where coarse sand covers the rocky ledges. At low tide it is nothing but mud flats. When the tide rolls in after a sunny morning, the water flows over the warm mud, making it the best swimming hole for miles. I parked on the grassy strip behind the beach. We got out and found a spot for our towels beneath a boulder half-buried in the sand.

The towel no sooner touched the sand than Robyn stripped down to her swim suit. She jammed her clothes into the picnic basket, kicked off her sandals, and lay back. She scissored her legs back and forth, burrowing first one foot, then the other into the hot, damp sand. "Ahhh!" she said. "Nothing like warm beach sand."

I disrobed down to my swimming shorts, much more slowly than Robyn's kick and fling routine. I let the sea breeze straighten out my towel, then dropped it onto the sand and fell into it. In an instant I relaxed; my body went limp. "I need this. Badly."

"Feels good to relax, doesn't it?"

"Long week?"

"Forever. I realized some things I wanted just won't happen before the premiere."

"Serious?"

"Nothing major. Nothing to worry about today, or even tomorrow. I don't want to push the cast too hard. Just enough to get a good show."

I looked up at the cotton clouds drifting across the sky, letting the exhaustion leach out of my body. I propped myself up on one elbow. "Go for a quick swim, while the water's still warm?"

"Sure." She didn't get up. "Race out to the ledge and back?"

Robyn swims extremely well. Had she not been so involved in other activities at college, she would have lead the swim team. Growing up beside the sea, I'm no aquatic slouch, but I know a match when I hear one. "Loser drives home?"

"Agreed." She inhaled deeply: I should have seen it as a warning. "Ready?"

"Ready."

"Okay. Go!" She leapt up and sprinted, sand and the towel flying in her wake.

She caught me completely off guard. I took off in pursuit, pumping hard against the sand. I could beat her on dry land. I had covered no more than half the distance to the water when she dove in. I knew who would be driving home, but I refused to give up.

The gorgeous weather continued through the afternoon. Reluctant to waste any, we lingered until the shadows chilled the air. Robyn repeatedly accepted my challenges for double or nothing. As a result, it would be a month before I had a chance to use the passenger seat. Around five we returned to her house.

I parked. "You want the roof up?"

She looked up. "It'll be all right. Car needs airing out."

"Suit yourself." I tossed her the keys, reached for my wet towel and bag, and tossed my gear into the truck bed. "Plans for tomorrow?"

Robyn leaned on the truck hood. "I told my mother I'd take her to Bangor. Then dinner with her and Dad. Want to come?"

"I have to work."

"Uh-huh." Matted by repeated cycles of sun, salt water, and sand, then blown dry by a dusty, fifty-mile-per-hour wind, her hair had more in common with a rat's nest than a coiffure. She put her long fingers through the tangle at the back, then slowly, carefully, pulled it out, creating a quartet of stiff furrows. "I'll have to soak my head." She pulled another hand through before surrendering. "Come by after nine, if you get a chance. I'm sure Mom can scare up a piece of pie."

"I'll do what I can."

"I know." She dragged a finger along the dusty truck, leaving a clean streak. "Needs a bath."

"I came by Potter's. It's still pretty dusty up there."

"So I see." She wiped her finger on her shirt, then stepped back. She had not bothered to replace her sandals. She ran one bare foot up the calf of the other leg. "Sure you don't want to come in?"

Smiling broadly, I stepped closer and slid my arms behind her back, pulling her tighter. "I didn't say I didn't want to."

She looked away. Robyn's eyes are dangerously captivating. Lush emerald in color, magically expressive, they hold the power to melt my stoutest resolve with an instant's glance. When I met her eyes again, they sparkled like the sun flashing on the waves behind her house. "Just for a minute?"

Denial did not come easily. "I have to get ready for work. Take a shower, iron my uniform. Grab something to eat."

"I know." I felt cool dampness as her hand caressed my back, pressing my moist shirt against the skin, then the gentle massage as she ran her fingers through the close-cropped hair at the back of my neck. "I have to ask."

"I wish I could stay."

"I know."

Robyn leaned forward and kissed me. She started to back away, but I held her tightly while we kissed again. A reassuring scent drifted off her body: salt water, a whiff of fabric softener, a hint of herbal shampoo. "Maybe I could stay a little while."

She slipped out of my grasp. "Get out of here. Don't be late."

"You can't get away that easily," I teased, reaching for her waist.

"Yes, I can." She pirouetted away, recovering her basket from the back of the VW. "I'll be here in the morning, if you want to call. You've got Monday off, right?"

"Monday off." I climbed into the truck. "Any ideas?"

"Maybe we can go camping?"

"Maybe." I started the truck, leaving my foot on the gas until the idle smoothed out. Robyn, the picnic basket behind her back, stood by my door, leaning on the window. "Find a place to stay."

"I'll see what I can find." She pushed her head into the cab and kissed me quickly. "Talk to you later."

"Bye." For a second, her eyes captured me before I reluctantly broke away. "Watch your feet." I backed up, pointed the truck toward home, and left her in a cloud of drifting brown dust.

Returning via the Potter farm, I reached home in fifteen minutes. I rent a one-room apartment over the old post office. The tiny, ill-fitting gable-end windows mean the place is dark all winter and stuffy all summer. The steeply pitched roof means you can stand up straight only in the middle of the room. It's nowhere near as nice as Robyn's place, but it is my own. I tossed my wet towel on the bathroom floor, quickly following it with everything else I had on. I started the shower and jumped in. I didn't bother with the hot water.

After the shower, I dug a two-toned brown uniform shirt out of the drawer and draped it across the ironing board. While the iron warmed, I shaved, found pants, and gave my uniform boots a quick Windex polish. I ironed the shirt, affixed pins and badge, filled the pockets with pencils, notes, and paper, then put it on. Downstairs I grabbed my hat and keys off the refrigerator and headed out the back door. In a minute I rolled down the road to the village.

What passes for Eagle Harbor is nothing more than the conflux of two roads, Routes 102 and the Cove Road. On that stretch of road sit the post office, O'Brien's Hardware & Marine, the Eagle

Diner, the dilapidated town hall and the new brick firehouse, and a pair of bed-and-breakfasts. A drive opposite the firehouse leads down a steep hill behind the diner, where the town dock hangs out into the harbor. I would have called it a pretty village even if it hadn't been home.

I found a space in front of the diner and went inside. No matter the season, Fridays are busy nights. I said hello to the people I knew and planted myself on a green vinyl-topped stool. A menu protruded from between the napkin holder and the sugar container, but I had memorized it long ago. As much as any of the furnishings, a three-some at the table closest to the door defines the diner, and the village. Not a single hair remains on Ed Berman's head: seventy-odd years as a farmer, church deacon, and volunteer firefighter emeritus have left him no more to tear out. It's hard to believe Murray Killing-ton can survive in the hot, humid weather of summer, dressed as he always is in a plaid wool shirt, heavy cotton pants, and Bean boots that end just below his knees. Without the costume he wears every day, he would not be recognized by people who have known him all their lives. The venerable Sam Adams rounds out the Eagle Harbor troika, lounging at their worn wooden thrones, surveying the realm beyond the glass.

A waitress, medium height, plump, dark hair and thick glasses, came my way. She swept a damp cloth over the countertop, plopping a water glass in front of me. "Hi, Jimmy. How's life been treating you?"

"Not bad, Rita. How've you been?"

"No complaints. Been a good day."

"Lot of traffic?"

"For June, yuh. I've been working since two and my feet are killing me." She smiled and shook her apron. It jingled loudly. "But the customers have been generous."

"Any plans for your summer fund?"

"First I'm going to buy a new pair of work shoes." She took a pencil and check pad from the apron. "What'll it be?"

"A number four. And coffee."

"No problem. I'll tell your mother you're here."

"Thanks." Rita scribbled something on her pad, clipped it up on the spindle at the cook's window, and disappeared through the swinging doors. The diner hasn't changed since I can remember: an L-shaped room with tables along the outer windows, a counter on the inside wall, the window and doors to the kitchen beyond the counter. Old pictures of the town dot the papered walls between the windows. The iron stove beside the door serves as the primary source of heat during the winter. The equipment, old as the building, blends perfectly into the simple design. Green, oval frappe mixer; a Taylor milk refrigerator kept mirror polished; a two-pot Bunn coffee machine, bought in the late seventies, which they still refer to as the *new* coffee machine. Only a stainless steel sink with a plastic hose threatens the rustic appearance. It's a cozy place, cooled by sea breezes in the summer, warmed by birch and pine in the winter, full of familiar people always willing to talk.

I swallowed some water and gazed out the window: many boats already tied up for the night. I scanned the harbor for the unfamiliar, older vessels of transient mariners or the newer boats freshly acquired by local residents. I didn't notice anything. The working boats of the Eagle Harbor fleet made up the majority. Wooden boats, thirty to thirty-five feet long, their sides scarred by years of bashing against the dock, endless days of hauling the traps over the side onto the long, flat quarterdeck. A huge cabin cruiser tugged at a distant mooring; I couldn't see the registration numbers, but I knew they didn't begin ME. At guest moorings bobbed a couple sailboats, including a black-hulled Hinckley sloop, built just a few miles away. Among the predominantly white working boats, some splashes of color stood out. A small red lobster boat bobbed at the demarcation line between commercial and recreational fleets, its seamless sides identifying the material as fiberglass, not wood. A pair of light-green cruising yachts moored near each other, a huge dark-green lobster boat beside them. A gray-hulled boat with a high prow and a new radar antenna was tied up at the dock. I could easily see a tall figure moving around the stern. The engine covers were open and I wondered if Dad had developed engine trouble.

"You're always looking out at the water."

I turned around to face my mother, who leaned on the opposite side of the counter. I noticed a large smudge of a coffee stain on her uniform. She kept a second uniform at the diner; she is an immaculate, fastidious woman. If she had not taken the time to change her blouse, it had indeed been a busy day.

"You should have gone into fishing," she added.

"Nah," I said quickly. "I don't like fish enough to want to spend every day with them."

She pulled a hairpin out of her hair, stuffing an errant wisp back into the bun on the back of her head before replacing the pin. The veins on the sides of her arms stood out as she worked the hair. She does a lot of manual work, from waitressing to sewing to helping my father pull traps on the rougher days. For a woman her age, she is remarkably fit.

"You in a hurry?"

I shook my head. "Not really. Why?"

"Sam—," the head cook, the one full-timer overseeing an ever-changing bunch of apprentices, "—is a little behind."

"Been busy?"

"No." She hesitated, thinking. "Just steady."

"Good."

"It's been a good shift." She looked past me, out the window. "Your father is still working on the boat."

"Guess so. Engine break down again?"

She sighed. "I don't know. He said something about taking it apart when he came in for lunch. He mentioned buying parts, but I don't know whether it broke or whether he's just catching up on maintenance. He got way behind installing the new antenna."

"He'll be coming in soon, won't he?"

"I imagine. I get off at seven. He said he'd come bring me home." She looked up at the round clock ringed by a neon light. "He's got plenty of time to finish tinkering."

Rita slipped around my mother's back, setting a saucer before me. She laid out some silverware and placed a coffee cup on the saucer. My mother stood beside the coffee machine; she filled my cup as Rita returned to the tables. I reached for the ketchup. "When you see him, tell him I can give him a hand tomorrow if he needs me."

"Not going to do something with Robyn? On a Saturday? Tomorrow is supposed to be better than today."

"She's busy," I replied between gulps.

"Well, that's too bad. For you, I mean." She leaned forward conspiratorially. Even before she spoke I knew some fresh gossip was about to be laid on my plate. Gossip was the lifeblood of the community, keeping all the parts connected to each other. "Margaret told me the Cole's neighbors—the new ones, from down south—well, they had a loud fight Tuesday night. It's not the first time, either. They're a pretty violent couple."

"I haven't heard anything. Police reports, I mean."

"Oh, I know. It hasn't got that far; not yet anyway. But Margaret says that the Coles are pretty upset about all the noise and commotion. And the parties—" She slapped the side of her face. "Anyway, I hear Rose is very disturbed by all this. Even mentioned selling the house."

"The Coles have lived there for three generations and those neighbors are at least a hundred yards away. They aren't moving."

"Fights travel a long way." Before she could continue, her gaze drifted over my shoulder towards a row of tables. "Excuse me, honey, I've got to work. Just a sec." She grabbed the coffee pot on her way out.

Rita came by and set out my dinner. I took advantage of the lull to eat. My mother loves to talk nearly as much as she loves to listen. I enjoy going down to the diner, having a few minutes with her before I go off to work. With my night shifts and her tourist season, I have no other time to see her. Still, eating is difficult when she directs a constant stream of rumor at me.

Before she returned, I had time to scrape the plate clean, but had only just returned to my coffee. She tacked a pair of orders up on the spindle, replaced the coffee pot, and planted herself at the counter. "Did you two go to the beach today?"

"Yuh. Down to the cove."

"You know, Jimmy, I haven't seen Robyn in a long time. Tell her to come over and visit some time. She doesn't have to come over just to see you."

"I'll tell her."

"Make sure you do." Sam set a plate on the counter and jammed the order underneath it as he called my mother's name. She spun around, picked up the plate, shoved the slip in her pocket, and deposited the plate in front of the customer beside me. "You eat too fast."

"I drink too much coffee, too."

She shook her head the way only a mother can. "You're worse than your father."

"It beats falling asleep on duty."

"I suppose." She left it at that, allowing me to ponder her words. In fact, I planned my route for the evening. I didn't get very far before she started in again. "Where were you working last night?"

"I was on the coast watch. Why?"

"I heard about a fatal hit-and-run near the lake. I was wondering if you knew anything about it."

"What have you heard?"

She took a half step backwards. "Well, nothing, really. I heard about an accident. Somebody hit a jogger."

I nodded. "It was a mess. The guy was killed instantly."

My mother's face wrinkled in distaste. The gruesome details were almost enough to get her to stop. Almost. "Any idea who did it?"

"I can't tell you anything, Mom."

"Police business?"

"I can't tell you anything because I don't know anything. I asked a few questions, but no one saw anything, no one knew anything."

"Somebody said it was a professional hit."

I know good gossip thrives on the unexpected, but she still managed to shock me. "A what?"

"A hit. You know, a contract murder." Her voice suddenly hushed, she leaned forward, her hand cupped beside her mouth. "The victim was a gangster. A man living a double life: nice man, good to his neighbors, but a Mafia don on the side."

I could barely avoid laughing. Gossip was nothing if not imaginative. "Where did you hear that?"

"I don't know," she replied quickly. "Some of the fishermen gabbed at the counter during lunch." She looked toward the ceiling, her gaze distant. "No, wait. That last part about the Mafia, I heard that from Margaret." She paused. "Or was it Barbara? Yes; it must have been Barbara. She lives up by the lake now, you know, and she'd be the one who'd know."

"If she does, she knows more than the police. We didn't even have a name when I left."

"That was hours ago, Jimmy. They should know more when you go in tonight."

"Maybe. And I'll be sure to pass along every scrap of dirt I can dig up."

She snapped her washcloth at me. "Don't be smart!" She folded the cloth and swept the counter. "Did you come by the house?"

"Yuh." I wiped off my face, crumpled my napkin on the plate, and pushed it forward. "Why?"

"Jenny home?"

"Didn't see her car. She missing?"

"She left in a hurry this morning, didn't take anything except that tiny little purse of hers." My mother carries a purse the size of a navy duffel bag. Anything smaller, including my sister's fanny pack, she deems "tiny."

"A couple hours ago Billy Foster came by and said he'd seen Jenny and some of her friends sailing toward the islands," she said.

"Steve's family has a boat. Was it that one?"

"Steve who?"

"I don't know his last name. Tall guy, skinny as a rail, braces, hair cut funny so it stands up in the middle."

"Oh, Steve. Yes, I think he does have a boat. Billy didn't have any details."

"What's the difference, anyway?"

My mother has a lethal, withering glare. When she fixes it on you, you knew you have traversed very thin ice.

"I'm her mother. Billy seemed to think they were going overnight. I want to know if my only daughter intends to come home tonight."

"Aw, Mom." I finished my coffee, and piled the cup and saucer on the plate. "She's old enough to take care of herself. This is her last summer before college. She's got to get in all the fun she can find."

"Fun is one thing. Irresponsibility is something else. She could have stopped by or left a note. If she's going to stay out all night, she should at least have taken a change of clothes."

If my sister had gone sailing overnight with Steve, a change of clothes would be the last thing on her mind. "Don't worry about it, Mom. She'll be fine."

"I don't see why she has to sneak around all the time."

"It's nothing personal." I laid a five, and whatever change I had in my pocket, on the counter. "I have to go to work."

"All right." She gave me a quick peck on the cheek. "You be careful."

"See you tomorrow."

I rotated the stool and slid off. From behind me I heard her say "good night" and clear my dishes off the counter. I strode through the double doors, climbed into the cruiser, and headed north.

I checked my watch. Just before six, close enough to sign in. "County one nine to dispatch, over."

"County nineteen. Go," came the reply. A Friday night meant the weekend crew manned the station. I thought I recognized the dispatcher's voice as one of the summer part-timers, but I couldn't be sure. I didn't know their voices as well as I knew the regulars.

"County one nine. Ten seven at 17:56. Location, Eagle Harbor, planning to patrol roads to north of Mount Desert Island, then heading east."

"Stand by, nineteen." The pause allowed the technician at the radio to check with the desk officer to see if anything more urgent demanded my attention. I expected no change in assignment. Patrol formed the bulk of the Friday and Saturday night workload. "County nineteen, Officer Hoitt, correct?"

I frowned. If they needed my name, I would probably be pulled off patrol for some inane duty. I liked patrol. "Affirmative."

"Right, uh, county nineteen. County one requests the pleasure of your company in his office at 20:00."

Involuntarily I straightened up, checking myself in the mirror. "Roger, dispatch." I let go of the mike. I didn't want to ask the next question, but I knew the next two hours would be hell if I didn't. "Dispatch, could you tell me the nature of this meeting?"

"No information available, county nineteen. I am only told it is urgent. I'd ask him, but he's busy."

"I'll find out soon enough. County one nine, clear."

I set down the mike. What did he want? I knew I had done nothing wrong. When Sheriff Walker thinks you have erred, he doesn't ask you to come by later—you report immediately. I didn't expect commendations, either. He doesn't make appointments for those. A peculiarity struck me. Why was the sheriff at the station on a Friday night? If I could solve that mystery, I might be able to figure out why I had to see him. My innate nervousness would intensify until I walked into the office, palms sweaty, stomach churning. Nothing I could do about it, I thought. I diverted my attention to patrol and left the future until later.

Even though it was a Friday evening after a beautiful day, I encountered surprisingly little activity. Whatever the reason for the meeting, the last thing I wanted to do was to arrive late. I kept my sidetracks minimal until I cleared the island, then used the back road toward Ellsworth, hoping to arrive early and attend to paperwork. I passed a lot of cars. Every business I passed had a parking lot full of kids and cars. I made a point of slowing down as I passed, but not once did I see anyone rush to hide anything, or abruptly turn their backs toward me. Too early for the hard core party animals, I thought. I went on.

The drivers behaved. During the drive to the bridge I trailed other cars, hampering my ability to use the radar. As I rounded a curve, a car in the other lane flashed by, a little fast. The radar fuzzed out, so I settled for flashing the blues. I looked back as he drove by: his brake lights stayed on a long time. I scared him enough to slow him down, and that was the point.

Across the bridge, the line of cars expanded. It usually does. Restaurants line both sides, their outdoor lobster pots boiling furiously. The flea-market tables and gift shops do a great business. Dozens of commercial ventures fill the ugly mile where all the roads into Bar Harbor and Acadia National Park converge. The passage is always slow. I made it through, heading for Oak Point at the first opportunity.

The radio stayed active as I wound slowly toward Ellsworth. Six patrolmen had Friday duty, and, in the time it took me to go from the diner to the point, I heard each of the others. Two of them signed on after me; I heard license plates run, calls to investigate disturbances, and reports of alarms, all the usual things for a Friday. The most interesting transmission came when Fred Hill, a Surry patrolman, called in. He also received a request to report to the sheriff at eight. Though close in age, background, and time on the force, we came from different parts of the county. Rarely do we see each other off duty, and on duty I hadn't done anything with Fred for at least two months. Why we would be called together made the mystery all the more perplexing. As hard as I tried to force it out of my mind, the inactivity pushed my mind into the same gutter. I hoped a call would come in to investigate something, but none came. I drove on, the car purring softly, the night quiet, broken only by the swish as a car passed by or the eerie symphony of frogs as I drove by wet ground.

Having accomplished little except raising my own anxiety and verifying the southern half of Hancock County was quiet, I pulled into the parking lot behind the stone county courthouse. My thoughts had become so amplified and frantic, they no longer made any sense. I no longer wondered why I had been summoned. I no longer thought about it at all. I didn't think, I just felt, and what I felt was sick. It was like I had been called into the principal's office: that feeling I knew too well to forget.

I grabbed my hat, taking the steps two at a time to the door. The dispatcher looked up as I walked by. I could not even guess her name. She looked me over, then resumed writing reports and reading teletypes. The sheriff's office was on the second floor, so I headed right up the stairs. They groaned as I tread the old boards, drowning out the murmur of radios and voices from the dispatcher's station and the soft babble from the coffee room. Upstairs was dead quiet. The naked bulb of the hall light cast clean silhouettes onto dark office doors. I hurried along to the far end, where the glass door panel read SHERIFF. Despite a door ajar, I knocked. I was told to go inside, so I did.

A man of sharp paradoxes, Sheriff Walker can be at once kindly grandfather and crusty curmudgeon, a man who looks ready to yell— or roll back his head and burst out laughing. He didn't look much like laughing or yelling that night, only tired, as if nearing the end of a long day. A hideous, sculpted-glass globe hung from the ceiling, but it was as dark as it was dusty. As far as I knew, the bulb had burned out long ago and had never been replaced. The sheriff worked by the desk light, a metal gooseneck lamp whose incandescent bulb cast hot, yellow light on the desk, reflected up into his face.

Buried behind a stack of papers, a pencil grasped firmly in one hand, he did not look up. A shiny pipe stem protruded from his lips, leading to a hand-hewn bowl balanced on his fingertips. The colorless lips parted to release a puff of smoke to curl haltingly toward the ceiling. The room reeked of the potent, vile mixture, staining the air in the room as it yellowed the paint above the desk.

Despite his immobility, he clearly knew who had entered. "Sit down, Jimmy. Relax."

I obeyed. He completed a form, initialed the top, signed the bottom, then pulled another off the pile and laid it on top. Still he didn't look up; he saw only the paper, his puffy, red eyes distorted by heavy black glasses. "Eight o'clock already?"

"A few minutes before, sir," I said. "I'm early."

He nodded. The second report must have been shorter, for it took him no time to read and sign it. "Fine, fine. We have to wait for a couple people, okay? Have a cup of coffee."

He pointed above the filing cabinet, to a machine that had once been white. Above the thick black liquid, lines of old coffee formed even sediment layers on the sides. I thought it better to wait for the fresher coffee downstairs. "No, thank you, sir."

He nodded, continued reading, signing, and shifting files from one pile to another. The smoke parted as he flipped papers around the circuit. Inside the little room a stuffy, airless heat pushed at me, melting my hot, sticky uniform to my body. After a few moments I could no longer breathe through my nose; I opened my lips to bring in enough air. Smoke danced in the light, roiling toward the chipped ceiling. I desperately wished I had something to do besides sit and wait, that Sheriff Walker would say something to which I could react, or offer something for me to read. Nothing happened. I baked slowly in the smoky oven.

I had left the door ajar. From the hallway echoed the hollow steps of someone else climbing the stairs, then treading down the hallway. His shadow preceded him, a rounded shape at the bottom of the frosted glass door panel that advanced upward until it became the shape of a man. A shadow hand rapped on the wood alongside the glass. The glass rattled with each impact.

Walker still did not look up. "Come in, Fred."

The door creaked on its tired brass hinges, opening enough for Hill to slip between the door and the filing cabinet. Patrolman Fred Hill stood a hand taller than I. A little older, he'd worked for the sheriff's department a year longer. Hancock County had more than enough room for two patrolmen to lose each other in it. I knew Fred by name, had worked with him from time to time, pulled over to the side of the road and talked to him when we passed. Yet I did not know him at all. I came from the island; he came from the neighboring peninsula. Only a few miles separated our homes—the distance by sea even less—but those miles made all the difference in the world.

"Have a seat, Fred," said Walker. "Coffee's on the cabinet. Relax. We have to wait for one other guest."

"Thank you, sir." He picked a styrofoam cup off the stack and filled it with the viscous coffee, then sat in a wooden, vinyl-covered chair in front of the blinded windows. Our eyes met, a gaze only long enough for us to realize that neither of us had a clue why we were there. He raised the cup; when it came down, his gaze focused somewhere else, examining the ceiling, the smoke, the floor. I could only guess what passed through his mind. I tried to find what we had in common, looking for the thread that might tell me what Walker wanted. I came up empty. Soon I, too, stared at the surroundings.

The telephone, an old black one that must have been installed by Bell himself, rang weakly. Walker picked it up, listened, said "thank you," then hung up. "Be just a minute."

Again the staircase groaned to announce someone's approach. The steps were quick and light, the tread of someone well-rested, with a clean conscience. A new shadow appeared on the door, growing rapidly until a hand stretched to grab the doorknob without knocking. A stranger joined us. Walker pushed his chair back and stood, prompting Hill and me to do the same. The stranger shut the door firmly, then strode to the desk. He was shorter than I but more heavily muscled, his shoulders wider, his stride longer, his hands open at his sides. He dressed well: new blue jeans, a camel jacket, white dress shirt but no tie, gray-and-purple nylon hiking shoes with plenty of wear on them. He had a short beard flecked with gray, thinning black hair that just touched his ears, and horn-rimmed glasses. He took Walker's hand with a firm handshake and a smile that implied the two had previously met. "Evening, Sheriff." Sharp, clearly enunciated words, but not a local accent.

"Evening, Tom." Walker twisted his glasses off his face and dropped them on top of the pile. "All settled?"

"We're set up, down the street. We're close to the station, off the main road."

"Good, good." Walker gestured expansively toward Hill and me. "These are the two men. Patrolmen Fred Hill and Jimmy Hoitt. Fred, Jimmy, this is Special Agent Wiley, DEA Boston."

The bearded man took our hands in a solid, dry grip. "Pleased to meet you," he said to both of us.

Walker sat down again. He leaned back until the chair springs screeched, dropping his booted feet onto the desktop. "Enough formalities," he said. "Do you want to start this, or shall I?"

Wiley cleared an edge of the desk and sat down. "You should tell them why we want them instead of anyone else. Then I'll review the case."

Walker nodded. "Fred, Jimmy, you're here because we have a major case on our hands. Our detectives are too busy to give Tom the help he needs. I needed two experienced, reliable, and proven officers. You two fit the bill."

I was relieved to learn I had avoided trouble Not only that, Walker regarded me favorably: what a break.

"You started the case last night, Jimmy. You recall a hit-and-run, about eleven last night?"

"Hard to forget, sir."

"Fred, as Jimmy witnessed, we had a gruesome hit-and-run last night. A car nailed a man on 102, late at night. No witnesses, just a dead body in the middle of the road. I don't think we had an ID when you went off duty last night, Jimmy. One came in early this morning." He rocked forward, rummaged through the pile of papers on the desk. He passed it to Wiley, who passed it to Fred. "Paul Martin, of Somesville. Know anything about him?"

Hill shook his head, handing me the sheet. "No."

I scanned it. The document contained a brief biography of the man, including a picture. "I don't recognize him," I said. "Not even his name. He's not a local."

"No. In fact, Martin is not even his real name. That biography you're reading—the work record, personal life, background, and so forth—it's all false. Martin was part of the witness protection program."

Words failed me. Hill spoke up. "How did he manage that?"

"He cooperated with a Federal grand jury," answered Wiley. He took off his glasses to rub the red spots on the bridge of his nose. "He was an accountant for a major drug smuggler in Florida. Couldn't touch him without an inside man. We managed to turn Frederickson, or Martin. He testified, so we rewarded him."

"How did he end up in Maine?" I asked.

"It's quiet here, remote," explained Walker. "A perfect place for a recluse. Portray him to the community as a nice guy, and within a couple years he's buried so deeply no one will ever find him." He tapped out the pipe against his chair. "Or so we thought."

"So last night's accident was no accident," said Hill.

"It goes deeper than that." Wiley replaced his glasses as he rose off the desk. "We were building a case against Frederickson. We suspected he broke the rules, declining to go straight after his relocation. There's a limit to what we'll tolerate."

"What did he do?" asked Hill.

Wiley paced the room, one hand jammed into his coat pocket, and the other sharply punctuating his words. "His old business. Drug smuggling. The economy is good, production is outstanding. Here in New England you have a vast, ripe, largely untapped market. Everyone with the cash to get in is trying to be a player. Frederickson either had a secret connection, or managed to acquire cash by some new method we haven't yet traced." Wiley shrugged. "He was damn clever. Smarter than we gave him credit. He used his funds to create a northern supply network. Didn't do any deals directly in Maine. He used this quiet, remote locale as a port of entry. He landed it here, then redistributed it to the big markets. New York, Boston, even as far as Philly or D.C. Volume business, put out to bid, highest bid got the whole load. We haven't determined the limits of his business, but our estimates indicate he did around seventy-five to a hundred million dollars a year gross. Since he'd been operating for less than two years, business could only improve."

"Why didn't we ever hear of this?" I asked. "This guy was operating in our back yard."

Walker shook his head. "You see, Jimmy, locally, we didn't see the business. We're merely a port of entry. The stuff came in, might have been stored here for a short time, then got shipped out. We never saw it, so we could never track it."

"Right," said Wiley. "Frederickson kept clear of the locals. The only way you saw what he smuggled in was from the guys who bought in Boston or New York, then returned up here on their own to sell it. In other words, your regular small-timers."

Hill shifted in his seat. "It sounds like the DEA knew a lot we should have known."

"We knew a lot." If Wiley felt at all guilty about withholding information, he gave no sign of it. "As I said, he was smart. His own hands were spotless. The money trail is crystal clear on the supply side; the trail is good even on sales. Trouble is, we ran into a huge gap. We traced some Colombian and Panamanian flake to the northeast coast. Followed transports, fishermen, all of it. We knew a lot of drugs were reaching New York and Boston via a new connection up north. In the middle had to be a connection linking the bulk transports to the streets. We couldn't find it."

Wiley sat down once more. "Frederickson learned a lot during his years as an accountant. He had so many layers of insulation we couldn't touch him. On top of that, Federal law requires us to have a solid case before pulling him from the protection program. We were close, tantalizingly close. New place, new name, maybe not prison—but no more freedom."

He rubbed his eyes again. "Someone beat us to him. Could be just coincidence that someone wanted him dead; we can't be sure. Looks like a pro hit. The question is, who? It may have been someone from his past. Maybe someone from the present. We can't be sure. We need to find out who did it and why he had to be killed now. Revenge? Competitive pricing? Someone else wanted control of his operation? We don't know. We damn sure need to find out, and fast."

I was impressed. My mother's sources were as accurate and as fast as anything the DEA had. I would not have been surprised if the gossip ring found out the killer before Wiley. I wondered how they had missed a drug smuggler right under their own noses. "Where do we fit in?"

Walker dropped his feet loudly to the floor. "You two are re-assigned to surveillance. Agent Wiley wants the local network rooted out."

"We want to question them," interrupted Wiley. "Some of the players may not even know their boss has been killed; they may not have known who ran the operation. But any recent shift in orders may be significant. We have to find out."

"You two are going to do the legwork," said Walker. "Agent Wiley has supplied a detailed description of the operation. We need to pry this network open, immediately. You two will be working with Sergeant Dickinson—he'll be coordinating. Got it?"

"Yes, sir," we answered.

"We'd like to watch any suspects before we decide how much they're worth, which ones to follow, and which to let go," said Wiley. "We want this port shut down. But first we want to milk all the information out of it that we can get."

Walker nodded. "You never know when you'll stumble across something."

"How are the drugs being moved?" I asked.

"By boat," replied Wiley. "That's what makes this area so perfect. A thousand small coves, lots of water, easy access to sea lanes. It's a smuggler's paradise. Big boats with large payload capacity are easy to come by up here. Everyone recognizes the fishing boats, but ignores them. They can meet a transport a hundred miles offshore, meet a delivery truck at some remote, rocky outcropping, then the truck goes on and the boat goes home. The truck can off-load it to a warehouse, or hide until they take it down to the city. Untraceable, even if the truck is stopped, searched, and the cargo found." Wiley shook his head. "By eliminating customs at the border they eliminate most of our chance to intercept."

"What about the Coast Guard?" asked Hill.

"They do what they can," said Wiley. "Now and then, they intercept one of the larger ships at sea. Rarely. Once it's off the big ship, forget it. In an area with a huge population of tourists and recreational boaters, like Cape Cod or southern Connecticut, they might run across a boat now and then. Maine has something like sixty thousand boats along its coast every year, plus visitors. There are five wardens, four Coast Guard patrol boats, and one cutter out of Boston to protect thousands of miles of coastline. Best setup I've seen in a long time."

"Sounds like a big deal," I said. "If you guys couldn't break it, what makes you think we can?"

"DEA didn't break it because they didn't have time," said Walker. "With Frederickson dead, they've got their hands full. DEA lacks time or manpower. So it falls to us."

"Okay with me," I said. "Where do we start?"

"There's a couple files downstairs, at the desk," said Wiley. "They're as up-to-date as the computers can make it."

"Over the next couple days, read the files, look over the case," ordered Walker. "Dickinson wants you to start watching the harbors tomorrow morning. He'll get in touch with you before noon."

"In the morning?" said Hill. "Does that mean a different schedule?"

"You'll be on duty twenty-four hours until further notice," said Walker. My heart sank as I thought of Monday's camping trip. I needed a few days away with Robyn. Obviously, it would have to wait. "Keep track of your time. We'll work out the details as we go."

"Speed is imperative," added Wiley. "I can't stress that enough. The whole operation could be shut down in seventy-two hours, leaving us with nothing."

"All right." Walker stood. "That's all you need for now. Don't worry about the rest of the shift. Go downstairs, have a few cups of coffee. The DEA agents and my men will brief you on procedures.

Have to check you out on some new gear, too. You should find all the details in the files: background, names, dates, places. Try to finish it all up by Monday. Got it?"

"Yes, sir," we replied.

"Before you leave, see the duty sergeant. Leave your cruisers, sign out unmarked cars. Draw portable radios, cameras, new armor, and some special weapons. Understood?"

"Got it," said Hill.

"Good. I'll be down later, after I talk with Agent Wiley. You'll be hearing from Agent Suarez soon."

"Very good, sir." Hill reached the door first. I followed him into the hallway, closing the door with a loud rattle. We strode down the hallway silently, lost in our own thoughts. As we descended the stairs, I said, "Looks like we hooked a big one."

"I think we hooked a goddam whale," answered Hill.

"Yuh. This one's going to take a while."

"No kidding." Hill slapped me lightly on the shoulder and turned down toward the basement as I headed for the desk. "I've got to call home, tell my wife I'm going to be late."

"See you in the break room."

"Right. Pick up my file for me?"

"Sure." He went out of sight below the level of the stairs. I leaned over the desk. "You got a pair of files for Hoitt and Hill?"

"Sure do." The clerk rolled backward to a work table and picked up two overflowing buff envelopes. "Here you go."

They must have weighed at least ten pounds each, I thought. "Thanks," I said. I took the files to the break room and tossed them on the table. The top one opened, spilling some of its contents: photographs, pages and pages of computer printouts, faxes, and dozens of grainy duplicates. I shook my head. I went to the coffee machine, poured a cup, and sat down. The file was thick, heavy, the pages loaded with information. I wondered what I had stumbled into.

Dawn splashed bright colors across the sky as I left the station. I remembered from my college all-nighters that, when you caught a sunrise, the following day seemed much longer. I looked forward to duty other than patrol, a chance to make a name for myself as a detective. It could be translated into an early promotion. On the other hand, the price I would pay included reduced sleep, greater personal risk, and less time with Robyn. I hoped it would all prove worthwhile.

Hill and I walked out into the lot, my gun belt draped over my shoulder, my hands full of files, radios, and other gear as I looked for my new car. I found the right blue sedan and dropped everything as gently as my tired arms allowed beside the trunk. I found the keys, opened the back, and tossed everything inside. Hill found his car, loaded it up, and slammed the trunk. "I was about ready for a new car."

"Isn't what I had in mind," I replied. "It'll do for now."

"It'll do for now," he echoed. He opened his door. "See you later, Jimmy."

I waved lazily. "See you, Fred. Good luck."

He started his engine, backed out, and pointed toward his home.

I fumbled with the keys as I tried to unlock the door. The inside was a lot nicer than my cruiser, more comfortable. It seemed ironic to me that the more comfortable car would be the one the officer spent less time in. After all, why shouldn't the guy on patrol, the one in the car for most of the eight-hour shift, have the more luxurious machine? One of the perks of promotion, I thought.

The car clicked smoothly into gear. It seemed strange not to have the rack of equipment stacked in the middle of the dash, to be driving a normal car. Probably not as much power, I thought. I resolved to test it out when I reached the open road.

At the end of the lot, I turned toward Route 1 rather than the back roads. That early in the morning, traffic would be nonexistent; the better road would get me home quicker. I wanted to get home as fast as possible, get as much sleep as I could before starting work. No way could I catch enough rest, but I knew anything would beat nothing. I did not expect a lot of sleep in the near future.

The stoplight turned green; I turned onto Route 1 South and pointed my new car toward my old bed.

3

Saturday Morning

Patrol Area: Eagle Harbor
Temps mild, light rain; wind
12–20 knots, N; seas moderate

That the spell of good weather would end was inevitable. When I awoke the next morning, the broken clouds that had been drifting past on my drive home had evolved into raging towers of stormy air, driven toward a low off Nova Scotia. The rain vacillated between an annoying drizzle and slashing droplets. The wipers barely kept up with the steady rumble against the car.

The first element of the surveillance would be gathering routine information: creating schedules, noting what tended to happen when. Against such an organized list of procedures, activities, and events, an irregularity, such as an incoming shipment, might stand out. By virtue of my connections, I was assigned to Eagle Harbor. Having lived there so long, I had a good idea of the standard routines. I knew who departed when and who did what. The fishing fleet set out between 4:00 and 6:30; most would return by 1:00. The Maine Shellfish Company truck came by on Wednesdays and Fridays. Shore Electronics made a regular supply and maintenance run every Tuesday; yet on any given day, he might show up for emergency repairs. If the Coast Guard stopped for an inspection, it generally came around two, during the middle of the week. As I thought about it, I realized there were plenty of others: deliveries to the merchants, tour busses passing through, church meetings and such. Collectively, they comprised life in Eagle Harbor. To detect a discrepancy, I needed more than basic schedules.

Before going to bed, I reviewed the files and set a preliminary timetable. Today I intended to start surveillance, and make cursory inquiries into what anyone knew. I sited my post on the point, just below the lighthouse. Among the rocks and trees I could remain undetected, protected from the sun, in a reasonably comfortable place to observe, read, make notes—and do a lot of thinking.

Then came the rain. Sitting under the lighthouse no longer seemed a good idea. I drove to the far side of the harbor, where an old shack nestles into the side of the glacial ridge that formed Eagle Harbor's east rampart. A widowed fisherman named Jack Baber had lived there until his death. Despite the thirteen years since, no one has bought the land or seen fit to tear down the shack. The weather has been unable to crush it. The shack has become a popular place among high school kids; secluded, good view of the harbor, with a clear view of anyone coming up the road long before they reach you. I needed the spectacular view, while the roof overhead offered obvious benefits. The shack would suit me just fine.

The shack had no proper driveway, just two grassy ruts snaking through the woods off Cove Road. The wide dirt skirt was well used, but narrow and overgrown—if you didn't know where to look, you'd pass it by as another hiking trail into the trees. I knew the right sign (a pair of birches immediately following a granite boulder), and turned up the path.

I hadn't been there in a long time. The quality of the ruts had seriously deteriorated; the grassy strip could have been cut for hay. Deep canyons appeared at irregular intervals, slamming the wheels to the limits of the shocks. I hoped the low car would survive.

Around half a dozen corners, up a steep grade, the ruts flattened out into a wide green meadow, surrounded by scrub brush. On the high side, beyond the trees, the ridge rises higher still; the harbor peeks through the trees on the downslope. A walkway leads from the meadow to the shack. I parked the car, facing the road. I gathered my equipment and headed for the shack.

When Jack had lived there, he used wooden stairs to drop thirty feet from lot to shack. Since his death, the stairs have been scavenged for firewood; only a rotten, skeletal frame remains. Sliding down the pine needle–covered slope was not easy, especially with my hands full, but it was safer than the stairs. The screen door has long since disappeared—the metal parts in a junk pile beside the house, the wood burned along with the stairs—but the main door, the last defense for those caught inside, remains essentially intact. The latch caught only partially, and the hinges didn't so much creak as bellow in agony as I swung it open.

The shack measures barely fifteen feet square. The old wood stove, surprisingly clean, occupies the corner nearest the door. Most of the cupboards have suffered the same fate as the screen door and stairs; the remaining ones are resistant to demolition. A few feet of linoleum-topped counter stretch away from the stove, empty bags, ashtray scrapings, and beer bottles stacked against the wall. At the other end of the counter is the bathroom, its door intact despite the fact it conceals only a fractured, useless toilet. The other side of the room Jack had used for his bed and chair; only the metal fossils remain. The bottom of a kerosene lamp still hangs from the wall, its globe long gone. With no wind, a medicine bottle full of kerosene can light the room for an hour or two, if you know how to keep the wick low.

I set my gear on the floor by the front window. Only one of the twelve filthy panes of glass had been shattered; a piece of sodden cardboard covered it. It would be easier to open than clean it. I bent to the base and forced the window open. Swollen by rain, it resisted at first, then gave way. I propped a beer bottle under the sash to hold it open.

Sitting on the floor, using the wall as a backrest, my position was only fairly comfortable, but the view was expansive and unparalleled. I scanned along the ridge following the cut of the driveway, back to where it joined the road. There was no clear view of the drive, but I could intermittently see any car passing behind the trees. Most important, it was dry. It would do.

The ridge slopes down below the shack, steeply approaching the water eighty yards below. The harbor spreads out from there, behind a thicket of hemlocks. From my vantage, I could see any boat entering or leaving Eagle Harbor. The town dock, and the village behind it, juts into the harbor from the right. Boats tugged on their moorings as I swept my view left. Green and red buoys march from the thicket of the moorings, delineating the channel. It is narrow, but deep. Three years ago a chartered sailboat, mishandled by some Massachusetts flatlanders, got broadsided by an outgoing fishing boat in fog. Everyone escaped, but when the fog cleared, only a mast tip leaning out of the water marked the yacht's resting place. Farther out, nearly lost behind a thick stand of trees, the mouth of the harbor yawns below the lighthouse on the far point. A granite breakwater separates the harbor from the sea. Only a vessel passing close to the ridge could escape my scrutiny. Because of the dirty water there, I didn't expect any traffic to pass unnoticed.

My view checked, I settled in. I wedged the radio beside the window pane where it could be easily heard and easily reached. The prevailing wind kept rain out of the window, except for a fine mist. It didn't bother me, but it could ruin the paperwork, which I kept back from the window. I set the binoculars on the floor, and poured a cup of coffee from my thermos.

I used the binocs and made a quick survey of the harbor. Just after ten in the morning; rather late. Half the local fleet was out. Three boats tied up at the dock, including my father, still making repairs. Three more bobbed at their moorings. About twenty pleasure craft reside in Eagle Harbor, from small aluminum runabouts to a big, beautiful sloop. I didn't know the local pleasure sailors as well as I knew the fishermen, nor did I know their boats. As far as I could tell, about four were gone, among them the Freeman's sloop: no doubt with Steve Freeman and my sister still aboard. Considering the rain, no surprise.

To profit from the transient yachtsmen, the town maintains twelve guest moorings, eight of which were filled. The visiting fleet on that day was a rich one; I conservatively estimated the value of the smallest boat at eighty thousand dollars. Eagle Harbor isn't exactly on the path from anywhere to anywhere; it is less known than places like Southwest or Bar Harbors, so getting a mooring is often easier. Like nesting birds, many boats returned every summer. A vague mist hovered just beyond the breakwater, limiting my view to half a mile outside the harbor. I could hear at least two boats maneuvering in the fog. Unable to see them, I had no idea whether they were coming in, or just passing by.

I made some notes, including a rough map of the moorings. I could not read registration numbers or boat names, but I noted anything remarkable about the boat: hull color, style, size, rig. If I knew the owner, I wrote it down. I noted the time of my first observation, and set the pad aside.

Before I could reach for the files, I heard the dull roar of an engine starting. I trained the binoculars on the harbor. For a moment, nothing; then one of the boats at the dock started to move, a red fiberglass lobster boat, around twenty-eight feet. I knew the owner by sight, but not by name. He'd moved to town only recently, in the last five or ten years, and kept mostly to himself. I watched it turn away from the dock, slip into the channel for a few hundred feet before it headed for a mooring. Only one man aboard: about six feet, dark slacks, probably jeans; either a beard or very dark skin. He had a good feel for walking over the boat. He gracefully swung out of the cabin onto the foredeck, climbed up to the prow, and bent over the bow chock to secure the mooring line. He yanked the line before returning to the cabin. Seconds later the engine died. He cleaned and locked up his boat before pulling up the skiff and rowing ashore.

I noted the time and actions. Barely half past ten, early for a professional fisherman to be back. Returning early did not constitute a crime, but it warranted inclusion in my notes.

My coffee had cooled, so I added some hot coffee to warm it. A quick sweep of the harbor revealed no more activity. I didn't have to read long before I realized a crucial fact: the story surpassed anything Wiley had implied. Whether you identified the corpse as Martin or Frederickson, the life that preceded his death made a convoluted story.

It began with Frederickson, the accountant, nearly thirty years before, a young man from New Jersey leaving a train in Florida. The young man who started working as a bookkeeper in a bakery could not have guessed the path his life would follow. Northwest of Miami, the bakery was a legitimate business owned by a very private man. Coincidentally, three things happened. First, the owner knew his business; before long the bakery expanded, opening a dozen other stores. The bookkeeping department grew as well, until Frederickson became not just a bookkeeper but Head Bookkeeper. Meanwhile, the market for illegal drugs exploded; the smugglers started looking for a new market and a new place through which to bring the goods. A new industry began in southern Florida.

Finally, the connection. While the private man who owned the bakery was totally legitimate, his brother lacked the same ethics. He saw the opportunity to make easy money. He acquired a little cash, enough to get a foothold in the growth industry. Business was good; as the sixties became the seventies the cash flow would have made a small country envious. He also acquired the paradoxical sobriquet Grandpa Joe. Somebody had to watch the money, and when Joe's aging accountant finally died, he needed someone reliable. What better person than his brother's head bookkeeper?

The bakery lost Frederickson, who had to learn the tricks of the new business. Grandpa Joe demanded that his accountant have a full understanding of the operation as the only way to ensure not a single penny escaped. If the new employee harbored any guilt about his new job, he buried it deeply. Frederickson would become a precise and demanding accountant who wielded a surprising amount of power within the corporation. In an industry where reputation meant everything, Frederickson earned an image as the accountant who never came up short. More than one rival enticed him to join them; it said much for his loyalty that Frederickson never considered the lucrative offers.

Shaking that loyalty would prove crucial.

I heard an engine catch. I traded the files for the binoculars. Sweeping over the moorings, I detected no signs of activity. I checked the boats at the dock, but none had moved. No one already in the channel should be starting up, but I checked anyway; I saw nothing. Must have been out in the mist.

I listened intently. I heard a single engine of reasonable size; that eliminated a few boats. It seemed bigger than an auxiliary motor, so I crossed off the sailboats. Scanning the boats that remained, I finally saw something: almost obscured by the high cabin walls, a man was moving about in one of the fishing fleet. I recognized the boat. It belonged to one of my father's best friends, Bert Duggan, but Bert was not the person aboard. The stranger crawled out to the bow and cast off. The weak current pushed the boat along while he returned to the cabin to drive clear of the mooring. Moving too fast, he swung past the nearest boats, setting the boats into a chaotic dance.

That wasn't right. I didn't know why the Duggan boat was not out fishing yet, but that didn't matter. Someone was stealing his boat. In all my life I can't recall anyone stealing a boat from Eagle Harbor; if it was happening now, I wouldn't be surprised if it was connected to the drug smuggling ring. I didn't have any time to lose. I toggled the radio switch. "County nineteen to dispatch, come in."

"County dispatch. Go, nineteen."

"Dispatch, I need a patrol car to report to the Eagle Harbor dock."

"Ten-four, nineteen. What's the situation?"

"I have a theft in progress," I said, proud to keep my voice so calm. "What's the nearest cruiser?"

"Stand by, nineteen," came the terse reply.

The boat was heading in. Strange way to steal a boat, I thought. Maybe it wasn't the boat he wanted, but something aboard it. An accomplice could be waiting on the dock. I trained the binoculars to the right, toward the dock, searching for the other half of the theft team. A red-headed man in white shorts and a yellow shirt walked to the end of the dock; he carried a big tote, and was heading right for a sailboat, so I discounted him. Next I checked the bait dock, and stopped dead. Talking calmly with my own father stood Bert Duggan. He looked up occasionally to check the progress of his boat, no doubt coming in to meet him. I remember my father telling me he had hired some summer help. It wasn't a theft; it was routine. I picked up my radio, and cleared my throat. "County nineteen to dispatch."

"County dispatch. Go, nineteen."

"Uh, county dispatch, disregard previous request."

"Disregard?" said the incredulous radio voice. "Are you sure?"

I sighed, then triggered the mike. "Mistaken identity, dispatch. My fault. No problem here. Over."

"Ten-four, county nineteen.

"County nineteen clear." Investigation was going to be a learning experience. I had to remember to gather evidence first, then reach a valid conclusion before calling in the cavalry.

I scratched a few notes, describing what I could see of the crewman as he pointed the boat toward the bait dock. Duggan, who I now noticed had a cane at his side, helped him tie up, then they loaded a rusty bait barrel. I wondered why he was getting such a late start. I made some final notes, then resumed reading the files.

Numerous DEA attempts to shut down Grandpa Joe's business barely slowed him. DEA reports indicated that, at best, they temporarily interrupted 3 to 5 percent of the business, and jailed a few minor characters. As profits increased, the business expanded. While increasing its scope of operations, the business became more violent: competitors regularly disappeared. Persistent law officials found themselves and their relatives susceptible to "accidents." Nothing could be proven, of course, but Grandpa Joe's import business spread as far north as Virginia, as far west as Texas, supplying dealers from New York to Chicago to San Francisco.

The DEA wanted very much to shut him down; to do so, they realized, they had to abandon petty interdictions and go right for the throat. They targeted Frederickson. Thus began two and a half years of surveillance, wiretaps, interrogations, and the pursuit of the money trail. A conservative Justice Department audit indicated it had cost nearly four million dollars to build a case against Frederickson, but they did it.

Duggan's boat pulled away from the bait pier. Duggan piloted through the channel, cleared the breakwater, and was swallowed by the fog. I marked the time.

They hauled in Frederickson. The DEA wanted Grandpa Joe; they hoped to use Frederickson to nail him. They laid out the situation, but he refused to budge. Questioning proved futile, and the U.S. attorney had no choice but to prosecute the accountant. It took seven months to set up the trial, which lasted five weeks before going to the jury. The prosecutor felt confident he would win a conviction, but the verdict never came. On the third day of deliberations, Frederickson, without the expensive lawyer Grandpa Joe had paid for, walked into the U.S. attorney's office and agreed to cooperate if they would halt the trial, grant him immunity, and hide him.

Naturally, the prosecutor was delighted to oblige.

Frederickson knew everything. It took nine days just to take his entire statement. Once they had it, the DEA, the FBI, and authorities from the state of Florida moved quickly. Within two months they crushed the entire operation. A few lieutenants escaped, taking some business with them, but over ninety percent of the business abruptly ceased. Grandpa Joe never served a day in jail: he died of a heart attack during pretrials. Frederickson, as promised, escaped prosecution. He received a new identity as a man named Martin, a quiet man, very good with numbers, and retired to Somesville, Maine.

Out in the harbor I heard another engine catch, or at least try. It sputtered, coughed, then died. The starter whined, the engine resisted. After a prolonged turnover the engine caught, ran roughly for perhaps thirty seconds—then died in a bang like the final fireworks on the Fourth of July. I took up the binoculars again and trained them on the dock. A cloud of thick blue-black smoke drifted over the water. My father stood over the engine compartment, shaking his head. As I watched he gave it a solid kick. Apparently, things weren't working out.

The monotonous droning beyond the harbor had increased; several boats were approaching. I looked at my watch: 12:40. Considering the interruptions an incoming fleet would yield, I abandoned the files and looked for lunch. I tossed my cold coffee out the window and refilled the cup. The box lunch from the diner was an adequate meal for my strenuous activity.

The rain had eased. The fog had thinned, allowing me to see the first boat before it passed the breakwater. The first boat became two boats in line: a big, white, lobster boat with a huge white wake behind her stern, and following the disturbed water, a smaller aluminum boat, modified for the lobster hunt with a lifting rig over the starboard side and a stand-up control console amidships. Both navigated the channel; the white boat headed for the dock while the smaller one aimed straight for its mooring.

A few minutes later the ugly barge owned by Eagle Harbor's fire chief chugged its way through the breakwater and pulled up to the bait dock. He had started with an old Boston Whaler, then added work decks, a cabin, bigger engines, more flotation, until he had something that looked less like a boat than a floating dump. Boats often returned around lunch. It gave them six to eight hours on the morning tide to gather their catch, then an afternoon to look for a buyer or make minor repairs. Though any of these men would probably vehemently deny it, they were creatures of rigorous habit. I relied on that to get an accurate portrait of harbor activity.

I finished lunch, crumpled the paper products, and flung them into the wood stove. I had no intention of starting a fire—despite the rain, the temperature was quite comfortable—but knew someone would. Someday the casual nature of the shack's visitors would cause its demise in a cloud of smoke. It would be a pity, but it was as inevitable as summer rain.

Back at the window, I observed that many moorings were now filled. Five boats had returned since I started observations; only three remained out. One of them, a large fishing trawler, probably spent the night on the banks. I used up four pages detailing the return of the fleet, including a short list of the order they came back. I also noted the two boats that returned together: no telling what that might mean.

I wasn't as sure about the recreational boats. I knew a few of them, like the Freeman's. Most of them I knew nothing about. Usually they could be counted on to stay tied up on rainy days, to go out in the afternoon on beautiful weekdays, and to leave in the late morning and return in the evening on the weekend. Deep down, I knew if anyone smuggled drugs into Eagle Harbor, it wouldn't be on the recreational boats.

The harbor quiet, lunch partly digested, I turned back to the reports. I had no sooner reached for the closer pile than I heard my name on the radio. It had been quietly squawking all morning with police traffic, but never with my name. "Hoitt. Go ahead."

"Jimmy, this is Dickinson." The portable radio mangled his voice even worse than the cruiser radios, but nothing could disguise it completely. "Where are you?"

"Eagle Harbor," I reported.

"Can you be more precise?"

"Do you know where Jack's shack is? Just below the ridge?"

"No. Tell me how to—uh, stand by." There was quiet for a moment. "Okay, stay there. I'll be there in about twenty minutes, half an hour."

"I'll keep the door unlocked."

"Ten-four. County three clear."

I settled back down to get a little more reading done before Dickinson arrived. As far as the witness protection program was concerned, the saga ended with the creation of Martin. Things remained quiet for a while. Naturally, they kept track of Martin's activities: watched him earn his real estate broker's license, observed his increasing proficiency, and saw what it did to his bank account. A gifted financier, Martin had great talent. Consequently, when he began to invest in larger and more expensive properties, the Feds were not surprised.

A report dated nine months ago made curious reading. A copy of an IRS record appended to the report stated that Martin listed just over one million dollars in assets. The report called attention to this, and to an independent assessment that Martin's net worth exceeded three million dollars. The size of this sum after only a few years in his new life was amazing enough, according to the author. But how could they believe such a meticulous, precise man could underestimate his own worth by a factor of three? Such a discrepancy unambiguously indicated that Martin wanted to hide something: land scams, insider trading, some kind of fronting operation. The author ended the report by recommending that a thorough investigation be initiated.

A page added after the report, clearly written by a supervisor, read "file for future reference." I looked through what I had, but found no indication that any action had been taken.

The sound of tires swishing over wet road drifted through the trees. I looked up to see a blur moving up the driveway. Dickinson had arrived. I put the papers in some order, pushed them out of the way, and went out to welcome him.

As I topped the rise, Dickinson parked and stepped out. "Afternoon, Jimmy."

"Hello, Sergeant."

He shook my hand. Dickinson stands six and a half feet tall and about 250 pounds, only a hint of fat on his fifty-year-old frame. His grip reflected every bit of that. "Secluded spot."

"Gets busy on summer evenings, if you know what I mean."

"I see." He may not have known about Jack's shack, but he probably knew a place just like it near his home. "Seems well known."

"What do you mean?"

"I called from Northeast Harbor. Checking things out there, talking to the harbor master and his assistant. He overheard you, and before I could ask you for directions, he told me. Then his assistant joined in and provided a short cut."

"It's kind of a local hangout." We started down the slope. "Seems to get a little more popular every year."

"I'll add it to my list. Why are you here?"

"From inside I have an excellent view of the harbor. It's dry. I can finish going through the reports."

"It looks leaky."

"It's just damp."

We went inside. The sergeant spared only a cursory glance around the room. He headed directly for the window, stooping low to look out over the harbor. He nodded slowly, picked up my binoculars, and looked again. "An excellent vantage, Jimmy."

"It has its benefits," I agreed.

"I don't suppose you've seen anything interesting." He checked my notepad. "Seems about right for a rainy day."

"Not much to compare it to yet. Seems quiet."

"Keep an eye out. When you get a good pattern, let me have a copy, okay?"

"Sure."

"How's the reading coming?"

"There's a lot of detail. I just finished the history lesson."

He nodded again. "Pretty grim, isn't it?"

"It's hard to believe this guy lived up the street, yet we didn't even know it. Scares me to think who else might be here."

"If half of what the DEA thinks is actually true, I can't say I'm sorry he's dead." Dickinson stared past me, his eyes cold. "We still have a murder to solve."

"Yes, sir."

"Let me tell you a couple things that aren't in your reports, Jimmy. They're all paper-thin leads, but they're all we've got. People working in the same office complex as Frederickson's agency report a lot more kids going to see a realtor than they'd expect."

"Kids?"

"Young adults, really. Late teens to mid-twenties. Mostly men; very few women."

"That's odd."

"Maybe, maybe not. It might just say the witnesses are mostly middle-aged women who notice young men."

That was of no help to me. "What else?" I asked.

"Bank accounts. Martin maintained bank accounts at nearly every bank or branch on the island. That's unusual. He also dealt heavily in his own real estate. Bought and sold large volumes all over Mount Desert Island and the mainland. But there were only four places where he bought large tracts of ocean frontage. They're all in excess of 150 feet of deepwater frontage, over five acres, well away from densely populated areas. He even paid top dollar for them, which is odd for a broker who should know better." Dickinson looked out over the harbor. "One of those places is on the west side of Eagle Harbor."

"I see," I said slowly. I could not believe a drug-smuggling operation could exist so close to my home. I would have known; if not me, surely one of the Eagle Diner gossips. I said as much to Dickinson.

"I know, Jimmy. But if I told you a week ago that Frederickson lived out here, you wouldn't have believed me, would you?"

I started to protest, then stopped. "I'll watch the harbor."

"Good. No one could possibly cover this place any better."

The unexpected praise from the taciturn Dickinson surprised me. "Thank you."

"You've earned it. If you find anything, call me right away. We don't want to let anything slip by. Francis wants to be kept notified, too, so don't be a stranger at Ellsworth. Okay?"

"Yes, sir."

Dickinson checked his watch. "I'm way behind my schedule. I'm not used to this duty, either. I thought I could cover a lot more ground. Take it easy."

Without waiting for comment he let himself out. I heard him run up the hill to his car. In a moment the car passed through the trees. Save for the rain falling on the roof, the wind softly sighing through the trees, and the buoy groaning off the breakwater, quiet returned.

I checked out the harbor to see if anything had changed, but it hadn't. Not much happens during afternoons. The fleet kept to their moorings; my father still struggled with his boat. Things were normal, and normal meant quiet. I returned to my reading.

While no one actively investigated Martin, a sequence of events began which would ultimately lead to him. One year before the discrepancy between the IRS records and Martin's estimated net worth, drug agents working in Boston first reported a new pipeline. When busts turned up some unexpected faces, the agents began to wonder why. Investigations revealed a new source of top-grade cocaine. Like any business trying to break into a market, the new source undercut the competition's price. Opportunists eager to take advantage of the cheaper supply precipitated a brief, bloody turf war.

The Boston agents wondered about the new source, but had no luck in tracing it, and had their hands full trying to cope with the consequences. They did, however, deduce two things. First, without a doubt, it came by land from the north; most likely through Maine or New Hampshire. Second, after about three months, the supplier, satisfied with his foothold, raised his prices to an appropriate market level. The battle died down, but the ground had been won.

If the Boston agents had learned of the next event, they surely would have made the connection, and commenced the investigation a year earlier. At a routine truck stop, Maine State Police halted a rental truck transporting bed furniture from Bangor to Boston. The manifest was flawless, the truck weighed in correctly, the driver proved fully licensed, but something "funny" about the cargo hold bothered one trooper. A closer inspection revealed a narrow false front. Behind the thin aluminum sheathing were stacked 150 kilos of cocaine.

The Maine State Police detectives found no link whatsoever to the driver, other than the circumstantial fact that he had been driving the truck. He had excellent character references, a clean record, and no sufficient motive to breach his personal beliefs to make some quick cash. They satisfied themselves he had no connection to the cargo and let him go.

The hidden compartment had been well built. The cargo could have been loaded a week prior to the loading of the furniture; it may have been there up to two months. The rental company's logs gave a long list of renters for the preceding two months. Not one of them could be clearly linked to the drugs. The truck had traveled from Nova Scotia to Boston and from Montreal to nearly every town along the Down East coast. With no reason to suspect any one area in particular, the task swamped the meager Maine State Police resources. No leads developed, and the case remained unsolved.

Highway inspectors examined all trucks, especially rentals, very carefully for the next few weeks. Nothing turned up. Soon they resumed normal operations. For another year the rented truck would remain unconnected.

A pair of murders at the beginning of the year provided the next piece. In Orrington, a village south of Bangor on Penobscot Bay, a brand-new pickup slid off the road and sliced a phone pole in half. Inside, police found a man slumped over the steering wheel. An autopsy found levels of poison five times the lethal level. The police never could decide where he had procured the fatal sandwich, its half-eaten remains found on the cab floor.

Local police found another man beaten to death aboard a rented yacht anchored in Camden Harbor. The renters disappeared. The boat had been rented from a firm in Marblehead, Massachusetts. It took only a short check to reveal that the people who had signed the forms did not exist.

While the public knew of no connections, the state police did. Both victims had been suspected distributors of illegal drugs. While neither could be called a "godfather," both had made a healthy profit and had employed similar operations: shipments came ashore on fishing boats, were repackaged, then sent down to Boston or New York. Neither constituted a major source, and neither excelled at it. Apparently, however, they had been good enough to get in somebody's way.

The Coast Guard got its licks in, as well. They caught a handful of the fishermen connected to the two dead men. The Coast Guard officers observed a change in the situation off Maine: more people were involved; shipments came more often, and in greater volume; and the hiding places became more cunning, yet similar, as if a single master brain orchestrated the entire affair. Already stretched by too many things to do, with too few men and boats, the investigation went no further then a memo sent to the DEA.

I put the papers aside and stood up, massaging my aching neck. Late afternoon meant dying winds, and the shack became humid and stuffy. I stretched my legs, then sat before the window. In the channel, a black-hulled sloop maneuvered toward the moorings, a good-looking boat with graceful lines. Scant wind swept over the water, but it didn't matter to the sailors aboard: sails trimmed in, no sign of fluttering sails, her course straight and true. They were good. The black boat passed the inner harbor buoy, tacked over, and deftly cruised among the moorings as they dropped the mainsail. Another tack and she swung back toward the breakwater. The genoa slacked as she coasted up to the mooring, stopping with her bow right over the pick-up buoy—an easy reach for the bowman.

I had almost completed my reading. Despite the calm harbor, I wanted to finish the paperwork before heading home. I stretched, pulling my arms far forward, and took up the final folder.

The Coast Guard memo did not reach a dead end. In fact, it proved to be the final piece of evidence that brought the DEA onto the case. The pieces were all there, but not yet on the same table. With a less regional view, the puzzle came together. The new supply in Boston connected to the rented truck, rented from a firm less than sixty miles from the two drug-related murders.

The reports said Wiley himself found the report of the IRS discrepancy. With this, the pieces fit perfectly. Martin was centrally located, enabling him to employ fishermen along the Maine coast. He knew the business well, having faithfully served Grandpa Joe for so long. Martin would have an excellent reason to want to conceal his worth if he ran such an organization. The reported discrepancy probably fell far short. Though insufficient to arrest him, the connections justified opening the case.

The DEA proceeded by the book. With a man as prominent as Martin in the witness protection program, able to afford phenomenal lawyers, the case had to be flawless. Such a case took time. They avoided the messy details of the operation, concentrating instead on the easier target of finances. Thursday afternoon, the U.S. attorney made an appointment with the director of the witness relocation program to sever the protection before filing charges. Normally, he would have charged and arrested Martin by Monday, but circumstances got in the way.

I sat back and thought. Martin's death, murder or accidental, came as a terrible inconvenience to the Justice Department. The money trail had yielded sufficient evidence to indict Martin, but little information about the network. With Martin dead, they had no case against anyone save the probate court.

The DEA doubted the organization shut down. Consensus held that Martin, like the two before him, had been killed to clear the way for another. The DEA wanted that man. Aside from the framework of his operation and Dickinson's lead scraps, there wasn't a hell of a lot to go on. The reports could reveal no more. The details of the prosecution I would leave to someone else. My task was perfectly clear: to find the connection to Eagle Harbor, or prove there was none.

Though the days were still summer-long, clouds and fog precipitated premature darkness. I could barely see to read. I could not make out details in the harbor, only fuzzy, white halos of the floodlights shining through the thickening fog. I had made some progress, if only in understanding the work ahead. A good day's work.

I gathered up my things, stuffed them into the canvas bag, and closed the door behind me. The night air hung thick and moist with heavy fog, but the rain had abated. I started the car, flipped on the lights, and bumped my way out to the main road. While the day may not have been perfect beach weather, Saturday night guaranteed a full load of night action. I had to wait for a line of cars before turning toward the harbor. One car flashed by me at a speed clearly exceeding the posted twenty-five. Working undercover differed from patrol; I instinctively wanted to reach for the blues and pursue, but my job lay elsewhere. I made a radio report to any cruiser in the area, and headed into town.

As I drove off the ridge, dropping closer to the water, the fog thickened. By the time I reached the village, I could not see the church steeple. The fog turned approaching cars into indistinct blurs. I turned into the gray murk after the diner, parking beside the boat rack.

Visibility deteriorated close to the harbor. I would not have wanted to take a boat any farther than the mooring. I walked out to the ramp and descended to the float. Since I had last seen the dock, another fishing boat had tied up and a pair of deckhands were off-loading green totes and stacking them on the dock. I knew the men by sight, but not by name. One of them must have recognized me, for he looked up to say hello. I returned the greeting and walked to my father's boat.

Still tied up meant no progress. The *Janet Kathleen III*—named after my mother and the previous two boats that had taken him from high school through two kids—rested against the dock, spring lines loose against the slack tide. Dad had built her from the keel up—a long project, but something he had long wanted to do. *Janet Kathleen III* had the classic lines of a Maine lobster boat: a high, blunt bow, sharply sloping sheer to a flat, broad fantail, a square cabin with large plexiglass windows set into the foredeck. He had built a sleeping cabin forward, with brass portholes along the deck. Two years of sun had faded its light gray paint to a chalky color, but no weathering could detract from the fine lines.

The engine hatches were propped up against the transom. From inside came the irritated sound of my father futilely arguing with the engine. As I passed the cabin I saw the greasy black lump in the center of the boat, parts splayed over the aft deck. I stepped down and swung my legs over the rail.

A head popped up from behind the engine. My father is a big man, tall, broad through the shoulders, with huge arms. A stiff Lincoln beard, flecked with gray, conceals his chin. Deep lines arrow back from his eyes toward the black hair slowly turning white. His uniform—plaid shirt, jeans, and a nylon hat with the Maine Shellfish Company logo embroidered on the face—carried stains from solvents, oil, bait, and grease. He waved. "How you doin'?"

"Not bad, Dad." I sat on the rail beside the winch. "How's it goin'?"

"Terrible." He set down a foot-long screwdriver. "My gawd, Jimmy, sometimes I wonder why I don't pay up the insurance, take her off the point, grab the shotgun, and blow a hole in the bottom."

"What's the matter?"

"I'll be damned if I know." He reached beside the wheel and pulled down his pipe, tobacco, and a book of matches. He started filling the bowl. "She was runnin' rough a couple days ago. I think I told you that."

"You said it was skipping."

"Yuh. That's what I said." He put the pipe in his mouth and struck a match, sucked down the flame and got the pipe going. "Well, I thought I'd take a look. I could spare a couple days. I took the easy route first and gave her a quick Mexican tune-up."

He had changed the plugs. "It didn't take."

"Nope. I looked at the old plugs when I pulled 'em. They weren't fouled, just normal wear. Except one. I figured my problem might be there."

"Burning oil again?"

"I should be so lucky." He took a long pull. A dense ghost of smoke drifted upwards. "I poured in some oil to check the rings. They seemed okay. I didn't want to see the results, but I borrowed a compression gauge and checked her out. Sure enough, I wasn't gettin' a damn thing on number three."

"Burnt valve."

"That's what I thought. So I pulled the head and had a look. Sure enough, the exhaust valve on the third cylinder, the edge was burnt right in."

"I thought you overhauled the engine last summer."

"I did, Jimmy, that's just what I thought to myself. I must have let out a cursing fit they heard for miles. It's them cheap valves from Japan they been sendin' me. Just like the three that blew last summer. They cost half as much, they look nice all arranged in a box, they work fine for a little while, but they last like shit."

"Did you get new ones?"

"Well, I went up to see Morgan soon as I had that thing out." Morgan ran the parts shop at the back of O'Brien's. "Took the valve with me. Shoved it in his face as soon as I got there and told him what I thought of his imported valves. He backed down right quick. Said he could get the original parts, 'cept he didn't have any in stock just then."

"And ordering them would take. . . ?"

"He said he'd phone in the order, but they still wouldn't be here for a couple weeks."

I winced. "Not good."

"You ain't kiddin'. Height of the season coming on, and all. So I fumed a little more, then had me a good think. The rest of the engine has a couple more of them damn things in it, so it's livin' on borrowed time. I figured what the hell? Fix it all now and get it done right. I ordered a full set of valves."

"Meanwhile?"

"Meanwhile, Morgan felt bad about it. Seein' as how it was just the one, he gave me a new one, free. So I thanked him, took the part and a couple things I got, and came back to the boat. Put his valve in, cleaned and replaced everything else, and put it back together."

Another tobacco ghost floated upward. "I had it back together just after noon. Been trying to get it to run ever since, but I'll be damned if it will. She usually fires right up. Not today. No, sir. Refuses to fire. If she does catch, she sputters, coughs, smokes, and dies."

"What are you going to do next?"

"I was just tinkerin' while I thought about it. Like it or not, tomorrow morning I'll take the head off again and have a look. Something must not be adjusted, or been put in backward. I don't know. I've about had it for today."

He sat still and quiet, puffing the pipe. I guessed he thought about the engine, and did not wish to be disturbed. After a while, he asked, "What time is it?"

"Coming up 8:30."

"Good time to quit. Give me a hand, will you? I've got to put a tarp over this."

"Leaving it here?" The rules said no boat could be left unattended at the dock for more than thirty minutes. I had never known the harbor master to enforce the rule.

"Yuh. Skip knows it's here, and he knows who owns it. If he wants to move it, he can call me or move it himself."

He hauled out a blue plastic tarp. I helped him drape it over the engine block. He kicked a few parts underneath the cover, and we laid trap-weight bricks around the edge to hold it against the wind. He gathered up his tools, stuffed them into a battered steel box, and put it inside the cabin. He slipped a brass padlock through the door panels. "She's down for the night."

"I'm sorry I can't help you, Dad."

He stuffed the tobacco into his pocket and slapped my back. "Don't worry about it. You got your own worries."

He had that right.

"How's the police work goin'?"

"Not bad." I saw no need to worry him that someone in Eagle Harbor might be smuggling drugs. "Quiet day of surveillance. Watching."

"Sounds better than wanging on that engine."

"It is."

"Glad you enjoy it." He looked toward the breakwater, as if his eyes alone could penetrate the fog. When I grew old enough to go fishing with him, he had sworn he had "special eyes," eyes that saw a different kind of light, unaffected by fog. That's how he explained his ability to return to the dock, even in thick fog, and never run into other boats or rocks. As I grew older, I learned the secrets of his special eyes: listening for breaking waves, for buoys, remembering who sets their traps near navigation buoys, and the magic of radar. But from time to time as he peered into a thick fog, I would remember what he told me—and wonder if perhaps he did have special eyes.

"Eaten yet?"

"Not since lunch," I replied. My stomach lurched as I recalled how many hours had passed since them.

"Got any plans for dinner? Goin' out with Robyn?"

"No."

He nodded. "Let's go up to the diner, grab a bite, pick up your mother. My treat."

"Done."

He swung his legs over the gunwales. I followed him up the ramp. I had been watching Eagle Harbor all day and felt full of the place. After what Dickinson told me, after reading about Martin and his business, I needed to return to the Eagle Harbor I knew from before. The best way to accomplish that would be to have dinner among my father's friends and my mother's sources, and immerse myself completely.

I deeply looked forward to it.

4

Monday Morning
Patrol Area: Eagle Harbor
Temps warm; wind nil; seas calm; clouds
building through the afternoon

By Monday, I had filled the pages of one notebook and begun a second. The tiny pages contained a condensed version of Frederickson's story, the vital details highlighted along with two days of observations. I knew the data from the weekend would differ from what I could expect during the week; nevertheless, the times and actions were significant. I knew who preferred to moor first rather than heading straight for the dock; who rowed to their boat and who used a motor; loading and off-loading procedures; and other segments of mundane harbor life. The transient yachts were more difficult. Any one of them, merely by their presence, might warrant careful watching. I did not know much about these boats, but at least I had a start.

The first day of the work week demanded my presence at the water before dawn. The sun rose around half past four. I hoped to be established no later than four. For some peculiar reason, my alarm chose that morning to fail, but despite its delay I reached the shack just after four. The day promised to be bright, warm, and clear, so I did not expect to require the shack. I saw no other cars, no trace of all-nighters lingering through dawn. Yet as I approached, I heard noises from the shack. I had no quarrel with them; that morning, the rocky shore below would suit me well. I made enough noise to convince anyone inside they were no longer alone, then picked my way through the bristled shrubs and damp earth toward the shore.

As I cleared the trees, dawn expanded over the Atlantic; grays and pale blues streaked the sky, forcing night's western retreat. Dimmer stars surrendered to the dawn, leaving only a few bright points. Over the far side of the harbor I could see one spot of light: Venus.

I could not see the sun; the ridge on which I stood prevented any direct view east. I had watched sunrises over Eagle Harbor before, had watched Eagle Harbor sunrises and sunsets from that very spot. That morning I had too much work to do to enjoy the spectacle. I walked along the ledge, cautiously working my way out toward the point. I found a large, flat granite outcropping, with a convenient backrest, and established camp.

The harbor lay quiet before me. A single boat tied up to the bait dock. Since mid-Sunday, two more transient vessels had arrived. The first measured about thirty-five feet, a sleek, pale blue sloop with a dark gray sailcover. Near it squatted a huge tricolored motor yacht, broad in beam and square in the stern. The mooring line dangled slack from her bow chock to the pickup buoy, as she bobbed gently on the windless waters.

The ocean lapped softly at the rocks below me; if the tide were higher or the sea stronger, I would have been soaked. To my left, the ledge stretched out to meet the sea, where the breakwater emerged from the cliff. The ridge soared up behind the rocks. To the right, the land curved slowly toward the inner harbor, the ridge dropping down to marshes near the village. About a hundred yards away, a skiff rested on the rocks, motor raised, painter secured to a rusty iron ring anchored in the rocks: some shack denizens preferred boats to cars. I tried to make my rock as comfortable as possible. Though I expected to stay only until eight, a granite ledge quickly gets uncomfortable.

Eagle Harbor slowly awoke. In the waning darkness, headlights swung beside the diner, dipping sharply as they approached the dock, joining the darkness before the rumble of the engine reached me over the still, quiet morning water. I plainly heard each car, from the time it peaked the hill on the far side of the village, past the diner, until it paralleled the harbor to disappear behind my back. Bell and whistle buoys sounded infrequently, the light swell barely sufficient to generate sound. The creak of oars in oarlocks drifted over. I heard conversations, but couldn't make out the words. Laughter carried well. One by one, I heard the boat engines catch as they prepared for another day. When the morning cook arrived at the diner, I heard the bass hum as he fired up the ventilators. On my ridge, I heard whispers and snapping branches as the shack's visitors made for the water, thudded into the skiff, and motored away.

Boats moved to the dock, loaded, then slipped out through the breakwater. By the time morning replaced dawn, I had watched the routine repeated more than a dozen times Only one of the visitors, an old wooden cruiser, left. I expected it would not return. None of the events struck me as unusual in any way. I was pleased to check my notes and observe each boat follow the anticipated routine. I could have stayed on the ledge and watched until the harbor emptied, but I had no way of knowing when or if any of the transients might leave. I had little to gain by putting my rear end into a deeper sleep. There were other things to accomplish. I pocketed my pad and pencil and headed up to the car.

The early hour allowed a swift passage to the village. Eagle Harbor is notorious for having too few parking spaces; once the fishermen arrived, it didn't take long for the few available spots to fill. I lucked into a spot by the church. Three hours past dawn nearly everything was open, with the exception of the bank. With no warrants and no specific questions, I did not expect to gather a wealth of information. Still, I needed any scraps I could get. My stomach growled. I had not eaten since waking. It wasn't easy to walk past the diner door, but I wanted to get started. Two doors down from the church, the plate-glass and painted-brick facade of the hardware store looks out on the harbor. I stepped onto the granite stoop and went inside.

That familiar smell greeted my arrival: light machine oil, oak floors, sawdust, and paint. O'Brien's Trustworthy adds to that fresh coffee, sea air, new rope, and fiberglass resin, to create a smell like nowhere else. Stock conforms to an unwritten hardware store standard: paint along one wall, marine hardware clustered in a corner, narrow, close-spaced shelves full of shrink-wrapped bolts, hinges, and fittings, and a scale to weigh nails. The cashier's desk floats at the center, an island of counters with sale fliers, cash registers, a key cutter, and meters for the dockside pumps.

Hardware stores don't have rushes; neither are they ever empty. A couple compared paint chips by the wall, brushes and a roller stacked in a basket on the floor. Duggan hunted around the marine section, so I assumed his assistant would manage the route that morning. Russ O'Brien leaned on the countertop, glasses on the tip of his nose, his lips moving slowly as he reviewed an inventory printout. He looked up as I entered, then continued reading. Mike Twitchell, his EHVAC radio mumbling softly, held two twenty dollar bills above a NAPA replacement headlight as Kathy, Russ's daughter, rang up the charges. He looked up quickly as I entered, then fixed his gaze on the register. "Hi, Jimmy," he said.

"How you doing, Mike?"

He nodded. "Okay."

"Eighteen fifty-three," said Kathy.

"Expensive bulb," I said.

Twitchell handed her the bills. "Odd size, I guess. It's halogen, too."

"At that price, it better last a while. How long did the old one last?"

"About eight months." He shrugged. "I misjudged my driveway and clipped a tree."

"Ouch." I knew his driveway: loose gravel, up the side of the ridge, with a vicious hairpin turn halfway up. It was never easy. "Damage the car much?"

Twitchell shot me an icy glance that told me it was none of my business. He is a proud, private man overly concerned with his image, and wouldn't want everyone to know he'd hit a tree in his own driveway. He turned back to Kathy to watch her count his change. "Dented the fender, bent down the bumper. Nothing bad. I'll bang it out and fill in the gaps with some marine-tex."

I smiled. "The universal remedy."

Kathy handed back his change, which Twitchell shoved into his pocket. "Sorry to be so talkative, Jimmy. We had another bad accident last night. I'm a little short on sleep."

"No problem. Take it easy, Mike."

He picked up the lamp and smiled. "See you later, Jimmy."

"Take it easy, Mike." The door chime jingled. I slid along the counter until I stood opposite Russ. "Got a minute?"

His lips stilled. "Sure." He looked over his glasses. He was round and squat, from the top of his shiny head to his extra-wide shoes. Amiable and friendly, he nonetheless harbored a pronounced distrust of people he didn't know. "What can I do you for?"

"A little information, that's all."

"Ah." He took off the glasses and leaned closer to me. "Police business."

"The pumps down on the docks."

"What of 'em?"

"How's business been so far?"

"Off a tad, I guess. Not much. When the truck came by yesterday the driver said the same thing. My shipments are down from last year, maybe a hundred gallons a month."

"Sounds like a lot."

"Around 5 percent, I guess. Little less."

"Not as many boats this year?"

He scratched his chin. "About the same. The fishing is good this year, so everyone's been saying. They don't have to go out so far to set traps. Saves gas. Last year we had a lot of cabin cruisers and a lot of big power boats. This year it's been sailboats. They don't get so much gas."

"But you think the traffic, overall, is about the same."

"From what I can tell." He looked sideways to make sure no one lurked nearby. "What're you after? Pirates?"

"Not exactly."

"Official secrets, eh?" He stood back. "I'm sure I'll hear about it soon enough."

"I'm sure you will," I agreed. I wondered how long it would take the millstones of the gossip machine to grind out a plausible reason for me to ask so many questions. "Thanks."

"No problem." He put up his glasses. "Hey, Jimmy, you going to see your father soon?"

I stopped in the doorway. "Maybe tonight."

"I special-ordered some parts for him. Tell him they're here when he wants them, okay?"

"Sure. See you later." The chime signaled my exit. Little of value there, I thought. Yet the trip had not been wasted: a reputable source had not noticed any major change in boat traffic. As I headed for the diner, I noticed two men on the dock. One of them looked like Earl Wilson; the other I could not identify. A quick chat with them might prove useful, so I headed down.

Up close I verified a stocky man, his green work pants hanging low, as Earl Wilson. Standing next to him, slowly puffing a black wooden pipe, stood a thinner, taller man. A sea breeze carried the distinctive, vaguely cherry smell of the tobacco to me, identifying Murray Killington before I could see him clearly. "Morning," I said cheerfully as I leaned on the rail beside them.

Murray nodded. "Mornin'," said Earl. "Ain't seen you in a while, Jimmy."

"I've been busy."

"Yuh, that's what I thought. Police always get busy, come summer."

Murray discharged a huge cloud around the stem. "Been a busy summer?" he asked.

I shrugged. "No more than usual."

He shook his head. "Seems like a lot more cars this year." The pipe went back between the uneven, stained teeth.

"How's the boat traffic been?" I asked.

"Not bad," said Earl. "'Cept the weekends."

"I got caught out last Saturday," added Murray. "Thought I'd never get all my traps in by dark."

"Yuh, but the days aren't so bad," finished Earl. "No worse than usual."

"How's the fishing?"

"Been good," said Earl.

"Yuh," said Murray. "Been good."

"Cold spring, so the water's cool. Brings 'em in closer."

"Course, the price suffers," said Murray.

The hollow clip-clop of shoes on the dried-out old planks signaled someone's approach. Together the three of us turned to see who it was. The man coming toward us, a confused look on his face, map in hand, clearly belonged with the large brown Cadillac idling in the center of the lot. None of us said a word as he came closer. "Excuse me," he said. "Can you tell me how to get to Northeast Harbor?"

Earl looked quizzically at me, as if waiting for a translation. Murray switched his pipe to the other side and stared blankly out toward the breakwater. I took the cue. "Where are you coming from?" I asked.

"We left Belfast early this morning, hoping—"

"No," I interrupted. "Did you come from the east or the west?" I asked, pointing.

"Oh," he said. "Uh, west."

"Keep going that way. Stay on this road, about ten miles. You'll pass through a town called Somesville. Just past it Route 3 goes off, right. Take it, stay on it, and you should be there in half an hour or so."

"Go to Somesville, turn right, that's it?"

"That's it."

He recited it once again for himself, thanked me, and returned to the car and its three other occupants. When the Cadillac disappeared, Murray shook his head. "Makes you wonder why they waste trees printing maps."

A loud thudding set the planks vibrating as a boat rapidly approached. A beamy white hull pushing a cascade of green-white water headed in at high speed. Despite the clamor of the engine, I recognized Aerosmith crashing out on the radio. One of the oldest boats in the harbor, it now belonged to the grandson of the original owner. Danny Hodgdon should have graduated high school that spring, but excessive absenteeism caused by a substance-abuse problem had dropped him into my sister's class. Danny cut the engine, let it coast a while, then slammed it into reverse. He touched the dock lightly, considering the speed of his approach, but it hardly qualified as graceful.

Murray again shook his head. "Never learned how to maneuver, I guess."

"Numb as a tire iron, but not so useful," added Earl with a sigh.

I clutched my stomach as it rumbled to remind me about breakfast. "I'll talk to you guys later."

"Take it easy, Jimmy," said Earl.

"Tell your father we're going to have a meeting Thursday," said Murray. "Heard about a new restriction on fishing coming up in the legislature."

"You'll probably see him first."

"If I don't, you tell him anyway."

They picked up the discussion they had been engaged in, as if I'd never interrupted. I climbed the hill, heading into the diner.

The regular breakfast crowd had already left and the latecomers were just arriving. During this mid-morning lull, the staff caught their breath and did the morning cleanup. Only three tables and two seats at the counter were occupied; everything else had to be swept, wiped, or washed. I picked a small table beside the bay windows and sat down.

One of the waitresses finished a corner booth, left her cloth on the table, and came over. Slender, outgoing, her figure and her face well tended, Denise is the diner's resident flirt. The diner uniform looks somehow different on her: the skirt a couple inches shorter, the blouse open one more button. Her nails are always long and glossy. She is my age. Most of my friends have painstakingly discovered that the war paint and the advertisements are a bluff: the flirt lurks only at the surface. That neither stops the unattached males from trying, nor Denise from carrying on. The ensemble works; without a doubt, Denise garners more in tips than anyone else.

She plopped herself in the seat opposite me and leaned over the table. Sometimes I wonder if the flirting comes automatically or deliberately. "How's it going, Jimmy?"

"Not bad," I replied. "How 'bout you?"

"Pretty good. A busy morning."

"Mondays are always busy."

"Yeah, I know." She looked past me as someone came in the front door. She smiled and waved. "A little more than usual, though. Maybe it was just my tables."

"A lot of tourists?"

She shrugged. "Five or six people from some boat. Nothing much."

"You're overworking."

She pondered the idea before agreeing. "I did a lot of subbing this week. Maybe I'm just more tired."

"You need a long nap," I offered.

"Yeah. A long winter's nap." She leaned back to retrieve her pad. "You having breakfast or just coffee?"

"Two eggs, bacon, muffin, potatoes."

She scribbled the order. "Okay. I'll get your coffee."

"Thanks."

I stared out the windows. The marine activity had quieted down since the initial rush to clear the breakwater. No boats had left since I abandoned my rock.

Denise quickly returned. She dumped a handful of cream containers on the table, then set a ceramic mug beside them as she regained her seat. "How come you're down here so early? And not even in uniform. Going out with your father?"

"I don't think he's going out today," I said. "He's got boat problems."

"Still? I heard your mother talking about that last week." She smiled coyly. "So you're not going to work."

"Nope."

"Going out to play? A little boat ride with dear old Robyn?"

I smiled. "Nope. Just bumming."

She looked skeptically at me. "I don't believe you. You're up to something. You just don't want to tell me what it is."

She'd hit it on the nose. While her flirting is harmless enough, her tongue remains her most dangerous weapon. Denise can spread gossip faster than fire through a tinder-dry forest. I sipped my coffee. "No, really. I'm just bumming."

"That's boring."

"Not if you've been working a lot."

She sighed. "I suppose."

"How's the summer been?" I asked. "Lot of customers, or what?"

"It's been good, so far. I've been making around fifty dollars a day in tips. That's decent for this place. If I wanted to work more dinner shifts, I could do a little better." She ran a fingernail quickly up my arm. "You know me, Jimmy. I like to keep my nights free."

"I don't get to see much of the town nowadays, working the night shift. A lot of tourist traffic this year?"

"A couple weekends, yeah," she replied. Someone else came through the door, again warranting the recognition smile and wave. "We had cars coming by all the time, and a bus or two. Seems like a lot of old foursomes out this summer. They just cruise the coastline. Stopping here comes naturally."

Her gift for gab made prying information from Denise easy. Once started, she just kept right on going. "You getting many repeat customers?"

"What do you mean, repeats? You've lived here all your life; you know what it's like. Most of the people in here come every day, same seat, same order."

"I meant the tourists. People who stop on their way somewhere, then again coming back?"

"No. Not really. I remember one couple. I think they took the ferry to Nova Scotia, then drove back. Stopped here about two weeks apart. Aside from that, I feed 'em once, and they're out of my life."

"How about the visiting boats? A lot of them?"

"Two or three every weekend, maybe one or two—" she stopped abruptly, leaned forward and grabbed my wrist, a seductive smile buried in the face paint. "Jimmy Hoitt, you're grilling me! You're not bumming, you're working!"

"No, no, I'm not, Denise. I was just curious."

She eyed me studiously. "You're lying through your teeth."

"I don't get to see Mom much anymore. I miss the details."

"Sounds like a professional curiosity to me."

"Well, it isn't." I took my free hand and pried her fingers off my wrist. "It's just idle curiosity."

"You're awful cute when you lie."

"I exude a natural charm."

"See? There you go again!" The desk bell on the counter rang; Denise obediently looked over. "Your eggs are done."

She went to the counter, impaled the slip on a nail and brought my order over. "Anyway, like I was saying," continued Denise as I eagerly dug into breakfast, "the boat traffic hasn't been much. Three or four boats on the weekend, though one weekend we had nine, I think. They were in some race out of Portland."

"Oh, I remember that," I answered between mouthfuls. "That was early in the season. Still cold."

"I think so. Besides the weekenders, we've had only a couple boats passing through during the week. That's really it."

"No regular boats?"

"Don't recall any. One boat in the regatta had a crew I knew from last year, but that's it." She leaned back, tapping her iridescent violet nails on the formica tabletop. "I still think you're grilling me."

"I'm just a real curious guy, Denise."

"Whatever your reason, Jimmy, I'm sure you won't tell me." She slowly rose, collecting her washcloth. "I don't see you so much anymore. Too bad." Her teeth flashed one more time. "You were always a lot of fun."

"You too, Denise. I'll bet you still are."

"So I've been told." She quickly toted up the pad, tore off the top sheet, and laid it on the table. She ran an enameled fingernail along my arm; this time it generated a potent chill. "You ever find that Robyn doesn't thrill you anymore, you give me a call, okay?"

"Don't hold your breath," I replied.

"Don't be a stranger." A lightning sweep of the cloth and a twist from her hips, and she was gone.

Information gleaned from Denise could hardly be called irrefutable testimony. Nonetheless, I accepted much of what she said. As it directly affected her income, her assessment of the summer business was probably accurate. Most of the boats that passed through had at least one single, willing Adonis aboard. If any of the crews returned for more, she would remember. Her appraisal of the reduction in traffic was the single most important item she offered. I mentally filed the fact away, resolving to transcribe it into the notebook later. Dickinson, too, might be interested in the traffic report.

I chased the last scraps of breakfast around the plate, drained my mug, put ample money on the table, and paid my respects at the register. The big wall clock read just after nine. By no stretch of the imagination had the morning been wasted, but neither had it been completed.

My half hour in the diner had been a crucial one for Eagle Harbor. The town was now fully awake. A steady parade of cars slithered along the main street, early tourists mingling with local traffic. The first boat had already returned to the dock. I recognized it as one that had left just after dawn. He could not have pulled all his traps, but he could have hauled enough to make a decent morning's income. I could faintly hear the hoist chain clanking and the fisherman's vulgar suggestions to the hoist operator.

A rocky bulge into the harbor holds the diner, the store, and a pair of houses opposite the church. As the road passes within twenty feet of the water, there is no room for structures on the ocean side of the village. Across the street, one of the kids from Scott's Market swept the asphalt around the gas pumps. East of the store's narrow parking lot, a carved wooden sign identifies the requisite bed-and-breakfast, unimaginatively called the Eagle Harbor Inn, from which floated the smell of fresh bread. Beyond the inn lurks a pair of tourist traps, one selling T-shirts, the other a purveyor of various "local" trinkets imported from Taiwan. Next comes an imposing, weathered Victorian building: the more imaginatively named, if more run down, Captain Sawyer House Inn. Past them squats an old house, well kept despite the annual war against the weather. Old chairs await recaning, desks expose their shredded veneer, and unfinished tables litter the front porch, spilling over onto the lawn. In a high-backed chair indistinguishable from the other junk, Sam Adams, silently puffing his pipe, rocks the mornings away.

A square granite-faced building guards the eastern approaches. With no particular agenda, I figured I might as well start there. The sign out front still says Eagle Harbor Bank & Trust, but it was long ago bought out by a much larger bank in Bangor, itself part of a financial group based in New York. The new owners elected to keep the name, hoping the good people of the village would continue to patronize their local bank.

Inside, the masonry walls preserve the morning chill. Two teller windows face the door; behind them, set into the wall, opens the vault. Actually more akin to a safe, it's just a steel box some three feet square, built into the wall. To one side are a pair of tiny offices for the head teller and the branch manager. If I was going to find anything, it wouldn't come from the manager. I went to the head teller's door and knocked. "Can you spare a couple minutes?"

Miriam Jouvet, head teller, looked up. She is five-two, with straight brown hair and translucent blue eyes; in her mid-thirties, she is still trim and athletic but slowly losing the battle. She punched a couple keys at her terminal before looking up. "Oh, hi, Jimmy." Her gaze returned to the keys. "I'll be with you in a moment."

"No problem." I slid inside, subtly pulling the door closed. No more than eight feet to a side, the tiny office nevertheless represents a sizable portion of the bank. A window looks out to the marsh and woods beyond, but aside from that break, filing cabinets, certificates, awards, photos, and a gray metal key box cover the walls. Crammed in between two cabinets, I found an office chair, which I put to good use.

After a long sequence of keystrokes, the printer began clacking. Miriam advanced the paper, examined it quickly, ripped it off, and clipped it to some others. She closed the file and pushed it aside.

"Now, what can I do for—" The phone cut her off. "Just a sec." She took the call, allowing me more time to examine the office. With very little to survey, I gained no more on the second pass than I had on the first.

She hung up. "Mondays are always like this. How can I help you?"

"I just wanted to ask a few questions."

"Ah." She reached for a styrofoam cup of clearly cold coffee. "Is this official?"

"Sort of." Unlike Denise, Miriam could be trusted with sensitive information. "I don't have any warrants. I'm not looking for anything in particular. I'm more interested in anything unusual, any transactions which seem out of the ordinary, or just surprises."

"Lately?" She tasted the coffee and quickly put it aside. "Last week? Last month?"

"Last few months."

Her chair groaned as she sat back. "A lot happens here in that time."

"Anything that happens all the time, I'm not interested in. Might happen just once a month. Maybe it only happened once, ever."

"Hmm." She took off her reading glasses and began gnawing the earpieces. "Can you be more specific?"

"It might involve large sums of money. Especially a transfer of funds in one day, out again within a week."

"How large?"

To me, a large sum of money was a week's paycheck. To Miriam, it might be the total of everyone's paychecks, deposited over a week. Who knew what Frederickson might consider large? "Something over twenty-five thousand dollars, I guess."

"Not huge, then. Just large."

I shrugged. "Big enough for me."

"Let me think." Her eyes glazed as she stared out the window. The eyeglass frames suffered as she thought. "Off the record, of course, Jimmy. You didn't get this from me."

"Understood. I'm just trolling for leads."

"We don't have many accounts here. You know that. Business loans might be that big, especially if someone's buying a new boat. Of course, we only take information. The processing is done in Bangor."

"I didn't mean the loan department."

"We handle the accounts for Island Realty; they flip-flop large sums once or twice a month. Outside of the loans, there are only four or five accounts with that kind of money. Certainly less than ten."

"I don't suppose you'd care to name names."

Miriam smiled. "Not without a warrant, Jimmy."

No need to push, I thought. If I needed to know, I could always ask my mother. "No, that's all right."

"A couple of those accounts transfer big sums around, every now and then. Like you said, no more than once a month. I know that's all rather sketchy. Does it help you at all?"

I had a lot more investigative work. "I think so." I stood up. "I'll let you know."

She rose also, and shook my hand. "If there's anything else—" The phone rang. She answered it, adjusted her glasses, and sat down. I mouthed my thanks, waved good-bye, and left the tiny bank behind.

There were myriad explanations for the circumstances Miriam had related. Most were legal. If Eagle Harbor was the base of a smuggling operation, then the one and only local bank might very well be involved. Even if the cash originated in a bank in Bangor, or Boston, even New York, the smugglers would need assets close at hand to pay the local help. I'm no banker, no financial wizard; my own checkbook is rarely balanced, occasionally overdrawn. The extent of the bank's involvement would have to be determined by someone else.

I headed up the street. I didn't expect to pass the antiques store without some questions from Sam. As soon as I passed his driveway, his gaze locked on me. "Mornin', Jimmy," he called.

"Hi, Sam." I leaned on the wooden railing. "How you doing?"

"Not bad. Back hurts a little." He rocked more vigorously and drew a long suction through his pipe. His lean, burnt face, deep ruts carved by more than sixty years of sun, wind, and salt spray, stretched taut over his cheekbones. "I try to stay off my feet for more than an hour at a time."

"How's Mrs. Adams?"

"Fine. She took the truck over to Manset this morning," he explained. "Picking up a couple wicker chairs. We'll re-cane 'em, clean the finish, and sell 'em. Brings a good profit."

"That's good."

He rocked forward and stopped, pointing the pipe stem at me. "You're not usually around in the morning."

"Routine business."

"Routine." He resumed rocking. "That's what gets to you after a while."

"What does?"

"The routine. Doesn't matter whether you're a fisherman, or a policeman, or an antiques dealer. After a few years, damn little changes. Takes the excitement out of it."

"Oh," I said politely. "I didn't know selling antiques was exciting."

"Used to be." He started coughing, a dry, painful hacking. He took out his pipe, leaned over the rail and spat into the rosebed. "Back when I started. There was a thrill in hunting for an item to refinish, as you re-created a thing of beauty." He calmly puffed a couple times. "And, of course, there was the thrill as I tried to sell it to some sucker for twice what it's worth."

"No more?"

He shook his head. "Ten years ago finding pieces was easy. And the tourists would buy anything that looked like it belonged here. But now—now, it's not like that. It's hard to find quality pieces that someone will part with. And the customers are smarter now. They know junk from antiques." He chuckled. "Most of 'em. The others just think they do."

Ike Morton, a venerable towner cut from the same bolt of cloth as Sam, walked up the sidewalk. "Mornin', Sam. Mornin', Jimmy."

"Good morning," I said.

"Mornin'," said Sam.

"Thought I'd come see you about that cider press. You want it or not?"

"What press?"

"My gawd, Sam, you was just up to the house last week to look at it. The cider press, the old one in the shack."

"Yuh, yuh," said Sam quickly. "I remember, I remember. Big oak thing, full of cracks. Tub broken. Dates from about 1925?"

Ike shrugged. "The building goes back to 1850. Least, the stone cellar does. I always thought the press was turn of the century, anyway."

"Nope," replied Sam. "Maybe back to 1919, but that's it. That press was built in Holden by the Shepard brothers, and they didn't make any 'til after the war. And that don't look like the first one."

"Why are you getting rid of it?" I asked.

"Tearing down the shack," explained Ike. "I'm building a new barn, replace the one that half burned."

"Presses are hard to sell," said Sam. If he had heard us, he ignored it. "People who want to use them buy new ones, or build them. Not many collectors. Even if it was in good shape, which it ain't."

"I'm telling you, Sam, we used it right up through last year when my middle boy broke the tub."

"The tub's all rotted away."

"Yuh, but the press is in good shape," said Ike. "Good and tight, works real smooth."

"Who's going to want a cider press that don't hold cider?"

"It's in damn good shape, except for the tub. Even that can be fixed, or the whole thing can be used for something else. "

"Well, I don't see how." He puffed calmly. "I'll still give you fifty bucks."

"Fifty bucks?" cried Ike. "If I burned it, it's worth more. A hundred."

"Nope. Too much. I've got to do some repairs before I can even try to sell it."

"Eighty-five, then. It'll take me some doing to get it out of there. She's bolted down pretty good."

"Take me more work than that. Sixty."

Ike sighed. "Seventy-five."

Sam puffed. He puffed again, then nodded. "You'll deliver it?"

Ike stepped back, tugging the bottom of his beard. "All right. I'll bring it down here, but I won't unload it by myself."

"No, no. Me and mother'll take it out. Might need a hand from you, that's all. Done at seventy-five?"

Ike thought a moment, then nodded. He stepped forward, and the two men sealed the deal. "Done."

"When you planning to bring it over?"

Ike looked up at the sky. "Weather holds, we can start taking down the shack today. I'll be over, say, Thursday. Weather permitting."

"Give me a call before you drive down. No sense driving down if we won't be here."

"Okay." Ike started back the way he had come. "Cash on delivery!"

"I'll have it!" Sam leaned further back in his chair, rocking slowly. During the heated negotiations he had rocked much more vigorously; now he relaxed again. "A good deal."

"A steal, or just a good deal?" I asked.

"Don't know. Things like that are touchy. Not too many cider press collectors. They don't drive around looking. Some people use 'em for other things, I guess. Never know 'bout that. It'll cost me a hundred or so to fix it up so's it looks good. I'll have to sell it for three hundred, anyway. Can't tell whether anybody's going to bite or not. I may be stuck with it. Funny thing is the last couple seasons I have had a lot of people asking about them."

"What for?"

He rocked a couple times before answering. "Beats me."

"How's business been this summer?"

"Average," he said. "Average. Course the traffic seems more to me, but I haven't noticed any change in sales. Why?"

"Just curious. Seems to me things are busier than usual. I was wondering if anyone else felt the same way."

"Nope. Course, the summer's not over yet."

Mrs. Adams returned, nosing a battered pickup into the driveway, a couple chairs strapped against the bed. She also hauled a pair of tables and what looked like a small chest of drawers. She waved at us as she disappeared behind the house.

Sam reached for his cane and stood up. "Oh, gawd. Looks like mother's brought back a bonus. Have to see what she's got us into." He leaned closer. "She's got a good eye for a bargain, but she can't tell something fixable from a dump reject."

"Need a hand unloading?"

He drew one last puff from the pipe before setting it down. "No. We can manage. Have a good one, Jimmy. Come by in a couple weeks. I'll show you a fine-lookin' press."

"See you." There was no telling what Sam's information meant. While he sat on the porch and watched everyone pass by, he couldn't tell how the boat traffic compared. Most of his customers were drivers, not boaters: it was not easy to bring home a maple chest of drawers when you came by boat.

Beyond O'Brien's I passed the fire station. Engine 5, a rugged all-purpose pumper built on a Chevy C35 truck chassis, parked in front of the white doors. The front gleamed in the morning sun; I presumed the two firemen sitting nearby on folding metal chairs were resting from the weekly waxing. They waved; I waved back. On the west side of the church is the cemetery, final resting place of pastors and parishioners back to the early 1800s. That's the town, from bank to cemetery. Having gone end to end, I'd extracted all I could by indirect questioning. Until I had more pieces and a more cohesive overall picture, I could do no more. The gossips would pick up where I left off; my work would only fan the flames. Perhaps someone might ask the right question of the right person and I might get an answer that way, through the Eagle Harbor Irregulars. They were a force to remember, but not to be relied upon.

When I opened the car door, a blast of stale, hot air told me to open all the windows immediately. I left the door open while I exchanged my chamois shirt for a lighter cotton one. My day was hardly over. I headed westward: some things along the shore warranted examination. The undeveloped properties Frederickson purchased could have served as his unloading areas, but they might have been mere investments. A look around might help.

I had to assume there were drug smugglers in Eagle Harbor. If so, they would have to go ashore somewhere. The municipal dock was too obvious, too exposed. With so much rocky Maine coast nearby, why take a chance that someone might venture down to the dock at an inopportune time? A boat could unload anywhere on the coast. But once ashore, the cargo had to go somewhere: that meant landfall had to be close to a main road. Landing at the base of a cliff or far out in a marsh would be inconvenient for more than a couple kilos, and Wiley spoke of much more than that. *If* the property had not been purchased for a port of illegal entry, then the unloading must have taken place elsewhere. Other than the dock, there were only three or four suitable places. I wanted to check them out.

The first place on my list was about a mile from the village, where a pond drained into a meandering stream that flowed through a pass between the rocks, slipping underneath the main road. On the sea side, the creek widened until it reached the marsh a quarter-mile downstream. At high tide, a small bay obscured the course of the creek. Even when low tide exposed vast mud flats, there remained enough water to get a good-sized boat through the channel as far as the roadway. The flat road provided enough room to see cars approaching a good half-mile away. Best of all, a gravel track descended from the roadway to the water. On a dark night with the tide low and the sea calm, only someone very observant would see anything at the water's edge, especially if approaching from the village. Though limited by the allowable draft at low tide, the location held great promise.

I parked just off the road and walked down. I had no idea what to look for, but I knew what I found wasn't it. Dozens of separate tire tracks scarred the gravel, the recent rain blurring but not eliminating the older ones. On top, in the fresher mud, at least three distinct tracks led to the water. The same things that would appeal to smugglers also made it desirable to the type of people who used Jack's shack.

I saw the burnt wood of a campfire and a pair of lobster carcasses jutting from the mud. Bottles, empty six-pack containers, and cigarette butts littered the area. There had been a lot of traffic down there. It was too useful a transfer spot to cross off my list, but I doubted any smuggler would bother with so busy a location. I saw nothing worth noting. I headed back for the car.

The next place came about three miles farther on. Just beyond a decaying family cemetery, a graying wooden barn braced against the wind, the house to which it belonged reduced to a stone foundation. Weeds overgrew both sites, riddled by wasps' nests and rodent burrows. Alongside the barn ran a pair of deep ruts, barely visible through the thick green undergrowth. If I'd had my own truck, I might have driven to the beach. As I had a car with a low clearance, I elected to walk. I hid the car behind the barn, though I really didn't know why.

It's a good hike to the beach, down a path barely wide enough for a car. Towering oaks as old as they were massive line the lane. The growth along the track told me the path saw no heavy traffic, but given the speed that thriving weeds can grow, if anyone had been down the path more than a week before I would not have known. Some of the garbage strewn alongside the path—beer cans, fried-clam boxes, half a pizza box—looked faded by sun, rain, and time; nowhere did I see any signs of fresh passing.

The road ends at a cobblestone beach. For about sixty yards, rounded rocks plunge sharply into the water. Each wave sent the stones moving, making a hollow popping sound as they shifted, followed by a hissing as the foaming sea flowed out again. A granite ledge climbs out of the ocean to the left behind a stand of spruce. Beyond the beach, to the right, the smooth rocks become sharp-sided ledge, rising gradually toward a dense cluster of houses about a quarter-mile away. Not a hospitable place to beach a boat—but if you wanted secrecy, the hardships could be overcome.

I checked out the beach, but found nothing. More litter scattered the area, the same, faded, soggy trash. Just at the tree line, I found a pile of charred wood, the remains of a beach fire. It had probably burned less than a month before. A storm a month ago should have washed out all the ashes. I searched for paint or rubber on the rocks from boats or trucks, but found nothing. I headed back to the car, empty-handed again.

Another creek bubbled under the road at the town line, open sea less than a half-mile away. The creek winds through the forest, beneath trees that meet overhead most of the way. It twists and backs on itself so severely that, from the road, I could see no more than fifty yards downstream, let alone to the ocean. A carriage path, abandoned by the park service but kept up by the neighbors, winds along the north bank until the creek merges with the marsh. I drove to the end, checking both sides, searching the creek. Again I saw nothing.

I checked my watch: almost noon. On my list, one place remained. As kids, we had named it Beaver Island. The beaver stream flows from the central ridge of Mount Desert Island, running through much of Eagle Harbor, including the back lot of the elementary school. It courses serenely through a tree-banked gorge, underneath a World War I–vintage iron bridge, through a kettlehole pond bordered by pine stands before flattening out into a wide marsh. Here, grassy fingers reach out into the bay. At the middle of the flats perches a lone remnant of the glaciers that carved Mount Desert Island: a flinty ledge about thirty yards long and less than ten yards wide. A layer of topsoil clings to the rock, just enough to support a healthy crop of weeds and bushes, grass amid the crags, and a few scrub pines.

Like a moat surrounding a medieval castle, the marsh encircles the ledge. From mid-tide to high water, enough water fills the channel to bring a small boat up to the island. Access from the shore is not so easy. No road passes within a mile of the island, though a narrow cow path snakes into the woods and halves the distance. Nowhere can you get a clear view of the island by car. Usually I would have borrowed the *Janet Kathleen III* to approach as close as possible, then taken the skiff and rowed ashore, but repairs made that impossible. At flat tide, a skiff could reach the island, although it would take nearly two miles of paddling through the meanders. Approach by canoe through the marsh would be far more subtle and less likely to attract attention. As it happened, I knew where to borrow a canoe. I backtracked to my car and headed for Robyn's house.

I pulled into the driveway and backed up beside the house. With no sign of her car, I figured she was not home. I scribbled a quick note on the back of an accident report form, wedged it into the doorjamb, and headed around back. The canoe, a hideous yellow Old Town, leaned against the foundation, exactly where we had left it a month before. A blue plastic tarp protected the hull from sunlight; I folded it, placing it beside the bulkhead. I flipped the canoe and dragged it across the grass. Cobwebs and dust competed for space by the thwarts. Easier to clean in the water than in the back yard, so I left the mess alone.

I had to get the rope, paddle, life jacket, and flotation cushions. Robyn kept them inside the bulkhead. Rarely locked—a sturdy door at the base of the steps prevented access—I had no problem finding what I needed. I took them back to the car, stowed the paddles and jackets in the trunk, placed the cushions on the roof where I would rest the canoe, and faked out the rope.

It's not a heavy canoe; I had little difficulty lifting it. Maneuvering around the house under sixteen feet of canoe was not so easy. The simplest way to carry the canoe meant bearing the weight on my shoulders. This spread the weight well, but placed my head inside the hull, rendering me blind except straight down. Following the patterns of grass, packed earth, and gravel I made my way. After grazing a pine tree with the after hull, I found the driveway without further incident. I caught a glimpse of bumper just in time to avoid pushing the bow through the rear window and precariously balanced it on the trunk while I repositioned myself.

Out from under the canoe, I was startled by the sight of Robyn's car, but I recovered fast. Rather than casual jeans and cotton blouse, she wore a long white skirt beneath a dark blouse. Such a disguise meant she had not been running errands. "Trying to steal my canoe?" she asked.

"Nope." I leaned over the car roof to arrange my tie-downs. "I need to borrow it."

"Why?"

"Work." Ropes spotted, I shouldered the canoe onto the roof, and set it down on the cushions. "I need to have a look at something I can't reach by car." I stepped back to check the alignment, then pushed the stern to even it up. "I didn't see you come home."

"I'm not surprised. You had that thing over your head as I drove up. I was pretty sure it was you, but all I could see was my canoe walking around the house. You looked pretty silly."

"These things weren't built as hats." Starting at the rear bumper, I began trussing the canoe in place. Since it was considerably longer than the car, it was an awkward arrangement. "Where were you? Obviously not working."

"Those sharp patrolman's eyes," she said, laughing. "I can't fool you for a minute. I've been sitting for a portrait for my parents. It's going to be an anniversary present."

"You couldn't just send a photo?"

"She only paints from life." She pushed off her car. "Artists are idiosyncratic, you know?"

"I love it when you use big words." I put a sheepshank knot in the line over the hood, passed the bitter end under the bumper, and used the loop to tighten the lashing.

"It's nice to see you, too."

"I'd love to stay, but I have a job to do."

"Protecting us from the evil among us," she said dramatically. If only she knew, I thought. She looked at the canoe, shaking her head. "With a canary canoe. Instills great confidence."

"There's a lot to this investigation," I replied, a little defensive. I could not tell whether she was kidding or not. "I have to get back to it."

"Where are you taking my canoe?"

"Beaver Island. I want to have a look."

"Sounds exciting." She shaded one eye with her hand as she looked up into the sky. "It looks like the rain will stay away for a couple more hours. Let me come."

"This is business, Robyn. I'm not going for a joyride."

"Business? Come on, Jimmy, it's me. It's the middle of the day. That island will be deserted."

"I have to search the island carefully. It's going to be tedious. You'll be bored to tears waiting for me to finish."

"I can help you," she said defiantly.

"You don't know how to search for things like I do!"

"I have eyes!" she snapped. "Besides, if you let me come along, not only will you have someone to talk to and help you paddle, but think what might happen if it starts to rain while we're out there. You'll have to wait for the weather to clear."

It was official police business, but it posed little risk. "All right. This is work, not pleasure. You do exactly what I tell you, when I tell you to do it. Okay?"

She ran her hand gently along the side of my face, smiling widely. "Don't I always?"

I took her wrist in my hand, removed it from my face, and smiled back. "Bullshit!"

"Let me get into something more appropriate for a canoe trip. I'll be right out."

"Hurry up," I said, the impatience only partly feigned.

"Only be a couple minutes."

I used the time to grab another paddle and life jacket and to re-arrange the ropes on the passenger side; I had not planned to open that door. Less than two minutes after letting herself in, Robyn locked the door and closed it behind her. She climbed into the car. "Let's go."

"Ten-four." I headed out to the road, down to the stream, and parked close to the bridge. By using beat-up trails, I could have shortened the range to the island, but paddling the extra distance would be easier than driving onto the marsh. Robyn helped me with the canoe. Opening the trunk, we traded ropes for paddles and life jackets, tossed them into the hull, and trudged down to the creek. I let her move forward, then pushed off, and hopped lightly into the stern. I gave the muddy bottom a firm shove and we were away.

The low tide had passed, so we paddled into a gentle current through the flats. More than enough water filled the channel for our shallow draft, though we had some difficulty twisting around corners. We scraped the edge several times. Sticky dark-gray mud encrusted the tip of my paddle as I gave three powerful strokes to force the bow onto the beach. Robyn jumped out, caught the bow, and hauled it up onto the grass. I stowed my paddle and followed her ashore.

With half the canoe on the shore, I saw no necessity to tie the painter. I didn't plan on staying that long. "It'll be fine."

Robyn took my arm in hers. "It's been a long time since we came out here."

I pointed a warning finger at her. "This is business."

From the beach, a well-worn path leads over the high grass, through a break in the junipers, and between a pair of weathered pines to the clearing. Almost directly in the center of the island is an area with no trees, the ledge covered by a carpet of soft, dense moss. The size of a small living room, the area can hold six to twelve people, depending on what they want to do. Surrounded on three sides by scrub and stunted trees, only the ocean side is open. Roofed by an overhanging canopy of pine boughs, the clearing shelters its inhabitants from the weather as well as from the prying eyes of nosy friends on boats or anxious relatives on shore. At the center of the clearing, in a natural bowl in the granite, a few charred pieces of burned wood and thick, sooty residue on the rock marked the customary campfire. Not big enough for a proper bonfire, but adequate for a romantic fire.

I gently pried off Robyn's arm and started poking through the ashes. No telling how many fires had been set there. I could discern not only common pine, but also birch, maple, and perhaps elm among the ashes. Firewood had to be imported to the island, usually taken from the family woodpile—hence the varied nature of the ash. The ashes were older than a week, but fresh since the soaking spring rains. Maybe a professional fire investigator could have told me more, but that was all I needed to know.

Robyn slowly walked around the edge of the clearing, looking down at the ground. "What are we looking for?"

"I don't know." I pushed aside the bigger pieces to sift through the powdery ash at the bottom. "Anything that doesn't belong."

She picked up a rack of empty Budweiser bottles. "None of this stuff belongs here," she said. "What a bunch of slobs."

"That does belong." From the ash pile I took a few shards of brown glass, the kind used in beer bottles; a size AA battery; three pennies, a nickel, and a quarter; an unburnt corner of a cellophane snack-food bag; chicken bones; mussel shells; what looked like the blade of a pen knife, snapped at one end; and a dozen bottle caps. "Things for parties are okay. If it's something you or I might have brought here, it belongs."

"I think I get it."

The fire pit yielded nothing further. I searched the rest of the clearing. The grass looked healthy, indicating that no one had been out there for at least a week. The moss was wholly unremarkable. As I looked over the ledge, however, a small piece of something off-white caught my eye. My fingers were too large to pry it out of the deep cavity, but a twig solved that. I examined it carefully. It was exactly what I'd thought: a half-smoked joint. While drugs were the ultimate object of my search, such a small find was of no significance.

The rest of the clearing yielded nothing else. Robyn had nearly completed the perimeter. "Find anything?"

She shook her head. "Only this." She held up a blue foil condom package, ripped in half. "There's a cache of these near the tree."

"A cache? Used?"

"I only found empty wrappers. Why?"

"There are some crevices in the rocks where some guys'll store a bunch of them. In case a sudden and unexpected need arises."

She straightened up. "I see."

"I'll start checking the shore. Fan out into the bushes and see what you can find, okay?"

"Sure." She took the head of the trail and ventured carefully into the bushes. "I'm glad I wore jeans."

Another path led to the shore from the other side of the clearing. I took it, carefully examining where I stepped, but found nothing. For no particular reason, I decided to go around the island clockwise. I trudged all the way around the leeward side of the island, and found, not surprisingly, nothing. I passed the canoe and continued.

Less than ten yards from the canoe, I came to an abrupt stop. Out in the water I caught a glimpse of something in the mud. I splashed into the cold water up to my knees. I had stirred up a cloud of silt, but through it I saw the green wire of a lobster trap. The water was far too shallow to fish, and in any case I could not see any line. I reached down and felt around the bottom. I closed my hands on the wire and pulled. The trap stayed stuck in the mud. I altered my grip, flexed my knees, and hauled. The trap came clear, splashing cold water all over me.

I carried the trap ashore and had a close look at it. A pair of small crabs clung to the inside, a starfish hugged the outside; I left them all alone. The two-chambered trap appeared to have been crushed, as if a boulder had been dropped on it. The side that should have contained the bait bag had been compacted into a tangle of twisted wire a fraction of its original height. Amid this mess were the remains of the netting and a few chunks of the weights. Most wire traps contain a pair of brick weights to keep them on the bottom: these are secured in wire baskets inside the trap. Both baskets were empty except for the shards, as if the trap had been cannibalized. The trap was past repair. Unable to find a tag to identify the owner, I threw it back into the mud.

I stood up and looked out to sea. Looking down into the water on a dark day from such an oblique angle isn't easy, but what I saw confirmed what I expected: On this side of the island, the bottom dropped off quickly.

"Why are you so wet?" I turned back to see Robyn standing on the ledge. "Find something?"

"No." I started back to shore. "Did you find anything?"

"Maybe. Come take a look."

I followed her into the trees. She stopped beside one of the larger pines. A flattened beer carton hung from a bush and a small pile of cigarette filters indicated someone had been there before. Aside from that, I saw nothing. I said so.

She looked up into the tree. "Now, look carefully."

"What am I looking for?"

"I don't know. It looks hidden, it looks new, and it's strange. It's also bluish."

I looked up, but saw nothing. "I can't see it."

"About thirty feet up, on the ocean side. About a foot away from the trunk. It's buried in the branches."

I looked again. At first I saw nothing, then I saw a faint glimmer as if something had moved. I watched, and saw the same thing again. The sightings allowed me to zero in, and I saw it. A small metallic object, roughly spherical, about nine inches in diameter, with a distinct blue tint, nestled inside what looked like a black rubber traffic cone. "Now we're getting somewhere."

"You see it?" she said. "What did I find?"

"A radar reflector."

"A what?"

"A radar reflector." I stared a little longer, then faced Robyn. "They use them on sailboats. Masts or sails don't show up well on radar, especially at a distance. They mount foil-wrapped plastic reflectors so they show up on radar."

"This island wouldn't show up by itself?"

"If you were close enough, sure. But if you wanted to find it from a long way off, you'd need help to know where you're going. That little piece of foil might do the trick."

"So anyone could find the place in the dark."

"Or in fog. Especially in fog. It's a perfect time to move around with a low risk of detection. With a good chart, a depth sounder, and radar, it's not that difficult, either."

"So I found something important?"

"You may have. Anything else?"

"No."

"Let me finish going 'round the shoreline. I'll meet you at the canoe."

It took me less than five minutes to complete the circuit. I found trash galore, but no more evidence. I returned to the canoe to find that Robyn had already turned it around. I climbed in, and, with one push, we were en route back to the road. The current at our backs helped cut the return time by half. We rinsed the canoe as we took it out, placed it on top of the car, and tied it down.

As easily as that, we had the canoe off-loaded at her house, the paddles and life jackets stowed. The day was nearly spent. I had accomplished something, but I felt tired and the day wasn't yet over. I still wanted to go to the dock after dark and snoop around. Robyn started up her front steps, unlocking the door. "Thanks for helping me paddle and search," I said.

"A little work with the police from time to time is stimulating," she replied. "You got plans for dinner?"

"No. Maybe grab a snack at the diner later." I could not stifle a yawn. "I have to work late tonight."

"How late?"

"After dark."

"There wouldn't be any point in asking to join you, would there?"

I smiled, but shook my head firmly. "No."

"What are you going to do until dark?"

"I don't know." Another yawn overtook me. "Perhaps I'll go take a nap."

She came down a step and laid her hand gently on top of mine.

"You can take a nap here. And I can make you a proper dinner. You haven't been eating well since you changed jobs."

"I haven't adapted to the new schedule."

"No excuse."

"It is too an excuse. It's just a feeble one. I'm too tired to come up with a good one."

"Then you're too tired to drive home." She tightened her grip on my hand and jerked it off the rail. "Come on. Sleep here."

I was tired of protesting; I didn't really want to fight her anyway. She hauled me up the stairs. I followed her inside, closing the door behind me.

5

Monday Night
Patrol Area: Eagle Harbor
Temps warm; wind 5–12 knots, SW;
skies clearing, seas 1–3 ft.

I left Robyn's house, fed and rested, just before eight. Endless phantoms drifted across the lawn as the falling temperature created a hint of fog over the water. For a day that had begun with rain, it ended perfectly. I intended to spend the evening on the water; a few hours of good weather would neatly end my day.

What I proposed to do danced around the edges of legality. I found myself increasingly unable to resist the emotion welling inside me. That I had been assigned to watch Eagle Harbor meant there existed a real possibility that drug smugglers lived in my home town. I could not rid myself of the thought that someone I had known for years could be involved. I wanted to clear the town and the people of Eagle Harbor, but if the ugly allegations could not be refuted, then it had to be me who brought in the criminals—not some distant, detached man from Washington. Unless you have grown up in a small, close-knit village like Eagle Harbor, I doubt that my motivations make much sense. I doubted Wiley could ever understand what I felt. He was exactly what I feared: a man from elsewhere coming in with his own ideas of the way things should be done. People like him first came to Eagle Harbor as visitors, then began to establish homes. They came because of the way of life, yet they inexorably changed the way I had known into what they came from. I had spent more than twenty years with the same set of friends, exposed to the same people day after day, year after year. I had a duty to the town, not just to serve them, but to protect them as well.

I formed a simple plan: examine all the boats in the harbor. I might have been able to secure warrants through the proper chan-

nels, and surely a call to the Coast Guard station on the other side of
the island could provide me a boat, a crew, and a reason to tag along
as an observer while they did "routine" boat checks. Yet either option would draw too much attention to the searches. I wasn't looking for *evidence,* I rationalized. I knew nothing I found would be
usable in court. I only wanted some feeble indicator to point the finger at a specific target. Whether the town was guilty or innocent, the
answer lay on the boats in the harbor. A quiet Tuesday night would
be excellent cover for a rowing tour.

As expected, I encountered no activity as I drove through town.
The stores were closed. The diner was dead and would be locked up
within a half hour. Only the red light between the doors showed at
the fire station. Lights showed in the parish house, but only a couple
cars, and anybody there would be too busy to spare a glance at the
water. As I nosed down to the dock I noted two parked cars; I could
not begin to guess where the owners were. I hoped they had their
own concerns.

I parked at the end of the lot, as far from anyone else as I could.
I put on a dark nylon windbreaker, not only to protect me from the
breeze but, along with dark pants and black Nikes it would limit my
visibility. The wind freshened, the way it does after a storm, and
kicked up the sea. Beyond the breakwater I could barely see the dark
rollers breaking on the rocks, but their muted roar was unmistakable.
Inside the harbor the swells were no concern, but they would nevertheless be noticeable in an open skiff. Low clouds completely obscured the moon. Directly overhead, I detected the faint glimmer of
two bright stars straddling the gray streak of a jet contrail. It would
be a very dark night.

I walked out the pier, quickly making my way down to the floats.
A big float bobbed at the end of the pier and two smaller floats
rubbed against the pilings, rows of small boats tied alongside. Tradi-
tional flat wooden dinghies and newer, smooth-sided fiberglass ones
competed for the tight space, quietly rising and falling with the
waves. The bow of one boat protruded sharply from the waves, its aft
end immersed in the shallow water.

I moved to the end, to my father's wooden dory. An old but
sturdy boat, it was built by my father and grandfather twenty years
back. Since then, it had bumped against boats and pilings, skimmed
the waves under tow, and beached on shores far and near. In the
worn spots, the history of paints could be traced, starting with the
original wood, working through several layers of white and gray, past
the year of electric blue (it had been on sale), back to white, and finally

the current battleship gray. My father had selected the color partly to match the paint on his new boat, but mostly to hide twenty years of damage. Whatever his reason, on that night it suited me perfectly.

I used the cut Clorox bottle to bail out most of the water, untied the painter, and gingerly boarded. I pulled up the oarlocks, slid the oars into place, and rowed away. Once clear of the pilings, the heavy boat sliced the waves cleanly despite the stronger push of the waves. I settled into a comfortable cadence, carefully feathering the oars. The water hissed softly as the dory plowed out into the harbor. I startled a seagull atop a buoy as I passed, nearly hitting it with an oar.

The harbor master maintains twenty-three regular moorings in Eagle Harbor. These are rented out each year, with first refusal going to the previous renter. Not all the residents require a mooring, and on the rare occasions that demand exceeds supply, the town simply drops another one, as the harbor could easily hold thirty to forty moorings. When I first ventured out fishing with my father, only a dozen moorings took up the harbor, all for fishing boats. The fishing fleet has since grown by four or five boats with the subsequent generation. Recreational craft fill the remainder of the spaces: chunky cabin cruisers, sleek racers, and graceful yachts. In the early seventies an attempt was made to start a yacht club. It failed, dissolving into bankruptcy within three years, but it left a legacy of six moorings reserved for temporary guests. As I set out that night, only two moorings, both for guests, were unoccupied. Three skiffs were tied up to moorings, their boats somewhere out on the ocean. The others would all require a visit. I had no particular priorities, and so elected to start from the sea side and work back toward shore.

The first boat swung at the end of a slack mooring line. Like many of the fishing fleet, her age was not easily determined by a quick visual survey. Materials and equipment vary slightly, but as a fisherman owns his boat longer, it eventually gets equipped like all the others. Damaged hull sections are replaced by whatever is handy and waterproof. After four or five years, the owner will still call his boat the "new" one, as it gets difficult to tell another year of wear from another five, or even ten. On this first boat, three spindly antennas reached toward the stars, a cake-pan radar antenna between them. Wooden slats protected the hull beneath the trap hoist dangling off the starboard side. A stub mast in the port quarter supported a tightly sheeted staysail, a small pile of traps stacked beside it, buoys spotted at the center of rope coils. Black plastic letters across the transom declared this boat to be *Miriam S,* identifying the owner as Russ O'Brien's eldest son. I coasted to a stop beside the seaward side, shipped oars, tied up to a stern cleat, and climbed aboard.

I first checked the wheel. A corroded chrome-plated throttle housing sat to the left of the wooden helm, controls for the hoist and a broad steel sheave to the right. Scattered over a shelf, forward of the wheel, were a carefully rolled chart and a pair of haphazardly folded ones, a wide-bottomed coffee mug, a log book, some pencils and pens in a tray. A crack bisected the windscreen. Behind the window post, a radar receiver hung from the overhead, its plastic-covered screen coated with caked salt. Beside it, a microphone dangled from the radio at the end of a long black coil. In front of the wheel were the speedometer, tachometer, engine temperature and oil pressure gauges, two fuel gauges—many newer boats carried two separate tanks—a black plastic circuit breaker panel, ignition switch with the key in place, and a covered compass. Nothing unusual.

I stepped over the engine cover. The hatchway leading below had been closed but not locked; I removed the panels and went below. It was very dark below and smelled of diesel fuel, wet rope, and stale beer. A narrow bunk hung off the starboard side, covered with blankets, charts, and notebooks, an old battery in a plastic casing, and stained foul-weather gear. From the sideboard hung four ratty life jackets half obscuring a first aid kit, a nearly empty bottle of whiskey, and a skeletal propane stove.

I searched for anything hidden, but found no clandestine compartments or loose boards. The boat had no secrets to reveal. I closed up the hatch, had a quick look at the log book, futilely searched the fantail, and returned to my dory. I cast off, pushing away from the *Miriam S.*

The next boat could have been a sister ship of the first: another well-used, appropriately equipped lobster boat. I found no more there than I had at the first.

On the next mooring I found only a skiff; no telling where the large boat had gone and no point in examining the skiff. Next came a broad fiberglass cabin cruiser with square, hard lines and every electronic device available. I boarded, but couldn't do much; the main cabin, engine room, and deck lockers were all secured by heavy brass padlocks. From the deck I peered inside the cabin, but anything hidden below remained hidden. The flying bridge allowed a look at the controls. Other than assuring me the owner had installed all the instruments or receivers he might ever need, I learned nothing. I took the name and homeport off the transom and rowed past.

I skipped the next boat. Even if the owner had been on my list of suspects I would not have been able to find anything I didn't expect aboard the *Janet Kathleen III*.

Just past, I came to a black-hulled racing sloop. About sixty feet long, broad-beamed, with long overhangs and a rounded, flush deck. A massive boom hung from an even more substantial mast, angling down to an oaken crutch just forward of the big stainless steel wheel. No cabin, and nothing more than a token toe rail edged the deck. At the junction of dozens of varicolored lines opened a deep, broad cockpit filled with winches, grinder handles, black plastic covers over the instruments. I didn't know much about her, but I knew her owner had moved to the island six years before. I went aboard and quickly looked her over. Nothing was locked, but neither was there anyplace to hide or store anything. Below decks I found a chemical toilet, line stowage, a battery compartment, and the auxiliary. Nothing.

Three more lobster boats, a beamy cruiser, and a skiff hurried me through the next section of boats. I had spent two hours rowing and searching. The hole in the clouds overhead had become a wide gap, through which many stars shined. The waves had flattened out, but the wind still blew fresh from the east. Clouds near the horizon obscured the moon, but I could see its faint glow trying to sneak around the edges. Another hour, and it would be plainly visible, illuminating anything on the water, including me. I quickened my pace.

I knew I showed some bias, but as I approached the next boat I felt that I had to look it over more thoroughly. It seemed exactly the boat drug traffickers would use. Long and low, the speedboat before me had a dark hull, her top covered by a piece of dark canvas snapped down to the sides. Two night-black Mercruisers dropped into the water from beneath a wide swim platform. At the stern of each side a stenciled black bird, its wings outstretched, hovered inches off the water. Forward of the birds she bore the name *Die Walküre*.

I tied up to the swim platform. The canvas boat cover tightly hugged the sides, but snaps are not locks. It took seconds for me to pry up the corner, crawl over the engine compartment, and drop into the cockpit. I took out my flashlight, quickly playing it around the boat. Nothing. I moved forward to check the helm.

A small padded wheel jutted out from the control cluster, the wheel of an Indy car, not of a boat. Instruments filled the space ahead of the wheel, status gauges for two engines, plus fuel, fathometer, compass, trim indicators, and a speedometer. Nothing unusual, and no room for something hidden. Wedged against the hull behind airplane-like throttles were a couple softcover books. I took them out and had a look. The first, the owner's manual, contained no marks.

The other was a marine guide, listing anchorages, moorings, and fuel docks along the Maine coast.

On the port side, a smoked-glass door led below. It was un-locked, so I had a quick look. Just inside the door a refrigerator held several bottles of beer, a bottle of wine, and five cans from a six-pack of cola. On the other side an empty shelfboard protruded from the hull. Not much room inside. A V-berth filled the bow. The deck, walls, and headliner were carpeted with a crushed-velvet material. I checked for concealed compartments, easily hidden under the car-peting. I ran my fingers along the seams to find the central hull joint. Beneath the berth my probes discovered a hollow, empty thud. I felt under the cushion, found where it opened, and lifted. I marveled that the boat's designers had managed to fit a toilet into such a small, confined space. I examined the fixture, but it was exactly what it ap-peared to be. Disappointed to find a secret compartment reserved for the head, I replaced the cushion.

As I headed for the open corner, I heard a boat approaching. The oarlocks squeaked loudly. There were at least two people aboard, for I heard talking. They could be the rightful owners re-turning to their boat. Trapped, completely blind, I tried to create a good excuse to explain my presence. I couldn't think of anything plausible and relegated myself to an asinine teenage story about wanting to see the boat. I sat, quietly hoping not to rock the boat, and waited.

The voices grew louder; I could understand some of the conver-sation. They were visitors to the harbor, just passing through, plan-ning to get underway at first light. The voices slowly faded, the squeaking oarlocks absorbed into the distant crash of the breakers and the gentle lowing of the wind. I poked my head out from under the cover. Two middle-aged men in a small fiberglass skiff rowed to-ward the first of the cabin cruisers, ignorant of my presence. When they paddled behind the *Miriam S*, I crawled out of the cockpit, snapped down the cover, and got underway again.

Rowing quickly to put maximum distance between myself and the powerboat, I approached the next boat smoothly and quietly. Another sailboat, this one a high-sided cruiser with a Massachusetts registration. No lights, and no boat tied up, although a rubber dinghy was lashed to the cabin roof. As I prepared to tie up I heard sounds from inside. There were people aboard! I looked more care-fully, and, through the veil of the curtains, saw the flickering light of a candle or a kerosene lamp dimly illuminating the cabin. A light din-ner or an early rendezvous. I gave the boat a wide berth.

Another uneventful but unlocked cabin cruiser, two more fishing boats, and I neared the end of my trek. Two fishing boats remained. From the shack I had evaluated them both as interesting. I approached the first, pulling in close for a once-around: a red 'glass hull, a trifle short but with classic lines, a high prow and a square stern. Gold letters on the stern boldly proclaimed this boat to be the *Aquila,* her home port, Eagle Harbor. I could easily picture the owner—five and a half feet tall, iron-gray hair, a thick beard, athletic and muscular for a man of fifty. I had spoken to him, could almost hear his name, but it wouldn't come. Something about the boat struck me as peculiar, though I did not know what. I tied up and clambered aboard.

A staysail stretched off the mast, snapping in the wind. Nine traps were stacked neatly at the transom. A quick survey verified they had never been in the water before. The deck showed no distinct wear, only smooth, clean white paint. I headed forward.

At the helm I encountered the same instrumentation I had seen so many times before. A new radar set hung from the overhead, radio and loran next to it, beside a device I did not recognize. It looked to me like another radio. Since many fishermen carried more than one radio, I did not give it a second thought. Compass, gauges, fathometer, depth recorder—all were spotted logically around the console. One peculiarity struck me: all the electronics were new and expensive, the latest in marine technology. The owner of this boat would require a healthy bank account. With fishing revenues in slow decline, this seemed odd.

I went below. Once inside the cabin, I realized what bothered me. This boat transcended clean; it was immaculate. Few marks marred the quarterdeck, every line on deck was coiled and secured, the boat nowhere littered with the residue of fishing. The helm position gleamed, the windows crystal clear, no stray gear out of place. The bunk was made, the blankets trampoline taut. This boat looked like no other I had ever seen.

I checked the chart station very carefully. Detailed records revealed trips up and down the coast. The trap inventory showed fewer than eighty traps. To afford such elaborate equipment despite so few traps seemed highly suspicious. The logs and records revealed no clear evidence of smuggling, nothing that wouldn't normally show up on a fisherman's documentation. I resolved to keep a close eye on that one. I buttoned up the cabin and left.

One boat remained, a chunky, wooden leviathan converted from a trawler to a stern-winched lobsterboat. I secured the dory to a gunwale cleat. Conversion had created a major alteration in her layout. A squat iron derrick dominated the center of the quarterdeck, leaning outboard over a gap in the transom. On either side were stacked traps, about twenty per side. Three guys in their twenties operated the boat, including my cousin Paul. They anchored the bottom of the high school class, but they had managed to stay out of most legal trouble. They worked hard, managing far more traps than any others. Uneven, not quite level block letters on the stern gave the name *Freebird*.

Forward, four bait barrels stood against the port rail. On the bow were strewn buoys, ropes, a pair of rusty, navy-type anchors, and a rusted windlass that did not appear operational. A skeletal mast rose from the control cabin, soaring to a crow's nest twenty feet above the deck. A pair of oblong radar antennas and an array of aerials finished the exterior search. Nothing unusual. I headed for the cabin.

Though it was locked, I could reach the lock through a broken window. Thickly cluttered, the cabin smelled of stale cigarette smoke and moldy, rotting wood. The wooden wheel lacked a sizable chunk of its circumference. Radar sets were stacked on the shelf, a fathometer on top; no loran, just an old Raytheon radio direction finder. A crude shelf for charts had been cut underneath the wheel, where I also found five empty beer cans, one full one, and a variety of butts. Mixed in with the Marlboros and Camels I found a pair of small, hand-rolled butts. I could not verify the contents, but when I found a third intact sample, a quick inspection confirmed they did not hold tobacco.

More interesting, I discovered a well-worn calendar. It seemed to serve as the ship's log: under the days were comments on the weather, fuel bought, time at sea, and frequent references to areas where they had fished, including some long cruises from Eagle Harbor. A ship so far out wouldn't be near any others—free to do as it pleased. More interesting was an inscription on every other Wednesday: a brief note describing a location ashore, followed, always in another hand, by inscriptions for weights. They were all in kilograms, I noted. Each Wednesday had a further scrawl: paid in full, paid on account. It was obvious to me something was being sold. What reason could there be to wait a week to sell lobsters? Not normal fishing, I thought. Only a bunch of burnouts like the ones who operated *Freebird* would have the audacity or the stupidity to write down illegal activities in uncoded language.

Certain I had found something, I examined the entries for the current week. I had blundered along at a most opportune time: the next day indicated a meeting at an abandoned quarry on the north side. I memorized the location and blessed my luck.

I checked the rest of the paperwork, but found nothing else. I knew the sheriff would be unwilling to make an arrest based on what I had found. A good man, an honest and efficient lawman, he would not approve my methods, whatever they produced. He was from away, and police work was different in a city like Westbrook. Investigations, procedures, and protocol were his stock in trade. He didn't understand the way the villagers viewed me, their own lawman. They depended not on locks or alarms to safeguard their property and their lives; they depended on me. They wanted to sleep peacefully at night. Walker would never comprehend that. Dickinson might; I would approach him first. I hoped I could convince him to at least watch the quarry.

I checked out the deck minutely, looking for physical evidence: nothing. I returned to the dory and rowed back to the dock.

Clouds draped a thin band across the distant horizon, the stars twinkled, the moon a silver sliver over the breakwater as I returned to the car. I felt a surge of excitement at the prospect of the next night. I would love to close the case so soon, even if the guilty included my cousin. We weren't all that close, anyway. After only a few days as a detective, I could be on my way to a distinguished career. No one wanted to stay a patrolman forever.

It was just before one. I passed no one as I drove through town. The town slept soundly. Too late to call Dickinson. The best time to reach him would be early in the morning. I could catch a few hours' sleep before then; no telling how much sleep I might get tomorrow.

I met Dickinson just before six. I told him I needed to see him in person. He did not question why, but set a meeting at a Trenton coffee shop at eight. I had ample time to shower, shave, and catch up on paperwork before leaving. Midweek mornings there is no traffic; transients from the previous weekend have left, while those for the coming weekend have yet to arrive. Tuesdays are only for locals and those with the full week off. I made remarkable time, arriving at the doughnut shop near Hancock County Regional Airport a quarter-hour ahead of schedule.

My coffee had just arrived when the door chimed to mark Dickinson's entrance. Undercover duty removed his uniform, but Dickinson retained a distinctive swagger, a way of swinging his arms well clear of his hips that told anyone watching that he didn't sell cars. He stooped over a booth near the door and chatted with the occupants, then joined me at the counter. He slipped onto the vinyl stool, planted his elbows firmly on the counter, and nodded. "Morning, Jimmy."

"Morning, Sergeant."

A waitress in spattered polyester approached. "Black coffee, apple Danish. Zap it," he said before she could ask. Before the double doors stopped swinging she returned, set down a brown ceramic mug on a saucer that did not match, and swept out of sight.

No one could debate Dickinson's size, but even on his own scale he has enormous hands, big enough to encircle the neck of a ten-point buck, powerful enough to hold him down until he stopped moving. The tiny coffee cup disappeared. Appearances aside, he is a remarkably jovial, friendly man. Anyone who knows him would swear to that. I know it, too, yet I don't think I would want to be on the wrong side of the law when Sergeant Dickinson came calling.

He downed half the cup in one gulp. "All right, Jimmy. What are you onto?"

"The last two days I've done a lot of looking around."

"Nothing illegal, I trust." He winked, as if he already knew.

"I've uncovered some inconsistencies. I may be onto something, but I can't make the pieces fit together."

"Puzzles are the hardest when you start," he said. "Especially when you don't know what it's supposed to end up like. Tell me what you found. Maybe both of us can make sense of it."

I condensed the previous two days into a concise report, telling him about my conversations and observations. He listened carefully, nodding every now and again. He seemed impressed. "You've laid down a good base. That's always important. What else?"

I told him about my visits to the likely beaching areas. Before I got to the last one, he interrupted. "Did you examine the trees surrounding these areas? Going back ten, maybe twenty yards into the woods?"

"I tried. Some of the woods on the shore are pretty dense."

"Find anything?"

I told him about the radar reflector. I omitted all references to my assistant.

He nodded. "We've found seven other sites exactly like that, covering nearly eighty miles of shoreline. We expected at least one on MDI. They're all the same pattern: deepwater close in, a radar reflector in the trees, restricted access, and limited visibility from the shore."

"What are they for?"

Dickinson shrugged. His order touched the counter before him, so he paused to take a bite before answering. "If we knew that, we'd be done. Wiley has told me that it's a common practice to set up many drop sites. A thick fog, a fathometer, a good chart, and a decent radar set can put someone ashore nine times out of ten, totally undetected. But one smuggler will use dozens of these things. Hard to watch that many drops every time the fog rolls in."

"But we may have something?"

Another chunk of pastry disappeared. "Unfortunately, when a drop is retired, the owner rarely removes the equipment. We could be looking at a site five years old, or one from last month. We've hit a trail, certainly. But is it hot or cold?"

"I don't think the reflector is that old. Last winter was pretty severe, and that reflector showed no chipped paint, no warping or wind damage."

"It would have been sheltered, up in the tree like that."

"An open tree on an exposed island on the shore of the North Atlantic." I shook my head. "It's new."

"Okay. I'll send out a DEA agent to have a closer look." I described the island's location in enough detail to allow a flatlander to find it easily. Dickinson wrote it down, still eating with his left hand as he wrote "If you're right, we've found a hot trail. Anything else?"

I hesitated. The night before, I'd been certain I had hit the mother lode. After a night's sleep, the whole connection seemed as frail as a spiders' web. Furthermore, there remained the problem of how I had acquired the information. How understanding would Dickinson be? I knew I had no other option. "Last night I went for a midnight row."

Dickinson raised an eyebrow. "Just for the view, I'm sure."

"I needed to round out my observations. I had to get a closer look at the boats."

The last scrap of Danish perished. "You carried a case full of search warrants with you, right?"

Before I could answer, he waved me into silence. "Look, I know how you feel. Maybe as a civilian you might have done exactly the same thing. But you're not a civilian. I'm not saying you ruined everything, but you could have. If we're going to nail these guys, we have to follow procedure. No exceptions. For God's sake, Jimmy, don't get caught. More observation, less participation, okay?"

"Yes, sir," I replied meekly. My information, whatever it was worth, would obviously be wasted.

"All right, then." What remained in the coffee cup followed the

Danish. A trace of a smile crossed Dickinson's lips. "No promises we can use anything, you understand. Tell me what you found."

I leaned forward conspiratorially, lowering my voice. Though I doubted anyone in the diner would be paying any attention, the action came automatically. I told him about the ordinary boats and the visiting yachts. I saved the best for last.

Dickinson found the calendar very interesting indeed. "Everything in kilograms, eh? That's peculiar. Any trace of other metric units? Maybe the owners are European."

"I know the guys who run it," I told him. "They're all local kids. They barely passed high school. They have enough trouble mastering pounds and feet, let alone meters."

"Everything paid up, too." He scribbled notes. "Find any indication of the sums?"

"No."

"Suppose they can't leave everything on their boat."

"It's unlikely these guys keep extensive records. They're hardly the type to write things down."

"Have you checked their accounts? Quietly, of course."

"No. I found a lot of new equipment aboard. They could have some money put away."

"Perhaps, perhaps. It's all circumstantial, of course. We may be seeing what we want to see."

I shook my head. "Someone on that boat is doing something he shouldn't be doing."

"Keep an eye on them. Pity we don't know in advance what they're going to do."

"We do."

Dickinson's eyebrows arched impossibly higher. "Do we?"

"An inscription for tonight. It's sketchy. Nothing about payment, no weights. A time and a place, that's all."

"That could be enough." He flipped to a fresh notebook page. "Where and when?"

"There's an abandoned quarry on the north shore of MDI. Nobody works it anymore. Kids use it for ATVs and dirt bikes. Around two, tomorrow morning."

Dickinson wrote it down. "Not much time," he said, closing the book. "Still, it's the best lead we've hit so far."

"Do we go to the sheriff?"

"Immediately." He stood up, threw a dollar and some change on the counter, and put his hand on my shoulder. "I'll give you the credit, of course, Jimmy. But I think I'd better do most of the talking. He's not likely to be so 'forgiving' about your . . . um, unorthodox . . . procedure."

"I think you're right."

"Follow me to the station. Bring your field notes."

"Yes, sir."

I followed him out the door, up to Ellsworth. He lucked into a spot by the front door, while I had to settle for a space near the back of the lot. I gathered up my notebook and went inside.

Three uniformed patrolmen and two desk sergeants were talking at the main desk as I entered. Their conversation was interrupted by two scraggly young men, each accompanied by an even scruffier associate, who eagerly tried to assault each other despite hand and leg restraints and the intervention of the larger sergeant. The patrolmen kept the associates out of the scuffle, holding them down on the hard wooden benches. The tide of the battle swung in favor of the officers as the associates reluctantly obeyed. The two men facing each other abandoned their taunts in favor of glares and meaningless feints.

"Need a hand?" I asked.

"No." The sergeant looked up long enough to recognize me. "We're okay." As the man on his right lunged forward, he pushed back, yelling directly in his face until he had the man against the wall. "Some campers had a little too much campfire juice this morning."

"Dickinson said you should go on upstairs," offered the nearest patrolman.

"Sure you guys don't need a hand?"

Each sergeant grabbed a combatant, maneuvering them to opposite sides of the long desk. "Sit!" commanded one sergeant. They obeyed, though not without a last glower toward the other. "We're all set here, Jimmy. Go on up."

The five men present were more than capable of handling the six captives. I headed up the stairs. Inside the upstairs conference room, a chaotic jumble of uniformed officers, suited Federal agents, and plainclothes detectives, were all conferring around tables, counters, and bulletin boards. Out in the hall, a trio of patrolmen listened intently to a pair of detectives. Through the next closed door drifted voices engaged in a heated discussion. I passed by, maneuvering around the clutter in the hall to the sheriff's office. The door was closed; beside it a DEA agent leaned over a cabinet. He looked up. "You Hoitt?"

"Yes, sir."

He jerked a thumb at the door. "They said you should go in."

I nodded my thanks and slipped inside. Dickinson stood over the sheriff's desk, leaning over him, speaking rapidly, one hand against the desk, the other flailing madly at the air. Walker leaned back, feet on an open drawer, one hand around the bowl of his pipe. Smoke slowly curled toward the ceiling as his lips parted and closed. His eyes barely diverted to acknowledge my entrance, then returned to Dickinson. I sat quietly in the chair beside the door.

Like Walker, I listened as Dickinson explained the location and use of the makeshift radar sites. He related my research at Eagle Harbor and two other sites. He alluded to several other drops around Mount Desert Island and the mainland side of Frenchman Bay. Other officers on surveillance duty must have been as active as I.

After a while, Dickinson paused and straightened up. "Are you still with me, Francis?"

"Still waiting for the point."

"I thought I made it clear," replied Dickinson.

"Not yet." Walker dropped his feet to the floor and put his elbows on the desk, pointing the pipe stem at Dickinson. "What you've told me so far confirms the DEA story. You have told me that while most of the landing sites in Hancock County are clean, some of them are suspicious and bear watching."

"It's worth more investigating, Francis, that's all—"

"Wait. I wasn't finished yet." He reversed the pipe to take one long draw, then aimed it again. "You've told me the good people of Eagle Harbor have no knowledge of a drug smuggler in their midst. I have the same report from at least ten other villages. So what is so important?"

I had to admit that from the other side of the desk, all my work added up to a tiny sum. The sheriff's systematic rebuttal only slowed the inexorable Dickinson. He took another step back, straightening fully. "There are a couple more details."

Walker smiled and spread out his arms. "I'm still waiting."

"For what?" The door opened, allowing Wiley to slip inside. Full-time on a case now, he had discarded the jacket and tie of his formal uniform. Instead he wore a shirt with its sleeves rolled up. A nickel-plated pistol protruded from a black nylon shoulder holster. He closed the door and slid into the chair beside me. "What have I missed?"

"Sergeant Dickinson was detailing the results of his men's weekend observations."

Wiley turned to Dickinson, who had retreated to the window. "And?"

"Sheriff Walker was unimpressed," reported Dickinson. "My

team has talked to the townspeople; aside from gossip, they've turned up little."

"Don't be too quick to discard gossip," said Wiley. "Some of our best tips come that way." I remembered the speed with which my own mother's network had identified the dead bookkeeper.

"Gossip aside, things appear normal. No one reports any strange comings or goings. No odd boats, odd people."

Wiley nodded. "I would be very suspicious if anyone did, Sergeant. This operation is no amateur job. It is professional and highly efficient. I wouldn't expect a couple days' legwork to run it down. What else?"

"We've checked drop sites. Most are clean, but we found several potential rendezvous points."

"Are you referring to the radar reflectors?" said Wiley. "I read a report about that yesterday. You found more?"

"Yes, sir. We've turned them up regularly, every few miles of coastline."

"Good work, Sergeant. Not conclusive, but indicative. It means there's probably something here. It's a good preliminary case, but we had that much before I arrived."

"Exactly what I said," explained Walker. "We've proven what we already suspected. No progress."

"Unfortunately, I must agree," said Wiley. "Anything else I should know?"

Dickinson looked quickly at me, then at Wiley before addressing Walker. "Yes. Patrolman Hoitt told me something this morning. I think you should hear it."

Walker's eyes narrowed as his gaze shifted to me. "What dark secret did you uncover, Jimmy?"

I opened my mouth to speak, but before I could say anything Dickinson began. "By a fortuitous circumstance, Hoitt acquired what we think is a rendezvous schedule."

" 'Fortuitous circumstance'?" echoed Wiley. "That sounds suspiciously like illegal search and seizure."

"I've warned you that everything, absolutely everything, has to be totally aboveboard," said Walker. "This has to be solid!"

"What Hoitt found," continued Dickinson, "was not, of itself, very valuable. It's nothing illegal, and nothing we have to present as any kind of evidence. It might be useful, that's all. Imminently useful."

"Imminent?" said Walker.

Imminent activity aroused Wiley's interest. "Where did this information come from? I have to know the circumstances before I can call the judge." His coal-black eyes bored in on me. "Tell me, Hoitt."

"Well, sir, during the surveillance—"

"Listen," hissed Dickinson. His long legs covered the room in two quick strokes. He leaned on the arms of Wiley's chair, pushing his face toward the agent. "My men know their jobs and they know the law. I know you want immaculate evidence, but we're not talking evidence here, only a tip. Okay? This tip came from the kind of sources anyone else in Eagle Harbor might use. It's a good tip. That's good enough."

Despite Dickinson's imposing presence, Wiley refused to flinch. "Tell me what it is. We'll see what we can do."

Dickinson backed down. "Tell him about the calendar, Jimmy."

I succinctly described the calendar, deleting any reference to exactly where I had seen it. I added that I did know who owned the calendar; I told them about the three owners of the boat. I added as much as I knew about them to complete the report.

When I finished, Wiley leaned far forward on his seat. He distractedly plucked at his beard, twirling clumps of coarse hair around his finger. Walker calmly puffed his pipe as he waited for Wiley to say something. The DEA, after all, would have to pass judgment. Dickinson watched the others. When our gaze met, he smiled.

After half a minute of thick silence, Wiley spoke. "If that tip's authentic, Hoitt, it's the kind of thing we wait weeks to find."

"I have no doubt it's authentic," said Walker. "But a calendar with a few vague references is hardly overwhelming. I don't think it's time to call the cavalry."

"I'm not so sure," said Wiley. "This could be the break of a lifetime."

"Let's keep things in proportion," said Dickinson.

"This is a railhead, not the summit," added Walker.

"No, no," said Wiley, his eyes distant. "The pattern is perfect. In the midst of these radar sites, you find a boat. Not just ordinary fishermen, but run by lower-class, undereducated kids. The same kind of person likely to be a user. That's exactly the way the operation works—local boats, local people. No one would notice."

"You're hanging a lot of weight on a very small hook," said Walker calmly. "Only last night you said you didn't expect to turn up anything for at least two weeks."

"I know, I know," said Wiley quickly. "But this is fresh. This could be a leftover meet from before the murder. It's exactly the kind of thing we might hit by chance, early on."

"It's your ass," sighed Walker. "What do you want to do next?"

Wiley turned to me. "Hoitt, you know this place?"

"Yes, sir. I've been down there more than once."

"Describe it to me."

I complied, including as many details as I could.

Wiley tugged his beard more frantically. "We'll move tonight. I'll have five of my men accompany me. Sergeant Dickinson, I want you to bring Hoitt and two more of your men, and report to me by midnight. Sheriff, I'll need four more men and a van. I'll have two snipers with me; do you have any marksmen who can be there tonight?"

Walker's jaw set tight; he loathed firefights as only a veteran could. "I have a good man named Bourque. Dickinson here is no slouch with a rifle."

"I'll provide the weapons. Have everyone at the scene before midnight."

Walker's pipe had gone out. He examined the bowl, then tapped out the ashes into a glass ashtray. The sharp rapping hung in the room like pipe smoke. "I think you're jumping the mark, Tom."

"Sheriff, an opportunity like this doesn't come every day. This is hot. If things don't turn out—there's always tomorrow. We can't let this slip away."

Walker nodded. He put the pipe in a drawer, closing it slowly. "I'll have the men there at midnight."

"Good," said Wiley. "I'll be in my office the rest of the day if anything comes up."

"I'll call you the moment we get another hot tip," said Walker.

If the sarcasm touched Wiley, he did not notice. He approached me. "Good work, Hoitt. I would appreciate a little more care in your pursuit of these tips—but this one will be all right."

"Thank you, sir."

"Sheriff, do you have topo maps for that area?"

"Downstairs."

"Hoitt, come with me. I'd like to have a look at the map with you. I need a better idea of the territory. We may need to scout it out."

Wiley quickly stepped into the noisy hallway. Neither Dickinson nor Walker gave any indication I should stay, so I rose and pursued the agent.

One A.M. found me entrenched with Agent Wiley, Sheriff Walker, and the compact tank of a man commanding the U.S. marshals.

Wiley rocked on his knees, constantly surveying the quarry, a lightweight headset with a microphone on a thin boom clamped onto his head. This Wiley differed from the laid-back, calm man who invariably sat on the sheriff's desk as he talked. His intensity increased geometrically with each passing hour, flirting with the border into frenzy. Since this was the first time I had worked with Federal agents, I didn't know if his reaction was unusual. Compared to the supercharged, clinical Maine State Police, or the methodical county officers, Wiley existed in a different world. Sometime around eight, while dinner subsided uneasily in my tight stomach, I had realized that those men were from a world infinitely distant from a patrolman from Mount Desert Island.

The whole company made quite a picture as we tried to melt into the background. Wiley's agents and the marshals used their black coveralls, DEA or U.S. MARSHAL emblazoned in gold across their backs. The state troopers used forest camouflage, like hunters without the blaze orange. Left out in the cold were the county forces: our tan uniforms stood out clearly, so we kept them covered under dark sweaters. We appeared dark enough, but the costumes made us look casual against the Federal and state armies.

The horseshoe-shaped quarry opened east, the narrow gap connected to the main road by a short gravel driveway. A winding service road spiraled to the pit bottom, while around the rim, pine trees stuck fast to dwindling soil atop the ledge. At the bottom, a black pool of still water flooded the deepest section of the abandoned pit. Wiley felt certain that whatever went down would happen near the pool. Consequently, he ceded the inside of the quarry to concentrate his men at the entrance and around the perimeter. I stayed with him at the command post, on the highest ground on the rim. We had three night scopes, a radiotelephone, and a powerful battery-operated spotlight. It was my job to point the light into the pit when Wiley called for it.

Behind us, invisible from the quarry, Dickinson perched in the lower boughs of a pine tree. Black greasepaint darkened his face; in his arms he cradled a high-powered rifle, with a night scope as big around as his arm, draped in night-camo cloth. Spotted around the rim were three other men equipped the same way. Near each crouched another man, armed like myself with sidearm and spotlight. Anyone caught below would have nowhere to go.

Well out of sight near the quarry entrance were two armed teams with flak jackets, automatic rifles, and night goggles. If a firefight erupted they would be our front line; otherwise they existed to prevent anyone's exit. A quarter-mile down the road, three vans loaded with guards would escort the prisoners back to the station. Finally, spotted a mile away on each of the three approach roads, unmarked cruisers, backed well into the woods, waited to alert us as vehicles approached the quarry.

Reports from these spotters continuously streamed from Wiley's radio. The unusual amount of road traffic annoyed him; I was not surprised. Wiley and his men kept talking about patterns, the need to vary routes, to avoid any obvious patterns. I kept telling him the suspects just weren't that clever. If they showed up at all, they would come from Eagle Harbor.

The Eagle Harbor volunteer ambulance crew waited near the vans. To handle immediate medical crises, Twitchell waited with us, a canvas bag of emergency supplies beside him. Despite the fact that his white uniform shirt clearly stood out, he refused to part with it. Instead, he kept his black jacket zipped uncomfortably high. Twitchell seemed excited, shifting positions every few minutes, trying to get a better view of the rim, the entrance, and the quarry floor. The prospect of imminent action must have tightened his nerves worse than it did mine.

The minutes edged slowly by, but nothing developed. Wiley checked his men, responding to each vehicle report. Walker settled back against a tree, his arms crossed. His pipe came out of a pocket. I wondered if he would light it; Wiley was bound to disapprove of the light and the smell. He seemed content to gnaw on the stem, his eyes fixed on some distant point below.

Around a quarter to two, a rustle of leaves and twigs came from the undergrowth behind us. Walker rolled to the ground and flipped down his infrared goggle, staring into the woods. I pointed the unlit spotlight toward the sound, waiting for the order. Wiley stood up so fast the headset ripped off his head and fell onto the damp pine needles. His sudden, jerky motions did not fit the smooth, practiced image he projected. I wondered if he was as nervous as I. He swung his pistol before him, seeking a target.

From the close tree came a soft chuckle. "Relax," soothed Dickinson. "Just a doe. She's been sniffin' around back there a while. She must have caught our scent."

Wiley looked up into the tree as if he did not believe him. He safed and replaced his weapon, then recovered his headset. "We don't have deer in Boston."

Walker brushed the needles off his shirt, picked up his pipe, and put it back in his mouth. "I'm not surprised."

"I wonder if she has any idea what's going on here," mused Twitchell.

Less than two minutes later, the southern spotter reported a battered green Ford F150 cruising northward, two men inside. Wiley looked at me. I nodded. "That's the truck. One of them must have slept in."

Wiley pulled the mike closer, speaking quickly and quietly. "All positions, all positions. Target is coming in."

I advanced to the edge of the cover, spotlight ready, thumb on the switch. There would be plenty of firepower on the targets; it surely would be unnecessary to use my gun. I found I couldn't resist. I drew it, clicked off the safety, and loosely balanced it in my hand.

The pickup arrived minutes later. They were either unconcerned about who might be watching, or worried about the path: high-beam headlights preceded them all the way down. They pulled up beside the pool, then doused the lights. The engine died. For a second, nothing; then the doors squeaked open.

Wiley held the night goggles over his headset. He described what he saw: "Two men. The driver is quite tall, dark hair, long dark beard. He's got a heavy plaid shirt, and old jeans. The other guy is about eight inches shorter, jeans, a pea coat. He's got a beard a shade lighter—it may be red."

I shook my head. "It's brown."

"Who are they?" asked Twitchell quietly. "They locals?"

"Yuh," I answered. "The boat is registered to Paul Carlson. He's the tall, bearded one. The other guy sounds like his best friend, Dick Gallagher. The missing guy would be Paul's little brother, George."

"George Carlson," said Twitchell softly. "That name sounds familiar. Did he have a motorcycle accident last year? Alcohol-related?"

"Yuh, in Southwest Harbor."

"They've opened the tailgate," continued Wiley. "One's in the bed. One's sitting on the gate. The one in the bed is taking off a blue plastic cover. They look gray, green. Boxes?"

Walker had the second pair of goggles up. "They're fish totes— the large, plastic stackable ones."

"Can't see what's inside." Wiley shook his head. "If those boxes are full, this is going to be one of the biggest busts I've seen."

"Wait and see," mumbled Walker.

"The tall one seems pleased with himself. He's standing at the back of the truck, leaning on the side. Looks like they're talking. One of them is smoking."

A stream of vehicles passed the quarry during the next quarter-hour. Any of them could have been the one we waited for. With each radio announcement my nerves tightened another notch.

The other truck did not arrive until after half past two. Unannounced by the spotters, a panel truck waited for an oncoming car to pass, turned off the main road, and bumped into the quarry. This driver must have known the way better: as soon as he cleared the road he went down to his parking lights.

"The game is afoot!" said Twitchell.

"This is no game," growled Wiley.

An out-of-place grin crossed the EMTs lips. "Yes, it is."

The van stopped by the pickup. The driver stepped out. A second man left the van from the passenger door, walking round back. "Looks like they're haggling," Wiley continued. "The van driver keeps waving his arms around as he talks. He seems excited."

"He's blaming someone else for being late," reported Walker. "He keeps pointing out of the quarry."

"The back of the van is open—all I can see are more of those damn totes. Means nothing to me. Make anything of the name on the door, Sheriff?"

"Dufours Seafoods, Yarmouth, Nova Scotia. I've heard the name, but it means nothing to me. I can't tell you how extensively they do business here, especially at this time of night."

"Right. They're clustered at the back of the pickup, totaling things up. The van driver is checking inside one of the boxes. He's smiling; he's a happy camper. Here comes the envelope. Odd," said Wiley after a moment. "It looks like a check. It's usually cash." He readjusted his mike boom. "All positions, stand by. As soon as the first box goes into the van, lights on. Twenty seconds."

Thirty-five seconds later the men lugged the first box to the van, unceremoniously dumping it inside, sending a dull thud to belatedly reach us at the rim. Wiley gave the order. "Go! Move, move, move. Lights on! Hoitt, turn that—"

I needed no more. My thumb moved up, and a brilliant white beam stabbed at the bottom of the pit in concert with four others. They wavered only a moment, then converged on the four stunned men staring upward with dull, vacant looks.

"Do not move. Do not move!" Wiley had traded his headset for a bullhorn. "We are Federal agents. You are surrounded. Lay face down on the ground, ten feet away from each other. Hands on top of your heads. Stay still! Comply immediately or we will fire." He needn't have added the last part; before the echo died away all four were on the dusty ground, clutching the hairs at the back of their heads.

From the quarry entrance came the heavy rumble of dozens of men running over packed gravel. I kept the beam on the prone smugglers, but turned to see the rest of our force double-timing in from the road, rifles ready. The first to reach the van kept well back, rifles up to cover while the others yanked hands behind backs, securing them with nylon wrist restraints. From high above I could hear the mumbling as the DEA agents Mirandized each suspect.

Wiley dropped the bullhorn. "Let's go." Walker fell in step behind as Wiley weaved his way down the steep sides of the quarry. Twitchell grabbed his bag and did his best to keep up. I picked my own way carefully, spotlight in one upraised hand, eager to arrive in one piece.

A thick, cold mist followed me into the quarry. The prisoners lined up against the side of the van. Wiley gave each of them a glance, then stood before Carlson. A rough man, Paul had started his share of fights. More than once he had stood toe-to-toe with teachers, ready to go to blows before surrendering to be hauled to the principal's office. Now he stood silent and immobile, looking nauseated, more surprised than anything. "Where's the envelope?" asked Wiley.

"Shirt pocket," answered Carlson quickly.

Wiley took the white envelope out of the pocket, ripping it open to find a check. "Stamp is Dufours Seafoods, dated today. Memo line reads 104 kg. Check is for $776. Hmmph." He looked it over again. "The wages of sin don't pay so well in Maine. Delivery boys never get rich." He handed the check to a marshal, who placed it into a plastic bag marked EVIDENCE. "Let's check the van."

Two men with rifles flanked the back of the van as he cautiously approached. Wiley, a victorious grin on his face, jumped inside. "This has been too easy." He bent to the tote he had watched them load, ripped the top off, and peered inside. The smile fled. "There are lobsters in here! I can't see anything else." He reached inside, then quickly withdrew his hand. "These things bite, don't they?"

"Not exactly." I went inside, and looked around. The lobsters were all pegged. I grabbed one big one by its back: it took two hands for me to lift the enormous crustacean clear. It must have weighed a good twelve pounds! "This is oversize," I said.

Walker joined me in a second. I pushed lobsters aside, pulled them out and examined them, while Walker did the same. Maine law requires that any lobster measuring more than 3⅜ inches from brow to base of tail has to be thrown back; that linear restriction limits legal Maine lobsters to a weight of about a pound and three-quarters; occasionally, a two-and-a-half-pounder might be caught when the molting season is on and the waterlogged softshells abound. Larger crustaceans thrive in the Gulf of Maine. I confess that now and then my father brought back a behemoth from the deep for our own family dinner. Yet never had I seen so many oversize lobsters in one place. "They're all way oversize."

"Check the bottom," said Wiley. "They're just cover."

The sheriff and I emptied the box. All we found were overweight lobsters, fresh seaweed, and chipped ice. We opened up more totes, but they were all the same: lobsters. "There isn't anything in here," said Walker simply. "Nothing but lobsters."

"Impossible!" cried Wiley. "That tip was gold!" He quickly examined the empty box, then banged and probed it. It didn't take long to figure out it was just a thin-walled plastic box. Wiley dropped it, then stared dully at the sheriff. "I was certain we'd hit something."

Walker smiled. "We did. We caught a bunch of lobster smugglers. This *is* an illegal operation. These lobsters are illegal to catch or possess, let alone sell, in this state."

Dickinson joined us. He stood by the back of the van, looking at us inside. "What we have here are fish smugglers, Mr. Wiley."

"Course," said Walker slowly, "I'll bet you probably don't get too many of them in Boston."

Wiley shook his head, staring at the melting ice at his feet.

The head marshal appeared beside Dickinson. "Find anything?"

"Not what we came for," answered Walker. "But we caught something else."

"What do you want done with the suspects?"

"Bring around the van," sighed Walker. "We'll lock them up tonight and give the Department of Marine Resources a call. They'll press charges. Customs may want to talk to them, too. Otherwise, you and your men are free to go."

"We'll have them loaded in a few minutes."

The marshal disappeared, instantly replaced by Twitchell. "You didn't catch them, did you?"

"We caught them," said Dickinson. "Not for what we expected, but we did catch them."

"Better luck next time." Twitchell peered into the truck and shook his head. "Sheriff, if you don't mind, I'll round up my team and be off."

"Sure," replied Walker. "Thanks for showing up."

"No sweat."

I felt sick. My work had started this, my tip—and the unfortunate ending had to return on me like a boomerang. I climbed down from the back of the van, sitting dismally on the bumper. "Jimmy." The sheriff's voice was quiet and calm. I knew that couldn't be good.

"Yes, sir?" I lacked the courage to look up and face him.

"I'd like to talk to you. In my office, tomorrow morning."

"Yes, sir," I repeated.

"It's been a long night. Get some sleep. Ten o'clock, all right?"

"Yes, sir."

I started to go, but a firm hand on my shoulder halted me. Dickinson turned me around. "It was a good tip, Jimmy," he said. "It's not your fault."

Arrayed around me were dozens of county patrolmen, federal marshals, drug agents, and the state police. They had come armed for a heavy battle, but caught only a batch of marine delicacies. "Look around you, Sergeant. Something went wrong."

"I think Wiley was a little anxious," replied Dickinson gently. "Your info held, didn't it? You never called it a drug deal, just a deal."

"Small consolation."

"I'll talk to Francis. He'll be in a more forgiving mood come morning."

"But I won't be on the case, will I?"

He patted my shoulder. "Let's wait 'til morning, Jimmy."

I looked up at the stars. "It *is* morning, Sergeant."

He abruptly changed tacks. "You live near here, don't you?"

"Nearer than Ellsworth."

He handed me a set of keys. "My car is by the vans. Take it. Go home. Sleep."

"How are you going to get back?"

"I'll ride in with Francis. When you come back to the station, drop the keys at the front desk. I won't be going any farther than Ellsworth this morning."

I sheepishly thanked him. He literally pushed me on my way, gently shoving me toward the quarry entrance. A promising morning had evolved into disaster. I knew the blame would fall squarely on me; it had to. I left the van, Wiley, and his smugglers behind as I walked dismally out of the quarry.

6

Wednesday

Patrol Area: Eagle Harbor to Bangor
Temps warm; wind and seas calm;
skies clear

I would have preferred root canal work to my meeting with Sheriff Walker. I didn't possess sole responsibility for the raid. I had provided only a tip, the slimmest of hunches. Dickinson had amplified my lead, the sheriff added his piece. By the time Wiley finished with it, we were prepared to apprehend the largest criminal organization in North America. Their overreactions were not my fault. My tip had been gold; the sting had not come up empty. Our presumed targets never showed, but the sale of oversize lobsters is no small matter to people who make their living catching them. Since the fish smuggling charges would stick, the raid had been successful.

I wished I could accept my rationalization, but I could not absolve myself. I had pieced together the scraps of available evidence. Not surprisingly, I found exactly what I expected. Even if Wiley and the sheriff had gone overboard, the fault lay squarely with the face staring back in the rearview mirror.

Two video trucks from Bangor were parked out front of the station. I wondered why they were there. I wanted to think there must be another reason. Prominent local trials could lure the trucks down to the courthouse. They frequented the fringes of Route 1 through the summer. I was kidding myself, I thought, as I parked out back. I knew why they were there.

Once inside, I confirmed my fears. In the high-ceilinged lobby, Wiley and one of his agents stood against the wall, facing two cameras and a flock of microphones. I had no desire to hear what he had to say. I had a vision of Special Agent Wiley stopping in mid-denial, pointing an accusatory finger at me as I hurried past, his eyes glowering as he proclaimed the whole thing my fault. The cameras would swing to follow his finger, and the microphones would point directly at me, pushing me against the opposite wall sticking me there like a fly to maple syrup. I just about ran past the throng to get to the dispatcher's window. "Buzz me in," I begged. As soon as the lock buzzed, I pushed through the door into the station, away from Wiley and the media vultures.

Before I said a word, the desk officer pointed a thumb down the hall. "Sheriff is in the main conference room," she said. "He wants you to interrupt him when you come in."

My spirits sank impossibly lower to know the sheriff wished to be interrupted no matter what busied him. I trudged down the hall, my lonely steps echoing on the wooden floor. As I passed the other office doors, I heard conversations stop, felt cold stares on me. The sheriff's office was hardly immune from gossip. By now they all must have known about the raid; they might even know my fate.

The last door opened into the conference room. I plainly heard Walker inside. He didn't seem angry as he discussed operational accountability with an unknown voice. Saving it all for me, I thought dismally. I drew myself up straight, took a deep breath, and knocked. I had permission to enter unannounced, but if a second's delay would attenuate the storm, I would take that precious second. "Patrolman Hoitt."

Immediately the talk inside ceased. "Come in, Jimmy."

I gently pushed on the door. Walker took up the far end of the table, file folders, papers, and an open statute book before him. A tired, bored DEA agent, file in hand, stood beside him, peering over his reading glasses.

Walker looked up at the gaunt face. "Five minutes, okay, Sam?"

"I'll just go get it started."

"Fine." Walker pushed back his chair. "Jimmy, have a seat."

The agent whispered past like a mortician. I pulled out a chair, and sat.

"It's been a very long night," said Walker. He massaged his neck. "Today will be a long day."

For lack of anything better, I replied: "Yes, sir."

"Pretty slick operation last night, wasn't it?"

"Sir?"

"Wiley's raid. Smooth, organized. A nice piece of work. He co-ordinated several unfamiliar groups very effectively."

"Yes, sir."

"He's not a bad officer. Overzealous, perhaps." Walker leaned forward and looked straight in my eye. "He's not alone there, is he, Jimmy?"

I could not meet his gaze. "No, sir."

He said nothing, idly gazing at the far wall while I sweated. Despite the cool morning, I could feel a solid line of perspiration beading on my hairline. I wished he'd come out and say it. *You're off the case, Jimmy. You're fired, Jimmy.* Whatever he was going to do, I wished he'd get to it.

Finally, he rose. "Wiley bought his own problems." He walked slowly around the room, his hands on his back above his kidneys. "He made the mistake of laying out grand expectations before we started. Told his boss he was on the trail. I doubt he mentioned any lobsters."

In spite of myself, I smiled. It fled momentarily.

"The district supervisor alerted the press. That's why Wiley is dealing with them now. Apparently, this is the first they've heard of the Frederickson conspiracy. I understand Wiley's boss is looking for someone's head on a silver platter. Frederickson's killer's, Wiley's, mine, yours—he doesn't care whose head. Somebody's. I had a brief talk with him this morning. He's more than a little upset that this will tarnish their image."

"Yes, sir."

Another long silence ensued. Walker paced his way around the room until he stood behind me. I dared not turn around. "Well," he said, "what's done is done. Tomorrow is another day."

He sat on the table, one leg still on the floor. "Jimmy, you're a good officer. I think someday you're going to make a good detective, if that's the path you choose to follow. You can't chase the big break, though. You won't always be on the front line. Case support is a respectable and important task. You understand?"

"Yes, sir."

He put his hand on my shoulder. "All you need is experience. Experience leads to a sense of perspective you can't rush to find. You had a good tip, but you should have done more work first, before you came up here. Checked to find any correlation between the dates and anything else. Checked bank accounts, gas bills, bait orders. You should have asked yourself a lot more questions and hunted relentlessly for the answers. Made sure there wasn't another explanation. You follow me?"

"Yes, sir. More caution, less style."

Walker smiled. "Jimmy, you've got a good style. Don't lose it. Try to put it to better use, okay?"

"Yes, sir."

"All right then." He shuffled back to his chair. "I've got a busy schedule ahead. I've got to fill out papers for the Department of Marine Resources and the state police. Everybody wants to have a chat with me later, too." He sat down heavily. "You've had a long night. You've worked hard. The harbor may be too hot to handle for a bit. Take today off. Relax. Catch up on some sleep."

"Okay." I didn't want to ask, but I couldn't not ask. "I'm still on the case, then, sir?"

"Hell, yes. But do us both a favor before you bring in any more tips. Do more groundwork."

"I will, sir."

"Good." He pulled his chair in, and picked up a sheet from the pile. "Now go home."

"Thank you." I needed no further prodding. I nearly sprinted down the hall, slipping out the door before Wiley or the cameras had a chance to mark my presence. I went to my car and left the station behind—I did not want to give Walker any chance to change his mind.

I barely slowed during the return to Eagle Harbor. Having the sheriff exonerate me for the previous night's mission was a mixed blessing. I would not be held responsible for Wiley's overreaction or the lack of results; neither would I get another chance. I had made my beginner's mistake and been forgiven for it. Now he would be watching more closely. The next time he would not be so forgiving. The next time he would want my badge. I could not allow a next time.

I didn't expect a vacation. I had no idea what to do with the free time. I thought it over during the ride home, but couldn't come up with anything to do. Back home, I parked and went inside. The phone hung right beside the door; I reached for it and dialed Robyn before the screen door slammed shut. I let it ring eight or nine times, but no answer. Robyn's home was too small to require more than eight rings. She might be out shopping, or down at the library; she could be out with her mother, or tending her flower beds. Summer leaves her schedule wide open. I decided to drive over later and leave a note on her door, hoping whatever busied her would not take all day.

First I raided the refrigerator for a quick brunch. On top of the fridge, beside an old fire department alert radio sat an equally ancient marine set. It was the original radio from the *Janet Kathleen II*, which I'd wired to 110 volts. The best weather came from the marine service, so I snapped it on and switched the channel over. The forecaster started near the Merrimack River, more than a hundred miles to the south. While I waited, I assembled what I had collected from the refrigerator into something resembling a sandwich, and mindlessly thumbed through the weekly paper.

The forecast moved northward. I put the paper aside and listened. The morning should start off cool and windy, but the sun would come out around ten or eleven, the winds and seas would die down, the temperatures would rise and the skies clear. The late afternoon should be good for boating, the evening magnificent. It sounded like an excellent vacation day. It would be dull if I had to spend it alone.

I cleaned up my mess and shut off the radio. Without thinking, I headed for the county Buick and had my hand on the door before I remembered I was off duty. I shook my head, going to the garage. Despite being untouched for three days—no, four, I realized—my truck fired on the first key turn with a reassuring roar, and chewed up the gravel driveway as my foot landed a little heavily on the gas.

I have traveled the roads between Robyn's house and mine so often they are as deeply engraved in my mind as the trip from bedroom to bathroom. I can travel them under any weather conditions and can recognize the turns ahead by the trees and signs before each. A consequence of that familiarity is that I am often barely conscious of having driven it. Before I knew it, I had stopped in her driveway.

I had my own house key, and used it. A quick search turned up nothing to indicate where she might be or what she might be doing. A large calendar beside the microwave held most of her plans. Aside from an untimed note to pick up some pictures, the sheet held nothing. She must be engaged in something that had come up on short notice. Probably her mother. She probably would not return soon. I took a piece of paper from her desk, scrawled a note that I had the day off and that I'd probably be down at the dock; I figured with the good weather my father could use a hand. I signed it, stuck it on the fridge, and let myself out.

The dock lot was full, so I parked behind the church again. I noticed *Freebird* tugged at her mooring—no surprise with two of her crew in the county lockup. The big racing sloop and the sleek powerboat were gone. Fred Dixon's *Susan Marie* took on reeking barrels at the bait dock. I abruptly stopped as I realized that even on my day off I could not stop investigating. As I expected, the *Janet Kathleen III* was tied up at the main dock, my father swearing as I approached. The pile of parts on the fantail seemed smaller than before, which should be a good sign.

Low tide necessitated a long climb down the ladder before I could jump onto *Janet*'s deck. I made my cautious way past the wheelhouse and planted myself on the gunwale. My father stopped grumbling at the engine block. "Mornin'," he said. "Thought I heard you coming."

"Just visiting."

"Thought you were working today."

"Walker told me I was working too hard. Gave me the day off."

"Uh huh." He exchanged the box wrench in his hand for a socket wrench. "How's the investigation going?"

I had not told him about my midnight search, nor last night's raid. I wondered what news had already reached him. "Slow."

If he knew, he showed nothing. I doubted he would. "Good."

"How's the repairs?"

"I might have her running before dinner."

"Really? That's great."

"I got a ways to go. I think I fixed the problem, got all the parts together. Can't seem to get the camshaft to seat just right, though." He picked up the irregular metal shaft. "Looks good to me. How about you?"

I examined it. While I knew something about engines, I was no mechanic. "Looks fine."

"A little excess wear on the third cam, but not so bad I'm ready to shell out three hundred bucks for a new one." He sighted along the shaft. "Doesn't look warped. But it won't fit."

"How did it come out? Did you have to pry it out?"

"She popped right out." He set it down on the deck beside him. "But I figured while I had it apart I might as well change the bearings."

"I hope you didn't raid the junkyard again. You bought new bearings, right?"

"Hell, yes. Saving twenty bucks won't help me when the engine quits thirty miles out. Ask Murray 'bout that." He reached between the cylinder rows and tugged. "I got a feeling he gave me the wrong set. They turn nice and smooth, but they fit like shit."

"Have him check the numbers."

"That's what I figured. Better change them now instead of after I've jammed them in tight."

"Do it now," I suggested.

"Yuh." He sighed, pushed the camshaft farther out of his way, traded some tools, and bent over the block. In moments both bearings were on the deck. Despite a coating of oil and grease, they still looked new. "I'll go have a chat with Russ. I'm sure we can reach some kind of an agreement. You coming?"

"No," I replied, rising anyway. "I'll be here when you get back."

A broad smile cracked his face, his faintly yellow teeth gleaming amidst the black beard. "Robyn's tied up, is she?"

"You got it."

He closed one big hand around the bearings and stepped up on the gunwale. "I'll be back in ten or fifteen."

"I'll hold down the fort."

He sidled past the wheelhouse and hopped onto the ladder, climbing quickly despite only one available hand. His tread boomed heavy, rhythmically, as he plodded over the dock planks. In a few moments the sound no longer reached me, leaving me alone with the dock, the sea, and the boat.

I sat on the port gunwale, in the shadow of the wheelhouse roof. Behind me the dock pilings trapped the morning coolness, preserving it in the flat water and gently undulating seaweed. After a long day of rain followed by a very long night's work, I craved sunlight. I abandoned the gunwale and headed forward. With her sharply raked prow, the foredeck of the *Janet Kathleen III* is not the most comfortable place to relax, but in sunshine it's warm and bright, with a spectacular view. I pushed aside a coil of rope and sat down, legs out, back against the cabin windows, letting the sun wash over me.

I stared dully out to the breakwater. The wind pulled the fleet toward the open sea, presenting me with a dozen bow quarters. Ever working, my mind tagged names and owners to the hulls. An image emerged from the water like a mirage from a desert: A black pirate ship, dark sails billowing, guns at the ready to guard her cargo—not newly minted Spanish gold or plundered Inca jewels, but a cargo worth its weight in either ancient currency. The phantom disappeared before me; the pirate ship did not belong in my harbor.

I had screwed up. My surveillance hadn't been faulty, just my interpretations. I ran into trouble when I stopped observing and began thinking. I had tried too hard to force the pieces together, like a frustrated kid with a cardboard jigsaw puzzle. What should the pieces of the case look like when correctly assembled? Did the pirate ship float inside the protection of the breakwater, or was the Great Secret of Eagle Harbor a boring lack of any secrets? For now, I had no idea. All I had was a pile of bent puzzle pieces.

My father returned. He held out a set of clean bearings. "Gave me the wrong set." He resumed tinkering and swearing.

Where to go next? Back to the beginning, I decided. The mangled puzzle pieces would have to be pressed flat and completely rearranged. No forcing them together, no preconceived notions of what the puzzle had to look like. Maybe the pirates were beyond the breakwater, but maybe it was moored only a few yards away. Maybe there was no pirate ship anywhere. Or perhaps it didn't look at all like what I expected. Whatever the solution, the first thing I had to do was to let go of the past.

I pulled myself more tightly around my knees, concentrating only on facts, contracting so tightly my muscles soon began to ache. Eventually the rocking of the ocean lulled me to sleep, aided by the gentle sounds of the waves lapping against the dock, the muted growl of the sea hitting the breakwater, and the screeching of the gulls. The clink of tools on metal and the cadence of my father's swearing became a kind of lullaby, carrying me into a deep, tired sleep.

I awoke as though I had merely blinked. My watch told me I had slept an hour and a half, yet I felt as if I had slept all day. Several days of nervous, fitful sleep had affected me more deeply than I had thought. My nap had been the best sleep since starting my new job. It felt good.

I eased my shoulders back and discovered that, while no longer tired, I remained tightly wound. An immense knot tugged between my shoulder blades; my upper arms ached; my neck felt sore, as if I had been clenching my teeth. Walker was right: I needed a vacation. The investigation could wait. I would be fresh, alert, and prepared in the morning. I knew Robyn would eventually find me. We could spend the evening and whatever remained of the day together. Until she arrived, a project close at hand begged for my attention. Engine reassembly was dirty, exhausting, consuming work. On such a day it would also be hot, sweaty labor. It was the perfect thing to help me relax.

I stretched my legs, then stood. I walked the narrow starboard gunwale back to the fantail and jumped onto the deck beside my father. New bearings had apparently been the answer, for he had the camshaft in place. "Need a hand?"

He nodded. "Maybe with two of us we can get her running this afternoon."

I flipped my shirt toward the wheel and knelt on the other side of the block. "What do you want me to do?"

Just before four, the sound my father had awaited for nearly two weeks finally bellowed across the harbor. The stone-cold engine did not respond well to the initial grinding of the starter. Dad advanced the throttle, punched the priming knob several times, and tried again. The engine coughed, sputtered, sounded as if it would catch—then didn't. A crack more throttle, enough primer to fill the fantail with fumes, and he hit the starter. At first nothing, then with a belch of thick black smoke and a dull explosion, it caught. It quickly wound up to speed, settling down to a hungry snarl.

Transfixed by the clacking, snarling engine, I sat on the gunwale, watching. Once it settled down, my father came aft, and sat beside me, as hypnotized as I was. He wiped his hands thoughtfully with a cloth barely any cleaner than his hands. A trace of a smile touched his lined, tired face. "I think we've got it."

It had been a long afternoon of laborious work. I was tired. Yet, in spite of my best efforts to immerse myself in the task, I did not feel purged. My mind still gnawed at the investigation. "Seems that way," I answered.

"Do you two have any idea," called down a voice from the dock, "how much smoke you just sent out?"

I looked up to see who it was, though I already knew. Robyn leaned on the rail, staring down. I raised a hand and waved. "I think we overprimed her."

"That's an understatement," she called back. "Are you going to come up here, or do I have to come down and drag you up?"

With those words she broke the trance of the running engine. My father pointed toward the bow, his gaze still fixed on the engine. "Go on," he said. "I'll clean up and put the cover back."

"I can help." I picked up the cloth and started wiping my hands. "It won't take the two of us long."

"You've done more than enough." He finally looked away. "I'll run her for a while, see if she's settled. If it seems all right, I'll go out for a quick spin."

It might take him an hour to finish the details, but it wouldn't be hard work. "Check the radio before you go."

"Yuh." He looked off the beam, where he could see the open ocean and the late afternoon sky. "Looks like it'll be a good evening. Maybe I'll see if your mother can skip out of work early. We can take a spin 'round the island. That'll break her in good."

I found my shirt hanging over the side, half immersed. I squeezed out as much water as I could before I put it on, wet and clammy against my skin. "See you later."

"Thanks, Jimmy." He went back to his engine as I slid around the deckhouse. The tide had nearly run its cycle, so a step and a half took me from deck to dock. Robyn met me, wordlessly putting her arms around me. I held her tightly, my fingers soothed to be touching the soft and warm back of her neck instead of the cold, hard steel tools and engine parts.

"How was your day?" she asked, her head still on my shoulder.

"Interminable," I answered. "I had a long morning."

"I'm sorry I wasn't around. I didn't know you'd get the day off."

"Neither did I."

She pulled back to look into my eyes. "Bad day at work?"

"A shitty morning of police work."

"What happened?"

I smiled. I felt buoyed simply to be with her. "Let's drop it, okay?"

She shrugged, and smiled. "Fine."

"How was your day?"

"Lousy." Her head fell against my shoulder again. "I spent the morning searching in vain for props and set pieces. I either couldn't find them or couldn't pry them away from their owners."

"How about the afternoon?"

"I had lunch with my mother and a couple of her bingo friends. Spent too much time arguing about what I was doing with my life. It gets to me after a while, you know?"

"I know." I said nothing for a while, a silence she readily joined. Finally, I said, "The afternoon's pretty well shot. What do you want to do tonight?"

"I want to get away from here," she said. "Let's go somewhere for dinner. Anywhere, as long as its miles away."

"You have any place in mind?"

"No. Let's just point the truck and go."

"I have to stop home, clean up and change. Take five minutes. We can still clear the island by five."

"Okay." We stood still for a few more moments, then, by unspoken agreement, we broke apart to walk hand in hand back to my truck.

Some six hours later, we returned to Eagle Harbor after our too-brief sojourn. Dinner had been okay. I spent most of it brooding, staring out a wide window at a lake far below. Normally, Robyn would have tried to draw me out, compel me to talk, whether I wanted to or not. But not that night. She was unusually quiet, lost in her own private world. Under other circumstances, I would have done for her what she'd have done for me. Instead, the evening turned into a night of few words.

As midnight dissolved one day to create another, I sat on the deck behind her house, nursing the dregs of a Shipyard Ale. The afternoon had evolved into a magnificent night—warm, cloudless: perfect. The moon, already sliding down the sky, extracted long shadows from the trees. The moon and the brilliant starlight illuminated the surface of the ocean five hundred yards away, tiny gems on waves as wind flitted over the sound. Setting spring stars filled the western skies over Blue Hill. Water, stars, wind made a soothing vista, purged of all boats, all duties and responsibilities. No smugglers, no suspects. A mild swell patterned Blue Hill Bay with harmonic regularity, undisturbed by rocks or boats. I wished I could be a boat out on those waters, with no cares about any investigation. Even if given the opportunity, I wondered, could I separate myself from my duty to absolve the village? It wasn't in my contract, nothing Dickinson or Walker enforced. Wiley could never even understand it. I carried it with me, inside me, all along the search for Frederickson's network. Probably I could no more ditch that emotion at sea than I could ashore.

That sense of duty had betrayed me at the quarry. As an investigator I had to approach the problem with no prejudices, no preconceptions, and no theories. First came the facts: only when they started to add together could I construct a theory. Yet what did I have so far? Tentative schedules and mere gossip. Yet based on that and the scant evidence of an innocuous calendar, I had called out the cavalry. Good God, I thought. If I looked hard enough, I could probably find such calendars on other boats, maybe at the diner or the hardware store, certainly in the bank. What had I been thinking?

I tipped the bottle all the way back, letting a trickle of lukewarm beer slide down my throat. The bottle hit the grass beside the garbage cans with a soft thud. I had not been thinking. I had been reacting emotionally, irrationally, and stupidly. It could not happen again.

Where to start? My vision glazed as I focused on the distant waves. By population, income, land, or any other criteria I considered, the town had no more to offer than any of a dozen other nearby towns. If Eagle Harbor held any guilt, it had to involve one of the boats in the harbor. There had to be something suspicious on the water that didn't fit the pattern I knew.

The boats. I mentally reviewed the lists and schedules I had compiled. None of the boats showed any glaring inconsistencies, but why should they? A boat that worked strange areas or operated at peculiar hours would be bound to draw the attention of the Coast Guard or at least the Department of Marine Resources. Such attention would be self-defeating.

While Denise's observations indicated no pattern among the transient boats, I had not yet personally checked them. A boat that made rounds, perhaps traveling the hot spots of Boothbay to Castine to Eagle Harbor to Machias, or several boats seen in the same company might signify a pattern. A little work could resolve that.

I needed a new working hypothesis. I had precious few facts to put into it, and some of my facts were bound to be irrelevant. The one theory that correlated the suspected fact of drug smuggling via Eagle Harbor with the maximum number of established facts had to be the correct theory. I closed my eyes in concentration. Fact one: proximity. Frederickson had lived in Somesville. Wiley believed that manager and business tended to remain close. This indicated a drop site somewhere on the island, a fact further bolstered by fact two: the geography of the island lends itself to smuggling. The third fact: Wiley had evidence of a drug connection reaching the United States on the Maine coast. If I believed Wiley's basic (and well-supported) assumption that Frederickson had not retired, then the first tenet of the solution could not be ignored. A network existed on either Mount Desert Island or the adjoining Maine coast.

I reluctantly accepted that. If not, a lot of people were wasting a lot of time, from Wiley down to me.

From there, the fact sheet grew increasingly nebulous. The next assumption: Frederickson had been murdered. Nearly a week of investigating the death had failed to prove a murder. The assumption was founded mostly on Dickinson's interpretation of the tire tracks. It was strong evidence, but not quite a fact. If it was an accident, it was a fortuitous one for us, but I couldn't call it a murder.

With the link to Boston through Bangor, Wiley had finally proven that Frederickson's network existed. I took that as a fact. If Frederickson had been murdered, it could have been by a competitor. How had Frederickson's network been revealed to the new operator? What had given it away? The operation ran so far underground that Wiley and his flock of agents could not break it. How did someone else come to know about it? Frederickson's operation should have died with him, unless it was being run by someone else (a fact Wiley did not accept), or the murderer had assumed control at once. No outsider could have discovered enough of the operation to take it over, not so fast. Therefore, it had to be someone inside. A lieutenant, a greedy delivery boy, a rival—whoever it was, he had to know the entire operation. That meant he had to know this area, my home. That meant it had to involve someone who spent enough time on Mount Desert Island to know it well. I didn't like the way that finger inevitably pointed, but there was no denying it.

Who knew enough? He had to know the shoreline intimately. Once ashore, the drugs needed to move to Bangor, according to Wiley. How did a shipment get from the ocean to Bangor? Whether by road or by air, this smuggling operation depended on local connections. He would know the business, the drop sites and dispersal plan, and the schedule. That man now ran the network. That was the man we hunted.

I reviewed my notes. Which vessels would be the most likely suspects? Almost immediately the image of the red boat jumped into my mind: *Aquila*. Why didn't anyone know much about the owner? Why was all the equipment new and well kept, as if unused? Why did he spend so little time at sea? Before I went too far, I checked myself. I was repeating my earlier mistake. I had not a shred of evidence, only gossip and guesses. I could be totally wrong. The fact that *Aquila*'s owner kept to himself might mean he was innocent. To blend in with the community, Frederickson's man could not afford to be a local pariah, isolated from the rest of town. Outsiders were far too conspicuous in a place like Eagle Harbor.

I put aside all emotions. Theories were fine, but until supported by evidence they were nothing more than matchstick bridges. One step at a time, I promised myself. I would restart my investigation by seeking the second man.

A creaky spring announced the opening of the screen door. Robyn, who had traded jeans and a button-down shirt for a light cotton sweater over cutoffs, stepped onto the porch, Binkley cradled in her arms. She stroked the back of his neck, which he evidently enjoyed; his insistent purr growled unmistakably above the lonely call of a whippoorwill. She looked out onto the bay, then up at the stars as she sat down beside me. "What a beautiful night."

"Yuh. I don't remember one like this since . . . since I don't know."

"Since last summer." She lowered her gaze to the shadow of Blue Hill. "Quiet on the water, too."

"Nights like this make me wonder," I began. I was glad she had joined me, glad for the chance to abandon the case. "No sounds to hear but nature's own. Nothing on the water but wind and waves. No engines, no cars, no lights."

She squinted across the water. "There's a bright one over there."

"Just a dock light. But imagine it's not. Picture a campfire, set just inside the woods by the native people. It must have been like this in Champlain's time."

"I wish I could have seen it then."

I nodded slowly. "It sure would be different."

The silence took over the deck. She continued to stroke Binkley, whose purring grew deeper. When she stopped, he purred on for a moment, expecting her to resume. When she didn't, he craned his neck backward and looked first at me, then at Robyn. He mewed once, softly, respecting the quiet. He rose to all fours, arched his back high in the air, his mouth gaping over sharp white teeth. He glanced once more at Robyn, then bounded off her lap, touched the steps once, and literally hit the grass running, disappearing into the shadow.

As if his departure had snapped some trance, Robyn shook her head quickly. She stretched out her arms, arching her back, gently lowering herself backward until her head rested against my chest. "Surely you weren't out here contemplating Samuel de Champlain."

"Nope.

"What then?"

"Guess."

"Work, isn't it?" She laid her hand on my forearm, slowly stroking it. "It's not much of a day off if you refuse to leave the job behind."

"Too much is happening. I need to stay on top of it."

"Is this case so serious?" she asked. "When you first told me about it, underneath your excitement, you seemed skeptical. You didn't put much faith in Agent Willy, either."

"Wiley," I corrected.

"You didn't trust him."

"I didn't believe him," I explained. "It sounded so fantastic. I couldn't believe a cocaine express whistled through my own back yard. I couldn't accept it, not in Eagle Harbor."

"Sounds like you've changed your mind."

"Maybe. I know more now. Wiley has a strong case. There remains a wicked lack of evidence, but I'm working on it. I think I reached a conclusion today. I have refined my strategy."

She half-turned to look up at my face. "A lack of a plan had you so quiet all night?"

"No. That stupid tip kept me so quiet. I realized I have to put it behind me. Immediately. I think I figured out how to proceed."

She smiled, squeezing my arm. "That's good."

Though still no further along than before, acknowledging to

Robyn that I had a definite plan dimmed the bitter memories of the quarry. With my problems pushed aside, I turned to hers. "What's eating you?"

"What do you mean?"

"It takes two to be quiet all night."

She sighed. "I suppose so." After that she fell abruptly silent. I didn't want to intrude on her thoughts, so kept quiet, waiting. "Afternoons with my mother really get to me."

"What do you mean?"

"She has an amazing ability to upset me," she answered. "Especially when I can least defend myself. This afternoon was a perfect example. I was already down because the morning hadn't gone well. At lunch I'm trapped with her and her friends. That's when she starts talking about me, asking me if I'm going to hang around town forever, what I'm going to do about you." She shivered. "Insinuating that I'm getting old and it's time I started thinking about her grandchildren. God, Jimmy, I'm only twenty-four. I'm still a kid, aren't I?"

I shrugged. "I'm still a kid. I'm older than you, so you must still be a kid, too." I wondered if I sounded as if I believed it.

"She can say it so sweetly, a smile plastered on her face. How can I argue with her when she's with her friends? They have me surrounded and outnumbered."

"You could have excused yourself."

"You know what happens then?"

"Can't imagine."

"The conversation goes on without me. A few days later, as I run into her cronies they pull me aside and whisper how upset I make my mother. Nothing about my life, of course, only that I should think about her." She lay quietly in my arms, staring up at the stars. I gazed up at them, too, weaving my fingers through her thick, soft hair.

"What set her off?" I said after a time.

"What do you mean?"

"When I get a lecture like that there's always a reason," I replied. "Usually it means someone else did something. Every time one of the waitresses at the diner brings in a new set of baby pictures, or wedding pics, sooner or later I get the grilling. My mother tries to be subtle, but she's about as subtle as a pair of bricks upside your head. So what set your mother off?"

"I'm not sure." She thought a moment. "Her sister called from Milbridge last night. My cousin—you remember, Rachel, the one whose wedding we went to last year?"

"The blonde who married a Neanderthal?"

"That's the one. I know they are trying to have a baby. Maybe she's finally pregnant."

"That would be plenty of ammunition for my mother. Might be enough for yours."

"Yeah." She shook her head. "I should have taken the job in Portland."

I pulled her closer. "No, you shouldn't have."

She clutched my arm tightly. "I know."

We reclined silently on the porch for a while. I don't know what Robyn thought about, but I gazed at the stars, the water, the dark mirror of the bay. For the first time in days, I was not thinking about the investigation. Binkley returned from the hunt, bounded up the steps, and settled in near my arm, nestled against Robyn's hair. He tucked his forelegs underneath him, closed his eyes, and began purring.

"How serious are you?" she said, barely more than a whisper.

"Serious about what?"

"About me, you moron."

I breathed deeply. "I don't know. I haven't thought about it for a while."

"You did once?"

"Sure. In the beginning, when I didn't know you well. We were still in school."

"School," she said. "That was a way back."

"Not so long."

"Long enough," she replied. "Since then?"

"I don't know. It's kind of weird. Every now and then, we'll be out driving, and it's so natural that I can't imagine being with anyone else. Once, maybe late last fall, we were up in the mountains. We passed an old barn, with a stone house, and horses out grazing. I thought it would be nice to have a place like that. It felt like you were supposed to fit into that picture, too." I paused. "Make any sense?"

"Yes," came her barely audible reply. "I've had thoughts like that, too."

"Let's take another tack," I said. "How serious do you want us to be?"

For a long time the moaning birds and Binkley's insistent purr were my only reply. "I think I'm ready to be a wife. But I'm not ready to be a mother, like my mother wants me to be," she said. "I have other things to do, first. How about you?"

I paused before answering, selecting my words very carefully. "I am not ready to be a father."

"Why not?"

"I don't know, exactly. It's just not a picture I can see myself in."

"Oh."

"Don't get me wrong," I added quickly. "I can't picture myself with anyone else but you."

"Good." She said nothing further for a while. Neither did I. "Do you want to get married?"

I looked out over the water. "Right now?"

"Soon."

I hesitated. "Robyn, I've had a lot of things on my mind lately. This is not the best time to ask."

"Think about it, okay? No pressure. I'll be here either way, 'cause I can't picture myself with anyone else, either."

"Okay." I looked up at the stars. A bright star that had been low over Blue Hill had disappeared, dragging the rest of the stars with it. "I have to work in the morning," I eventually said. "I'd better head home."

"It's too late to go home." She put both hands on my arm, holding on tightly. "Stay tonight. Please."

"All right," I replied quickly. Too quickly, I thought. "Let's go. I need some sleep."

She rose. I stood up, extended a hand and helped her up. I opened the door. She prodded Binkley with her toe, then followed the cat, and I trailed her. The investigation could wait.

I did not reach the harbor early enough to watch the departure of the fleet. Instead I had to settle for a boat inventory and consult my notes to determine the most likely disposition of the missing boats. As another weekend approached, the fishing fleet would be desperately competing to supply fresh lobsters to all the local pounds and restaurants. I happily noted that at long last the *Janet Kathleen III* had slipped her mooring. I doubted my father would be able to do much more than set some traps, but that beat hanging around the repair dock. Only the trawler *Freebird* and Ed Wilson's *Beth Anne* still bobbed at their moorings. *Freebird*'s presence I understood. A nasty summer cold laid Ed low, so he, too, could be excused. The big cruisers were all gone. As I watched, the racing sloop got underway and slid past the breakwater, leaving only the two fishing boats and the sleek *Die Walküre*. This last was curious on such a beautiful day. I decided this was the time to find out more about its owner.

I parked with the other trucks and headed for the dock. The diner provided limited data. I had to go to a direct source for a change. An unfamiliar form showed on the dock as I approached. Based on the one evening when I had caught a glimpse of *Die Walküre*'s master, I knew I had an opportunity to meet him again. I quickened my pace, not so much that anyone would notice, but not so slowly to allow him to escape.

I need not have rushed. He was studying the NOAA chart for the harbor and adjoining Blue Hill Bay, which he had spread out on the dock rail and held down by a brick. Standing beside him, listening intently, pointing occasionally, one of the local kids leaned against his bike, popping his gum. The man made insistent inquiries concerning a section of the chart about which the boy displayed no knowledge.

I purposely approached him from his blind side, stopping several feet down the rail. The man stood just shorter than I, pale yellow shorts exposing well-developed, deeply tanned legs terminating in boat shoes so new the white rubber soles gleamed. A brightly colored tropical shirt protected his shoulders and back. Black plastic sunglasses that likely would cost me a week's salary dangled from a nylon cord around his neck. A fluorescent neon Playmate cooler sat between his feet. His hip pocket bulged with the rectangular shape of a bundle of bills tied together with a money clip. Even without seeing it, I knew the clip would be gold and the bills inside it would not be singles.

I let the two argue a few more moments while I checked the harbor again. The wind and tide blew *Die Walküre* broadside-to. In full daylight the nearly straight sheer and bright colors gave her the appearance of speed even while she was sitting still. On the foredeck lay a sun worshipper, clearly female, a light sheen of oil reflecting the still-rising sun, the smooth body contours interrupted by narrow cloth strips. The red bow of *Aquila*—another boat I wanted to watch—cleaved the water at the edge of the granite breakwater. With any luck, I might be able to meet her owner as well.

"Can I help you?" I asked.

The stranger snapped around. "Lord, I hope so." He spoke slowly, his voice thick with an accent from well south of New England. "You know anything about Blue Hill Bay?"

"A bit," I said.

He ignored the boy on the other side, dragging the chart closer to me. "I wanted to do some touring. Head up some of the creeks, see what it's like."

"Sounds great," I replied. "Some beautiful marshes around here."

"Nice and secluded, too, I'd wager."

I smiled. "You'd win."

"Anyhow, this chart doesn't have the detail I need. I'd like to know more about these inlets," he said, pointing to the chart.

I bent over to have a closer look. An odd place to select for touring, I thought, less than a mile from where Robyn and I had found the radar reflector. Perhaps this man intended to do some daylight reconnaissance while his companion deepened her tan. "What's your draft?"

"I need one meter of water," he explained. "At mid- to high tide, it looks okay. What I can't figure out is the width of the channel. I need a channel about three meters wide. Is this good enough?"

I surveyed the harbor again, as if for the first time. I kept it up until I was sure he'd noticed. "That your powerboat?"

"Yeah," he replied proudly. "Brand new. Set me back a bit, but this trip north makes it all worthwhile."

I'll bet, I thought to myself. "Who's on the deck?"

"A friend," he said impatiently. "Look, you gonna help me, or just stare at my girlfriend, hey, pal?"

I pointed at the chart. "I wouldn't be too confident about trying here at mid-tide." I checked my watch. "High tide will be in about four hours, so you might want to wait another two hours."

"Once I get in, I need a place to turn around. I hate long backing. I can pull the drives up and pole her around—do it back home all the time. But I need a wide channel."

"You can get up some of these as far as two miles. They narrow fast. When you're at the end, you'll know it. Don't push your luck."

"Thanks for the help." He started rolling up the chart.

As long as I intended to be direct, I thought I might as well push my luck. Even if he only dropped the name of another place which interested him, it might be useful. "Why you want to go up there? Better visitin' along the ocean, if you ask me."

"I didn't." He tucked the chart under the cooler handle, picking them up with one hand. Without another word he showed me his back and strode away. He took the walkway down to the main dock, jumping into a gray rubber boat. He stowed the cooler forward, flipped off the painter, fired up the tiny engine, and powered away. In less than a minute he pulled alongside the big boat. The cooler went over first. With the help of his shapely crew, the boat came aboard to be lashed over the engine cowling. Less than five minutes after talking to me, he fired up the first engine, then the second, then I stared after the white foam bubbling back from the outdrives, their echo booming off the dockside buildings.

Startlingly rude, I thought, for a man seeking assistance. Perhaps he was in a hurry. Perhaps he didn't appreciate the small talk. Perhaps. . . . There might be many legitimate reasons why he'd rushed to return to his boat. Aside from the curtness, he'd left the impression of a self-sure, powerful man who undoubtedly would do whatever he had to do to accomplish whatever task he gave himself. His appearance and his bearing spoke as much for his tenacity as they did against his courtesy or compassion. He could make money the easy way, using his boat and his cold side. He could also extract his needs from a bank, a brokerage, or real estate. I could not guess his business; yet I felt certain that, whatever it was, he was no pushover. Abrasive personality aside, his link to Frederickson was speculative; I had zero evidence. I would not eliminate him from my short list of suspects, but I wouldn't promote him, either.

The lobster raid had proved that the Carlson brothers were involved in illegal transport of fish; it did not prove they were innocent of any other crime. For the moment, however, they were off my list. It would take time for them to resume their activities. There remained the red boat nosing against the dock. I headed down to meet the owner.

Aquila drew up alongside the main float. The driver chopped the throttles, letting the tide nudge the boat into position. He stuck his head overboard, carefully watching his approach. He wasn't a young man, but placing his age was hard. He could have been anywhere between forty and sixty. A thick, close-cropped red beard edged his chin. Dark eyes, centered between deep crow's feet, gauged the distance from hull to float as *Aquila* coasted. As the gap of green water diminished to a sliver, he stepped over the gunwale, picked up a line, and walked the boat forward. Before the stern could swing out, he took up the aft line. In a few seconds both lines were fast to the iron bollards. He reboarded, killing the engine as I approached. Despite my previous failure, I still felt that courtesy would be the best plan. "Good mornin'," I said amiably. "Need a hand?"

"Boat's secure." His voice came out short, clipped, commanding my attention. He spoke with a trace of an unplaceable accent. I knew it did not come from within two hundred miles. "A hand with the trays would be much appreciated, if you don't mind heavy lifting."

"No problem." I knelt alongside his boat. "My name's Jimmy."

"Peter." He lifted the top plastic bin off a stack, and set it on the gunwale with a grunt. "Peter Smith."

I hauled the bin up to the dock. "You're not from around here, are you?"

"Why do you ask?"

"I've lived here a long time. Long enough to know most people. I don't know you."

"Uh huh." He leaned back and had a good look at me. "You're not a fisherman, are you?"

I debated lying about my profession, but saw no point. "No."

"I've fished out of here for a while. Long enough to know most people. I don't know you." Smith set another tray on the gunwale. "Did you go away to college?"

"Yes. Why?"

"I probably moved up while you were away. It's no wonder we don't know each other."

He hadn't moved "down," I noticed. "I guess."

"Your last name. What is it—Hoitt?"

The recognition startled me. "How did you know?"

"Easy." He went to a second pile of bins and brought over the top one. "You look like your father."

"God, that's what everybody says."

"Maybe it's time you left."

We finished the second stack and began the last without another word. While he wasn't exactly secretive, Smith was far from open. "When did you move up here?"

"Couple years back."

"From where?"

"Florida." He set the last bin down with a resonant thud. I barely heard the sound; it paled against the grinding mechanisms starting up in my brain. "You ask a hell of a lot of questions, Jimmy."

"I'm very curious."

"You're damn nosy."

"I didn't mean anything by it. I was just trying—"

"I know you're a cop," he said simply.

He caught me by surprise. I'm certain I showed it. "What?" I stammered.

"You're a cop. I've seen you at the diner, and around. Lately you've been hanging around during the day. You're investigating. That's why you're asking me questions."

"I wasn't—"

"At least be honest about it," he sighed.

I clamped my mouth shut and forced myself to think before I spoke again. Denying the obvious made no sense, especially since asking any one of a hundred people would blow my cover. That didn't compel me to confess. If he wanted to find out, he would have to do his own investigation. "Does this mean our conversation is done?"

"You want to chat, let's chat. You want to interrogate, we'll wait for my lawyer. Deal?"

"We'll chat later."

"You can find me if you want." He moved forward to the deck-house and pushed the starter. He shouted over the engine: "Mind casting me off?"

I let go the aft line and tossed it aboard, cast off the bow, and handed him the line. He accepted it with a smile. "Thanks for the help, Jimmy." The boat backed clear, heading for the mooring.

My morning had gone poorly. My great plan of the night before had rapidly deteriorated. My main suspects were far from coopera-tive, while the trail of facts remained stone cold. Perhaps my next plan could circumvent the—a sudden scantling of a scent hit my nose, arresting all other thoughts. I sniffed again: blueberry muffins. Time for a break, I thought. I skirted Smith's totes and trudged up the pier toward the village.

I headed straight for the counter, swung a seat around, and plopped down beside the register. Inside, the aroma of baking muffins hung thick in the air like a fall fog. I waited only a few mo-ments for service. "Hi, Mom," I said cheerfully.

"Hi, Jimmy. How's work this morning?"

"Work's been better," I admitted. "But I'm feeling too good to let it get me down."

An inquisitive eyebrow arched toward the roof. "I take it, then, you spent the night with Robyn."

I inhaled deeply. "Smells like fresh muffins."

We knew each other far too well to miss the signals between us. She knew that if I wanted to talk, I would not have abruptly changed the topic. She smiled warmly, more mother than waitress. "Blue-berry. Want one?"

"Oh, yeah," I answered slowly. "And a coffee, please."

"You mind one of the broken ones?"

Occasionally, the bottom of a muffin would stick to the pan more strongly than to the rest of the muffin. This resulted in a muf-fin split into two warm, delicious halves. Teflon was heard of in Eagle Harbor; cast iron was tradition. "I don't mind a bit."

"Coming right up."

She returned in seconds, a muffin split in half, buttered, on a paper plate. She slid it in front of me, took a coffee cup from the clean rack, and had it beside the plate before I could touch the muffin. "I haven't had one of these for too long."

"Maybe a month."

I picked up the bottom—I preferred to save the sugared top for last—balanced it on the tips of my fingers, and took a deep bite. The sweet taste of warm cake mingled with the tart wild blueberries and salty butter. Heaven had to have fresh blueberry muffins. "A lot has happened."

The counter bell rang. "You enjoy it, honey. I've got work to do. Come over for dinner?"

"Probably."

"Okay. See you later, Jimmy."

I savored my snack, wishing each bite could be huge to capture all the taste, yet wanting to keep them small to prolong the wonderful sensation. In the end, taste won.

Denise drifted over from a distant corner to ring up a check. "Hello, Jimmy."

"Hey, Denise. How's it going?"

"Good." She smirked. "Have a good night?"

As I said, news travels fast. I grinned. "Can't complain."

"How's work? Still on that case you were pumping me about?"

"I never said I was on a case."

"You didn't have to." She counted her change, then slammed the drawer. "Besides, I saw you talking to Smith down on the dock just now."

I made a mental note to take more care in my interrogation techniques. My lack of training and experience might lead to trouble. "Friendly talk."

"And the other guy. The one you asked me about—with the nice boat."

"More friendly talk."

"Fine." She headed back to her table. "If you don't want to cooperate, then I won't tell you—"

A quick, firm hand on her arm stopped her. "Tell me what?"

"About Smith."

I could not conceal my interest. Denise had read me so well I didn't think a little more revelation could hurt. "What about him?"

"Joy—from the bank—she just left. Coffee before work, you know. You were talking to Smith, and we started talking about him."

She paused as if I should respond. I sipped my coffee. "Go on."

Her voice lowered, and I knew the best part would now begin. "She told me about two weeks ago she had to go out to his home for some special paperwork. I guess he has a lot of special paperwork. Some Federal forms, things like that. She didn't want to elaborate much. Anyway, she says he has a beautiful spread. Up on the side of the ridge, near the top. About twelve acres: house, barn. He raises horses; at least, he boards them, she says. He's got a new house, a new truck, a new boat. When I saw you, and she told me that, I put it together with the dead man the other night. We figured we'd done all your work for you."

"Very funny." I finished the cup. It would be premature to blindly accept the information without corroboration. Not again. Joy's word as a bank employee I could accept. Her reputation as a property appraiser remained open to question, however. There might be a good reason for Smith's recent purchases. I needed a look around the Smith place, I thought. I could try to talk to him, apologize for my clumsy questioning. Not only lower his guard, but also get a look at his property. These thoughts flashed through my mind in a second. None could be repeated to Denise. "Is that all?"

"All?" echoed Denise. " 'Is that all?' Isn't that enough?"

"Jesus, Denise, everyone who moves into town and doesn't talk to anyone gets a reputation as a thief, dealer, or some other social leper. It's always about money."

"I think you should get right on it," she said indignantly.

"I'll ask around. See what I can dig up. Don't hold your breath."

Denise, clearly unwilling to waste any more time with me, abruptly broke clear of my arm. The tart, sweet muffin lingered on my tongue, despite being nearly drowned in coffee. Another one would be a welcome end to breakfast, but there was too much work to do. Underneath the register I found a phone book. I reached for it and searched for Smith. There were, of course, many; but none of the three P. Smiths listed an Eagle Harbor exchange. An unlisted number did not surprise me. There were other ways to get an address, short of tailing him. I put two bucks on the counter and headed out.

I left the diner in the bright midmorning sun. By the time I arrived at Smith's home the sun had peaked and then drifted down into the soaring trees along the ridge. It had taken only forty-five minutes to go through the town records—all public access—to find an address for Peter Smith. His tax bill validated Joy's estimate of the property. Unfortunately, I could find no more information. En route to his ridge-top aerie, I got a radio call: I had to report to Ellsworth at my earliest convenience. I didn't want to get anyone even the slightest bit mad at me, so I headed north immediately. The afternoon passed filling out paperwork. All the agencies from whom Wiley had requested help had their own separate forms for me to recount my evidence leading to the quarry stakeout. I was the original source, and they wanted to make sure they got the story right. The afternoon proved as tedious as the morning had been fruitless.

Before I went home I drove up Smith's ridge, found a driveway with a plain steel box marked with the correct number, and turned up. A long, winding drive led up the side of the ridge, precariously balanced above the trees. After passing a long piece of weathered granite, the drive hooked sharply left. I came out into a wide yard between a house and a barn. Behind the barn was a fenced-in pasture. Peering between trees and rocks, I could trace the fence to the top of the ridge. A good spread, indeed.

No sign of another car, not even in the open-doored barn. I parked well clear of the buildings. The house came first. It was an attractive, comfortable-looking place constructed of logs: common enough Down East. It was not large, but more than sufficient for a man living alone. The front porch was clean and orderly, a stack of wood against one side, a canvas chair on the other, beneath a kerosene lamp. A massive wooden door prevented casual entry. I knocked, receiving no response. I went around the back side of the house, which revealed no more than the front.

The barn could conceal a wide variety of evils, so I headed there next. As I passed the fence, a large, dark horse with white boots and a triangular blaze ambled toward me, followed by a slimmer, lighter-colored animal. A thick wire topped the fence between us, preventing much communication. I continued to the barn, the horses pacing me. Taking the open door as an invitation, I passed inside. It smelled and appeared as old as any other barn on the island. The faint scent of mildew, the stronger, sweeter smells of hay and lumber pervaded the dusty interior. The planked walls showed some cracks, though the rafters overhead weren't yet sagging. At the center a wide bay stretched all the way to the roof. Judging by the parallel ruts in the wood floor and a dull patch of old oil, the barn had long doubled as garage. A workshop covered the right wall: a long table, rows of tools attached to magnetic holders or arranged neatly in trays. Power tools on a shelf, track lights overhead, sawdust and metal shavings on the table; the work area obviously saw extensive use. Along the other wall I discovered more stacked firewood, a massive iron stove, a dusty, worn ladder to the loft, and the remains of a few lobster traps—whether awaiting repair or consignment to the fire I could not say. The back of the barn belonged to the horses. Two broad stalls, each with their own entrance, opened onto the pasture, tack and gear arrayed around them.

The barn exuded that aura barns acquire only with time: the edges of the board worn smooth and round; creaking floorboards; the snapping of the planks as the wind rose and fell. But almost everything *in* the barn looked new. Smith spared no money on his equipment, and it looked like he used everything he bought. All the tools on the workbench added up to a lot of money, even had they been collected over a lifetime. The horse tack, even the horses themselves, added more. High up along the roof ridge an electric winch hung from a steel girder. Whatever he used it for—auto repair, hoisting hay—it certainly did not come cheap.

I stood motionless, thinking. I needed and wanted something more substantial, some indisputable link to Frederickson. A barn is a magnificent place to hide things. If nothing jumped out at me, I would have to look more carefully. I borrowed a crowbar. Many of the floorboards sounded loose when I tapped them, but I could not pry any of them up. The walls were solid, no place to hide anything.

A neatly coiled leather bullwhip hung on a wall peg by the window. Curious, I reached for it. As I stepped on the woodpile to get closer, an angular, out-of-place shape caught my eye. A tall, dusty, dark-green plastic case nestled between the wall and the woodpile. Gripping it by the top, I hauled it out over the woodpile.

I dusted it off with my hand. Two brass catches held it closed. They were not locked. I snapped them open and had a look inside: an M16 rifle. It was well cared for, clean, oiled, polished. Judging by the wear on the trigger, guard, and barrel, it had been used. Four clips, two short, two banana, flanked the rifle on the foam cushions. None contained any shells. The foam around the rifle appeared packed down, as if it had once been stored with a short clip loaded in place. That clip might contain ammunition, but it must have been stored elsewhere. I wondered how Smith had come to possess it, and why he wanted to.

I was lost in thought when an iron hand clamped onto the back of my shirt. I had been squatting down, balanced on the balls of my feet. The hand caught me completely off balance. It took very little effort to flip me over. Before I could react, both my arms were pinned behind my shoulders. I tried to face my adversary, but could raise my head only a few inches off the floor. That sufficed to feel an ice-cold piece of metal lightly contact the back of my neck. People may tell you this area of skin is insensitive. I assure you it is sensitive enough to distinguish the shape of a gun barrel.

7

Wednesday–Thursday
Patrol Area: Eagle Harbor
Hot, dry days; warm,
clear nights

D on't move." The voice was clear and distinct: not the voice of a hesitant homeowner but the calm voice of a professional, confident that he had the situation well in hand. I hoped.

After a moment the barrel withdrew. He released my arms, forcing them down to my sides. Certain the gun had not gone far, I left them there. A single hand frisked me down, rapidly, expertly. I felt the bottom of my shirt ripped over my pants, then a tug as he removed my gun. A quick pull at my belt, a snap of the catch, and the hunting knife hanging from my belt was gone as well.

A foot wedged into the middle of my back, with enough weight behind it to keep me still. I heard the sharp click as he opened my knife. "Nice knife," he said. "Sharp, light." I jumped as the blade sunk into the split floorboards not four inches from my face. "Not very well-balanced."

My gun replaced my knife as the object of curiosity. First, the clack and metallic rasp of the magazine dropping clear. It hit the floor with a hollow clack. I heard the hammer pulled back, then a snap as he dry-fired it. I was glad I kept the chamber empty.

The foot pulled back. "What the hell are you doing here, Hoitt?"

I shrugged. "Just looking around."

"If you were just looking, you wouldn't have been behind the woodpile." He abruptly tossed back my gun. "Why are you snooping around?"

"I'm not snooping." My pistol was intact, though unloaded. He showed no intention of offering the magazine. I wouldn't ask. I replaced my empty weapon in its holster. "I'm on a case."

143

"Warrant?"

"No."

"So, why are you poking your nose in here?"

"I told you, I'm on a case."

"I'll bet you are." He stepped forward, but only enough to intimidate. He kept his face in shadow. "Let me tell you something. This is still the United States, even up here. That means you can't go snooping anywhere you please. I don't appreciate uninvited guests." He stooped to the floor to recover the rifle. He examined it quickly but carefully, butt to muzzle. "Don't like people playing with my toys, either."

"That rifle is illegal in this state," I said quietly.

"As a matter of fact, this particular weapon is illegal in every state." Satisfied with its condition, he replaced it in the padded case. "It damn well should be, too."

"Why do you have it?"

"A lot of big things that go bump in the night up here on the ridge."

"I could place you under arrest for possessing it," I said.

He restacked the wood. "Hoitt, do the words 'illegal search and seizure' mean anything to you?"

"As much as possession of an illegal weapon."

"Look at it this way." He finished with the woodpile, then replaced the crowbar on the rack. He leaned against the bench, his arms folded. "Arrest me now, I'll hire a lawyer. The case will get thrown out, and you'll be up the creek with the sheriff. If you confiscate this one, I'll get another. What will you have accomplished?"

"My job." I bent down and picked up my knife, then the magazine from the floor, and put them away.

"Your job, eh? How long have you been at it?"

"Three and a half years."

In a flash of movement so quick it took me completely by surprise, he charged me, backing me against a heavy oak post. He shouted in my face like a drill instructor, cutting off all retreat. "Bullshit. No one could be a detective, even a county one, for three years and still blunder as much as you."

"I've been a patrolman for three and a half years."

"How long have you been investigating? Snooping around barns, hanging out by the dock?"

I hesitated. "A while."

"How long, Hoitt?" he barked.

"Five days."

"Five days!" he echoed. "Five days? And you're out on your own? What kind of an ass-backward place is this?"

"We're short-handed," I explained. "Something very large came up. We had no time to waste."

"Very large? What could be so important that a sheriff who should know better would throw an inexperienced kid out on his own investigation? Even if it's not dangerous, it's damn stupid."

Even if he hadn't been one of my prime suspects, I would not have answered. "That's not for public discussion."

"Bullshit," he laughed. "There are damn few secrets in Eagle Harbor. Even someone from away hears things."

My throat tightened, leaving a bone-dry tongue choking my words. I had tried diligently to prevent myself from becoming the gossip mill's grist, but evidently I had failed. "What do you mean?"

"I'm no idiot. Maybe you are, Hoitt; I don't know. I can add two and two." He finally backed off. "One: a stranger is killed in a hit-and-run accident. His body isn't even cold before I hear rumors that he was a very rich, very powerful criminal. Second: within forty-eight hours, there are people like you crawling around, asking questions, watching. That adds up to four. Add a Bangor news crew reporting that drug agents have set up shop in Ellsworth, and announcing a bust that went bad. What the hell is anyone with a brain supposed to think?"

"Good God," I said slowly. "Is it that obvious?"

"You're lucky," he replied quietly. "I doubt there are that many people around here who can add. Your secret may be safe."

Who the hell was this guy? I thought. Who did he think he was? "Don't think much of the locals, do you?"

"You can be friendly, open, and warm. Cold and mean, too. Not real long on brains, that's all."

"I suppose you're vastly different?" I snapped.

"Not for me to say. I'm not very open, and I suppose I'm more prone to being cold and mean than most." Something went out of him: his shoulders dropped, the voice calmed abruptly like the eye of a hurricane passing by. He sighed heavily, massaging his brow before he went on. "Sometimes I'm not too bright, either."

"As long as we're being honest," I began. "I'm a cop on a legal investigation. I could still report that rifle."

"It wouldn't stick. And I'd *still* have one around."

I remembered I had come for information, and realized he had delivered me an opening. "I can save you the trouble of buying another."

"How?"

"Answer my questions."

He pondered it, then stepped closer. "All right. But you've got to answer mine, first."

Anything he might learn from me apparently already existed in the public domain. A little "leaked" information might trap Smith, too. I had very little to lose. "If you promise to repeat nothing."

"Done," he agreed. "I don't know anyone to tell. What is this serious crime that you're investigating?

"Drug smuggling."

"What kind? How much?"

"Cocaine. Maybe more. We're not sure how much. Roughly ten to fifty kilos per week."

"That's a good load."

"That's a huge load for around here."

He nodded. "I guess. Where's it coming from?"

"The DEA thinks its direct from South America."

"By sea, I presume."

"As far as we know."

Smith nodded. He retreated to his tool bench, looking through a dusty window upon the ghostlike shadows of his horses, drumming his fingers on the wood. "The dead jogger. He started this, didn't he?"

"Yes."

"He wasn't from Maine, was he?"

I wondered where he was headed with that. "No."

He stared out the translucent pane as the specters of the horses walked through the adjacent pasture. He stood perfectly still, arms tightly crossed over his chest, head held rigid, his back straight. His sparkling eyes danced with life as he focused on the world beyond the window. The muscles at the back of his jaw worked back and forth, the only sign he was not a statue. "I came here for the horses, you know."

Whatever I had expected, I was surprised to hear about horses. "What?"

"I've always loved horses," he said. "Work horses, draft horses. Never had much interest in thoroughbreds. This is the kind of climate, the right area, where you can raise them, work them, use them. It's why I came here."

"How about that." What else could I say?

"That's what brought me up here. The horses. Had to find a place for them, and somewhere to get away. A quiet place to start again." He blinked; that's when I realized he hadn't been blinking before. "You're in way over your head."

"How do you know?"

He finally turned to look at me. He wasn't angry, or detached. He looked more tired than anything else. "Trust me, kid," he said.

There was an indefinable familiarity to his movements, his actions, his words. It struck a resonant chord with me, though at first I didn't know why. Then it struck me: he was like Wiley. Not identical, they were hardly built on the same mold. They moved deliberately, pensively; their eyes betrayed a mind always working a problem. Yet it was easy to imagine Wiley twenty, thirty years down the road, and see the man before me. My eyes narrowed. "What are you? FBI?"

Smith shook his head. "Not exactly."

"City detective? Customs agent?"

"No." He looked out as one of the horses whinnied. "You drink coffee, Hoitt?"

"Of course."

"Come inside, then. We'll talk." Without another word, he walked away. I followed him into the house.

From outside, the peeled logs, interlocking corners, and snugly fitting windows imbued the house with a rustic, immovable, albeit chunky look. Inside, all vestiges of cold, detached architecture evaporated before I could close the door. The regular patterns of spaced logs and tight corners were instantly recognizable, yet those features retreated to the outer edges of sight. The heavy logs encircled me with mute strength and safety, warm and comforting. In one half, an overstuffed sofa and an elegant leather armchair flanked a low mahogany coffee table with legs carved more intricately than a ship's figurehead. A stone fireplace fit into the wall beside them. A lonely Shaker rocking chair, worn smooth by use, faced the fireplace. The far end of the house served as kitchen, dining room, and office, assignments denoted by appliances, table, and desk. A narrow, steep stair, almost a ladder, led up to a bedroom loft.

Around the edges, artwork, mementos, and curios covered the walls. I am no expert on diverse cultures, yet I thought I recognized items from many regions. A blanket from the Southwest concealed a large part of the wall near the door; an even larger quilt of more local origin draped down behind the desk. It was like standing in a heritage museum, compressed to fit into the confines of the logs, a lot of life hidden behind the big door.

I absorbed the setting in a second. I had no more time to spare, for immediately I was drawn to the stone mantel. Carefully arranged on the wide black slate were photos, clippings, and candles, arranged with a peculiar, ordered randomness that spoke of great planning.

While the objects were meticulously cleaned and dust-free, smooth wear on the finer engravings indicated they had been frequently, though gently, handled. Heavy white candles in brass bases flanked the mantel and thick, chunky drips had cascaded down the sides to merge with the brass. As I approached, I sensed the presence of the collection more strongly than anything else in the house, far more powerfully than any cold item in a stale, lifeless museum. The mantel was no museum; it was a shrine.

There could be no denying the Madonna of the monument. At the center, a large photograph in a silver frame leaned against the brick. It could have been taken anywhere between two and twenty years ago. The portrait captured a strikingly beautiful woman with a shy, inviting smile, leaning comfortably but seductively against a tree. The glowing, honest smile illuminating her face created a radiant beacon at the center of the indistinct, unfocused background. I could no more guess her age than I could date the photo; probably she was about thirty-five. She must have been happy when photographed, for she exuded a warmth too potent to be anything but sincere. Bright blonde hair danced onto her shoulders, the soft ends merging into the geometric patterns of a sweater. Emerald eyes looked back at me, bright eyes so alive that even transfer to emulsion could not dim them.

The other photos contained this same woman: different poses, different locales. Whether she played with animals or children, or mugged for the camera; whether dressed in summer shorts or yellow rain gear, she always appeared cheerful, vibrant, ready to jump off the picture and alight on the floor. Although I had never seen her before, I found her image arresting, because I recognized the vision, if not the individual. To the tiniest detail, she could have doubled for Robyn Cole. Ten, fifteen years older, wiser, but adding that time to Robyn would have produced this image long before creating Robyn's own mother.

I stumbled backward to take a broader view. In doing so, I startled myself as I bumped into Smith. He stood silently, his colorless eyes gazing at the mantel. Not at it, I thought. Not at the pictures, but at the subject herself. I desperately wanted to ask him about the woman, why she was enshrined that way, but I could not bring myself to interrupt his private thoughts.

"My wife, Beth," he muttered softly in response to my unspoken query.

I nodded, signifying an understanding I did not possess. I knew the answer to the next question, but I asked. "What happened to her?" The question sounded cold, callous.

He hesitated. I thought I caught a glint in his eye—twinkle of happy recollection, or tear of memory? In an instant it faded. "She is dead."

His voice sounded as harsh, abrupt, and final as death itself. The silence hung between us, keeping us apart in our own thoughts, our own worlds. After a time, he pointed toward the kitchen. "I ran out of regular coffee a couple days ago. Hope you don't mind instant."

Some time later, I finished the cup as I sat at the table opposite Smith. Not another word had passed between us while we waited for the water to boil and let the coffee start to work through us. He noted my empty cup and rose to refill both of them from the iron kettle. "You knew Frederickson," I said.

"Not exactly," he said. "I knew *of* him would be more accurate."

"Why?"

"We . . . we tilled the same field. Different sides, you understand, but the same field."

"Smith," I mused. "Is that your real name?"

"What?" He seemed surprised by the question. "Oh, hell, yes. Never thought to change it. There really are people named Smith in the world, you know. That's me: Captain Peter Smith."

Many fishermen accepted or commandeered the title "captain." Even though I didn't know him well yet, I sensed it was more than just a word to Smith. "You don't just mean captain of that red boat."

"That's all," he shrugged. "Now. Not always, if you haven't figured it out yet."

"Navy?"

He laughed. "Coast Guard. Retired."

"You were based in Florida?"

"Six years ago, yes."

"You ran into Frederickson before, then."

"Me? Hell, no. Florida's a big place, not like up here. There's plenty of room for a big-time drug smuggler and one Coast Guard officer to never run across each other's path. All too easy to be busy with other people, other crimes."

"But you knew about him."

"I knew the name. Not much more, I'm afraid."

He knew more than he was telling. I didn't know quite what it was, but I was certain there was more. "So you knew Frederickson was Martin?"

"Why would I know that?" he suddenly snapped. "He was a character from another play, lost in the witness protection program. I had no idea."

"But you must have known a lot about his cartel, their work, and how—"

"Look, Hoitt," he said sternly. "I was just a sailor, caught in the middle of a war we couldn't possibly win. I learned what I needed. I followed orders. I did my job. We ran into a boat on the high seas, we boarded it, searched it, and prosecuted the owners for what we found. That's all. No big headlines, no parades or press conferences. Just like you, Hoitt, except we were patrolling the seas instead of the roads."

"How long were you down there?"

"Around ten years, altogether."

"In all that time you must have learned something. We're shooting in the dark up here," I pleaded. "We don't know what we're working with, what we're looking for. Someone with your experience with smuggling and familiarity with the area could be invaluable to us."

"You don't need me." He finished his coffee, and took our cups to the sink. "You've got the damn DEA, all the marshals you ask for, and every county cop within a hundred miles. The last thing you need is a washed-up old sailor."

"Any help would be—"

"Look," he said patiently. "I came here to get away from all that. I came to start a new life for myself, to find a community where I didn't have to let everyone into my own private hell. That's all. Let it go."

I didn't know very much about Smith. In fact, most of what I knew about him I had learned in the last hour. Yet I got the unmistakable impression there was something he was holding back. I let my gaze wander around the house. It confirmed his story for me. The immaculate order of the belongings, the way nothing was left out; marine hardware for decoration, a ship's clock that chimed each half hour of the watch; pictures of palm trees and beaches—pictures. The shrine on the mantel, all those pictures of his wife. I was pretty sure I knew what he was keeping in, and I thought I knew why. "What happened to your wife?"

Smith showed me his back as he leaned over the sink, mechanically rinsing the coffee mug. The setting sun glowed red, limning his figure in flame. "One night, after hitting a big shipment, me and my wardroom staff were down at a bar, celebrating. Dumb luck had put us in the right place, the right time, and we took about four million dollars worth of cocaine away from its rightful owners. While I was out celebrating, three men broke into my house. By a stroke of good luck, my daughter was out that night. But not Beth." He set the mug gently in the drain tray, and froze, staring out at the sunset. "Not Beth. They took some cash; loose change, really, less than a hundred bucks. She was shot five times, by two different guns."

I didn't know what to say. *I'm sorry* came to mind, but it seemed so hopelessly inadequate. "They ever find who did it?"

He shook his head. "No."

"Grandpa Joe? Frederickson's cartel?"

"Who knows?" He shrugged. "It doesn't matter. There are so many."

I nodded with slow recognition. "I see why you think we're in over our heads."

"I don't just think it, Hoitt. I know it. I've been there."

"We're not back-country yokels, you know," I said sharply. "We've been known to solve a case or two from time to time."

"Relax," he reassured. "I'm not implying you're idiots. Just don't fool yourself into thinking you're up against idiots—because you're not."

It was not easy to dismiss what he said. After reading all the reports, observing how hard it was to find any evidence, realizing what problems we would face, I had wondered myself if the sheriff's department was not tragically overmatched. "I'll proceed carefully."

"Watch every step," he admonished. "Because I guarantee you someone else is."

"Believe me, sir, you've convinced me." The discussion spooked me; I wanted to push the investigation, end it soon, and return to my peaceful life pulling over speeders, tracking the occasional car thief. One aspect in particular ripped at my stomach. My eyes wandered back to the mantel, the photos of a woman long gone, and the thoughts of one close at hand. "Do you have any ideas who killed Martin?"

"Why should I? Could be anyone. Could be just some drunk driver, or a hit-and-run. In this business, it's awful easy to see ghosts behind every gravestone."

"I can't believe it was just an accident," I said thoughtfully, with more conviction than I would have thought I felt. "It doesn't explain enough facts."

He smiled. "Then you've got some work to do, my friend."

"Yes, I do." I stood up. "I'd best get to it."

Smith ushered me to the door. "Don't let me stand in your way. I wish you the best of luck with this."

I stopped in the door frame, facing him. He had a presence that made him seem bigger, more powerful than in fact he was. I was actually a little taller than he. We stood eye to eye, my determination reflected in his wise and gentle eyes. Behind those eyes was a vague reflection of a spark whose inspiration I could only imagine. "Agent Wiley might want to talk to you."

"Listen, Hoitt," he said sternly. "Don't say anything about me. Keep me out of it, all right? I came up here to get myself out of this crazy game. After six years, I think I'm finally starting to feel like it's over. Don't drag me through it all again."

"With your knowledge of the two sides of the case, you could—"

"Let me out of this madness while I'm mostly in one piece."

I reached into a pocket, removing a calling card. "Think about it. If you change your mind, give me a call."

He looked at it only a second and refused to take it. "I'm sorry, Hoitt."

My mouth set firmly. "Yes, sir. Wouldn't want to disturb you, Mr. Smith." I opened the door, stepping out on the porch.

"You're not married, are you, Hoitt?" he abruptly inquired.

"No."

"A girlfriend, then?"

I knew why he was asking, but felt compelled to answer honestly. "Her name's Robyn Cole."

"You'd better be careful for her, too. I lost Beth because I was careless," he stated. "Simple as that. I let my guard down for a minute, just one damn minute—and my life was changed forever. Her future was taken away, and there wasn't a thing I could do to get it back. Don't let it happen to you." He held my eyes transfixed for a moment; I could not look away. From his eyes flowed an empathy and a sadness that he couldn't have meant to show. He seemed about to say something else, then he closed the door quietly but firmly in my face. The spell snapped. I left the porch and headed for my car.

I had not eliminated Smith from my suspect list yet, but his story would be easy to verify. Then I would drop him from the list or promote him to the top. I had no reason to doubt a word of his story. I knew my research would exonerate him. The spirit that illuminated those eyes was no lie. I headed down the ridge, back to the harbor. My investigation, like my trip, seemed to proceed dismayingly downhill. Every lead I followed began promisingly, then veered sharply into a blind alley and ended up a cold, dead end. Either I had missed something or I chased phantoms. Maybe I chased phantoms because there was nothing tangible to flush out. Good news as it might be, that solution was too easy, and did not take into account enough known facts. It was far easier to believe that my investigation had missed a major point. The question—again—was which direction to head now.

There were three possibilities. Smith could be lying, or at least revealing only part of the truth. That could be easily verified back in Ellsworth. Second, my initial search had been so narrow I had failed to uncover all the possible suspects. The third option, the one I felt the most promising, concerned *Die Walküre* and her short-tempered captain.

I doubted the boat would return early on such a magnificent summer day. Night would soon arrive, but nothing useful would come from another look at the moored boats. Investigations, I had already learned, do not take place solely in the field; work has to be done in the office as well. I had to go to Ellsworth. There I could check out Smith and *Die Walküre,* and review my notes and Wiley's reports to spot a gap. If Eagle Harbor had anything to hide, Ellsworth would be the place to find out.

I had one thing to check before heading inland. I went into the village, slipped into a parking space beside Scott's Market, and went inside. Customers were nonexistent so close to closing time. The plastic drapes had been pulled over the refrigerated sections, while behind the meat counter a white-aproned clerk put away the perishable stock. I nodded in reply to the clerk's wave and passed behind the swinging door. Behind the butcher's counter, beside a bright metal slicer, I found the office door. A yellow trapezoid of light spilled onto the uneven wooden floor, telling me the owner hadn't left.

I poked my head around the corner. Wes Scott bent over his desk, poring over the ledger, rimless spectacles precariously balanced on the edge of his bulbous red nose. His lips moved slowly as he checked receipts, bony fingers reaching out to touch the calculator keys. Two bloodshot eyes met me when I knocked. "Spare me a minute, Wes?"

"Just a minute," he said. The glasses slipped further down his nose. "What can I do you for?"

"A semiofficial request."

A yellow-toothed smile cracked Wes's face. "I'll try to give you some semiofficial help."

"Can I have a quick peek at your gas records?"

"Sure." He spun around, the wooden chair creaking loudly. "I only have the ones since April up here. The others are put away."

"These will be fine."

He pulled three heavy binders off the shelves and dropped them loudly on the desk. "This one's the roadside pumps," he said, sliding off the top one. "These two are the dock pumps. The bottom one's April first through late May, early June. The other one is current. Enough?"

I pulled the most recent marine records closer. "This'll do fine, Wes."

I scanned the pages. In one column, Wes listed how much fuel he had bought from the distributor; next to it he listed what he had paid for it. In the last two columns he listed how much he had delivered, and what he had received for it, indicating cash, credit card, or store credit. Each entry included the date, who had delivered the fuel, or who had purchased it. This last column interested me most, for the listings were by boat. A quick survey of Wes's book told me which villagers were buying gas, and which visitors came back.

The first date logged in this book turned out to be June third. Starting there, I searched for the name of the Florida boat. The first entry occurred on the sixteenth, which showed 163 gallons of fuel had been pumped aboard "*De Valkoor*." The book also listed the Florida registration, which I copied into my notebook. The owner, whose name did not appear, paid $260.81 in cash. A lot of money to carry, I thought; but anybody with such a boat must have it.

After that initial entry, another appeared every three to five days. The volume of the sale ranged from 130 to over 200 gallons. Those were large tanks, yet with those huge engines, he needed every pint. Based on his frequent visits, I judged it unlikely the boat had arrived before June twelfth.

One more treasured scrap of information surfaced. After one refueling the man's wallet had come up dry; a credit card with the name J. Philipe Devereaux had been used to pay. That name went into my book along with the registration.

I picked through the book a while longer, looking for anything unusual, finding nothing. Smith, who kept a well-tended account with Wes, fueled about once a week. Usually he bought around fifteen gallons—barely a third of my father's consumption. It confirmed that Smith didn't make a living fishing.

I thanked Wes, handing back the books. I snagged a pack of gum and a Snickers bar, paying at the register on my way out. A quiet Eagle Harbor greeted me at the door, the street empty, the stores silent. The black sloop tied up to the dock, her crew folding sails and securing gear with practiced efficiency. Ed Berman and Murray Killington laughed raucously in the diner, their booming voices carrying clearly though the open windows. The village was calm and peaceful at night, whatever demons possessed it by day. Detective work was a challenge; it was fun, in its own way but I missed night patrol. I longed to cruise the secluded shadows of the island again. I returned to the car, aiming north for the mainland.

Judging by the Ellsworth parking lot, little business transpired at the station that evening. Three decked-out cruisers, a pair of unmarked cars, and a visitor's Cherokee constituted the only additions to the duty staff. I had grown so used to the trucks and vans used by the drug agents that the familiar lot now seemed empty. I passed inside the building less than an hour after leaving Wes to his tiny office.

I waved at the dispatcher, who buzzed me inside. Two doors down, opposite the cage, I headed into the lunch room. A row of vending machines along one wall, a refrigerator, microwave, and a sink allowed employees to prepare a reasonable snack. The battered, threadbare couch offered hope of a brief respite. That night, the long table interested me more. I dumped my notes on the corner and pulled out a chair. I looked through the sheets until I found what I needed, then took them with me to the cage.

Jaime Ganem, the night dispatcher, looked up as I let myself in the back door. Petite and efficient, she had chestnut shoulder-length hair and penetrating eyes. She was deceptively strong for her compact frame, and more than one overly amorous suitor had found she could take them down faster than they could blink. She completed a call, then swiveled her chair to face me. "What's up?"

"I need to run down a couple names. Computer up?"

"Yuh," she said. She tore the top sheet off a pad and slid it toward me. "Long delay on out-of-state tonight, though."

I scribbled down the data. "Top name is Maine. Check the license and criminal record, please."

Jaime took it. "Okay. The other?"

"Bottom one is a Florida boat reg. I'd like to know the origination date, and in whose name. It should be listed as pleasure, but see if you can verify the type of registration."

"That will take some time."

"When you get that name—"

"*If* I get a name," interrupted Jaime. "Could be owned by a company. I can't tap into those records this late."

"If you get a name, check it for records, too. If you can, I'd appreciate a picture."

Jaime made some notes. "See what I can get. You want a picture of the first guy?"

"No. I'm pretty certain I know him."

"Okay, Jimmy. I should have the Maine license in ten minutes or so. The other one might take hours."

"No hurry," I replied. "I'll be in the lunch room." I left her to do her work.

My first task reminded me of college finals: data organization. I realized if the pile of notes was to be worth anything, I had to cull through them and extract significant facts from the garbage. Only then could I detect something that might put me back on the trail. The trail began with the paper on the table. I sat down, bent my head over the stack, and began to sort.

I felt like I had barely begun to dent the pile when Jaime came in fifty minutes later. "Got it." She laid the papers in front of me, and moved toward the coffee maker. "A little delay, that's all. You got what you wanted."

I picked up the computer sheets and had a look. The top sheet detailed Peter Smith; it revealed nothing unusual. His age, address, and description checked with the man I had met. His driving record was clean, no criminal record, nothing for ten years. I had no reason to suspect that even if I had ten more years of records I would have found anything more.

Devereaux's fax photo stared back at me with the same flat, vacuous eyes I had met on the dock. The next sheet listed information about FL 797 DA, the boat I knew as *Die Walküre*. Her owner matched Wes's records: J. Philipe Devereaux. The boat registration contained nothing remarkable, simply a word description that corresponded perfectly with the boat I knew. The registrations came due every year, so I could get no data on when the boat had been purchased, other than the year of manufacture: two years ago. No restrictions or warrants tagged along with the boat.

Jaime used the name off the registration to track him down. My knowledge of Maine geography is exceptional, and of international, passable. My knowledge of Florida geography doesn't exist, so the address provided by Florida DMV meant nothing. Since the town name ended in "Key," I presumed Devereaux lived on one of the islands off the southern tip of the state. His license record made interesting reading: his driving tended to excessive speed. Over five years, there were eleven citations for exceeding the posted limit, in one case more than fifty miles over. He evidently liked to park his Porsche wherever he wanted. Though not an exemplary driver, he currently drove free of suspension.

His criminal record proved mildly informative. He had trouble getting along with people: the report included six citations for disturbances or assaults. None had resulted in more than a fine. He had spent a weekend in jail for drunk driving. Most enlightening, he held five convictions for possession of drugs. Four times he had been caught with an ounce or less of marijuana, once with a "trace" of cocaine. Never had he been found with sufficient quantities to justify prosecution as a dealer. He had been severely fined, issued a six-month suspended sentence, and sent on his way. That had been nearly a year ago. Devereaux might have abandoned his habit since, but I doubted it.

Jaime stirred her coffee. "Get what you were looking for?"

"I guess so." I put the latest data into an appropriate pile. They, too, would have to be boiled down.

"What you expected?"

"Pretty much." I sat back, massaging my neck. "No surprises. What it means, I haven't figured out yet."

"You know," she said, pointing the mug like a gun, "There are a lot of guys around here saying the same thing."

"What do you mean?"

"The other detectives bring in suspicions, and run them to ground. They come out true. But then what? You can look at some pieces of a jigsaw puzzle, and know that they're all from the same puzzle, but can't figure out where to put them."

"Yeah," I said. "That's exactly what it is."

The buzzer sounded. "Got to answer the door," said Jaime.

I bent forward to re-attack the notes. "See you later," I said to a closing door.

An hour and a half later, I had not moved. The files and notes before me had begun to assume a subtle order. I had created larger sections of the puzzle, but I still labored with no distinct idea of the final picture. In the hallway, feet pounded up stairs, voices exchanging scraps of information, men hurrying around without direction. Whatever they were up to sounded more promising than my notes; after two hours, anything would. I abandoned the stack and slipped into the hall.

DEA agents dashed through the hall, running past me to the conference room out back. I caught a glimpse of Wiley as he ordered a skinny agent to fetch a case file. The men in the halls carried or wore their flak jackets. They were too busy to talk, so I headed for the dispatcher's office. The placid, quiet office had become a boisterous, crowded command post. Jaime manned the radio; I heard her calling in all free patrolmen. Call, the night sergeant, leaned over the counter, barking rapidly at patrolmen who had just arrived. A detective and a plainclothes patrolman sat at the desk, each bearing a phone. The excitement was contagious; merely standing close by infected me, though I had no idea what was happening.

The patrolman at the counter nodded to Call before disappearing around the corner. As the sergeant turned around his gaze fell on me. "Hoitt! Why are you here?"

"Paperwork. I needed the computer, so I—"

"Can you spare a couple hours?" he interjected.

"Sure."

"Good. You're with us." He took a brass key ring from his belt and tossed it to me. "Go back to the gun closet. Take out four rifles, the green ammo box, take them to conference room three, and give them a quick once over. Got it?"

"Yes, sir."

Rae Greene, a patrolman from Trenton, approached the counter. Call told her to wait. "We should be ready in about fifteen minutes. We'll pick you up on the way out."

"Yes, sir." I still had no idea what action waited, but now I had a part in it. At the far end of the hall a steel cabinet contained ample firearms to repel virtually any foe. One key opened the lock; another allowed me to remove the restraining bar. In seconds I had four rifles on the floor. Tucked into the back corner I found the ammo box. I took it and set it by the rifles, locked the door, and managed to juggle everything into the conference room.

A cursory inspection of the rifles indicated they were in perfect condition. I opened the bolts and peered down the barrels, looking for dust or obstructions, but they were all clear. Inside the ammo box were twelve ten-round clips. I selected two for each rifle, and loaded the clips before I replaced the box.

When I returned to the conference room, I no longer had it to myself. A pair of DEA agents had slipped in. They unfolded a topographical map on the table in grim-faced silence. On my heels came Tom LaBlanc, another patrolman. He hefted one of the rifles on the table, repeating the simple exam I had just done, checking the bolt, barrel, and clip. "All set?" he asked.

"Looks good to me. You going to use one?"

"Call told me to come get one."

I pointed to the table. "Take a spare clip, too."

"Thanks." He slipped the nearest one into his pocket.

"You know what's going on?" I asked.

"We're going on a raid."

"What kind of raid?"

"I don't know."

The agents at the table guaranteed we weren't going after lobster smugglers. Not intentionally, anyway. "Any idea where?"

"Yeah," spoke up one the agents across the table. "A place called Verona. I think it's on Verona Island, wherever the hell that is."

I stretched over the table to assist. A large scale map of Hancock County, it detailed most of the ocean shoreline. The agents were concentrating on the southernmost region, where Penobscot, Blue Hill, and Frenchman Bays merge into the Atlantic Ocean. While it was a region liberally sprinkled with islands, they would not find the one they sought. "Verona's up by Bucksport." I ran my finger north, up the Penobscot River, until it diverged around an oblong ellipse. "Verona."

"Ah," said the other agent. "How far?"

"Twenty miles," replied LaBlanc. "Half an hour."

"Hell, that's just around the corner," he answered.

As we studied the map, twenty men entered the conference room in as many seconds: patrolmen, agents, Wiley, with Sergeant Call bringing up the rear. Wiley exhibited the same vaguely bored look he sported whenever I saw him; yet his eyes sparkled more brightly than usual.

Wiley and Call stepped behind the desk and lectern at one end of the room. Immediately the murmuring died. Call ran a hand through his thinning hair as Wiley leaned against the blackboard, hands clutching the metal tray, fingers drumming the aluminum in brittle stereo. "All right, listen up. Here's the dope," said Call.

Wiley took over. "We've run down a tip on a shipment of cocaine coming into Verona or Bucksport in about two hours. As far as we can tell, it's not much—between two and ten kilos. Whatever it is, it's almost certainly a direct link to Frederickson. I want to nail this thing down."

A link to Frederickson at last! In a town about as far from Eagle Harbor as it was possible to be while remaining in Hancock County. Perhaps I had been chasing phantoms.

"They'll be coming up the Penobscot," continued Call. "We're not sure exactly where they'll land, but we've narrowed it down. At this time we are not sure how many people we're facing, or how forewarned they might be, so we're going in with full battle gear. Waldo County sheriff will cover the bridge. Coast Guard will seal the river. We'll be coming in from Bucksport. If the information is good, we'll trap them in the middle."

He paused long enough to check the paper in his hand. "Agent Wiley will take his agents in first. Sheriff Walker will meet us east of Bucksport. Any questions?"

None came forth. If they were anything like me, they were too keyed up to ask questions. Wiley scanned the officers before him. "Surprise is ours. We don't expect trouble. We don't think they'll be heavily armed, no more than hunting rifles. We want these people alive. We need them to find whoever killed Frederickson."

"Assignments," said Call. "Harris, take my cruiser and agent Diaz and lead the way. The sheriff will meet us in Orland, at the end of the Castine road. LaBlanc, Barrows, Greene, and Hoitt—grab a rifle and join me in the van. We'll be the last out. The rest of you, find a car and follow Harris." His last words were nearly lost among the noise of shifting feet and chairs, as the men exited through the single door. I joined the crush, grabbed the last rifle and clip from the table, and headed for the parking lot.

By the time we reached Bucksport, I could not remember ever being so tense, so coiled up and ready to spring. The justification for the raid sounded more solid than the information I had given Wiley, instilling confidence that we might actually find who we wanted. That carried with it the kind of danger a county patrolman in Maine just doesn't see much. The last of the convoy, we pulled up behind the others in a Mainway parking lot at the east end of the bridge to Verona Island. At Call's request I slid back the van door, latching it open.

We parked beside Walker's car. He stood in the open door, radio mike in one hand, Wiley beside him, waiting for an unseen cue. Both stood silently, staring across the black water at the dark island. After a few moments, a quiet, calm voice came over the radio. "You guys set?"

Walker pulled the mike closer. "All set."

"I think they're coming," said the voice. "They don't seem panicked. Send in the advance team."

"Ten-four." He turned to Wiley. "I've given the driver directions. You'll be there in five minutes."

"Should beat the boat."

"No problem. Get going."

Wiley waved his men back to their cars. In seconds they rolled quickly but quietly across the bridge. Walker waited until they cleared the far side. "We're going to cross the bridge and make a roadblock," he said. "Then the van will follow me down to the drop." He slipped inside his car, and we followed.

We crept across the bridge to the base of the hill, where the bridge met a concrete abutment. Walker spoke with an officer standing watch, then joined us in the van. "Take the third left, go down until we reach the other cars."

Headlights off, we bumped along the narrow, barely paved road. We sat on the edge of our seats, tense, fingers hovering over safety catches, feet drumming on the floorboards. A hint of a cool breeze blew up from the river; the whispering rustle in the trees merged with the soft crunch of the tires and the steady drone of the engine to escort us to the target. The houses we passed were dark; only one showed the blue flicker of a television.

The van maneuvered around a corner, slowing to a stop. Through the open side door I saw a thinning of the trees as the road came close to the river. Just below a couple boats moored well offshore, beyond a weathered, sagging pier. Barely visible in the dark distance beyond the pier, a third boat swept toward shore. She showed no running lights. While there were no spotlights to guide her, I knew the night provided ample light to allow an experienced mariner to safely return home. The boat itself, painted forest green, moved slowly, with no bow wave, the wake hidden by the hull, a barely visible wraith on the river. I knew Wiley's men waited below us, yet I could see no sign of them.

Walker, who had been gazing out the passenger window, turned to the four of us in back. "Keep quiet. Move slowly, pick your way cautiously. Greene, go fifty yards ahead of the van. Find a tree, get behind it, and cover the dock and boat. Hoitt, go up the bank ten yards and do the same. LaBlanc, Barrows, lay down on the floor of the van and cover. Everybody we have has labeled jackets, but it's quite possible a civilian or two might wander by. Do not fire the first shot. Pick your targets with extreme care. Now move out."

Greene and I checked our rifles and jumped out. Starlight helped me pick my way back along the roadway. I measured off twelve paces. I figured that was near enough ten yards, and crouched down behind the vee of a white birch. I shot more accurately from the crouch than prone, and I did not feel I needed the extra cover.

The boat engine died away as it drifted toward the dock. I could just discern the shadow of a man at the helm; another one leaned over the port gunwale, preparing to grab the dock. With the engine at idle, the scene became hushed as a cemetery. The muted snarl of the engine, a sibilant swishing as water sluiced past the hull, distant cars humming along the opposite side of the river were all I heard. I thought I heard the sharp snap of a branch breaking, but when no follow-up sound came I attributed it to my excited imagination.

The bow touched the dock, rebounding gently off the fire hose chafing. The crewman stepped across the narrow gap of water, landing on the dock with a delayed hollow thud. He walked the bow toward a cleat on the corner. The shadow behind the helm cut the engine, removing the most obtrusive sound from the evening cantata.

Muted voices came up from the boat, too distorted for me to detect words. A roaring laugh bellowed from the boat as the helmsman tossed a dark fanny pack to the crewman. The crewman waved as he started up the bank.

He hadn't gone two paces before a brilliant beam of light pinned him against the slope. "Do not move!" boomed Wiley's voice, mangled by an electronic bullhorn. "Federal agents. Stop where you are! Hands on your heads!" From somewhere to my right, another spotlight came on, flooding the boat with stark white light. A second later two more snapped on, both to my left. A brighter, more powerful light illuminated the aft end of the boat from the Coast Guard patrol covering the back door. From my high position I could detect silhouettes emerging from the trees and bushes, advancing down the bank.

The men on the boat complied without hesitation: they became motionless as stone. The crewman dropped to his knees, then fell forward to lie face down. The man at the helm, his hands bolted firmly to the top of his head, shuffled sideways to the gunwale, squinting into the light. In seconds two of Wiley's men planted themselves at the end of the dock, rifles up to their shoulder, aimed unwaveringly on the two men. Three agents with sidearms ran down the decaying wooden ramp to the boat. While one covered, the other two moved in, roughly and rapidly frisking down the suspects before securing their wrists with nylon restraints. The agent on the boat tossed the stern line to the armed agent, who threw a couple hitches around the nearest cleat. The helmsman stepped off the boat, the crewman rose; all five marched up the dock and waited on shore. I could not help but be impressed. Less than ninety seconds ago, the boat had been drifting into the dock. Now it sat immobilized and impounded, its operators prisoners.

"Hoitt!" I heard a cry from the left. Walker had stepped out of the van. "Greene! Down to the dock." He seemed to say something else to those in the van, but I could not hear as I picked my way down the loose slope.

Wiley had already begun searching the fanny pack. A quick check revealed it held nothing it shouldn't: a wallet, loose change, insulated gloves, car keys, a notebook, and a black prayer book. Wiley tossed the bag to an agent, then marched down the dock to stand, arms crossed, before the suspects. He continually fired questions: who were they, who did they work for, where was the shipment. The only satisfactory answers concerned their names. His initial look of triumph evolved gradually to one of frustration. The two men were mere boys, eighteen years old, perhaps twenty. They appeared confused, frustrated, and bewildered by the whole event. They could have been fine actors, but already I had to ask myself if the Verona raid was any more successful than the quarry assault had been.

"All right!" said Wiley finally, flinging up his arms. "Keep your stupid mouths shut! I will personally ensure that your lack of cooperation plays a role in your trial. Hunter, Diaz, take these idiots to the van. The rest of you come with me. Corsetti, bring down George."

Two agents escorted the boys up the slope as Wiley and his agents took to the dock. I waited for Walker and Greene. "We go with them?" I asked.

"No," said Walker tiredly. "We'll wait here. If Wiley needs us, he'll call. They're already getting in each other's way." He took his glasses in one hand, pulled the end of his shirt out of his pants, and wiped them off with a deliberate circular motion. "I don't think this is Wiley's day," He found a convenient outcropping of the ledge, sat himself down, and proceeded to methodically fill, light, and puff his pipe. The scent of his tobacco—strong, tinged with spice—drifted lightly on the night air.

For the next half hour the agents didn't so much search the lobster boat as ransack it. Corsetti came down with George, a trim, eager German shepherd. They emptied every stowage compartment, dumping the contents all over the deck and the dock. Cushions and life jackets were slit open, every buoy attached to the pots on the stern was tested and probed for hollowness. Anything that seemed mildly suspicious passed before George's nose, but the dog alerted on nothing. The hull and decks were carefully knocked for secret compartments, then George took a final tour of the boat to make sure. Two agents were given the unenviable, messy, and ultimately fruitless task of poking around the engine compartment. They came up as filthy as they did empty.

After a while, watching their search became boring. I surveyed the area around the dock. There didn't seem to be anything remarkable about it. The dock was not new, and it was located evenly between four houses which obviously shared it. I knew the water was deep there: three-hundred-foot tankers passed up the Penobscot to Bangor, cruising only a few yards off shore. The shore was steeply sloped, making it hard to move anything to or from the dock. It was isolated by the slope; the dock was fairly well hidden from the road. You had to drive onto the island to even realize there was a dock there. I looked overhead: the canopy was quite thick. Birches mostly, with some pines farther up the slope. A flash of silver caught my eye. It took another puff of wind to show it again: a silver radar reflector, hanging twelve feet up in the trees. An easy way to find the dock in the dark or fog, I thought.

I diverted my attention back to the search. Eventually it became clear the boat had no secrets to surrender. Wiley stepped back, frustration and anger fighting for time on his face. He paced the narrow planking, scratching the back of his neck. "Elias!" he called. A tall, thin, sandy-haired agent separated from the pack, approaching reluctantly. "This is your tip. The boat is clean. Are you sure it's tonight?"

"Yes, sir. A hot trail."

"I can see how hot!" snapped Wiley. "There is nothing on the boat. Not even any goddam cigarette butts! They could have picked it up and stashed it. Maybe they came in earlier. Could it be anywhere else?"

"Why stash it once, then come back, unless—"

"Don't ask *me* why!" yelled Wiley. "You want why, go ask them. Is there anyplace else?"

Elias pondered the problem a moment, nervously tugging a red beard. "There should be a drop, off the dock," he said. "For temporary storage."

"Great." Wiley's features brightened slightly. "What do we look for?"

"A lobster trap near the dock," Elias explained. "It should be accessible from the dock. It's tied to a buoy, a short post, all black with a narrow gold stripe near the top."

"All right." Wiley looked up the slope. "Mason, bring your light down here." A burly, muscular man with a battery-powered spotlight in his hand shouldered his way past me and Greene. He stomped to the end of the dock and played his light over the water. He scanned along the sides of the dock, but came up with nothing. The water was so shallow that rocks, bottom scum, the dark shadows of fish, a brown reflection of mud and a half-buried outboard stood out clearly. No one would drop drugs there.

Starting at the edge of the dock Mason swept the light left and right, each sweep a little farther out. The depth of water quickly increased, and the swirling murky waters of the Penobscot hid all traces of anything more than two feet down. As the beam swept an arc fifty feet to the right of the dock, a shadow twisted in the current. It pivoted again as Mason concentrated on it, flashing a gold stripe.

"That's it!" said Wiley excitedly. "That's what we want! Bring that buoy and whatever it's attached to in," he called to the patrol boat.

"No problem," called a chief on the bow. The boat backed out into the current.

"Watch yourselves," called Elias through cupped hands. "It may be booby trapped."

The chief waved as the white boat advanced on the buoy. Two crewmen sized up the situation, beaming a spotlight into the water, conversing briefly, before one grabbed the post. They hauled it aboard, trailing sticky, black-green slime and seaweed along the pristine sides of their vessel. They led the line forward and wrapped it round the bow cleat. While the crewmen peered over the side, the chief gave directions. The boat crept ahead. Moving across the current with a line off the bow was not easy; but the helmsman expertly delivered the buoy and line to Wiley.

The patrol boat backed down, its searchlight aimed straight down into the water. Wiley examined the buoy while an agent held the line. After a moment's examination, Wiley shook his head. "Ordinary buoy," he proclaimed.

The crewman on the side pointed into the water and called out: the chief gazed down with him. "Mr. Wiley!" he yelled. "You're not going to like this."

"What's down there?" called back Wiley.

The officer shrugged. "Looks like a lobster pot."

"All right." Wiley rose. "Let's pull it in and see. Lee, Hunter, give Taylor a hand."

Two more agents joined the one on the line. A weighted lobster pot can put up enormous resistance to being dragged over the uneven river bottom: the three men clearly struggled. The work became harder as they pulled the lobster pot in close and started lifting it from the bottom. Walker's pipe had gone out. A round of sucking in a lighter flame restored the smoke before the agents hauled up the trap, dripping, onto the dock.

It looked like an ordinary wire trap. The nets appeared intact; it did not appear very old. As soon as the trap hit the dock, George had a sniff. Immediately he began wagging his tail violently, barking insistently. Corsetti pulled him back to facilitate a closer look. The only thing inside were two brick weights. Corsetti fiddled with the unfamiliar latches to open the trap, reached in, and removed the bricks, handing one to Wiley. Bricks, evidently, were bricks. George continued to bark at the empty trap until Corsetti pulled him away.

After looking it over carefully, Wiley angrily flung the brick into the river. A column of water jumped up, drenching the front of his shirt until water dripped down his pants. "God damn it!" he cried. "There was something here! The dog knows it. They took it out before we showed up."

"Maybe it was never here," said Elias sullenly.

Wiley whirled to face him. "Make up your mind. Are you sure about your contacts, or not?"

"I was sure," said Elias. "I'm not now."

"Fantastic," grumbled Wiley. His hand went to the back of his neck and started kneading. "Something was here. They knew we were coming and cleared out. Whoever is running this had ample time to sink his tentacles deep into the locals. He's better connected than we are."

"He couldn't have found out from me," said Elias defiantly. "I'm certain."

"No," said Wiley. The hand moved from neck to beard. He raised his head and looked at Walker, who calmly puffed his pipe, watching. "If there's a leak, it wouldn't be through us."

Walker pulled the pipe from his mouth and spat on the ground. "Careful, Wiley. Don't let your bad luck sour our relationship."

For a moment, Wiley said nothing. Resignation displaced the anger and consternation in his face. "Lee, cart this trap to the van. Hunter, take the buoy, too. Clean up the dock a little. Put everything aboard their boat. Chief Ranzoni," he called to the patrol boat. "I would like to confiscate this boat. Can you tow it back to Rockland?"

"No problem," came the cheerful reply.

"Thank you." Wiley started ashore. "The rest of you, collect your gear and clear out. I want to see everybody at the sheriff's office at 9:00."

He stalked up the slope to stand before Walker. "Sheriff, if you don't mind, I'd like to have a talk with you. Privately. Can we share a car to Ellsworth?"

"Fine." Walker rose, tapped out the pipe against the ledge and dropped it into his pocket.

Wiley, who looked tired and beaten, nodded. He gestured up the slope. "After you, sir."

Two hours later I returned to Eagle Harbor, a long night's work drawing toward a close. From running down Smith and Devereaux to participating in Wiley's raid, I had done a lot. Still, as I drove home, I wanted to do one last thing. There were parallels between Verona and Eagle Harbor. Enough to justify a quick dock search. I did not honestly expect to find anything. But a failure to locate anything could be a boost to clearing the village.

At 3:30 in the morning, only silence inhabited the village. In about an hour the fishing fleet would wake, pushing out the solitude. I could get only a quick look. As I parked in front of the diner, I noticed lights behind the fire station door. I had not given close attention to the radio all evening, but I didn't think I would have missed an emergency call. I drew my pistol and went to have a look.

I approached from the church side, where the deeper shadows offered thicker cover. Anyone looking toward the church would see only his own reflection in the glass. I kept below the window level until close enough to slip off to the side of the building. My back tight against the cinder blocks, I moved closer until I could peer inside. A quick glance revealed no one looking out. I ventured a more detailed look around the inside.

The second look drained away the adrenaline instantly. I holstered my gun, walked around the front and tried the door. It was unlocked; I went inside. Twitchell and an attendant worked behind the open rear doors to the ambulance, cleaning. Twitchell looked up, startled. "Jeez, Jimmy, you scared me. I didn't hear the door."

"Sorry," I said. "What's up?"

"We made a run," he explained. "Bunch of kids out on the beach, having a good ol' time. Cops found them and had just started to disperse them when one starts barfing his guts up." Twitchell shook his head. "First-time drunks are always rough. He's small, couldn't weigh ninety pounds. We took him over to the hospital. He managed to hit the ambulance floor a couple times."

"You guys get all the fun," I said.

"Tell me about it." Twitchell stepped back to survey the process. "Looks better now, let me tell you. How come you're up and about?"

"Busy night," I replied. "We had to help Wiley make a fool of himself over to Verona."

"Oh, yeah," he answered. "I heard about that. Another shipment locked up?"

"Just like up to the quarry."

Twitchell grinned, shaking his head. "You guys in the sheriff's department are all right. But this guy Wiley—he just doesn't have his shit together."

"I know what you mean."

Twitchell yawned. "I could jaw with you all morning, Jimmy, but I've had a busy night. You look tired, too. You should go home."

"Soon enough," I replied. I could not stifle an echoing yawn. "I want to have a look around the dock first."

He patted my shoulder. "Don't work too hard."

"Catch you later." I headed outside, down to the dock.

Unlike at Verona, floodlights thoroughly lit the Eagle Harbor dock. The greenish-white glow allowed me to see the boats moored close in and provided a dim glow on the sides of those boats farther out. I had brought a flashlight, but it would be useful only for close inspections.

I went out to the end float and proceeded to search the water. If Verona served as the example, which I hoped it did, the buoy might be in sight. The water was deeper here, which meant the buoy could be closer, but it wasn't. The channel twisted to the right, into the moorings. To keep clear of them, the buoy might be far left; I found nothing there. The dock lights shed useful light out to about seventy-five feet. Past that, the black buoy could easily be lost amid the shadows of waves, moorings, and boats. I needed a closer look and so headed under the dock to the skiffs.

I found the familiar dory, cast off the painter, and headed out. I decided to search in concentric circles, so I rowed about fifty feet away from the dock before circling. Since the boat cast dark shadows seaward of the dock lights, I concentrated inshore. The first semicircle revealed not a thing, as did the next two, ten to fifteen feet seaward of the previous one. With my next tour, I began to encounter moored boats, and the semicircle became ragged. Buoys appeared, but only the individually marked buoys of the locals. Two more passes yielded nothing.

Two-thirds of the way through my next tour, about 120 feet off the end of the dock, I detected a dim shadow near the long shape of *Die Walküre*. I scrabbled around the bottom for my flashlight, found it, and pointed it along the beam. I still could not identify the object, but it warranted a closer look. I pulled the right oar twice to start a turn.

When the bow bumped against the buoy, I immediately back-paddled until I sat dead in the water. The boat rocked wildly as I searched for the buoy. I found it near the transom, stuck in close as if the line had caught on the dory. With equal parts of elation and despair I recognized it: a short-posted black buoy, a single gold stripe around the top. In the calm darkness it bobbed gently in the water, a deceptively innocent marker unmistakably linking Eagle Harbor to Frederickson.

I desperately wanted to know who owned it. A quick look revealed no name stamped onto the buoy. I peered over the side, aiming my light into the water. The sea water absorbed the beam after three or four feet, only enough to see the line snaking toward the bottom. It had taken three strong men on good footing to haul up the Verona trap. I had been pulling traps most of my life and knew I probably could not manage it alone from the dory. My father was notorious for leaving his keys aboard; sometimes he even left them in the ignition. I hoped he had done so that night, so I could bring the *Janet Kathleen III* over and haul up whatever was down there in minutes. I looked around for the familiar mooring.

Without warning, the dock lights went out. I knew my night vision would return, but the darkness momentarily blinded me. The eastern sky brightened with dawn, but it was too early for the lights to go out automatically. On the other hand, the automatic lights were known for random failures. The town council had bought them, on sale, from an electrician who promptly went out of business. My eyes gradually adapted to the predawn starlight. I found the *Janet Kathleen III,* got my bearings, and bent over the oars toward the far side of the harbor. I gave a single pull. In that awkward position, feet out, back poised over nothing, arms close to my chest, I heard the startling report of a gunshot.

Caught off balance, I tumbled into the bottom, the oars loose, feet high in the air. I stared past my feet at the stars as a second report echoed across the harbor. This time water splashed close by. The lights had not failed by accident. I was not only a target, but a sitting duck. My first reaction was to stay low, below the gunwales. I did not hear the third shot, but I did hear the crackling of wood splintering: I covered my face as a bullet slammed into the dory. When I looked out again, I saw a ragged hole beneath the oarlock. Another shot came out of the darkness; this time less splintering, but a hole opened closer to the waterline. As I moved around and tilted the dory, water trickled in.

I grabbed the oars, scrambled to a crouched position, and began to pull as hard as I could. For the moment I did not care which way I headed, I wanted to get away. I pulled away from *Die Walküre* as the next shot whined past, burying itself in the hull of the speedboat. A trickle of fluid accompanied the smell of fuel spilling from the tanks. The boat was behind me: I realized I now rowed toward my enemy.

Turning would present a broadside, but advancing toward the shots sounded worse. I pulled hard on the right oar, pushed on the left, pivoting the dory as tightly as its long waterline would allow. I straightened on a reciprocal course, hoping to pass under the bow of the powerboat. I felt exposed with my face toward the shooter. An orange light flashed among the trees on the far shore: the report followed as another shot went by. I rowed on, pulling irregularly as I tried to jink the dory to throw off the aim. It must have worked. Two more flashes, two more reports, but no hits.

I scored the next hit: the dory slid under the bow of the powerboat, but my head failed to clear. I bumped painfully into the sharp prow. I did not want to waste time, so kept rowing to put the boat between me and the flashes before I took a moment to rub the back of my head. I pulled the oars in and dragged myself alongside *Die Walküre*. The intensifying stench of gasoline made me anxious to leave. First I needed to know I was at least clear to reach the next boat. I cautiously stood up, looking toward shore. Nothing. I bent down and picked up my pistol, snapping off the safety. I peered over the gunwale again, and this time a flash erupted on shore; fiberglass flew as I dove to the bottom again.

From the bottom of the dory, I realized the hole in the side was serious: two inches of water flooded the bottom. I put away my gun. I could not hope to hit a target so far away with only my Beretta. My boat was flooding and I was defenseless. In half an hour it would be light and others would show up; then I might be safe. The dory would fill, and though it would sink only to the gunwales, it would not provide even a scrap of cover. Time was my ally. Someone had to have called the sheriff's office about the gunshots; a patrol car or state trooper couldn't be more than fifteen minutes away. The early fishing crews would soon arrive. In time, I'd have plenty of help. But before anyone arrived, whoever fired from shore could move wherever he liked to try again. How long could I hold out?

Another shot came from shore. He must have been shooting at phantoms, for I could not be visible. I could not wait until morning. I found the bailer and furiously flung water over the side. A desperate plan gelled in my head. I hesitated a moment, for I knew my plan relied on no one lurking at the dock. I had a better chance on land than waiting out on the water, so I jumped into the harbor with a splash.

With my 160 pounds removed, I hoped the dory would float a little longer. I made my way to the bow, and grabbed the high prow. I kicked until my feet came up under the keel, then thrashed to pull me and the boat ahead. I made slow progress, but I moved. In a few seconds I cleared *Die Walküre*. The shooter seemed confused; no shots came. Then came three shots in rapid succession: my cover held. One shot hit the transom, but the other two missed.

Now I needed direction. The dock was almost directly off the beam. To head that way meant exposing the side of the boat to the shore. I stopped kicking and swam to the side, hoping to stay invisible from shore, I reached an awkward but tenable position. I kicked hard to turn the dory toward shore, then kicked to start moving. Two shots boomed across the harbor: both slammed into the side of the dory, one near the waterline. The boat started settling more quickly.

With no idea how long my cover would last, I kicked harder, trying to reach land. Each kick tipped the dory a little more: each time I felt my arm sinking lower as it settled deeper. Another shot took off three inches of planking along the gunwale, sending a shower of splinters into my face. My eyes were spared, but I felt the sting of sharp wood in my cheeks, amplified by salt water.

I advanced within thirty feet of the dock. The dory had sunk so deeply that it provided pathetic cover, and dragged heavily as I tried to proceed. The time to part company had come. I took three deep breaths, sighted on the dock, and dove as deeply as I could. I kept my arms along my sides; a diver had once told me that you can make better time kicking alone than by swimming as you would on the surface. I kicked hard, tightened up, and kicked even harder. I held all my breath until I had to start exhaling or explode. Eventually I had nothing left to blow. I fought the urge to inhale, kicked twice more, aiming for the surface. I slowed down, resisting the desire to broach; if I came up short, a man on the shore could not fail to notice.

I surfaced with great restraint, gasping. Immediately I checked my position. I had done better than I thought: I had passed the end of the dock, swimming as far as the riprap around the parking lot. Through the pilings, I looked toward the far shore. I saw no flashes, and heard nothing. I had a good view of the dock and the parking lot. Anyone up there would have been silhouetted against the stars, but I saw nothing. Behind me, the top of the dory just barely hung above the surface.

I still felt exposed and did not want to linger. Still panting, I swam toward the rocks. One leg touched the bottom at the same time as the opposite hand. I dropped to a crouch, walked along the bottom to the far side of the riprap, and crawled out of the harbor. I clung to the rocks, breathing heavily. I snapped open the thong of my holster and pulled up the Beretta. I hoped it would fire; I hoped it wouldn't need to. I pulled the hammer back, braced myself, and made my way up.

I stood, dripping, gun in hand, scanning the dark lot. No one looked back. The harbormaster's office was a small shack near the end of the dock. On the outside wall a gray box controlled the lights. The door hung open: the light switches were off. With dawn imminent, throwing the switch would only make my location obvious. I kept the gun in hand, though it fell to my side as I stumbled tiredly to the road. Near the top, just as I prepared to fall on my car, I saw headlights coming from the west. I realized the flashes had been from that direction. I shuffled to the front of the car and crouched. Resting the gun on the hood, I held it in both hands and sighted above the right headlight where the driver sat.

The lights hauled behind them an ugly, battered Volkswagen. The car parked behind mine, the lights went off, and Denise stepped out. I suppose I should not have relaxed until I confirmed she was not the gunman, but I was too tired. If Denise was the mastermind— that was a joke—then she could have me. I dropped the gun on the hood and fell onto the curb.

She was startled as she came round the fender and saw a dark, wet shape huddled on the curb. She gasped, stepped back, and reached into her purse. I remembered she carried a can of pepper spray. The thought jump-started my exhausted body. My arms covered my face as I rolled away from her. "Denise, it's me! Don't, please. It's Jimmy!"

"Jimmy? Jimmy Hoitt? Is that you?"

I cautiously exposed my face. I mustered as much of a smile as I had left. "Afraid so."

She dropped her purse, and knelt down. "My God, Jimmy, you look awful. What happened? Is that blood?"

"Yes," I answered simply. "I've had a long night."

8

Friday

Patrol Area: Eagle Harbor
Hazy, hot; sticky wind
from SW; seas flat

I perched uncomfortably on a stool, my back pressed tightly against the countertop, head leaned far back. My eyes shut, I could see none of the treatment. Feet shuffled on the linoleum floor, the stove ventilator fan roared and rattled, but no one spoke. Even so, I could feel the heads shaking around me.

Even with my arms supporting some weight, I could not endure the position for long. I squirmed toward a more comfortable position. With the squirming came admonitions to cease. "Stop that," said a clinical female voice. "You've got to hold still."

"Okay, okay," I mumbled. "Try to hurry."

"I'm doing what I can," replied Ellen. She is about seven years older than Denise, and the added years bestow on her an unspoken authority. Her work as keeper of schedules and supplies gives her jurisdiction over the older waitresses as well. Ellen is cheerful, friendly, and surprisingly smart, and when she gives orders, you obey. "This isn't easy, you know."

"I'm sorry."

"Stop talking."

The steel tweezers delicately probed my cheek bone. At first a gentle tug, then a sharp yank extracted what felt like an old phone pole. I stifled a yelp, setting my teeth hard.

"Dammit," she said. "It broke."

"You want the knife?" asked Denise, just a little too eagerly for me.

"No. I think I've—" the tweezers probed again. "Oh, hell, let me have it." I felt a feather's touch: the knife was so sharp it sliced cleanly. I probably bled profusely, but the razor-sharp blade cut with little pain. Another yank with the tweezers and another piece of blood-smeared wood came free.

"Got it!" exclaimed Ellen. "You can open your eyes now."

I obeyed. At the bottom of my vision I detected jagged shadows, the bloody remnants of the dory shrapnel. "I think I got them all."

"Thank God that's over."

She took my face in her hand, rotating it side to side before the light. "I don't see anything. Could be something buried in the cuts, under the blood. You feel anything?"

"No," I replied. That wasn't exactly true. I felt a lot. A dull, persistent pain pounded behind my face. I felt tired, shocked, angry, and threatened, but I did not feel any more splinters in my face. "Thanks."

"Let me wipe it off," said Denise, shoving me backward. "Just a second." She gently dabbed a damp cloth over my face. "It looks clean, I guess. Sure you don't want to have it bandaged?"

"Yuh, I'm sure." I pushed her hand away and sat up straight. "I'll clean and bandage it later."

"You're frightfully ungrateful," she said.

"No, I'm not." I generously kissed her hand. I winced: using my lips stretched something that did not want to be stretched. "Thank you."

Dickinson, obstructing the doorway, shifted his weight to lean against the other frame. "You up for a walk?"

"Where?"

"We're checking the woods where you reported the flashes. Thought you might want to look for yourself."

When I slid off the stool my knees buckled, but I grabbed the counter, recovering before hitting the floor. "I think so."

"I'll drive."

I managed a smile that minimally hurt. "Lead the way."

Dickinson's car waited right outside the door. The rumble of a heavy truck climbing the road from the dock made us pause as I worked the door handle. Lights flashing, the EHVAC rescue unit hauled up the slope, attendant Scott Bishop at the wheel while Twitchell rode shotgun. I climbed into the cruiser. "That wasn't for me, was it?"

"No." Dickinson executed a tight 180 in the road and headed for the woods. "One of the fishermen hurt his back. They're taking him over to the hospital to have him looked at."

In the deepest recesses of my mind a subdued alarm rang. There had been no one in the parking lot when I came out of the harbor. A good half hour had passed since then. That meant a remarkably fast response from the ambulance corps to be evacuating a fisherman who had not yet arrived when I first reached the diner. Something didn't ring true. "What's his name?"

"Wilson? Whitman?" Dickinson struggled to recall. "Winthrop?"

"How about Winter? Dave Winter?"

"Yeah, I think that was it."

"He's young for back problems."

"One bad fall is all it takes," said Dickinson.

"Yuh." I checked my watch: 4:45. Winter was a little early, I thought. I began to ponder why—then realized there were many possible reasons for a deviation. Maybe he was in a hurry and that's how he hurt his back. Made sense, for the moment. I'd look into it later. We reached the edge of the woods lining the western shore. Straight spruces, lower branches stripped and dead, filled the narrow strip between road and water. The dense stand permitted only glimpses of the harbor through the trunks. Thick briars, ferns, and immature spruce prevented a clear view of the water. Four cruisers, three unmarked cars, a pair of DEA vans and the State Police Crime Investigation Unit took up the shoulder on both sides. The men fanned out everywhere: guiding traffic through the gauntlet, questioning bystanders, running into the communications van, or searching the woods. Dickinson parked, leading me right into the trees.

As we neared the shore, we penetrated far enough through the woods to provide a clearer view of the harbor. I shaded my eyes against the glare, with a view all the way to the eastern side. The boats still in port, including Dave Winter's battered *Margaret B.*, remained at their buoys, half-heartedly pointing into the wind. Even at three hundred yards, the sleek shape of *Die Walküre* revealed a pronounced list to starboard as a Coast Guard patrol boat rigged a small boom to contain the spilled fuel. The fiery Devereaux would be irate when he came down to the water. For a moment I had a sharp image of how I must have looked in the gunman's sights. My small dory maneuvering amid the moorings, far from any cover, the only movement in the predawn shadows. No wonder I had been under constant attack.

Dickinson called, motioning me to join him. Two patrolmen and Deputy Harris stood among the shrubs, talking in the clipped speech of an investigator. Near the base of a gnarled white pine, flattened bushes and trampled earth identified the firing position. "Hello, Deputy," I said cordially.

Harris, a gaunt, stretched man of fifty, nodded, smiling a tight, restricted smile. "Hello, Jimmy. How are you?"

"I'm all right. Face stings."

"Imagine it does."

"Deputy Harris thinks this is where the shots were fired," explained Dickinson.

I looked out on the harbor with a hunter's eye. "The angles seem about right." I knelt, running my hands lightly over the area where someone had tried to kill me. "Find anything lying around?"

"A lot of lousy footprints," replied a patrolman. "Took a cast of the best, but I wouldn't hold my breath."

Harris dug into his pocket; what he removed gleamed in the morning sun. "Found this."

I reached up and took the plastic bag containing the small piece of brass. It didn't seem like much. "Just the one?"

" 'Fraid so."

"I counted at least nine shots," I pleaded.

"I believe you," said Harris sympathetically. "He policed his brass. We found this one buried in the mud, under the impression of a knee. He probably lost it."

"Not much to go on," I said.

Dickinson displayed an open hand, and I set the bag in it. He examined the shell closely. Dickinson was an expert at identifying ammunition; fifty years of experience using various firearms can do that. "Standard round," he said. "Twenty-two-caliber rifle. Probably a stock hunting rifle, but maybe an old sniper rifle. Machine-made Remington round. He didn't roll it himself."

He handed it back to Harris, who examined it briefly before putting it away. "That's all we've found."

With five men still in the woods, Harris clearly thought there might be more. "You looking for anything in particular?" I asked.

Harris shrugged. "We're looking for whatever we find. It would be real nice to figure out how the gunman got into and out of here. We're close to the main road, yet no one saw a thing. No tire marks, no sign of a beached boat."

"I don't believe in ghosts," I said flatly.

"One of the waitresses drove past within minutes of the shooting," explained Dickinson. "She said she saw nothing."

"Any luck with the buoy?" asked Dickinson.

"Not a nibble. We've watched it since fifteen minutes after Jimmy came out of the harbor. We've had our eye on it."

"That was thirty minutes after the last shot," I said. "That's plenty of time to pull up the trap and throw it back."

"Sure, I know," replied Harris. "But nobody's been in or out of the harbor who doesn't belong here."

I pointed out to the listing *Die Walküre*. "The speedboat is owned by a guy from Florida," I said. "A little shorter than me, bleached hair. Usually wears sunglasses and shorts. Seen him around?"

Harris and Dickinson both shook their heads. "Nope," said Dickinson. "Can't say we looked for him, though."

From the scrub along the shore came a shout. We walked quickly through the brush, dew-moistened plants spattering our clothes. Just above the rocks, a patrolman pointed at a flat slice of charcoal-gray slate. "See that?"

Dickinson bent over the rock. "Droppings?"

"No," said Harris. He probed at the moist brown spot with a finger. "It fell out of the cleats of a shoe. Shallow cleats. You can just see a hint of the treads."

I twisted my head to line up with the shore. "Looks like half a heel print."

"Not even half," added Dickinson. "But it wasn't here last night. It would have dried up."

"Search for more," ordered Harris. He sighted on the harbor and the trees where we had just been standing. He pointed toward a boulder offshore. "Check the rocks below. The tide's coming in, so hurry. Follow this line back to the road. See what turns up."

As the patrolmen scrambled off, Harris checked the print again. "Not much point in bagging it. We'll destroy it if we touch it."

"Take a picture," said Dickinson.

"I'll call down the troopers." Eyes on the ground, he followed the line he had just marked back to the road.

Dickinson straddled the print, his eyes narrowing as he scanned the harbor. "Perfect shot at that buoy from here."

I sat on a granite outcropping. "There must have been something in that trap when I went out. They pulled it out before you guys could cover it."

"Nobody passed us except the locals," said Dickinson.

I dropped my chin into my open palms. "I know."

Harris came back not only with his camera, but also with Special Agent Wiley. I started to get up, but a firm hand on my shoulder kept me down. "How are you feeling, Hoitt?"

"All right. Nothing that won't heal."

"Good." He stared out to sea. He had changed, as if the Maine climate had prematurely weathered him. Enormous brown smudges hung below his flat, lifeless eyes. Even hidden by the bushy black beard, his cheeks were more hollow, his usually cold thin lips three shades grayer. "If we're on the trail of Frederickson's assassin, I'm surprised it hasn't come to this sooner. We must be getting close."

Harsh white glare flooded the woods and rocks as the trooper fired the camera flash, moved slightly, shooting again, repeating the process. "I forgot my scale," he said. "Put your boot next to it, will you Dickinson?"

Dickinson planted his polished boot tip near the mud. "Sure."

Wiley still stared. "Where was the buoy?"

I stood beside him, pointing toward *Die Walküre*. The ever-changing patterns of tide and wind now presented her full broadside. A boat's length off the bow a black spot bobbed on the gentle swell. "Just off the bow."

"Why didn't we haul it in?" asked Harris. "Dust it for prints, trace the materials. Anything we can get."

Wiley shrugged. "You'll find it's a trap like any other. If we leave it alone, they just might bite at it again."

"But they know we've uncovered the buoy system," I said. "They must, or they wouldn't have shot at me."

"The best hiding places are the most obvious ones," mused Wiley. "They could be back to use it for another drop."

"They might also booby trap it," said Dickinson.

"We have little to gain by leaving it out there, but absolutely nothing to gain by bringing it in," replied Wiley. "At this point, we'll take what we can get."

"Yeah," agreed Harris. "What's our next step?"

The empty eyes traversed from the water to Harris, then fixed on me before returning to the harbor. "It looks like the operation might be folding. They took a big chance shooting at Hoitt. I'm sure the gunman knew he was a cop. That means they're desperate. Since the only thing they can't buy is time, they must be in a hurry to pick up."

"I was really hoping we wouldn't find anything," sighed Harris.

"Never thought to check our own yard," added Dickinson thoughtfully. "All the cocaine and marijuana must be coming in elsewhere, we thought. In Maine, a kilo of cocaine is a huge bust. Used to be. Before this."

"We haven't found anything yet," I said.

Wiley snapped out of his reverie. "You haven't heard?"

"Heard what?"

"Last night was a big night," he explained. "While the Verona raiding party debriefed in Ellsworth and you were being shot at, a routine safety inspection on a truck in Kittery turned up twelve kilos of uncut Bolivian coke hidden in the gas tank. Another tip aimed us at a Bar Harbor Airlines commuter plane. Customs searched the plane and found another ten kilos."

"Biggest bust in Maine, if you connect them to one investigation," said Dickinson.

"We traced them both as far as Bangor, consistent with Frederickson's operation," continued Wiley. "They had bar codes printed on them, which leads us to believe they were parts of the same shipment. Either the volume is far larger than we expected, or they're trying to empty the warehouse before we move in."

"Damn it," I said. "If it goes to ground, we'll lose it."

Wiley nodded. "I'm convinced whoever killed Frederickson intended to take over the operation. I don't think he expected us to come down so hard so fast. Now he's selling off the inventory and getting the hell out."

"For now," said Harris.

"For now," echoed Wiley.

My own gaze wandered out to the harbor. I had denied the inevitable for a long time: now I could not avoid it. Someone had shot at me in my own harbor. At least one person I knew had to be involved. Along with the rest of the village I had been betrayed. With the network closing down, the traitor in our midst would be able to hide in the safety of the village. He would be safe. But eventually word would leak about his anonymous existence, just as the village always knew what transpired within. Growing fright and distrust would dissolve the close bonds built up through generations of shared hardships. The familiar, friendly social order would become extinct. I could not picture Eagle Harbor as the fearful result of that process. "Is it closed down yet?" I asked.

"I'm not sure," replied Wiley after a moment. "I don't think so, but I can't support that with hard evidence. It's just a hunch."

"How long until everything's gone?"

"He can't move easily. He's too hot," said Wiley. "He wants out fast, or he wouldn't have risked the shooting. In a hurry, he could easily make a mistake."

"So could we," said Dickinson.

"How long?" I repeated.

"He could be out in an hour. He could lay low, take it easy, and move out slowly over a couple months."

"You're the expert," said Dickinson. "What's your best guess?"

Wiley breathed deeply. "This sea air is remarkable. Invigorating, fresh." He inhaled again. "Pity you can't bottle it."

"It's been tried," replied Harris tiredly. "How long?"

"Thirty-six to forty-eight hours. If he's not gone already."

"Damn it!" exploded Harris. "We've made no progress in seven days. Now we've got hours?"

"We've got to step up the pressure," said Wiley. "The shooting was a mistake. He's shaken. All he has to do is hear the dogs; they don't have to bite him. If we keep pushing, keep closing in, he'll choke. We'll get him."

"He's mine," I said quietly to the steel-gray waters.

Neither Dickinson nor I spoke as he took me back to the diner. I rested my arm on the door, letting the thick sea air blast against my throbbing face. A range of distasteful thoughts coursed through my head. If someone from Eagle Harbor was involved, as could no longer be denied, it was someone who had shared our family dinner, someone I took coffee with at the diner. That was too close to home. I wanted the blast of air to purge my thoughts, but I knew no hurricane ever could.

Dickinson didn't bother to park, stopping in the road by the door. Just eight o'clock, yet the long night had already evolved into a long day. My arm was leaden as I pulled the door handle, my biceps screaming quietly as I stepped out. All traces of the morning's cool, damp air had dissipated, replaced by the heavy, slow-moving air of a day destined for haze, heat, and humidity. "It's gonna be a hot one."

"Weatherman said it might hit ninety today."

Even in Maine summer can bring oppressive humidity that frays everyone's nerves and saps their strength. It's hard to get anything done on days like that. I ran a hand through my tangled mat of hair. The already rising temperature drew out my sweat, mixing it with caked salt from my morning swim. With that mess topping a face bruised and bloodied, I was glad not to have a mirror. "That would make everything just perfect, wouldn't it?"

"Just about." Dickinson leaned across the seat. "You okay, Jimmy?"

"Yuh. Dead tired, but I'm all right."

"We're not through yet."

"Hell, no," I replied. "We've got at least thirty-five hours, if Wiley's right. He's been right about everything else so far, hasn't he?"

Dickinson smiled. "Let it go."

"Sure." A yawn crept up, overtaking me before I could stifle it. "I think I'll go home and take a shower. Talk to you later."

He sat up straight again. "I'll be in touch."

I waved as he merged into traffic. Another yawn came up. I had ample warning to do something about it, but with no one around, didn't see any point. I searched my damp pockets for my keys, and drove off, turning left just beyond Dave Winter's house onto a side road to sneak back home.

I parked in my driveway a few minutes later. I gathered up my paperwork from the back seat and floor, intending to bring it into the house, then changed my mind: I had no particular reason to go inside. I dumped the paperwork, closed up the windows, and exchanged the official keys for my own. If nothing else, driving my own truck would provide air conditioning for the hot day ahead. I threw my jacket on the passenger seat, locked my gun and holster in the gun case under my seat, fired her up, and pointed for the north-western shore.

I was awake enough to realize how exhaustion had drawn away the edge from my skills. I did not want to tax my driving any more than I wanted to engage in a firefight. I kept to the main roads, letting the traffic float me along, and reached Robyn's house a quarter-hour later. I popped up the sun roof and jumped out onto the gravel, bounding up the steps with surprising energy. As I pressed the bell, I felt something furry crawling around my ankles and looked down to see Binkley. He mewed silently, flicking the tip of his tail. "It's Jimmy," I called.

"It's open," came the reply.

I pulled back the screen. Binkley slipped inside, forcing the front door open wide enough for me to follow. He scurried around the corner as I peered in. "Hello?"

An arm rose above the couch. "Hello."

I closed the door and advanced on the couch as Robyn emerged from behind the couch back. She looked quite comfortable, head propped up on three massive, ugly, fringed pillows, a bright red T-shirt stretching down to mid thigh. A paperback, *The Optimist's Daughter*, rested on her chest; I could just see the tops of her reading glasses over the binding. Her eyes rolled upward to catch a glimpse of me, but as soon as they reached my face her friendly glance changed to a shocked stare and the color drained from her face. She bolted upright, the book falling to the floor. "My God! What happened to you?"

I sat on the couch. "I had a rough morning."

"You look like you lost a fight with a coyote."

"I lost," I said. "But not to a coyote."

Doubled up so tightly her knees pushed against her chest, she reached out gingerly to touch my face. "Are you okay?"

"Just splinters, sprayed liberally over my face." I touched my face, letting my finger slide slowly over the wounds. It hurt to do that. "Does it look that bad?"

"Did you have a car accident?"

"No." I knew she wasn't going to like it, but I had to tell her the truth. "I was shot at."

For a second she did nothing. Her eyes probed mine, seeking denial, or more information, or reassurance. The emerald circles didn't waver, not to look at the rest of my face, or anywhere else. Her eyes began to blur. With no more warning she exploded into me, encircling me with her arms. Her hair, soft and sweet, was the one thing that touched my battered face that morning without causing pain.

I enclosed her in my arms. "I'm all right," I soothed. "No big deal."

"It's that case, isn't it?" She did an excellent job of maintaining control, but the forced, constricted voice belied her effort.

"Without a doubt," I said.

"I'll be glad when this is over."

"Soon," I said. "Soon."

"Not soon enough."

"Too soon," I said.

She pulled away. Moist, red-rimmed eyes silently interrogated me. "Too soon?" she said. "You sound as if you're enjoying this."

"That's not what I meant," I explained quickly. "They're closing down the operation. In less than two days it will all be gone."

"Two more days," she repeated. "Two days of the most desperate action yet?"

I shrugged. "Perhaps."

"Two days can be a lifetime."

"May not be enough time."

"Let him go," she said sharply. She put her head against my chest. "Better to let him go than get killed."

"It's not my decision. Anything could—"

"Shut up," she snapped. "Shut up and hold me."

Thoughts and emotions swirled in search of vocabulary, seeking a way from my mind to Robyn's ear. The thoughts checked behind each door, but nothing yielded. The thoughts would not die, but the words refused to form.

"You don't understand what it's like," she said. "Waiting around, never sure when you're going to show up. I know what you're doing, and I know it's dangerous, but I can't do anything. I'm reduced to a shaking, shivering fool."

"I remember waiting nights when a storm blew up and my father wasn't in yet," I replied. "My mother would feed us, but she couldn't eat or do anything except sit in the living room by the fire, staring at the door. But he always came home."

"It's not the same with you," she said. "We all grew up knowing the force of nature. We've survived hurricanes, storm surges, floods, and blizzards. We don't understand them, but we have learned to cope, how to survive." She shivered. "But you go man against man—unpredictable, dangerous. You never know what you're up against. God, Jimmy, cops are killed on traffic duty. They're killed chasing speeders. You're trying to match heads with a drug lord!"

"I'll be all right," I said, hoping I sounded more positive than I felt. "I can manage."

"I hope you can." Her grasp tightened. "I don't want to lose you, Jimmy."

The thoughts still echoed inside my mind, but I had no words for them. I wanted to say something, anything—but nothing came. I could only sit silently, holding her, caressing her.

She held me a few seconds longer, then, as abruptly as she had started, she pushed away. "I think I've blubbered enough."

"You can blubber some more, if you'd like."

"No." She sat on the edge of the couch, rubbing her face. She picked up the book and soundlessly deposited it on the table, staring at the closed cover.

After the silence passed from extended into uncomfortable, I stood up. "If you don't mind, I thought I'd borrow your shower. My hair's a mess."

She turned toward me, then looked above my eyes at my hair. A smile all the more beautiful for its frightened spontaneity drifted across her face. "It sure is."

"Take just a couple minutes." I passed behind the couch, letting my fingers linger on her shoulder.

"Use the gray towels," she said.

The hot water hitting my hair trickled out salty, cascading down my face to fall on my chin. The solution stung as it soaked into the cuts, but the soothing, relaxing sensation of being clean and salt-free easily compensated for the pain. I lathered up, rinsed off, and stepped out. A ratty, enormous red beach towel hung off the door rack. I took it, vigorously toweled off, then wrapped it around my waist. I gathered my clothes from the floor and tracked into the bedroom. I sat on the edge of the bed with the intention of drying more thoroughly, but instead fell backward. I was asleep in seconds.

When I awoke, I discovered two things. First, I was not alone; second, my towel had fallen off. I rolled alongside Robyn, who was snoring softly, to steal a glimpse at the clock radio on the headboard. Half past four: I had slept for six hours. I sat on the edge of the bed, yawned, stretched, and relieved a sudden itch. I felt rested.

I had no more recollection of Robyn's joining me than I did of falling asleep, but neither circumstance bothered me. She was peaceful in sleep, her head buried in her pillow, hair streaming onto the white linen as though a breeze blew through the window. She looked very comfortable and very deeply asleep. As much as I wanted to rouse her and spend some time awake with her, I knew I still had a lot of work to do and that Robyn had earned her rest. I hung the towel on the nearest bedpost, dressed quickly, kissed her as she slept, and slipped silently out the front door.

I recovered my gun case from under the truck seat. Out on the back deck, I field-stripped the Beretta, flushed it thoroughly to get all the salt off, then painstakingly re-assembled it. I put away the case, then slipped on the holster. What to do next I did not know. With so little time left, I had no idea what progress Dickinson, Wiley, or anyone else had made. I hoped the entire task force had not spent the afternoon asleep. I needed an update first, and would let that determine my next move. I headed for Ellsworth.

When I pushed through the double doors, no one familiar greeted me. The station was quiet. A tall, balding man brandishing a sheaf of papers argued with the desk officer, while a shorter, calmer man in a plaid shirt waited his turn. I passed inside to find the offices as empty as the parking lot. Strangely quiet for a Friday afternoon, I thought. A vaguely familiar patrolman, out of uniform, changed the coffee pot in the kitchen. As I saw his pallid face, I realized how much younger than me the newest officers were. "Where is everybody?" I asked. "Something up?"

"That's what I heard," he responded, his voice tremulous. "But I don't know when, or where, who's going, or who they're after."

I smiled. The futility of further interrogation was immediately plain. "Thanks."

"I think there's a DEA agent in the conference room," he said. "You might ask him."

In the conference room I found a lone figure, jacket draped over a chair back, poring over papers and pictures. He had been along for the venture in Verona, but I did not recall his name. He gave no notice of me as I stood in the doorway. He picked up a photo from the pile and held it up for inspection; only then did he see me standing beyond the fax machine. Cold eyes narrowed as he tried to place me. "Hoitt, isn't it?" he said in a gravely but not angry voice. "Can I help you?"

"Yes, sir. Another officer told me something was up with the Frederickson investigation," I said. "He thought you could fill me in."

The chair creaked as he shifted his weight, letting the hand with the photos fall as he put his feet up on the next chair. "Wiley has changed his strategy. We're going on the offensive, simultaneously hitting three targets. Same as last night. From what I hear, he's getting the same results."

"Where?"

He shook his head. "Don't recall the name. I think they're around Blue Hill."

I moved up to the table, leaning over the back of a chair. The defeated manner, coupled with the fact that he pored over a pile of papers while agents were in the field, indicated he had no confidence in Wiley's success. "You don't expect him to find anything, do you?"

He leaned farther back, flipping a pencil end for end in his fat fingers, tapping the tip at each cycle. "Wiley is desperate. He's been running this case for a long time, and now he feels it's slipping through his fingers. He's drastically lowered his attack threshold; he's jumping at anything. He still feels there's a little time, but this guy is just half a step ahead of our intelligence."

"Maybe he's just lucky." I stood up, staring thoughtfully into the distance. "Or maybe Wiley's not looking in the right place."

The agent shrugged. "Who the hell knows?"

I lingered for a moment, evaluating my options. If Wiley's current assault proved successful, then the case could be finished. I wanted to see the case closed as much as anybody, but I didn't want it closed because the suspects escaped. If Wiley was too desperate, that ending was too likely. If Wiley could pursue a long shot, then so could I. I had little assistance to offer an assault in Blue Hill anyway. I knew where I had to go.

I established myself on the rocky coast beneath Jack's shack one more time. I could not have clearly explained why I wanted to watch the harbor. I figured, if you want to find a predator you can find his prey or watch his den. I left the prey to Wiley and his resources. I intended to watch the den. I relied purely on intuition, on a detached feeling that did not clearly align with facts. But I didn't have anything else to go on.

At dusk, the sun dropped slowly into a dark cloud, drawing a premature blanket over the harbor. The dock lights ignited on schedule, casting greenish light onto the sheltered waters inside the breakwater. The bright moon was high enough to remain clear of the clouds. The wind direction shifted, and now flowed offshore. The resulting warm breeze warded off the evening chill, but forced out the sweet smell of the ocean with the mustier, thick, vibrant scent of the forest and the stale, hot smell of the village.

I brought up my binoculars. Three-quarters of the fishing fleet had tied up for the night. Almost exactly at their center, I could just see the flash of gold on the black buoy. The racing yacht had slipped her mooring. *Die Walküre* hung limply at the end of her mooring line. She showed no sign of any attempt to repair or even assess the damage. Had Devereaux skipped away? For so many days I had seen him on his boat; yet on this crucial day, his absence was suspicious. A long, straight-decked ketch tied up at the main dock, her running lights lit, sails furled but uncovered, lights burning inside the cabin. Looking at the darkened hull four hundred yards away I could barely make out the registration, but it appeared to be from Connecticut. Nothing moved, and no boats other than the ketch seemed in imminent danger of moving, making an unusually peaceful Friday night. My luminous watch read 7:20.

At half past eight, five people escorted an obviously intoxicated sixth down to the ketch. They boarded cautiously. While three assisted the one into the cabin, a statuesque woman and a tall man dressed head to toe in white peered and pointed over the stern pulpit. They seemed to argue. The woman started the engine and pulled away from the dock to their guest mooring. Their mooring hid from me behind a pair of lobster boats, but by watching the masts I marked their course. The masts stopped moving; soon the engine stopped, leaving the harbor again quiet. Across its still waters, I could hear voices as they secured their vessel for the night.

Almost exactly a half hour later, the stillness fled as a heavy rock beat, distorted by distance but still recognizable, floated in on the night wind. The shifting, echoing sounds made it hard to isolate the source. I suspected a house with all the lights blazing on the western shore. I had to admit it was a great night for a party. I wondered if my sister was there. Probably.

Just before ten o'clock, the lights of the diner went out. Three cars fired up to take the evening shift home. The diner was the last thing to close; the town quietly went to bed.

At 10:15 I detected the plodding of a diesel beyond the breakwater. I saw nothing for another ten minutes until the dock lights caught the white bow wave of Don Porter's boat clearing the breakwater. Porter had painted his long, wooden boat gloss black, unique in Eagle Harbor. Very late for him to return home, I thought. As the boat approached the mooring, the light revealed two people aboard. Don Porter's youngest son, Eric, stood at the helm, one hand on the wheel, one hand around the blonde girl at his side. Theirs had not been a night fishing, I thought. I resumed my vigil.

Half an hour into Saturday, a muted sound close by drew my attention. Nothing moved in the harbor. For a moment I had no idea what to look for. I heard a different sound, as if someone close by blew his nose. I shifted my view to the shore beneath me. A pair of harbor seals roiled the surface less then ten yards off, oblivious to my presence. I watched them for a while, until they abruptly turned toward open water and dove.

The distinctive growl of another diesel yanked me out of a quick snatch of sleep. My watch read 2:15; I wondered who would be out so late. I swept the harbor with the binoculars, but could find no lights or movement. The echoes off the ledge made localization by sound extremely difficult, even without the intrusion of the party still raging across the water. If it wasn't in the harbor, it was either coming in or passing by. Passing boats did not concern me. I shifted my attention to the breakwater.

Slicing through the black water so slowly it made no waves, a gray prow slipped through the passage. Cruising without running lights was suspicious; it also made it hard to recognize the boat. It passed no more than four boat lengths inside the breakwater before I identified it as Dave Winter's. Strange indeed to be returning at this hour, silent and dark. Stranger still from a boat whose captain had been taken from the dock by ambulance that same morning. It might not be Dave, just as it had not been Don Porter; yet the lack of running lights bothered and excited me. I stood up as I followed the boat.

The engine died away as the boat drifted into the moorings. I held my breath. All my suspicions and fears for Eagle Harbor were at once realized when a hook emerged from the side, dipped into the black water to pull up the gold-striped buoy. The set of the wind and the tide hauled the boat bow-on to me. The bright dock lights glared off the plate glass windshields, effectively preventing me from seeing inside the cockpit to identify those aboard. Lobster boats carry a power winch, to one side of the helm, with which to haul up traps, but I could hear no clanking, grinding winch; the line attached to the buoy came aboard by hand. Someone did not wish anyone else to hear anything.

Soon the trap came alongside. A hand pulled it onto the gunwale. Whatever had to be done didn't take long, for within seconds the trap went over the side again. It disappeared with an inaudible splash, yanking the line behind it. The engine coughed and restarted, then the boat was underway again, circling. I knew it was headed for the mooring. I wanted to have a chat with whoever had pulled that trap. I wrapped the strap around the binoculars and scrambled up the rocks.

I was on the road into town in less than three minutes. I wasn't quite fast enough. As I signaled and slowed to turn down to the dock, a dark green pickup climbed up the hill. Barely slowing, the truck turned east and accelerated up the road. I stood on the brakes, clamping the wheel to hold it straight. As blue smoke drifted past, I quickly scanned the harbor to make sure the truck whose taillights were just disappearing held the person I sought. No cars remained on the wharf. The truck held my answers. I spun the wheel hard, jumping up onto the sidewalk, barely clearing the diner as I pursued.

I had caught only a glimpse of the truck, not enough to verify it as Winter's. I had seen enough to know the older, heavier truck would not have a higher straight-line speed than mine and would be less maneuverable in the turns. As I juggled brakes, wheel, throttle, and shift to make the sharp curve, I also realized speed alone would not win this race. The road twisted and curved over the ridge before pirouetting back to sea level. The other truck had a good start; if he knew I followed him, he could probably hold his lead long enough to lose me. I drove as hard as I dared, then pushed a little harder.

About two miles out of the village I found my portable radio, snapped it on, and brought it to my face. "County nineteen to county, come in. Over." No reply. I repeated the message, dropping the radio as a turn tighter than expected demanded both hands. The truck fishtailed, sending a shower of sand and gravel into the red glow of the brake lights as one wheel dug into the soft shoulder. Fighting the resistance, I held the wheel firmly. Abruptly the rear end grabbed, dragging me straight. I recovered the radio. "County nineteen to county, come in please. Over."

"County nineteen, this is county, go ahead," answered the bored, tired voice.

"County, I am in high-speed pursuit of a suspect in the Federal case," I said. The next turn I expected, and so better prepared for it. The radio stayed in my hand, held tightly against the wheel. "Now heading northbound on Cove Road, about three miles out of Eagle Harbor."

A different voice came on the line. "Copy, nineteen. Vehicle description?"

"I only got a glance," I said when I could. "Looked like a GM pickup, three to five years old, dark green. One occupant."

"Any idea where you're headed?"

"None at this time."

"Ten-four, nineteen. We will close off Thompson's Island and bring in assistance. Keep us informed of any change in course, over."

"County nineteen. Ten-four." I threw the radio onto the passenger seat and turned full attention to the problem of driving. I had cleared the ridge; the descent down the other side raised speed beyond my own confidence. The birches along the roadside became a gray-white blur as my headlights swung past. Every so often a gap opened between the trees where narrow trails led down to private homes or cottages on the water. Any of them could have accommodated the truck, hiding it out of my sight. There was no time to check every siding; I hoped the truck kept to the highway.

I cruised through a sweeping turn at the base of the eastern ridge. The trees fell away, opening onto a long public beach. The road edged the beach before it disappeared into the next cluster of houses. About a half-mile ahead, brake lights glowed as the truck slowed to negotiate a sharp left. Not only had he not turned off, but I was closing. Did he know I was there? Did he care? With the quarry so close, I jammed down the pedal to make up time.

The radio on the passenger seat crackled. I scrambled after it between maneuvers. "County nineteen. Go."

"Jimmy, this is Dickinson," said the disembodied voice. The wail of his siren echoed hollowly over the radio. "I'm on 3 North near Hull's Cove. What have you got?"

"I watched the buoy. About half an hour ago a boat came by, picked it up, hauled something aboard." A strip of crumbled pavement caught me by surprise, jarring the wheel momentarily out of my hand. "I'm following the truck the suspect entered at the dock."

"Any ID?"

"No," I replied quickly. "I recognized the boat, but I'm not close enough to make out the driver."

"Still headed north?"

"Affirmative. We keep this up, we'll hit Thompson's in ten minutes."

"Ten-four, nineteen. I should intercept by then. County three, clear."

During my conversation I had inadvertently slowed down. Certain I had lost distance, I pushed harder. I had been trained in high-speed driving, but that had been in a heavy cruiser with a low center of gravity, not a lightweight, top-heavy sport truck. The feel of the road from high up in the cab was a lot different than from the cruiser. I was learning: the speedometer indicated twice the legal limit.

Less than three miles from the last sighting, I reestablished contact with the green pickup. As I rounded a turn, a pair of brake lights glowed ahead, swinging out of sight behind the next curve. I was gaining.

I kept up the pressure as the houses grew denser and we crossed into Somesville. He led me east on Route 198, then bore left onto 233. Another piece of straightaway opened up, giving me an excellent view of my quarry and a chance to catch up. I had closed to within four hundred yards. Still too far to make out details like license plates, I could confirm the truck looked like the one Dave Winter owned. The shadow of the driver changed shape: a pale blur looked back up the road toward me, then hunched over the wheel again. There could be no more doubt that he knew I followed.

With no warning the brake lights glowed. The truck's rear end swung wide as he turned right. With the rear tires spinning and smoking, the truck turned perpendicular to the road, diving off the pavement onto a gravel trail as I jammed on my own brakes. I pushed into first and followed. "County nineteen to county," I broadcast. "Suspect has turned off 233 approximately two miles east of Somesville. I believe it's a fire road leading into the park."

The much narrower road made my job increasingly difficult. My speed was cut in half, and I had to constantly move the wheel to hold onto the track. I trusted the truck ahead not to stop; if it did I might careen around a blind corner at full speed and smash into it. I reached under the dash and flicked on the rooftop light bar. Dust spun up by the first truck reflected most of the light. I was extremely glad I had taken the truck rather than the patrol car, which would not have survived this jarring, crashing foray through the trees.

The fire road plummeted into a ravine, rising on the other side to join one of the myriad park carriage roads that meander across the eastern half of the island. These gravel roads are kept in magnificent condition for foot or horse traffic, but they were never built to carry a three-thousand-pound truck hurtling through the woods. Gravel, fallen limbs, and dirt flew everywhere as I tried to catch up to the other truck, only barely keeping my own vehicle under control. Ahead in the dark dust loomed an arched stone bridge far too narrow for my comfort. I clutched the wheel in a death grip, lining up as best as I could on the low stone curbs. The front end lurched upward as I hit the paving stones flat on. I swear the truck never touched the other half of the span on the way down.

The carriage road turned out to be a lot longer than I expected, though it ended where I thought it would: on the loop road through Acadia National Park. A timber gate across the end of the carriage road had been smashed through, the gates still swinging. I aimed for the center of the gap. A piece of the gate slammed into the fender, but didn't slow me in the slightest as I reached the relative safety of the loop road. The green truck was nowhere in sight. Through most of the park the loop road is one-way, circling clockwise through the easternmost parts of Mount Desert Island. In this section, however, it was two-way, giving me a choice. His overall direction had been eastward, toward Bar Harbor. I sped off to the left.

After the passage over the ruts, pavement offered relief. I made better time, but continued to wonder if I closed or opened the range. As the loop road slalomed through the forest, gaining altitude as it crossed the glacial ridge, visibility never extended more than two-tenths of a mile. I had no way of knowing whether I had selected the proper turn. Second-guessing myself would only make matters worse. I pushed as hard as I could.

Distracted by the pursuit, and traveling far in excess of any safe speed, I did not comprehend the significance of a sharp-curve sign until too late. For a moment I forgot the pursuit as I juggled two feet over three pedals, white knuckles locked on the wheel, my right hand clasping the gearshift tight enough to lift the transmission into the cab. The rear end swung wide, the tires squealed, the engine raced, but none of it did anything to check my progress toward a row of picturesque white birches guarded by a line of granite boulders. I was out of control, skidding to an impact with the trees. I dared not turn harder; the truck was already on the edge of toppling sideways. Without warning, the cab jarred suddenly as the front tires gripped the pavement. Another jerk and the hood began to move away from the boulders. Finally the rear tires fell in line. Almost too late, the truck headed for the road, not the rocks. Metal screeched, the empty bed reverberating as the rear quarter ricocheted off a boulder.

Ignoring the pounding in my head, I shifted and pulled away. From then on, I paid closer attention to road signs. A relatively smooth stretch opened before me: a good opportunity to call in. I groped for the radio, but came up empty. When further hand searches yielded nothing, I risked a glance. One glimpse sufficed: pieces of broken gray plastic mixed with the circuit boards on the floor. The corner had claimed a single casualty. I hoped the information I had supplied to the other officers would suffice.

Three corners in quick succession prevented me from lamenting the radio. I refused to accept I had come this far for no reason. After the last turn, a long view showed a pair of taillights. Though I could not positively attribute them to the truck, in my mind they could be no other. I cranked on a few extra turns.

Around another pair of corners the road not only straightened, but flattened. Something ahead caught my attention: my halogen headlamps and four bar spotlights reflected off a cloud of dust drifting from the road leading off to the right. I had no idea why the driver would want to go to the summit of Cadillac Mountain, but I hesitated only a moment before trading the brake pedal for the accelerator and turning onto the summit road.

The curving alpine track up the mountain arced back and forth along its way to the summit. Often, the only thing between my speeding truck and a plummet down the rift were pink granite coping stones. Thankful for the night that hid the abyss beyond the road, I pushed as fast as I dared.

About two-thirds of the way up, the road took a sharp cut into the mountain, then back out along the west flank. As I rounded the corner and turned into the mountain, the broadside of the truck on the next switchback reflected the moonlight.

Before I knew it, the road cut sharply to the left, then gently right, widening into the summit parking lot. What next? At the corner farthest from the summit road, I saw the truck: lights out, engine off, driver's-side door opened, no sign of anyone nearby. I slowed and turned, using the battery of lights on my truck to sweep the area. My truck and the green one joined two cars already in the lot, doubling the number of unauthorized vehicles. A rusted old Mercury was parked near the center of the lot, one side low over a flat tire. Beside the gift shop, conveniently close to the cover of trees, a late-model Honda merged with the shadows: the other half of an illegal drop, or just a couple teenagers desperately seeking some privacy? The car had a local plate. Quiet and empty, it posed no immediate threat. I advanced on the truck.

I parked behind it, aiming my lights at the open door. I withdrew my gun, checked and cleared the chamber, then flipped off the safety. The harrowing pursuit had ended. I felt like a cat who pursued a moth all over the house, and finally caught it, only to wonder what the hell to do with it. I opened my door and looked briefly around. My floodlights revealed nothing, only serving to blind me. I switched them off and jumped clear of the truck, running for cover behind a granite boulder.

I crouched behind the boulder for several minutes, waiting for my eyes to adjust to the bright moonlight. When I felt ready, I moved slowly, cautiously, silently away from the rock. The only clue was the truck itself, so I headed for it. I checked all around, looked through the bed, eyeing the ample space below it. I found nothing. The flat, rocky ground in front of the truck offered no concealment for anyone within twenty yards. Whoever had driven the truck to the summit had left.

I opened the passenger door, yanked open the glove compartment, and rifled through the contents: owner's manual, four or five maps, papers that felt like gas receipts, and a flat vinyl case containing a yellow auto registration form. I took the papers and registration in hand and moved away from the truck, not only to reduce my exposure but also to better use the available moonlight. From the relative safety of another rock I scanned the papers. The registration had faded, and with light only as bright as a good dinner candle I could just make out the name: Winter, David P. My suspicions were confirmed.

A sound behind me arrested my attention. I closed my fist around the papers, raised the gun, and flattened out against the concrete sidewalk. I waited. In a few seconds I heard a muted rasping— no, it was a voice. Whispering voices meant at least two people. Only one had come up in the truck. The voices continued, then a snap as a twig broke. Immediately I heard a hissed, "Sssh!" In another second the door of the Honda clicked opened. A quick turn of the starter and the Honda began down the mountain. So much for their privacy, I thought. The lovers were gone. I could concentrate on Winter.

Winter could go anywhere but up. I had no guess which way might be better than any other. To my right, an aggregate path led to an observation platform built on top of the rocky summit. Not merely a potential hiding place, it commanded the summit's high ground and was surrounded by a low, masonry wall: good cover, excellent visibility. I crumpled the papers, jammed them into my pocket, and abandoned my rock. Rather than running the straightest route possible, I zigged and zagged up the path, hoping to prevent any unseen gunman from getting a clear shot. I began maneuvering so rapidly I lost track of my position and failed to see the last of the stone steps, caught the tip of my sneaker on it, and fell forward onto the ledge.

Sudden, numbing pain obliterated any thoughts of where next to run. I doubled over, grabbing my knee, rocking and twisting, my teeth clenched against an unvoiced scream. In seconds, more serious questions of survival took over. When I tripped, my gun had flown out of my hands. I crawled over the ledge, keeping the knee high, probing with alternate hands. My gun had landed on the path, ten feet ahead of me. I looked it over, felt for proper operation. It seemed okay, but the only sure way to find out would be to fire it, and I wasn't about to betray my position yet.

I jammed the gun into my belt and hobbled to the edge of the low wall. My back against the cold stones, I flexed my knee as I listened for the sound of anyone nearby. I waited, flexing, listening, tensing, for several minutes. A whistle buoy moaned pitifully in the bay; cars speeded by on the main road to Bar Harbor fifteen hundred feet below, sounding like the distant rustling of trees. Up behind the gift shop, a pair of owls exchanged hoots. I did not hear what I expected.

I shifted, poking my head over the wall, quickly drawing it back. Nothing appeared unusual. I peeked again, searching more carefully. The summit sloped away, a few straggling tufts of grass and weeds striving for the sun between the broken rocks and the walkway. The slope ended abruptly forty yards away, where the gentle incline became a steep cliff plunging three hundred feet to the granite scree below. The cliff surrounded three-quarters of the observation area; the parking lot and a walkway to the gift shop completed the circle. I detected no cover between my position and the cliff edge except the deep shadows offered by the moon. Many were large enough to conceal a man.

I lowered my head below the wall, sliding to the right six feet, in case I had been noticed. I raised my gun, ran my hand over it once, and prayed it was intact. From the other side of the wall came a sharp sound. Definitely no buoy, passing car, or owl, but hollow, as if a rock had been disturbed and bounced off the walkway. I popped up to look over the side, just in time to see a blur dive into one of the larger shadows. I took aim. I could have fired, but was reluctant to shoot first.

My opponent moved, so I did the same. Placing a hand on the wall, I vaulted over the side, trading protection for mobility. My injured knee collapsed as I landed, but I had anticipated that, and my hands took the strain as soon as they touched the ledge. The same shadows that protected him, served me. I took advantage of the long shadow of a park information sign and moved well away from the observation area.

The shadow man did not like his spot; I had no sooner stopped and turned to look back when I saw him rise from the shadows and run nearly straight away from me. I was relieved to see no rifle or shotgun in his hands. I figured he could see behind him only poorly, so I ran directly into the moonlight, taking advantage of the nearby walkway to advance twenty yards closer before leaving the path and flattening behind an outcropping.

Though well protected by my shadows, I was also blind. I ventured farther out to look ahead. As I looked up, he ran again. This time he ran toward the cliff edge, perpendicular to his last jaunt. From that angle, his peripheral vision had a better chance of picking me up if I ran at full speed. I rose to a crouch and, using whatever cover I could find, moved slowly, diagonally toward him. I had the mixed advantage of the walkway for my own use. It offered no cover, but gave me no surprises to bump into, either. He dropped out of sight behind a huge shadow with such square, straight edges it had to be manmade. I stopped to see what he would do next. He must have thought I was still on the summit platform. He kept in the shadow from the summit, but clearly stood out against the lights of Bar Harbor. At least eighty feet separated us. I wanted to close that distance by at least half before revealing myself. Back in a crouch, moving even slower than before, I followed the path around the cliff edge.

I halved the distance, then did a little better, bringing myself within thirty feet. I was close enough now to recognize Dave Winter. Winter and I had gone to MDI High School together. We weren't exactly friends, but we were united Eagle Harbor residents against the denizens of Northeast Harbor, Bar Harbor, Somesville, or Southwest Harbor. He had assumed his boat after his father, an Eagle Harbor man from birth, died in an accident. Dave was a regular at the Eagle Diner, a constant member of the Congregational Church, a dedicated husband and father with three kids, and as tightly knit into the fabric of the community as my family, or Wes Scott, or Ed Berman. I didn't want to accept the evidence so plain before me, but there could be no denial. Through his use of the black buoy, Winter was connected to Frederickson's murder. I would have felt furious, dismayed, and even frightened at who else might be involved if I had had a moment to think. Fortunately, I didn't.

A granite dike led from the parking lot to the cliff face, passing within twenty feet of Winter. I moved along it, hoping to avoid the cliffside end. My eyes remained fixed on Winter with every silent step, my feet probing the ground cautiously before claiming it. I took up my position, braced myself, and lined up the gun on a man with whom I had taken more than one cup of morning coffee. Part of me wanted to fire unannounced, an involuntary response to the revulsion I felt. The baser response caved in to training: I knew I had to order him to surrender. I opened my mouth to speak, but before I could say a word, Winter leapt to his feet and ran, diving behind rocks and out of sight. I never learned what gave me away.

For a second, I did not know what to do. My pursuit had been so cautious and undetected, I could not immediately believe I had been discovered. From there, I could not see behind any shadows: no sign of Winter. Looking back the way I had come, I saw it would have been impossible for Winter to have seen me. As the walkway started up the slope, however, the boulders afforded excellent cover. He had disappeared into those rocks. The more time he had to maneuver among them, the poorer my chances. Gun ready, I stood up and started for the slope.

Winter blindsided me from the top of the park map display behind which I had crouched. He hit me with enough force to send me sprawling. For the second time that night, the Beretta flew out of my hand as I crashed to the ledge. I landed on my back, knocking the wind completely out of me.

Apparently more scared than brave, Winter had no inclination to finish me off. He rolled to his feet, and turned to run up the slope. Still breathless, I couldn't pursue, but one arm outstretched to its length covered just enough distance to yank his ankle as he began running. With his weight so far forward, he had no hope to stop himself before he toppled forward onto the rock.

For a moment I owned the advantage. I got to my feet, hobbling as fast as I could. His hands cradled his head the same way I had cradled my knee; I wondered if he had been knocked senseless. I quickly discovered he had not. When I passed within range, one leg flashed out, catching me on the knee. The blow would have been more effective if he had waited half a second: the tip of his work boots just touched me. Even so, I went down.

I crumpled immediately, teeth gritted tightly, a salty taste in my mouth assuring me I had bitten my lip. Winter scrambled into a crouch and rushed me. I was in no position to kick him as he had kicked me. I tried to roll out of the way, but instead of escaping I merely rolled into his fist. The resulting blow stunned me. I was only partially conscious as he grabbed me, hauled me to my feet, and began to pound my midsection. I would have fallen if he had not supported me. Winter held me firmly, and, with him to worry about my weight, I concentrated every bit of strength I could summon into a short right to his jaw.

A howl of pain coincided with my release. I managed to stay upright, retreating as he swung powerfully but blindly at thin air. He seemed unaware of my position. I ran toward him with all I had left, which is to say I stumbled in his general direction. A roundhouse swing connected with the top of my head as my right shoulder jammed into his stomach. He fell back, but a table-shaped rock prevented him from going down. He screamed hoarsely, pushing off the rock. I found myself shoved backward, shoulders locked in his grip, feet scrambling for footing until I realized there was none to find. He held me a moment, then cast me away. I fell slightly outward, mostly just down. Blindly I scrabbled to find his legs, but they weren't there. As I slid down the cliff face, I clawed at the crumbling ground. One hand found a sturdy tuft of grass, clutching it desperately. I doubted it could hold all my weight, but I had nothing else until my right hand found a notch in the rock that made a good hand grip.

Winter remained out of sight, but his panting breath told me he hung close by. Not that there was a damn thing I could do about it. We stayed immobile, me hanging, him panting.

"Sorry, Jimmy," he said, finally. The clopping of his boots on the walkway replaced his fading panting.

Winter had left me with few options and even fewer hopes. I was tired. My arms consumed all my strength just to support my weight. I had no chance to rest, thereby draining my reserves faster. As much as I wanted to avoid it, I had to look below to see if there was any hope. The shadow of the mountain immersed everything underneath me in absolute darkness. I could discern nothing five feet below me any more than fifty feet or even five hundred. If there was a way out, it was not that way.

I checked the face. If I could find a foothold, I could at least rest a minute, then try to drag myself up. I probed with my right leg, then switched to my left. In my current position it would be fatal for my injured knee to collapse. I moved the toe of my shoe methodically along the face, seeking anything that would accept it. Pebbles and rocks fell into the blackness. I found nothing. Reluctantly I searched again with my right foot. A promising notch initiated a small avalanche as soon as I put any weight on it, dragging all my hopes down the mountain with it.

The tuft of grass began to fail: the roots were never meant to support an extra 160 pounds. I slid another two inches down the mountain. I tried to find a lower purchase on the tuft, but only managed to uproot it. I cast it aside, clawing at the ledge for any handhold. Rocks, pebbles, another tuft—none of them held more than a few seconds. My left hand tested its way to the end of the cliff, then dangled, useless, alongside my body.

The fingers of my right hand, already cramped, began to lose feeling. A loss of control would inevitably follow. What would happen next I could clearly imagine. That handhold was solid, though. Perhaps if I put both hands in the crevice, I could stay on the cliff long enough to find a secure foothold. Any attempt beat letting go. I swung my left arm toward the right, but couldn't reach the notch. I shifted position slightly and tried again.

Suddenly my left hand flew up over my head as a firm, strong hand locked around the wrist. I was momentarily startled, and my exhausted right hand began to ease its grip. Instantly, a second hand as strong as the first latched on.

"You hurt?"

"No," I said quickly. "But I can't haul myself up."

"Hang on. This will hurt a little."

"Less than going down," I said.

The tension on my wrists increased and I groaned like a weightlifter as I rose. It did, indeed, hurt as my chest, protected only by a thin, quickly ripped shirt, scraped over the granite edge. It still beat the alternative.

In another thirty seconds, I topped the slope with only my feet dangling over the edge. I drew them in and lay panting, face down, heart thumping, on the ledge. I looked up into the face of Peter Smith. "Don't think I'm ungrateful," I said between gasps. "But what the hell are you doing here?"

Pale moonlight reflected off white teeth as he broke into a relieved smile. "I thought you could use some help."

9

Saturday Morning

Patrol Area: Eagle Harbor
Early morning fog, dispelling
to hot, humid day

That is one hell of an understatement." I sat on a ledge near Smith, well above the edge. "Do you always loiter on isolated summits at night?"

"I have to admit I like it better by night." Smith reached down for a small rock, weighed it in his hand, swung back, and heaved it over the cliff. He counted the seconds aloud until a sharp, clipped report echoed back up the cliff. "Three hundred fifty feet," he said flatly. "A healthy drop."

"Seemed like a mile," I replied.

He leaned back against the mountain. With the moon behind his shoulder, a baseball cap low over his eyes cast abysmal shadows over his face. "You surprised me the other day," he finally said. "I didn't expect to hear what you told me."

"Yeah," I said. "I couldn't believe a huge smuggling ring existed here, either."

"Not that," he snapped. "After living in the middle of it for fifteen years, I know how drugs pervade everything. No matter how idyllic the setting, how peaceful the village, how cheerful and friendly the people, as soon as you think it can't happen here, you realize how tragically wrong you are."

It made me furious to think he might be right. "Why didn't you do anything before? Why did you have to let someone die first?"

"I never knew the details," he protested. "I only knew the potential existed. Frederickson's death shocked me. I was dismayed but not surprised to hear that the industry had penetrated Eagle Harbor, but I didn't expect a guy like Frederickson to be involved. I figured it was all local talent: small-timers working the tourist traps and the high schools." He paused, shaking his head sadly. "I thought it was right up your alley, Hoitt. I never expected to be drawn into this mess. I thought I was free."

"We don't have time for personal vendettas," I said bitterly.

"No," he replied quickly, before lapsing into prolonged silence. He didn't move, black eyes staring at the granite beside me, idly tossing a stone from one hand to the other. "No, we don't. I want to see justice finally, properly served."

He abruptly stood, stepping onto the trail. "Parking lot's empty, except for us. The truck hot-tailed it out of here."

"Winter," I said softly. "His name's Dave Winter. He's a fisherman down in the harbor."

"Tall guy, with stringy, sun-bleached hair?"

"Yeah," I replied. "You recognize him?"

"He's got the mooring next to mine." Smith nodded. "He just ordered a new boat."

"I don't wonder."

He returned to kneel beside me. "I spent yesterday thinking. You were right: I came here to get away from people like Winter and Frederickson. That's why I selected Eagle Harbor. It would be a great tragedy if this place became as paranoid and frightened as the place I left. Tragic for me, tragic for you and everyone else who lives here. I can't sit idly by waiting for more tragedy. I don't know about you, but I've had all I care to." He rose, staring off into the night beyond the cliff. "What was her name? Robyn?"

"Huh?"

"Try to stay with me, Hoitt. Your girlfriend."

"Robyn. Robyn Cole."

"Local girl, I suppose."

"Same as me."

"Got a picture?"

I withdrew an aging print from the clear plastic sleeve in my wallet. As Smith held it up to the moonlight, I thought I saw a trace of a smile. "A beautiful woman."

"Yuh. She is."

"Don't let her get away, Jimmy. Trust me." He handed back the photo, his eyes glazed over. "I had a wife. She looked a lot like Robyn. I thought I could handle myself back then. Just like you do now. It cost me a lot to learn how wrong I was." Fire displaced the dead look in his eyes. "My Beth is dead because I lowered my guard. I just pulled you off the cliff. So don't expect me to say I'm sorry I hurt your feelings when I call you inexperienced. The cost is too damn high."

The pictures on the mantel came back to me. In my mind, the pictures of Beth Smith mingled with the familiar image of Robyn, and behind those two bright and lovely forms a nebulous but deadly presence seemed to loom.

"I was heading to the harbor to have a look at the sea," continued Smith. "I saw you whip around as I approached town, saw you tear off down the road, then heard your report on the radio. I added things up and followed."

"I never saw you."

He shrugged. "You were too busy. I wasn't trying to hide. Winter couldn't see me, and I figured you'd write me off as your backup. I kept you in sight, waiting for another radio report over the scanner to lead me on."

"My radio died back on the fire road," I explained.

"That explains the radio silence," he said. "They were trying like hell to get hold of you. Probably still are."

"There's a pay phone by the gift shop. I'd better call in."

"Now there's a good idea." He gave me a hand up to the trail.

"First thing they'll want me to do is to report to Ellsworth and give them all the details. That should tie up the rest of the day."

"You never told me why you were chasing Winter," Smith reminded me.

"They're using lobster pots to transfer the cocaine," I explained. "I found one in Eagle Harbor. I watched it all night, until Winter took it. He threw something back, then bolted, so I followed. . . ." I shrugged. "We ended up here."

"Damn. Too bad he got away."

"We can track him down fast enough," I answered. "He won't get off the island."

Smith pointed to the rocks on the left. A pencil-thin beam of light from his palm-sized flashlight glanced over the stones. "I think your gun's around here."

A few minutes of searching revealed the barrel protruding from a wide crevice. I recovered the Beretta, checking it quickly. When I looked up, Smith was already five paces ahead. "First thing he'll do is call his boss," he said. "By the time we find Winter, he'll have spread the word about you. The operation will snap shut like a Venus flytrap."

"Wiley thinks it was closing down anyway," I said. "He thinks the last shipments are all going out immediately. There'll be a brief delay for redistribution, but it will all be boarded up within hours."

Smith nodded. "Doesn't leave much time, does it?"

At the phone booth, I dialed the operator, who put me through. "Sheriff's Department."

"This is Hoitt," I said. "I lost Winter on the summit—"

"Jesus, Jimmy. Thank God!" exclaimed the other voice. "Hold the line, I'll get the sheriff."

I held out the phone. "Back from the dead, yet I'm still on hold."

Smith's deeply furrowed brows worked intensely. "Didn't you mention lobster pots?"

"Yes," I said. "They appear to be the drops."

"Maybe. It all works." Smith stroked his chin. "Hoitt, listen. It takes only a couple of phone calls to halt everything, even in mid-shipment. It will take a lot longer to clean up all the drops. They were active an hour ago, or Winter wouldn't have hit the bait. Are you with me?"

"Yuh," I answered slowly. "If everything was all done, they wouldn't have bothered to pull the trap."

"You caught them when they're vulnerable," mused Smith, his eyes dancing. "They have inventory out there, waiting to move. If they run without it, they lose a lot of money. Those buoys, Hoitt. They've left us an opening."

"We've only discovered two after searching all week."

"Then you haven't been looking in the right places." He vaulted onto a rock to get a better view of the sea. "It'll be dawn in an hour. We've got to be out there before then."

"What do you mean, 'we'?"

"This is my home, too, now. As much as you may not want to admit it, I belong here as much as you. I don't want this in my home. If we can clean it up now, and be done with it—good."

The phone clicked as the hold snapped off. "Hoitt?" bellowed Walker. "Are you all right?"

"Yes, sir, I'm fine." I clapped my hand over the receiver. "Out where?"

"On the water. We'll have to look somewhere else. Assemble the pieces together in a new way." He jumped down. "We've got to go. Now."

"Hoitt? What's going on?"

I had no time to decide which direction to follow. I had to decide quickly. With so little time, emotion played a large part in my decision. "Sheriff, I have a hot lead. White hot. I have to move fast.

A man named Dave Winter picked up the Eagle Harbor buoy. Before I could ask him about it, he ran. I followed him up Cadillac, and lost him there. Telling the sheriff about Smith would not aid my case, so I omitted any reference. I felt only slightly guilty. "I have to go back to Eagle Harbor right away. Find Winter; don't let him get off the island. He's deep into this."

"We need your evidence," insisted Walker. "Jimmy, you're part of a team. This is not a lone-wolf operation."

"If I take the time to report, my tip will go stone cold dead." I took a deep breath. "I'm certain it leads directly to the man we want."

"All the more reason to report what you've got. We'll move immediately, set up a command post down there. Meet me at—"

"Sir, I have to go."

"Jimmy, you listen to me, God damn you!" roared Walker. "You play this against me, and I'll have your ass for breakfast! Do you understand me? Are you listening, Hoitt? Get in here right now or—"

Directed by parts of my mind I did not understand, my left hand depressed the hook.

"Let me guess," said Smith cheerfully. "The good sheriff did not approve."

"The sheriff vehemently objected." I hung up the receiver. "I don't think I'll be a detective much longer."

"If we can pull this off, you may find yourself bypassing the county sheriff's office entirely."

"If we fail, I'm going to need to buy a boat, because the only person who'll hire me will be me."

Smith grinned, a smile that failed to convey any warmth. "If we fail, we'll be dead." He slapped me on the back and started to jog down the road. "We'll take my boat. Meet me at the dock as soon as you can get there."

I stared after him, wondering why the hell I was chucking a promising career with the Hancock County Sheriff's Department to pursue a murdering drug smuggler with an old man I had not known a week. As I stared after Smith, I realized two things. He was a fit and athletic man, who appeared younger than I knew him to be. If his mind was as sharp as his body, he was acute indeed. He also had a confidence and conviction that could not be easily shaken. He was damn sure of himself. Wiley tried to project such confidence, but failed to inspire it. I ran to my truck as Smith jogged to the other lot.

Less than a half-hour later I knelt on *Aquila*'s high prow as Smith manned the helm, one hand on the wheel, one hand on the throttle as he backed clear. He checked astern, watching the water pass alongside. I let go the line; the mooring buoy dropped clear, splashing into the harbor. The engine hesitated as Smith shifted gears, swung the rudder over, and powered away, rounding the outer moorings and aiming for the breakwater.

I kept low, one hand on the cabin rail as I made my way aft from the bow. I landed with a heavy thud in the cockpit, joining Smith in the deckhouse. The air was thick and stale, utterly windless except for the reluctant wind created by our speed. It would be a hot, sticky day when the sun rose. A thick, clinging fog lurked in wait for us beyond the breakwater.

Smith concentrated on maneuvering around the obstructions between us and the open ocean. He split his time between watching the starboard side and looking ahead. When the gray outlines of the dock had long since disappeared, off to starboard the flat granite blocks of the breakwater slid past. Smith smiled broadly, focusing all his attention forward. "That's the hardest part." He reached past the polished mahogany wheel and snapped on his instruments: fathometer, radio, radar, and a brand new sat-nav. He advanced the throttle, eliciting a deeper snarl from the deck, a broader wash behind the transom, and a sharper incline to the deck as the prop bit more deeply into the water.

"Where are we headed?" I asked.

"Out."

"Anywhere in particular?"

"Yup." The farthest instrument back of the helm was a CRT screen surrounded by flat film controls. He switched it on, punched three buttons, and a small chart etched in green appeared: the outlines of the islands, harbors, and positions of navigational aids I knew too well to miss. I'd seen the electronic charts only at boat shows or in the shop. "We need a starting point."

"We could throw a dart at the chart," I said, only half joking.

"I'm connecting two facts. One: If they're using lobster pots, they must be so isolated that when the illegal contents are withdrawn, it can be done in privacy. Therefore, we head to a sparsely populated buoy zone. Offshore, away from most other traps."

"Deep water," I said.

"But not so deep that it looks suspicious. A lone trap laid in a hundred fathoms would look damn strange."

I checked the fathometer. It read only eight fathoms, but increased rapidly. "So we go deeper, but not too deep."

"Two: It's clear the lobstermen are the middlemen. Another

boat makes the drops, probably at night. Fog, rain, low cloud, any-thing—the worse the weather, the better. No one to see them. With the right boat, they could reach the drops in any weather. To make sure everyone knows where all the buoys and traps are, they need a common, reliable reference unhindered by weather. Why not a navi-gational buoy, regularly maintained by the Coast Guard?"

Assembling the same pieces I had juggled for days together in a new way, Smith reached a solution that made a lot of sense. The quarry Smith hypothesized was far more clever than the plodding one Wiley chased. I began to uncover a deeper respect for the former captain. "I suppose there just happens to be one off Eagle Harbor? Deep water, remote from everyone else?"

"Off Mount Desert Island, anyway." He pointed to a spot on the map around nine miles east-southeast of Bunker Head. "A navi-gational buoy. Well out, so the delivery boat, whatever it is, never has to approach too close. Can be located in all weather. A large buoy makes the perfect marker."

I squinted at the chart. "It's in 120 feet."

"Deep, but not too deep."

"All right, I'm convinced," I replied. "Once we reach the buoy, where to?"

He shook his head. "I don't know. We'll have to wing it."

We made rapid progress through the swell. Concealed by fog and without needing to avoid any other vessels, we headed directly for the buoy from the moment we cleared the breakwater. I had fished those waters, but I was a day sailor. When I ventured forth at night, I did not go far. I stayed in port in bad weather. I knew the essentials of using radar, but rarely needed to. Smith made finding the big buoy easy despite the poor visibility. About forty minutes after dropping the mooring, Smith pulled back the throttle. The tall red buoy coalesced before us, shrouded in fog. "Hard to miss, isn't it?" said Smith.

"Easy to find, under all conditions."

Smith nodded. "That's what buoys are for. They're hardly secret weapons."

Our momentum fell away. With no wind and a calm sea, the dis-tance between us and the buoy opened slowly. "Now what?" I asked. "I could go aboard and search it."

"You'd be wasting your time."

"Then where to?"

"A damn good question." He walked aft, set his foot on the transom, and stared out into the fog. "Think like they do. Once you've made it this far, how do you find the right location. Where do you look for the next marker?"

I tried to view the problem from the other side. The next marker had to be impossible to miss in all weather. Sighting by landmark was out of the question. The marker also had to be easy to use, easy to conceal. I tried to consider my own skills. I realized I knew next to nothing about detailed navigation.

"Simple," said Smith. I thought he had the answer, but found he had merely echoed my own thoughts. "It has to be a simple, easy method anyone could employ."

"How deep is deep enough?" I asked. "We've got 120 feet here. Should we head toward deeper water, or head in?"

Smith shrugged. "Hell, I don't know. I'd say anywhere around a hundred feet would be perfect, and here we are—"

He looked past me, when suddenly his eyes locked on something. The sparkle I had seen on the summit returned. "Jimmy, you've hit it." He surged past me to the instrument cluster. He flipped a switch on the fathometer, changing the readout to feet. "That's the key."

"One hundred and thirteen feet of water? What the hell is so significant about that?"

"Not a damn thing. The best thing about a fathometer is it works in all weather, under any conditions. It can't be fooled, and any idiot who can tell time can read one. Plus, everybody's got one. Nothing suspicious about it. This is it."

For the first time during the investigation I finally realized how brilliant the whole operation must be. No trivial solutions would solve this problem. I'd need to give the other side a lot more credit. "They get dropped in 113 feet?"

"You're missing the big picture. The other traps all get dropped at the *exact same depth* as the buoy," he said excitedly. "Under any condition, you can follow the contour."

"About every boat has radar, too. Why not take radar bearings?"

"Bearings on what? For radar to work the buoy would have to stand out—then everybody would notice. If you go by bearing—say Duck Island at one hundred—you have to know the target and the bearing line. The contour is easy. Nothing to remember or write down. Just find the buoy, read the depth, and follow the contour."

I began to understand. It was clever, yet easy to follow. "So we follow the depth?"

"We return to the navigational buoy, take a sounding, check the chart, and follow the contour. Maybe we'll find something."

"Worth a shot," I said.

"Good. You watch port, I'll take starboard."

Smith leaned out the starboard side of the deckhouse, one hand on the wheel. I mounted the gunwale, grabbed the rail, and hung over the port side. The tide set had pushed us out of sight of the buoy. A quick radar fix and a minute's thrust put us back on it. "One hundred twenty-two feet," he called.

"What happens at high tide?"

"Doesn't matter. Whatever the depth is right here, the same depth will be found all along the line."

Subtle, I thought. Brilliant.

"Which way?" he asked. "Northeast or southwest?"

For no particular reason, I replied, "Northeast."

He accelerated, rounded the buoy, cruising on our new course. It took Smith a while to adjust to waves, wind, and the contour of the bottom so we stayed on the line. We didn't make much speed, but we didn't want to miss anything. The rising sun suffused the sky with a luminous glow, like a flame through smoke. The temperature began to climb, dragging the humidity along with it. I threw my light jacket into the boat.

The fog prevented me from seeing more than twenty yards. Consequently, I spent most of my time searching the sea out along the beam. We occasionally passed buoys, but none were the right color. "Any luck?" I called.

"Keep looking."

I concentrated so hard on penetrating the dingy fog well off the beam that I nearly missed the buoy when it passed close alongside. Had it not bounced off the side, I might have missed it entirely. "Ho!" I cried. "Buoy alongside!"

Smith quickly checked the radar, looked all around, shifted into reverse, and swung the wheel hard. "Keep your eye on it! Don't lose it!"

I moved aft to keep the buoy in sight. "It's dead astern, now."

He juggled the throttle and helm as I kept my eyes fixed on the buoy. We had not been moving quickly, but by the time we slowed, I lost it. "Can't see it."

"Keep your eyes fixed on its last location," said Smith. "I'm backing down."

The boat gained sternway, Smith carefully manipulating the controls to keep us moving slowly. The buoy suddenly materialized out of the fog, just a few feet from where I had been staring. "Buoy twenty feet aft."

Smith killed our progress. The prop-wash sent the buoy spinning, but it did not drift. "Which side?"

"Port."

"Good."

I found an eight-foot boat hook while he backed slowly. I anchored myself in the closest corner, leaning farther out over the side than I should have. An inopportune wave pushed the buoy away, then the suction off the stern drew it closer. I grabbed the post. "Got it!"

"Bring it up to the winch."

I dragged myself into the boat before hauling the buoy forward. Smith hung the buoy on a hook, then pulled enough line to get three turns around the drum. "Twenty fathoms means around 135 feet of line. This'll take a couple minutes."

It seemed longer before an indistinct shape showed beneath the waves, just before it splashed out of the ocean. Smith halted the winch and swung a lobster trap aboard. I helped him lower it onto the deck. We had snared an ordinary trap of plastic-coated wire mesh, two wide hoops enmeshed in netting inside the frame. Inside the trap parlor we found no lobsters, only a ripped, empty bait bag and two bricks to weight down the trap.

"Looks a lot like a regular trap," commented Smith.

"Maybe it's a decoy," I said, disappointment thicker in my voice than the coating of green, weedy slime on the trap. "Maybe they reached it first."

Smith stroked his chin thoughtfully. "Remember, it's important to look uninteresting." He opened the two latches and reached inside. He removed the bait bag, gingerly holding it to his nose. "This bag has never been used."

He reached in again to remove a brick. He weighed it in his hand, carefully running his fingers around the edge. "Hmm," he said. With no warning, he slammed the brick onto the deck planking.

Except for occasional training sessions, I had never had occasion to see cocaine. When a state police instructor came down to lecture us at our annual drug-enforcement training session, he brought a small sample so we could see what we were seeking. The sample came in a small, sealed glass container the size of a test tube. As an ordinary patrolman, even when the county sheriff's office made a bust, I never saw the evidence. Less than a week after elevation to detective, however, I now stared at it in the wild. I was numbed. I looked up at Smith, who nodded. I tentatively picked up one of the small polyethylene-wrapped bags. The plastic felt as cold as the water from which it had just been plucked. The powder inside filled the bag so densely it felt like a solid mass. "I think we're onto something," I finally said.

"Prosecution Exhibit A." Smith picked up the second brick and smashed it: another package popped out. He looked over the brick in his hand. It was hollow inside. The shell of ceramic was only a half-inch thick. He set the piece down, recovering the bag of white powder from the crumbled brick remains. He held it up to his nose. "Just smells like plastic." Grasping the bag firmly in hand, he moved his hand up and down to gauge the weight. "A pound or so. Probably half a kilo."

"A key of coke in every trap," I said dully. "What a deal."

"With wholesale at around two thousand an ounce, someone paid about seventy thousand dollars for this lobster trap," said Smith. "Even after paying the fisherman to bring these in, and the cost of having it brought to New York or Boston, there's a lot of money in here. Not a bad day's haul."

The files and the scope of the DEA operation gave me a good idea of the money involved in this operation. Not until uncovering part of it, physically touching it, did the incredible magnitude reach me personally. Even with just ten traps hauled once a month, someone earned eight million dollars a year in the Eagle Harbor drug trade. Ten traps a month for the police to find, scattered over an area where on any summer day thousands of traps were hauled up, cleaned, and set again. It needed only a handful of fishermen out of the hundreds around. No wonder the sheriff's office had never investigated. The drug traffic would blend into the legitimate operations of the local fleet even if increased tenfold from my meager projections! We never had a chance. I gingerly replaced the package beside the brick it had come from. I looked at Smith, who seemed as transfixed by the substance in his hand as I. "Where do you get bricks like that?"

He shrugged. "Homemade, most likely. Make a form, press 'em out, then bake 'em. Pack the coke so it's dense, and the weight is about right. A little epoxy to hold it all together and you're in business."

"If we can find the kiln where they make these, we can—"

"Forget it. You don't need a kiln for this. You can form them in a wine press, bake them in a gas grill, and that's that."

"A wine press?" I asked.

"Anything to crank up the pressure. A wine press is easy to get, easy to hide."

"Or a cider press," I groaned.

Smith nodded. "I suppose so. Why?"

"There's been a business in cider presses lately." I told him what Adams had told me, all the while wishing I'd asked myself more questions. "Now what?"

Smith placed his sample beside mine. "I don't know."

"If everything is being rolled up, why is this trap still here?" I asked. "Could it have been missed?"

"You don't misplace a hundred thousand dollars. I know I don't." Smith leaned against the gunwale. "As far as we know, the operation hasn't been rolled up yet," he said pensively.

"We can't be sure, though Winter's actions imply it's still an open pipeline."

"Sometimes there's a huge delay between placing an order and receiving the merchandise," said Smith. "If the man now running the operation did kill Frederickson, which is likely, he might not have expected such furor so soon after the accident."

I nodded. "If he had placed a large order before the murder, he might be unable to halt delivery."

"Right. For a few million on a last score, he might be tempted to hang around, stay low until it comes in, and send it down the line. Then he could leave safely and profitably."

I picked up the bag. "This might be the last shipment for a while."

"With all the heat Wiley has laid down, this could be the last shipment forever."

"Why wasn't it picked up?"

Smith shrugged. "Fog. Broken engine—who knows? It might be here because it just got here. To maintain the cover, it wouldn't be pulled at night. Lobstermen don't go out at night, so that would be suspicious. The rightful owner could be headed out now."

I stared at the deck, at the jagged, broken edges of the bricks. "Can't put it back, can we?"

He shook his head. "We'll have to lose the buoy and the trap." He went to the winch, pulled a long knife from a sheath on his belt, cleanly slicing the line about three feet below the buoy. He kept the bitter end in his hand, knelt on the deck, and hacked away with the knife.

"What are you doing?" I asked.

"This way, it'll look like a prop cut. It'll stand up to a cursory examination, if it ever gets found." He finished hacking, then flung the buoy overboard. Deprived of the drag from the line, it flopped on its side. "Anybody finds that, they'll figure someone ran over the line and cut it. Happens all the time."

"What about the cocaine?"

"I'll stow it below. It's useless in court, but might help you convince Walker or Wiley that you're onto something. When you need it, you'll know where it is. Throw the fake bricks over the side. Take four or five of my bricks," he pointed toward the far corner of the fantail. "Toss 'em in the trap, kick it over the side. No one will ever find it."

"Done." He went below. I picked up three bricks, took a fourth to make sure, and put them inside. I tossed in the bait bag, lifted the waterlogged trap onto the gunwale, and shoved it over. I pulled all the line off the winch and let the dead weight of the trap pull it down. The brick pieces followed, all the evidence eradicated before Smith returned topside.

"I had a thought," he said. "If a shipment did arrive recently, there's no reason to think it's only a couple of keys. There's bound to be more of these things around. Even a small shipment would need, say, ten traps."

"Some might be empty," I said. "After all, Dave Winter came in last night."

"But a few extra could be decoys. Even if half the shipment is in, there's likely to be five or more out here."

"How the hell are we going to find even one?" I said. "There's miles of coastline to search, even if we stay on the contour."

Smith shrugged again. "Maybe they're spaced at even intervals."

"Of what?" I said. "A thousand feet? A mile?"

"We'll follow the contour until we find another one."

"In this fog it will take us an hour to search a mile or two," I said. "If they're spaced out around Mount Desert, then traps could be separated by five miles or more."

"We have to start somewhere." He took the helm, squinting at the chart. "This contour runs up into Frenchman Bay. Goes in pretty close before heading out again. Worth following, at least for a while."

"All right." I pointed at his electronic chart. "Can that thing tell you how far we've come from the navigational buoy?"

"That's what radar's for." He snapped on the ACTIVE button, illuminating the screen with a sickly green glow. He set the scale at 1.2 nautical miles. The navigational buoy showed up clearly off our port quarter. Another button imposed range circles on the screen. "It's three-quarters of a mile back." He checked the fathometer. "We drifted a little deeper, maybe fifty yards. Back on course quick enough."

"I don't see many other boats," I wondered aloud. Business was too profitable in the early season to let traps sit idle, fog or no fog. "In fact, I don't see any."

He pointed at an indistinct smear near the edge. "There's one. Open runabout, probably. Maybe a sailboat. It's a foggy Saturday; there won't be too many boats around." He gunned the throttle and gathered steerageway. "I'll head back to the buoy so we can measure the whole distance."

"Can this thing show how many boats are out?" I asked. "Especially close in?"

"Change the scale. Top corner."

I pushed a button at the corner. The picture disappeared for a second, then rematerialized behind the unseen wand as it swept the circle. The corner read 36 nm. "That should do it." At long range, the ghost of a sailboat shrunk to a fuzzy point. The buoy showed clearly, a hot white point of light; five other oblongs denoted boats. None was more than three miles beyond the ghostlike line of the shore.

An unexpected point caught my eye. Along the shore, near the Eagle Harbor breakwater, a fine pinpoint of light glowed. I lacked the skill to read a sophisticated radar set; the one on the *Janet Kathleen III* was more like something from a U-boat. I pointed out the anomaly to Smith. "What's that?"

He squinted at the screen. "I'm not sure."

"Lighthouse?"

"There isn't one there. Besides, it's too small." He stared at the screen. "Look: there's a glitch above it, too." Nearer the top of the screen a second point, well inland, just barely stood out of the ground clutter. "They align."

"Range marks? Antenna?"

"Antennas aren't so sharp." He cocked his head. "Looks like a radar reflector."

At first I missed what he said, then a distant memory aligned with his statement, and another piece of the puzzle fell into place. "It *is* a radar reflector."

"How do you know?"

I briefly related the story of the radar reflector Robyn and I had found. "That's how they find the buoys."

Smith stared at the screen. "Of course. I should have known. Line up two points—the oldest nav aid in the sailor's inventory." He tapped the screen near the upper contact. "I'll bet that's on high ground—up Bernard Mountain—visible from the entire southern quadrant. Your reflector down on the shore, this one here—a whole set spotted radially around the island."

Like the range marks showing a channel, aligning the two points would give any boat the same line. Follow the depth contour until the points aligned, and claim your reward. Simple, efficient, subtle— it was pure genius. "Jesus, that's clever."

Smith put the boat back in gear, swung the wheel hard, and powered away. "I'll run us on the contour. You watch the radar. The reflectors are low; they'll only be visible along a narrow arc." I remembered the cone with the rubbery coating. These guys were thorough. Maybe we were hopelessly outclassed, I thought. "Tell me if any boats head our way. Keep a sharp eye on the radar for faint echoes forward, cause I'm running blind."

We headed into the fog, our foaming wake merging with the swirling fog to close our passage astern. Smith pushed hard, hauling us into the fog where we could never see more than fifty feet. I kept my eyes glued to the radar while he checked for buoys and watched the fathometer. Between the two of us, I figured, we had a good chance of avoiding any obstructions.

After we had cruised easterly about half a mile, the pinpoint on the screen abruptly dropped out of sight. I drew Smith's attention to it. He spared the radar a glance. "Tight, narrow focus. That means quality equipment, which means a lot of money."

Smith made small course adjustments to keep us on the contour as I advised him about traffic. Two solid contacts and a blurry one headed for the open sea. A tiny heading alteration could bring any of them dangerously close. Any boat that ran along the twenty-fathom line could legitimately be classified a suspect. The three boats continued advancing, never deviating from their outward courses. Meanwhile, no reflectors. "Maybe there aren't any more," I said.

"We've only covered two miles," replied Smith. "Too soon to give up."

The words had no sooner left his lips than another pinpoint flashed on the shoreline, approximately three miles east-northeast of Eagle Harbor. "Got one!"

Smith chopped the throttle immediately, scanning the screen. "Looks good." He took a clear plastic ruler from the tray beside his wheel, laying it over the screen. "Another quarter mile, I guess. Still no boats close by."

"Nearest boat is still three and a half miles away," I said. "He rounded the end of Cranberry Island and arrowed on about 120. If he holds his course, he'll pass a mile astern."

"The farther the better. When the ruler cuts through the center, let me know. I've got to watch the depth."

A gentle kick from the prop pushed us into the light swell with just enough steerageway to maintain control. I kept my eyes glued to the screen, unblinking, my eyes starting to sting in the salty air. The point slid closer to the center, closer still, then seemed to jump to one side as the ruler cut the center. "On the money."

Smith killed our way. "Still on the beam?"

"Yuh."

"You take port and aft."

Mounting the port gunwale, I grabbed the pilothouse wall and leaned over the side. The rising sun had burned off some of the fog, increasing visibility to around two hundred feet, with rare patches twice that. It was just past six in the morning. The fog would be completely gone in less than two hours. Soon the ocean would be alive with recreational and commercial vessels, just like every other summer Saturday. We had little time.

Precise navigation and clearing fog were on our side. Before I had completed even one sweep off the port side, Smith yelled from starboard. "Got it. I'll run in closer; you grab it."

"Aye, aye." I jumped onto the deck, hopping across to the far side. We came up very close. It took only the merest goosing of the throttle to put the buoy alongside. I grabbed the post, held on tightly, and dragged it over the sheave and around the drum of the winch. As I hauled, Smith took a strain on the line, then kicked on the winch. The dripping, seaweed-covered trap bumped against the hull soon afterward. It looked exactly like the last one, down to the worn but empty bait bag and two identical bricks. I grabbed the trap and set it on the gunwale. Smith knelt beside it, studying the bricks. He picked up one of his own, stared at it for a moment, then re-examined the others. He grinned as he put his brick away. "I think it's loaded. They don't look like standard masonry bricks."

"Seen enough?"

"Kick it over the side. Let's see if anyone bites."

"That could take hours," I morosely pointed out.

He shrugged. "We don't have anything else to do. We could look for others, but who's to say they'd be taken any sooner?"

"It could take days."

"If they're in no hurry, then neither are we."

He was right. "We drop it, then linger?"

"Half right." He removed the line from the winch, threw the buoy over the side, then kicked the trap after it. "If we stay too close, the runner will see us."

"We can hide in the fog, at least until it clears."

"Obviously, they have radar, just like us," said Smith patiently. "Don't think they're backward or stupid. It will get you killed."

He'd caught me again. "Then what now?"

"We'll drop a couple traps," he explained. "I've got plastic reflectors down below. We'll put them on the posts. We'll get a decent return, and they shouldn't arouse suspicions. We'll surround this buoy, then cruise around watching our buoys. We'll never have to come within five miles. If a boat goes inside our triangle, we'll have the guy we're after."

"You're as devious as they are," I said.

"You have to be." He pointed aft. "The traps on the port side should have enough line. Take three off the rack, check the hitches. I'll get the reflectors."

It took us a half-hour to set the traps in a large triangle around the target. By then the fog had lifted a little more, raising visibility another hundred feet. Smith switched to a low scale on the radar, showing me the reflectors' images. They were not as distinct as other boats or even the shore marker, but they clearly stood out from the clutter. Switching to the ten-mile scale as the buoys receded into the fog, Smith accelerated toward shore.

We patrolled aimlessly up and down the coast, Smith navigating by computer chart as I kept an eye on the radar. Our distance from the target varied from two to six miles as we killed time, waiting. By half past seven, all vestiges of fog were gone and a baking, hazy sunshine grilled us mercilessly. Mount Desert Island became a shimmering lump off the beam. Visibility was good, but the haze limited acuity to about five miles. We increased our range from the buoys, up to twelve miles off. We spent the morning using fuel, getting hungry, and missing the sleep we had not had the night before.

At 11:30 all vestiges of hunger and tiredness evaporated like the morning fog. A boat with a hard radar signature like a lobster boat's cruised at high speed, straight out to sea. While we could no longer see the onshore bearing marks, from what I remembered of the topography, the target followed the radar line dead on. Smith brought *Aquila* around in a long, graceful turn, then settled onto a new intercept course. "I'll aim for his base course," he said. "When he heads north for home, we can get him."

The target held its seaward course as we paralleled the shore. After five minutes, Smith abruptly cut power, swinging the rudder hard over to pivot his boat in a tight circle.

"What's the matter?" I asked.

"Nothing," he replied. "If he's watching, I want him to think we're pulling traps. We'll stay put for five more minutes, then go on."

Before we restarted, the other boat penetrated the triangle. I couldn't believe how tightly wound the morning had made me. My hand trembled as I activated the radar range finder. "He took the bait."

"Good," said Smith. If he suffered the same excitement, he hid it from me. "Time for us to get moving."

The second hand on my watch seemed to stop. I slapped my wrist, but the watch did not run any faster. Finally, the target began to move. The boat closed a circle, retracing his course toward shore. Then the dream of an easy intercept died: only a hundred yards from the triangle, the blip turned away and accelerated.

"Damn it!" cried Smith. "He's going west." He swung the wheel hard left, advancing the throttle to the stops. The engine roared, the bow jumped up as *Aquila* surged to the pursuit.

I braced my legs wide, clutching the deckhouse roof. I had to lean forward to read the radar, but the thrust kept me from falling. I had to yell over the engine, even though Smith stood only a few feet away. "What's the rush?"

"He's going too far west," hollered Smith. "We're going to be five miles astern of him, instead of on his beam. We wasted too much time playing fisherman."

Aquila hit her planing speed: the bow came down, the deck leveled. Smith retarded the throttle, knocking the roaring engine down to an insistent clamor. The deck vibrated as a foaming white wake snaked away from the stern. The frothy white water turned green farther back, merging with the waves angling back. "Can we catch him?"

"We'll try," said Smith, his mouth set grimly. "We're in a flat-out speed race. It's pretty much up to the engines now." He tapped the radar set. "Keep an eye on him. If he changes course, we'll need to act quickly."

"Yes, sir." We flew over the ocean. Only when the bow crashed into a wave flat on did we slow momentarily before we surfed through the water again. The radar contact did exactly the same thing. It was difficult to gauge their speed; watching them pass Swan's Island I estimated it at about twenty-five knots—fast enough for a lobster boat. A glance at Smith's speed log read thirty-three knots.

Other boats were green blips flashing by the edges of the screen, their courses holding them well clear. As the range closed to the target, I kept the scale at a minimum to catch any course variations. Our course became an arc as we approached the island, but the target course remained laser straight. "He's steady on course," I said. "Want to guess where he's headed?"

"A stab in the dark: Eagle Harbor."

"On the money."

Smith checked the radar. "You sure?"

"Pretty sure."

I was beginning to learn the man's subtleties. I knew from his sudden silence and distant gaze he considered a new tactic. "I'm going to run for shore. If he suspects he's being followed, that might fool him. We can reach the breakwater before he closes within a mile. We'll be lost in the clutter, even if he is still watching."

"Then we watch him once he reaches the harbor?"

"That's my plan."

Our superior speed brought us off the east ridge of Eagle Harbor before the target closed within two miles. As Smith eased back the throttle, the bow fell and the towering wave that had chased us advanced, lifting the stern as it slipped under the hull and made its way into the harbor without us. After the high-speed run, it seemed like drifting. I missed the speed, the sense that we were actively doing something.

Smith killed the engine short of the daymark atop the riprap. He went aft and leaned on one thigh as he wedged his foot into the corner where the transom met the gunwale. Crow's feet at the edge of his eyes deepened into canyons while he squinted into the blinding sun. The rolling crash of waves breaking against the rocky base of the breakwater replaced the drone of the engine. A light breeze nudged us toward the rocks. I wondered why he waited.

"I never completely trust any instruments," he said. "Before we commit ourselves, I want to visually verify that he's heading in."

I checked the radar, selecting a lower scale calibrated in yards. "He should be about fourteen hundred yards away, just aft of the port beam."

When Smith didn't reply, I began to repeat my message. "I heard you," he said.

Drifting, we covered half the distance toward the breakwater before Smith resumed the helm. "He's heading in. We'll go first."

The engine turned over with barely a touch of the starter, settling into a muted snarl that stuttered as waves covered and uncovered the exhaust. Smith rounded the daymark and brought us into the harbor.

Midday brought a clutter of people, boats, and gear to the cramped dock. Smith avoided it all, sliding into the moorings. Maneuvering in a long, sweeping arc, he approached the pick-up buoy from downwind, reaching neutral so accurately it took barely a second's reverse power to halt the boat with her prow directly over the mooring buoy. I pulled it up, slid the eye over the cleat, and secured it with a lighter cord. "What are we going to do when he comes in?" I asked, as I joined him in the deckhouse.

"Depends on him. As soon as he does something, I'll tell you what we'll do."

"That's pretty defensive."

He shrugged. "We have so little to go on. We can't risk going out on a limb." Abruptly Smith turned away from the helm. "We can cover him better if we split. We'll take the skiff in. You stay on the dock and I'll row back here."

It seemed exactly the wrong time for us to split. "What will that accomplish?"

"If he heads for shore, you get your truck and pick me up at the dock. If he heads back out, I'll bring the boat and meet you at the dock."

Three minutes later I stood alone, watching Smith row back. I posted myself on the end of the main dock, where I could lean comfortably against the rail, with an unobtrusive, unobstructed view of the harbor. The municipal landing consists of a single large float, able to accommodate three boats, plus a small, one-boat fuel and bait dock on the side opposite the launch ramp. A big cabin cruiser, its crew using the dock freshwater hose to clean off the foredeck, took up the seaward side of the main float. An unoccupied lobster boat, its engine cover up, used the east side. On the west, a thirty-foot cruising sailboat that smelled rented awaited the return of her crew. Over on the fuel dock waited George Carter's green-hulled Newman. Just beyond the breakwater, a gleaming white boat pushed a thick wave before her as she arrowed for the channel.

A rumble close by took my attention. Alongside the dock a stretch of cracked gray pavement led down into the water. Extremely active during launching season or before a hurricane, this launching ramp saw little use during the summer. Today the wounded *Die Walküre*, listing, exhaust coming from just one port, nosed its way toward the ramp. A massive white-and-black Peterbilt from Southwest Harbor backed a hydraulic boat trailer down the ramp to meet the boat. The driver climbed down to operate the cable controls at the front of the trailer. Yelling back and forth between driver and skipper brought the bow into the trailer yoke. The truck driver threw across a line, with which the lithe woman secured the shackle to the bow cleat. The winch whine took over from the boat engine, easing

Die Walküre onto the trailer bed. I still didn't trust him; I noted the name of the boat hauler and made a mental note to call later and find the disposition of the speedboat.

I looked out again. The beamy white boat, her bow high out of the water, was headed toward the dock. I glanced out at Smith: his foot braced on the gunwale, he watched the boat pass. The newcomer approached dead on. I could see only its bow. Sunlight diffracted off dozens of scratches and salt-spray splotches on the plexiglass windshield, which prevented me from identifying anyone aboard. I thought there were two people inside, but I couldn't be certain. The bow numbers began to resolve. I ran through them several times to memorize the registration.

Carter's boat roared to life. Behind a huge patch of roiled water, he cast off, leaving the fuel dock open to allow the suspect boat to take its place.

As the boat came closer, she showed her broadside. There were indeed two people aboard. A pale, gaunt man with a beard peered over the side as he came up to the dock. Standing behind him, in an identical uniform of faded blue jeans and a worn T-shirt, an equally tall woman stood ready with dock lines. A pile of traps filled the stern. I wondered which contained contraband.

Criminal or not, the bearded man handled his ship well, touching the dock with only a tiny bump. The woman jumped across the narrow gap to land firmly, lines in hand. After tying up, she spoke to the man. He nodded. She shrugged, then headed up the walkway toward me.

I hesitated. I had not expected them to split up. Who should I follow? I looked out to Smith. He had found a better view by sitting on the deckhouse roof, looking busy with some frayed lines in his hands. He appeared as unsure as I felt. Unlike me, however, he had no decision to make. While the woman carried nothing in her hands, during the ride in she'd had plenty of time to stash the cocaine on her person. It only had to be invisible against a cursory glance; she would not expect an inquisition at the dock. Yet she might have left it aboard.

Behind the deckhouse, a black buoy at the end of a short length of line hid behind a trap loaded only with a bait bag and the ubiquitous bricks. Were they real, or did I stare at a hundred thousand dollars worth of fake brick? I wanted to stay with the drugs, but where the hell were they? The boat did not appear likely to leave soon. If it did, Smith would have to follow it. When the woman stepped off the dock and started toward the road I followed, four steps back.

She walked confidently, looking only ahead. If she felt any nervousness, she didn't show it. She was about five-nine, 140 pounds, with short brown hair that curled close to her head. In the small world of the lobster fraternity, I knew many and recognized even more. I didn't know these people. I used to feel it was a tight, close-knit community sharing a common cause. Despite my personal ties, I'd had no inkling that some in my community smuggled millions of dollars' worth of cocaine into Maine until an outsider told me so. It made me wonder just how well I knew these people. The woman before me, the man in the boat, and who knew how many more were complete strangers.

Wearing his starched apron with the Scott's Market logo, Ned Tobey came down the hill. In his late teens, Ned was delighted to work close to home at a job that guaranteed free nights. He had once been my sister's boyfriend, and I knew him pretty well. His small, black eyes darted back and forth from the parking lot to the water, searching. He knew me. He knew who I was, and might even know what I was investigating. Would he run? I braced, ready to chase him if he bolted, trying to decide what to do with three suspects. His roving gaze fell on me. An instant's hesitation hung there, then he cheerfully waved, and moved on.

He approached the woman in jeans. They exchanged a few words. The thought of Ned implicated in the smuggling ring hit me hard. How deeply had this plague penetrated? Could we ever uproot it all? Ned nodded to the woman, following her to the fuel dock. Trying to appear unconcerned, I pressed against the rail and contemplated the sea as they passed. Ned took a key from his pocket, using it to turn on the fuel pump. He handed her the nozzle, which she dragged over to the boat, where the bearded man guided it into his tank. Ned had nothing to do with the smuggling. My overactive imagination would soon incriminate everyone.

The tank must have been pretty full; the nozzle came out in two minutes. Installed in the late sixties and only repaired, never modified, this was known as the slowest marine pump on the island. My father, who inevitably let his tank run nearly dry before refueling, would spend twenty minutes topping off. The *Janet Kathleen III* had been built just before the gas crisis of 1974, so she had enormous tanks. Even so, she could be refueled almost anywhere else in half the time.

Ned noted the readings, shut off the pump, and locked down the nozzle. The woman paid him in cash, waving off the receipt. She reboarded. Ned headed back to the store. The bearded man started the engine. Dirty brown water drifted forward along the hull as she backed clear, then pulled away. For the first time since picking up the boat, I had a clear view of her nameboard: *Susanne L*, plastered in unimaginative black block letters across the transom. Smaller script underneath revealed Northeast Harbor as her home port.

I headed for the float, preparing to meet Smith. Clearly, nothing had happened in Eagle Harbor. They'd come merely to refuel. I began to wonder if we had followed the right boat. I also wondered for the first time what sort of job I might seek after police work.

As she headed back out to sea, the *Susanne L* did a curious thing. Instead of aiming directly for the channel, she headed in amongst the moorings. She passed directly off the red bow of *Aquila*, then cut left through the midst of the moored boats on her way out. For a moment she disappeared behind *Freebird*. When she came back out, she finally turned toward the breakwater, sliding into the main channel. I wished Smith would hurry, or else even with his boat's speed we would lose them. That's when I noticed a subtle change on the quarterdeck: no trap balanced on the side. That trap had been attached to the black buoy. Seeing it gone, I instantly understood the transfer.

I watched the *Susanne L* pass through the breakwater, staring so intently that I did not notice Smith rowing in until he yelled to me. I met him as he nosed his skiff into a narrow space, tossing me the painter as he shipped the oars. He gingerly stepped onto the float as I tied it up. He grinned broadly. "You saw that?"

"Hard to miss," I replied.

"Not a bad plan," he said. "Works any time, at any port. Very subtle."

"Maybe they finally made a mistake," I said optimistically. "I think we should leave it alone."

"Definitely." Smith arched his back, stretching. "I guess we wait and see."

Another opportunity to sit around killing time, I thought. I had heard how tediously mind-numbing detective work could be. I well knew the portrayal given by TV and movies was terribly inaccurate; many detectives in Maine never fired their weapon in the field through an entire career. In the past week I had been fired at, pushed off a cliff, and involved in two raids and two high-speed chases, one of them on the high seas. Yet if you added up the time devoted to those activities and compared it against the rest of my time, fully 95 percent of my waking hours had been occupied with reading files, writing reports, waiting, and watching. Another stagnant afternoon watching a damn buoy—what a challenge. "Want to stay on the dock?"

"Too obvious." He started toward the lot. "We'll go by the sea-wall, past the bank. It's close to your truck. The shadows will provide some cover, both from the sun and from whoever grabs that buoy."

"Sounds good," I lied. "How about a bite to eat?"

"Now, there's a plan."

A take-out window offered diner service for those who chose not to go inside. While I placed our order, Smith leaned casually against a post. Anyone noticing him might think he waited for lunch. Few would observe he could see not only the take-out window, but also the entire harbor.

Marie Fickett, a protégée of Ned's, handed me two grease-stained bags and a cardboard tray with two cups. I thanked her and started for the sidewalk until Smith's hand on my shoulder stopped me. He pushed gently, aiming me toward the water. "Let's walk along the water. The buildings would block our view."

Eagle Harbor had nothing even remotely approximating a beach. Jumbled rocks made walking the shore difficult at any time. Doing so while holding two bags and a tray would be even more difficult. "Only for a moment," I said. "We'll reach the seawall soon."

"Do you want to take a chance? It would take only a couple seconds to scarf up the buoy, and only a little longer to raise the trap."

I handed him the tray. "You carry these."

We picked over the rocks. I thought we looked extremely suspicious, if anyone bothered to notice. We had no place to eat on the wet, seaweed-covered rocks, and the sidewalk offered such an easier passage that anyone seeing us must assume we were up to something. I kept glancing over my shoulder every few seconds both to make sure Smith did not lose my soda as well as to check the buoy.

I set down the bags on the white-painted seawall, braced a foot on the tallest rock I could find, and pushed up. Smith handed me the tray, which I laid beside lunch before lending him a hand. I planted myself on the softest tuft of grass at the foot of a great old pine, and opened my bag. Smith shaded his eyes from the glare, staring out at the harbor. I popped my soda out of the tray, and pushed the rest toward him. "Here."

He didn't reply. The fried, greasy smell of the clams assailed my nose. I suddenly realized I was starved. I ripped open the bag, attacking delicate, sweet clams that were the tastiest around. I plopped one on my tongue. Just out of the Fryolater, it was extremely hot. Tossing it back and forth inside my mouth, I ignored the burning while exposing most of my mouth to the perfect flavor the cooks could only realize in the afternoon, between the lunch and dinner rushes, when they had time. I leaned against the tree with a satisfied smile on my face. "Ahhh." I grabbed another succulent sweet clam.

Out of the corner of my eye I saw a dark-green hull moving amidst the moorings. It began to head straight out, then slowly turned back toward the buoy. This was the one time I had actually looked forward to having a chance to sit and wait, but my respite was clearly going to be short-lived. "Uh-oh. Here we go."

Smith gazed intently toward the moorings. "That's a local boat, I think. Fletcher?"

"Paul Fletcher?" We had graduated in the same year from MDI High School. "Taller than me, blue eyes, sandy hair. He had a droopy mustache last time I saw him."

"I guess." Fletcher brought the trap aboard, then returned to his mooring. Smith grabbed his bag. "Come on."

As perfectly prepared as the clams were, when they cooled the grease congealed. I knew from experience the taste would die. I picked off another, then closed up the paper bag. They might be edible for another half-hour. "Let's go."

"Get the truck." He handed me his lunch. "I'm going back over the rocks. Park in front of O'Brien's. I'll meet you."

"Done." While he vaulted back over the seawall, I ran across the street to the truck. I threw the bags inside, placed the tray on the floor, and climbed inside. With another pursuit imminent, I had to make a conscious effort to relax, drive cautiously and safely to O'Brien's. I parked by the fire hydrant, left the engine running, and stole a couple more clams.

Smith crossed the street and climbed in beside me. "He's rowing in, alone."

I pointed into the parking lot as I munched. "See the old Monte Carlo? The cream one with the basket wheels?"

Smith squinted. "Yes?"

I nodded. "Fletcher's."

"Looks fast. If he bolts, we'll lose him."

"It's not as fast as it looks."

"You can stay with it?"

I smiled proudly. In my younger days, Paul and I had faced off more than once. "No problem."

Smith took his bag and sampled its contents. "Not bad."

"They do good work in midafternoon."

Smith chewed, gazing pensively at the lot. "I wonder if we have time to make a phone call."

"Who?" I asked.

"You should let the sheriff in on this."

"Not now." I rolled up the bag again. "Paul's on the dock now. That's him, right?"

Smith watched him walk up, then nodded. "That's the guy."

"Paul Fletcher. Damn!" I would have bet a week's pay on Paul's innocence. He drank, often to excess, but that was not unusual. He didn't smoke, and in a school where rumors circulated faster than official notices, I never heard anyone say Paul did drugs. Yet he had been more than willing to make a fast, easy buck. He'd gamble on any school function, even the drama festival plays. Morals and money never meshed with Paul. Evidently, they still didn't.

Paul threw a gym bag through the open window of the Monte Carlo, then hopped in and fired it up. He seemed in no hurry, as calm as on any other day. Only one back-up light lit as he maneuvered onto the Cove Road, heading east. Rather than make a blatant U-turn that would only draw attention, I took a slightly longer route through the church parking lot and came out onto Route 102 behind a rented Ford full of middle-aged tourists. If Fletcher drove hard, I would have to pass it on the winding road, a dangerous trick that would also give us away. Ahead, Paul kept to the legal limit. For now, at least, I had no need to pass the Ford.

Our three-car convoy meandered toward the top of the island, close to the speed limit but never exceeding it. Over the ridge, Route 102A broke away to the right. A long half-circle that rejoined 102 farther along, it ran beside the ocean and touched a part of Acadia National Park, offering many places for a clandestine meeting. Fletcher might go that way. I moved up close, where I could see Fletcher beyond the Ford. He bore left, staying on 102, but the rental elected for the scenic route. I no longer had a shield; we were open to a rearview mirror inspection. Fletcher never noticed. We plodded northward.

As we approached the village of Southwest Harbor, 102A rejoining us, Fletcher could again turn right to reach the ocean, but didn't. I kept well back, leaving room enough between us for a rusty, full-sized pickup to pull onto the road ahead. Even though the tight spacing didn't safely allow it, a dusty white Subaru with Massachusetts plates stayed on the tail of the pickup and joined the parade. I fell back farther, treading the line between riding the Subaru bumper and losing sight of Fletcher.

Our four cars passed through the stores, houses, motel, and the pair of inns that formed the town center of Southwest Harbor.

Fletcher's brake lights ignited as he drew into a streetside parking spot. The truck slowly passed through town, followed too closely by the overeager Subaru. Phillips Street led off to the right just shy of the parked Monte Carlo. I turned there, passing out of sight as Fletcher, gym bag in hand, hopped out and crossed the street.

Smith opened his door and ordered, "Let me out." I quickly obeyed. "Turn around and park on this street as close to the main road as you can," he called through the open window. He ran toward the corner as I searched for a place to turn around and park.

As I returned to the corner, a red Taurus wagon turned into traffic and pulled away. I slipped into the vacated space. Smith stood across the street at a phone booth, watching the street. I had no idea who he was calling, but crossed the street to find out. "Who are you calling?"

"No one." He hung up.

"Where's Fletcher?"

"The pharmacy up the street." He pointed to a cluster of three shops. The middle one had a large orange-and-white prescription sign hanging over the door. "He went right in."

"What now?"

"I'm going across the street." He pointed to a glass-fronted store. "I'll be in the hardware store. They've got a good window."

"And me?"

"Call the sheriff. Fletcher took the bag with him; this is the place." Without waiting for a reply, he crossed the street and went inside. I dialed "0." The operator connected me with the sheriff's office. "Hancock County Sheriff's Department."

"This is Patrolman Hoitt. I need to speak—"

"Jimmy?" said the voice. "Jeez, they been looking for you all day. Where are—"

"Shut up and listen," I snapped. "Agent Wiley and the sheriff will want to hear this. I have followed a half-kilo of cocaine. It is now being transferred at Bodwell's Pharmacy in Southwest Harbor. Tell them to move, immediately!"

"All right, Jimmy. Stay on the line—please!" The line clicked. Down the street the glass door to Bodwell's opened up. Fletcher came out, minus the gym bag. He jogged across the street, got into his car, and drove away. Smith ran across the street as the Monte Carlo went round the corner. "Are they coming?"

I held out the receiver. "I'm on hold. What do we do? Follow?"

"No." Smith watched the pharmacy. "He left the bag, we have his name. Let him go. We want what's inside."

"Why would he—" I broke off as a voice came on the line. "Hoitt? You still there?"

It was neither Walker nor the dispatcher. The voice sounded strained and distant, as if the line had gone bad while I waited. "Yes. Who's this?"

"This is Wiley," he replied. "I'm on my car phone. What do you have?"

"I have two suspects and a drop," I answered.

"Where are you?"

"Southwest Harbor. There's a pharmacy called Bodwell's, in the middle of the village."

"How do you know it's there?"

"It's a long story, sir," I said quickly. "I followed a hunch, which led to a couple more traps marked by a gold stripe. I have—"

"Where were they?"

"About three miles off Bunker Head. I also—"

"Bunker Head? Where's that?"

"Cranberry Island. South of MDI. I looked in the traps and found—"

"How many traps?"

"At least two."

"Only two?"

"We didn't have time to look for more. I confirmed the traps contained cocaine. I'm now—"

"How much?"

"What?" I snapped in frustration.

"Weight, Hoitt. How much?"

"About a kilo in each trap. Look, I can fill in the details later. Right now, I have a lead. If you want it, you'd better get down here fast."

The line buzzed and clicked a while before he spoke. "I've chased a lot of wild Maine geese, Hoitt," he said sourly. "I don't want to bag another one."

If Wiley refused to show, the case was done. Walker would be too busy chewing me out to respond, and the operation would fold before another chance came. This was it. "I am certain, sir."

"All right, Hoitt. All right. Do they know you're watching?"

"I don't think so."

"Okay. Watch it. If anybody leaves, get a description: plates, direction, all you can get. Under no circumstances rush the place yourself, no matter what. Got that? Stay outside. We'll come in and take it. When we arrive, find me. Got it?"

A burning surge of adrenaline infused my insides, quickening my pulse and filling the pit of my stomach with a ball of lead. "Yes, sir."

"We'll get some backup down to help in about ten minutes, but it'll take an hour to get everything ready. Can you hold out?"

"Yes. I'll be here."

"Keep your eyes open." The line clicked again; he was gone.

I turned to Smith. "They're moving in. It will take about an hour. Meanwhile, we watch."

"I'll go back to the hardware store. Go past the store, up the street. Try to cover the back door."

"Right." I took my Beretta from under the seat before we went our separate ways; me up the sidewalk, right past the pharmacy. I resisted an urge to stop and stare inside. I kept my vision straight ahead, walked past the block of stores, then went down a narrow lane. A magnificent hedge provided good cover. I propped myself beside a mailbox and watched.

Ten minutes later, after an older couple went inside, a Dodge Intrepid pulled up beside a hydrant across the street. The man inside, clearly a plainclothes officer, spoke briefly into a radio. I wished I had a radio to hear him. Working blind was worse than the waiting. As long as he covered the front, I decided to improve my stand. I walked along the street, past the hedge, behind the store. A metal door with triple locks guarded the back of the brick building. I couldn't see the closed door from the hedge, but if it opened I would not miss it. I settled on a rotten stump to wait.

I lost track of time as nerve-wracking excitement attacked my sense of its passing. Up the lane a blue-haired woman let her dog out; it yapped constantly at me until she opened the door to readmit it. A family of chipmunks invaded the dumpster; I saw more rodents than humans as I waited. I tensed as the back door opened. An unseen hand tossed a collapsed cardboard box onto a pile, then closed the door.

Without warning, an iron grip locked onto my collar, lifted me off the stump, and flung me down on the ground. The first thing to go was my gun, quickly and deftly removed. The hand pushed my head against the gravel, while a heavy heel on my back kept me from moving. "Keep still, keep silent," urged a voice. "You got any ID?"

I reached for it, but a lightning hand stopped me. "Back pocket," I said.

I felt my wallet lifted out, heard the Velcro fastener ripped apart. The heel in my back went away. "Okay, let him up," said the voice. I found myself between two men in black overalls covered by stiff flak jackets, each bearing an automatic rifle, big yellow letters DEA printed on their backs. "Sorry, Hoitt. We had to be sure."

"Understood." I reclaimed my wallet.

"Stay behind the trees," commanded the agent. "No telling what's going to come out of that door. Just sit back and enjoy the show."

I crouched behind a thick red pine. In addition to the two who had taken me down, three other agents covered the back of the pharmacy. They each established their position, trained their rifles, and froze. Nothing moved. There was no sound.

The quiet lasted seconds. There were no shots, no yelling or screaming from inside the pharmacy. Out front, five cruisers, lights ablaze, pulled up, trailed by the sheriff's van. I heard three shrill blasts on a police whistle, and from the relaxing of their stances I knew it was over. The back door cracked, prompting an immediate return to their firing stance. The butt end of a rifle poked through, pushing open the door to reveal another flak-jacketed DEA agent. He waved us inside. One of the agents tossed back my gun as I followed the others up the iron steps.

The door lead into the pharmacist's stockroom, a well-lighted area lined with fully stocked shelves. Two men in white jackets held up the wall as officers patted them down, cuffed them, then took them away. Out front by the register, a wide-eyed, loudly protesting clerk was being ushered out the front door. DEA agent Corsetti came through the door as she left, with George, the big German shepherd straining at his leather leash. Corsetti ordered the dog to sit, bent beside his head to whisper instructions, then released the catch on the leash. George put his nose down low to the ground and began to search, walking quickly, his tail flipping wildly at the shelves.

Wiley and the sheriff stood beside the cash register, talking to a flak-jacketed man bearing sergeant's stripes. I passed through the pharmacist's counter to join them. Wiley looked up, but I barely noticed him as Francis Walker fixed me with a gaze as hard and cold as all his experience could summon. "Hoitt, even if this works out, you are still in one hell of a deep hole. I don't like mavericks working for me."

"Yes, sir." I replied.

"When we're done here, you and I are going to have a long talk about your performance. No more independent investigations for you. Is that clear?"

"Yes, sir."

"What exactly are we looking for?" asked Wiley.

"A kilo of cocaine."

"It's a start," he said. "How did you find this place?"

I briefly detailed my work since the previous night, starting with Winter, up and down Cadillac, through the search on the bay, the traps found with the special bricks, then the surveillance that lead to Bodwell's. I omitted all reference to Smith. As irate as Walker was, I knew he would be even angrier if he knew I had been working with a civilian. I told him I'd hidden the coke on a boat, and hoped he assumed it was mine. I ended my tale by giving Wiley the name, home port, and registration of the delivery boat, as well as Paul Fletcher's name, description, address, and the direction he left town.

Wiley took exhaustive notes. When I finished, he ripped off a sheet and handed it to the sergeant. "Go to the communications van. Call Ellsworth. Have these three people arrested for possession and brought to the station. I'll take care of them personally when I get back." The sergeant took the sheet and left.

Wiley opened his mouth as if to add something else, but George's barking cut him off. As if he understood canine speech better than English, Wiley ran down the aisle, Walker and I right behind. Surrounded by shelves of various legal drugs, we found George running his nose over the floor where the linoleum met the counter. Corsetti knelt beside the dog, reattached the shackle, told the dog what a good job he had done, then gave him a ratty, torn cloth toy and led him away.

A uniformed officer bent to the floor, probing along the tiles. He tapped and prodded, but the floor revealed nothing. Impatiently Wiley knelt beside him, did exactly the same thing, with the same results. He stopped probing aimlessly and dug his fingers into the crack between tiles. He pulled harder, and a narrow steel blade sprang up. When he pushed the lever, a snap catch let go and a section of the floor popped open. An enormous grin illuminated Wiley's dour face as he reached into the hole, withdrawing a package of plastic-wrapped white powder identical to the one I had seen that morning. He held it up to his mouth and kissed the plastic as he sat on the floor. "Bingo."

Walker advanced, a hand on Wiley's shoulder as he peered into the hole. "Jesus Christ," he said. "There's more than . . . than thirty keys in there."

"Progress at last." Wiley, evidence still in hand, issued orders for evidence bags, contact this person, contact that one, firing his words with machine-gun cadence. He pulled out packages, probing under the floor for more. "There must be fifty, sixty kilos under here."

Walker fell back to the counter. He drew a stained handkerchief over his sweating forehead. "Good God."

"We've hit them for about two million." I'd never seen Wiley like this: happy, almost giddy, issuing orders to everyone around. When he looked up at me, a toothy grin split his beard. "Good job, Patrolman. You have led us to the biggest bust in the state of Maine."

"Thank you, sir."

"I'll see you get a commendation," he said. I glanced at Walker, whose glare reminded me I'd need one. An agent appeared with a handful of zip-lock bags marked EVIDENCE. Wiley returned to the hole in the floor, counting aloud as he transferred packages to the evidence bag.

The sight of the cocaine should have thrilled me; it should have ignited fireworks at the prospect of a job well done. It didn't. The fact that Walker still seethed was only part of the reason. Something was missing, something that eluded Wiley. While he might have come in with more than a kilo, no way had Paul Fletcher come into that pharmacy this morning carrying all that cocaine. This was just a drop-off, a transfer station on a long line. If Fletcher and Winter simply dropped off at Bodwell's, who picked it up? While at least one of the pharmacists must have known about it, every other detail of this elaborate operation told me the leader would not be so stupid to leave his entire stock literally underfoot. The pharmacists, Winter, Fletcher, the crew of the *Susanne L*—they were just couriers to insulate the head. I wanted *him,* not merely those who held the bag. Wiley seemed willing to settle for the runners, but I wasn't.

I headed for the door, but stopped when Walker's large hand closed around my upper arm. "Good lead, Jimmy," he said. "That was good work. Remember what I said."

"Yes, sir," I answered.

"Take the rest of the afternoon off. Rest up. You've had a long day. I've got some follow-up to do. Meet me in my office around eight tonight. Okay?"

"Yes, sir," I repeated. I took one more glance at the growing pile of bags on the floor, then went outside.

I found Smith leaning against my truck, waiting. He looked up to recognize me, then stared off down the road. In the second our eyes met, I knew the end results did not meet his approval, either. "What did they find?"

"At least thirty kilos under the floor. All packaged just like the ones we found. They came by bricks."

"Pretty good haul," he said. "That's going to make someone very upset."

"Yeah, but who?" I said. "Wiley is so excited, he's lost sight of the big picture. Walker is mad as hell at me, and shocked to find out Wiley was right. Neither one is searching any further right now."

"Too bad," observed Smith. "There's so little time."

"By moving in here, we killed this trail."

Smith nodded. "Word will get back, if it hasn't already. A bust this size will set him back. If he was planning to bug out, he'll probably just grab his own stock and run."

"Who the hell *is* he?" I cried, all my anger and frustration, restrained for the last week, erupting. "Who are we looking for?"

"Look at the facts. It must be somebody local, maybe from Eagle Harbor. Someone clever, observant, who can move above suspicion, go anywhere, any time. Someone who could devise a quick and easy way to move a lot of cocaine as he pleased. Someone who also, incidentally, may have an inside line to the sheriff's office, so he can stay out of their way."

"Jesus," I said. "I know dozens of people like that. Hell, you've just described my father."

The intense, abstracted stare infused his eyes again. He was thinking. "Why a pharmacy?" he said thoughtfully.

"What?" I replied, too angry to think.

"Why not a hardware store or a gas station?" he continued. "There are only three or four pharmacies on this whole island, including the hospital. A pharmacy is therefore inconvenient. Yet here we are. So why a pharmacy?"

Reason began to cut through the fog of anger. He was right. On an island loaded with surreptitious meeting places, why select an obvious, rare pharmacy in the middle of a large village? The piece did not fit; it must be the key. Why here? "Of course, there are a lot of pharmacies in Bangor," I said.

"Once it reaches Bangor, it quickly leaves by truck or air. Here it's different."

"The rest of the plan must hinge on the pharmacy," I said slowly. "A pharmacy is essential to the smooth execution of the rest of the plan."

"It's probably cover," said Smith. "Through this pharmacy, and maybe a few others, they get it out of here quickly, safely, completely above suspicion. Who can go to a pharmacy, anytime, without drawing attention?"

"A doctor," I said.

Smith pondered my solution. "Most doctors don't go near them, let alone frequently. Delivery men?"

"Most of the deliveries come by UPS. The rest of the stock comes by freight from out of state. No locals who fit the other categories." I thought again. "The police come by here often enough, to fill up crash packs. So do firemen and paramedics."

"EMTs. Ambulance attendants," said Smith.

As he spoke the words, an explosion of light flooded my brain, dispersing the shadows in the corners. The scattered segments of the puzzle finally fell together into a recognizable picture. "Oh, my God."

"What?" said Smith. "What is it?"

"It all fits," I replied, my voice low, almost imperceptible. He'd been around all along: I talked to him just before the harbor shooting, had even told him what I was going to do. He knew Winter well, and Fletcher, and moved deftly and freely everywhere around Eagle Harbor and Mount Desert Island. He'd been with us at the quarry. He had been on the scene of the original accident. "My God, he stood there right beside me, right over Frederickson's body."

"Who?" hissed Smith.

"The killer," I replied. "The smuggler. The traitor. The man behind all this." I paused, took my breath, and swallowed hard. "The head of the ambulance corps."

"Who?" replied Smith. He dropped his voice as if he were afraid of who might hear. "That fool who always wears that damn beeper?" Smith tapped his head as if trying to remember. "What the hell is his name?"

My unseeing eyes stared past Smith at the image of a man I'd thought I knew. He'd gained the trust of everyone in Eagle Harbor and the sheriff's department. He was so intricately woven into the fabric of the community, no one would ever have failed to vouch for him under any circumstances. He was our neighbor, our local rescue chief, our friend. We all trusted him, literally trusted him with our lives. He had betrayed us all. "His name is Mike Twitchell."

10

Saturday Evening
Patrol Area: Eagle Harbor
Temps warm; humidity high;
wind increasing from SW

S mith stared into the empty truck bed for some time, his jaw set, his hands draped over the side. The muscles around his eyes jumped as he considered my conclusion. "Twitchell, huh?"

I nodded. "He fits."

"Be wary of evidence that fits too tightly," he replied.

"With his ambulance, he and his crew can come and go as they please," I explained. "Never searched, never questioned. He can travel any time of day, appear anywhere on the island. Especially here. He can go to the waterfront, transfer the shipments to the ambulance as easily in Eagle Harbor as he can in Bangor or anywhere else on the island."

"Others fit the same profile," said Smith. "Starting with his own EMTs."

I paused. The theory had only coalesced a moment before. I had not yet had a chance to work out all the bugs. "Twitchell's a peculiar guy," I said eventually. "He has to be involved in everything. He can't let a town committee buy an ambulance, he has to do it himself. He had to check with the builders to make sure they followed the plans right."

"I'll bet he did," interjected Smith.

"He shows up on most calls, whether he's on duty or not. Even when they wash the truck, he's around to supervise, if not to help. Even miles away, off duty, he carries his radio, so if anything happens he can respond."

"Sounds obsessive."

I shrugged. "Maybe he's just dedicated. But I can't imagine any of his EMTs doing anything with the equipment that he didn't know about.

"If it is one of his men," pondered Smith, "he would go to every length possible to make sure Twitchell couldn't find out."

I shook my head. "You don't know what a parasite this guy can be. He made a nuisance of himself spring before last, pestering the council for a new ambulance. He haunted the council members, managed to run into them at least twice a week, telling them everything the Ambulance Corps did, emergencies, mutual aid, charity work. He had detailed lists of the people involved and all the work they did."

"Tenacious," replied Smith. "Many men are nuisances without being criminals. He's obnoxious, conceited, a pest. None of which proves he's the mastermind. You haven't even convinced me—you'd have no chance with Walker or Wiley."

"Let me finish," I said. "With his ambulance work, he has a perfect opportunity to be anywhere, any time, without raising even the slightest suspicion. He has access to the whole coast. Just last week I saw him and Winter sharing a table at the diner."

"I share a table with many people," said Smith. "Not only does it not mean we're all smugglers, it also doesn't mean I know what they do the rest of the day."

"Okay," I conceded. "But given what we do know about Winter and what we suspect about Twitchell, it is indicative."

"All right. A very unconvincing Exhibit A duly logged. Next?"

"Twitchell has lived here all his life. However, he did leave for a while, about ten years back."

Smith drummed his fingers on the steel bed. "I don't imagine he went to Canada?"

"He traveled the country for a while," I said. "Didn't stay anywhere too long. The last place he stayed before returning north was the seven months he spent in South Florida. You wanted a link between Frederickson's Down East operation and Grandpa Joe's old Florida work—I offer you Twitchell. He was in the right place at the right time."

"Exhibit B."

"Three more points." I was beginning to convince myself. "He has a direct line to the sheriff's office. We all know him. He's a regular at the station. He often hears of our projects in advance. Half the time, we invite him along on raids for the medical assistance. That would explain how our raids keep coming up empty. He has ample time to move his stuff out of danger before we strike."

Smith nodded, staring up the street at Wiley's army. "Maybe you keep coming up empty because you're on a cold, dead trail."

I shrugged. "It's the only trail we've got. Better a cold trail than none at all."

"You don't have an airtight case, but I admit there's some merit in it," said Smith. "What else?"

"I decided to check the harbor just after I came back from the Verona raid." I tried to remember the sequence of events, wanting to get everything perfect. I realized how tired I was; I hadn't had a good sleep in a long time. "I thought it up on the drive back. I didn't tell Dickinson or anyone else in Ellsworth. I said nothing to anyone, talked to no one on the way down. Except when I reached Eagle Harbor. Twitchell was cleaning out the ambulance. He'd had a run that night and had just returned."

"Why did you tell him?"

"How should I know? I didn't know any better. It was just idle talk, that's all. But he's the only one I said anything to."

"And you were shot at later that night?"

"That morning, yuh."

"An hour later?"

Seemed about right. "More or less."

"While you rowed out on the harbor?"

"Yes," I said, more than a little exasperated. What was he driving at now? "Why?"

"You were exposed out there," said Smith. "Anyone watching the buoy would have seen you, had plenty of time to call for help, or move around and take a few shots. Whether they wanted to kill you or scare you doesn't matter. They had time."

"Who's going to be watching the harbor at three in the morning?" I protested.

"Someone with seventy thousand dollars' worth of cocaine sitting on the bottom, that's who." He tapped the side of the bed. "Still, you could be right. You said there's one more thing?"

"Yuh. Two days after the murder I was talking to Russ, down to the store. Twitchell was in there buying a headlight—big old round one. He said he'd hit a tree and broke the lens. But he drives a Chevy Suburban: it has rectangular headlights. He owns another car, a big mid-seventies Chrysler. He doesn't drive it much, usually only for special occasions. I've never seen him driving it around at night. At the scene of the murder, we did find glass shards, as if a headlight had been broken. And—here's the kicker—the Chrysler matches the general description of the car that killed Frederickson."

Mention of the murder perked up Smith's attention. "The murder is the key to the whole case. Without it, this is a routine drug case. Maybe kind of big for around here, but still routine. Frederickson's killing connects all the pieces on the table into one enormous operation."

I had convinced myself. "I'm telling you: it's Twitchell. It all fits."

"Is that all you've got? That's not evidence, that's a collection of petty suspicions."

I racked my brain for more connections, but right then, I had nothing else to go on. I had a deep-seated suspicion and a gnawing feeling that I was right, but that was hardly evidence. "I'm afraid that's all I have."

"That's precious little to indict a man for."

"I agree it isn't much," I said sheepishly. "But it's all we have right now."

"It's damn slim, Hoitt," scolded Smith. "It'll never stand up in court."

"Maybe not. So let's get more. We have to investigate him directly."

"If it *is* Twitchell, he knows you've been investigating the case for more than a week. He's had plenty of time to leave."

"Saw him this morning."

Smith frowned. "He's still here, huh?"

"Still here."

"A man clever enough to run this operation should have fled a week ago."

I pointed to Bodwell's. "He was waiting for one more score."

Smith shook his head. "He stood over the body right next to you, did he?"

"He did."

"Took you a week and a half to see him as the murderer. Well, better late then never."

"Not if he's already gone."

"If he's left, our work is done. If not . . ." His brow furrowed in thought. "Bought a new ambulance, did he?"

"Yuh. Chevrolet. Cost around seventy-six thousand dollars. Delivered last fall. Brand new, built to his own specifications, under his personal supervision."

"I'll bet." The eyebrows worked harder. "It's no coincidence that Frederickson's operation, according to Wiley's report, stepped up about the same time."

"Coincidence?" I said, not following. Then I understood: the drugs moved in the ambulance. "No coincidence."

"I think we need to check out that ambulance," said Smith.

In front of Bodwell's, the DEA van headed north, trailed by a three-car escort. Wiley and Walker stood together in the doorway, each bearing an evidence bag. A Bangor TV crew had already arrived; I knew others would soon follow. If Twitchell did not already know of his setback, he would soon. Walker had not expressly forbidden me to work, I rationalized. I was only barred from individual investigation. I promised myself I would call in whatever I found. "Let's go have a look."

Smith spared one last glance at the agents and reporters moving around the pharmacy. "Time's a-wasting." It took only seconds to start the truck and aim back toward Eagle Harbor.

We made the drive in silence. I had not the slightest indication of Smith's thoughts. He sat still, moving only from the vibrations imposed by the bumping truck, chin sunk upon his chest, eyes closed, arms folded. I didn't know him well enough to read his thoughts or interpret his body language. He could as easily have been considering his grocery list as continuing his search for the grand unified theory; he certainly could have been pondering the case. Or, I realized between quick glances, he could have been napping.

I left aside all consideration of Smith as we passed the town line. Whatever he had to ponder, I had at least as much. I had a case to be quickly solved and proven before the principals could clear town. Though I'd convinced myself, I still didn't want to believe Mike Twitchell was at the heart of it all. So friendly and familiar, so trusted by everyone—how could he have changed so much from the man we thought we knew?

I wondered about the town itself. Eagle Harbor had been home all my life. It is impossible to live in a coastal village for so long without understanding the secrets lurking close to the surface. Sooner or later, word gets around that arson is behind the sudden demise of abandoned houses; before long everyone knows the arsonist is the fire chief's son. Everyone knows that the married waitress at the diner has been quietly seeing one of the guys from Russ's store while her husband hauls traps; meanwhile, she is the only one who does not know he gave up unprofitable evening fishing long ago and spends his time in a different port. Ninety-five percent gossip with a tiny grain of truth, the secrets were public within the village, but held strictly within those bounds. The tales possess little interest or relevance to people from away. Rarely do they concern breaking the law. None of those reliable, comfortable, small-town secrets had touched on Twitchell or his operation.

Eagle Harbor would not have been the same place without Mike Twitchell. He had been the prime motivator behind the creation of the Eagle Harbor Volunteer Ambulance Corps. Some years back, Robyn's cousin Tommy had fallen through the February ice into the subfreezing winter water. It took an hour for the nearest ambulance to respond over icy roads. When he died at Eastern Maine Medical Center, the doctors said he might have been saved with better, earlier care. From the seeds of that tragedy, Twitchell had grown a reliable, well-trained, fully equipped, and highly regarded troop of volunteer EMTs. Many residents owed their lives to the rapid, efficient response of the EHVAC; I doubted there was anyone in town who didn't know someone that had been aided by Twitchell's volunteer corps. The town would be forever indebted to him for that contribution, however self-serving it might appear now. He shared the common foundations of so many of us. He could trace his direct family lineage back to one of the original four families that broke from the mainland in search of new fishing grounds to call their own. He'd gone from Vernon Aldridge Memorial Elementary to MDI High School, the same as Paul Fletcher, Dave Winter, Denise, or me and Robyn. His parents and grandparents were buried in the Congregational cemetery in town, just a few plots away from the Coles and the Hoitts. He was part of the same church, kept his money in the same bank, and shopped and dined with all of us in the village. He was one of us, a trusted and deeply integrated member of our community, and he had betrayed our trust.

On the other side of the truck cab, Smith kept his silence. If Twitchell's involvement distressed or surprised him, no trace of that reached his face. I caught myself. What did I know about Smith? Next to nothing; most of what I knew I had learned from his own mouth, and only in the last week. I knew little about his past, and had only the barest idea why he had ended up in Eagle Harbor. A cursory check of his background had indicated everything he said was the truth, but if he was as clever a deceiver as he was a detective, I knew he would have taken pains to protect his personal truth. Here was a man who was everything Twitchell wasn't: a complete enigma, with a past full of shadowy secrets and unknown tales, a man with no local history and few friends. I wondered how many of the residents knew any more about him than his name, if they even knew that. I also wondered how many of them knew about Beth. The shrine on the mantel stayed with me. It was more than a passing similarity to Robyn that held it in my mind. The passion and intensity of feeling that must have gone into assembling those mementos was tangible, and undeniable. I could not believe he could have created that monument without sincerely possessing the emotion and pain it so obviously displayed, and I was convinced no one who had lived through that could possibly stand to allow it to happen to anyone else around him.

I trusted him. I had to. I couldn't deny my own visceral reactions, and they were quite clear. So, surprising as it sounded, I found myself riding off to arrest a man I had known all my life in the company of a total stranger.

Towering storm clouds rapidly obscured the sun, bringing on a premature twilight as we entered the village. The day slowly drained away, leaving traces of heat drifting up from the asphalt and a sludgy, used humidity. Despite the coming night, I refused to ignite my headlamps, drifting cautiously through the village. As the brick firehouse facade came into view, I abruptly realized the implications of my actions. This was no longer mere investigation. I had taken the next step: seeking direct, specific evidence that would lead to an imminent arrest. My facial muscles relaxed as all vestiges of emotion drained away. Involuntarily my gun hand left the wheel, slowly flexing, stretching, preparing. I liked the darkness; the oppressive humidity suited the occasion.

A surprising volume of activity flows through Eagle Harbor on a sticky summer Saturday night. The evening was still young enough for the diner to remain open, encouraging guests to come inside, enjoy some homemade ice cream, and borrow the air conditioner. Boat parties were just getting started. Judging by the cars in the parking lot, most of the boats in the harbor were in use. And why not? If I hadn't been working, I would probably gather up Robyn, borrow the boat, and take a cruise. My mind drifted away from the case to the water. The distraction lasted only a second.

I passed the dock, the diner, Russ's. Smith kept his eyes on the white firehouse doors. "Why didn't you stop?"

"Too obvious." I pointed up the street. "We'll park in the cemetery. Short walk to the back door. No one will notice we're even there."

"Any reason you've decided to play it so safe?"

"I did some thinking on the way down," I answered. I had done a lot of thinking. I suspected he knew I had been thinking about him, too. Would he trust me enough to step into danger with me covering his back? "I thought I knew Mike Twitchell. He's in church most every Sunday, which is more than I can say for myself. Helps around the docks, knows everyone in the diner. Everybody knows him."

Smith's eyes roved over the roadside as we passed. "Sounds like one hell of a guy."

"That's been my problem," I grumbled. "I've been searching for a barbarian, a vicious, merciless drug smuggler. At the trail's end I find, instead, a kindly neighbor. He doesn't fit the profile."

I shivered, my knuckles whitening on the wheel. "I can't believe it's Mike. Yet a creepy feeling crawling up my back tells me he's the one. My God, he stood right next to me, calm, almost bored, as we investigated. I was horrified, my stomach churning up a hurricane. But not Mike. And he'd done the killing not an hour before." I took a moment to catch my breath. I relaxed my hands, returning to a state of battle-ready tension. "A man like that I want to give a lot of leeway. If I can go in there and do what I have to do without being detected, so much the better."

Smith turned toward me. A passing car spread light over his face, and I saw him smile. "You play this very well, Hoitt. Keep it up." He faced forward again. "You'll live longer."

Just on the other side of a hanging wooden sign, a break in the stone wall and an open iron gate allowed access to the old graveyard. I headed for the back corner, aimed the truck for a quick escape, and parked. I pocketed the keys and leaned forward, cradling my face in my hands, breathing slowly and staring off toward the distance. "Well," I said.

"Well," agreed Smith.

"Let's go." I stepped out, reaching under the seat for a spare clip before closing the door. I sidled along the truck until my foot touched the stones. Past the wall, dense briars, shrubs, and young trees formed a fence about thirty feet wide between the graveyard and the parking lot behind the station. I cut through as quietly as leaves and twigs would permit. I came out of the woods onto the grass, turning to find Smith close by. "Still with you," he said.

Thirty yards away was the back wall of the firehouse. A naked quartz light burned over the door, forcing us to stand in a pool of bright light as I fumbled for my key chain. I found the chain, first tried the wrong key, then the right one, and we were inside, protected again by the dark.

"Sheriff's patrolmen have keys to all the local fire stations?" asked Smith.

"Back in Ellsworth, sure," I replied. "I'm an inactive member here. I've been letting it slide; they'll probably make me quit soon. Meanwhile, I still have a key."

"You must know Twitchell pretty well, then."

I crept into the truck bay. "Not so well as I thought."

I heard shuffling behind me, then a loud clang as something heavy and metallic struck the concrete floor, almost obscuring a muffled exclamation. "Listen, Hoitt," said Smith. "You may know you're way around, but I don't. Turn on the lights. We can pull the curtains."

"Can't. The front doors have uncurtained windows. Anyone driving by would notice."

"We can't find anything in the dark."

"Wait here." I reached out to touch the wall, following it to guide me to the side of compartment E5. I pulled out a heavy-duty flashlight. A flick of my thumb flooded the compartment with light. I picked up another. Careful not to let the beam rise far off the floor, I returned to the work room. "Here."

He switched it on. "Where to now?"

"This way." I led him back into the bay. The firehouse dated from the fifties, when it had been spacious. Over the years, as equipment grew larger, the dimensions appeared to shrink, until barely enough walking room remained. Instead of the two trucks originally envisioned by the architects, the garage now held three. Closest to the door was the wide, shiny-chrome rear end of the American-LaFrance pumper. Hose nozzles, an oversize extinguisher, and bolt cutters were lashed to the hand rails. Neatly coiled rows of yellow hose, piled into four compartments along the top, peeked from under a canvas cover that did not quite fit. On the other side of the garage, a Dodge pickup chassis loaded down with compartments and a water tank served as the town's general-purpose truck. It parked so close to the back wall that the round ball of the trailer hitch fitted neatly into a matching gouge in the concrete wall. The front bumper just touched the rear bumper of the ambulance before it, a vivid orange-and-white van still showroom new.

Though the trucks nearly filled the bay, it contained more than trucks. Suspended from the roof hung an aluminum boat. In a village on the water, it was as vital as the pumper beneath it. Dents and scratches along its hull testified that it did more than simply hang. A triangular wooden rack hugged the wall beside the pumper, drying hoses draped over the apex. Empty raincoats, surmounted by bright orange fire helmets, hung on the opposite wall, ready for the next alarm. Between the trucks, nestled into the rear wall, a tiny alcove barely larger than a phone booth served as the base station. Three separate radios clung to the wall, clipboards and notebooks dangling off pegs or thrown on top of the filing cabinet beside the door. The

flickering light of a scanner cast shifting amber shadows on the office.
"Tight spaces," said Smith. "Where to?"

I aimed my light at the radios. "We check the logs."

The glass door was closed but not locked. I picked up the nearest clipboard to find only a duty list, not what I sought. Three boards in a row contained maintenance records for each truck. On the desk, beside the telephone and standing mike, a narrow clothbound notebook caught my attention. I handed it to Smith. "Station logbook. Look through it."

He took the book, flipping the pages quickly. "Did you have anything in mind?"

"Every time the ambulance goes to the pharmacy there should be a record."

"Unless he's sneaking off to do it," said Smith.

I sighed. "Doesn't make sense to create such a detailed and accurate cover story only to risk it all with an unauthorized, unreported pharmacy call."

"Who's going to know?"

I opened the top file drawer. "Too many people have keys. Too much gossip. Somebody would notice. Someone else would ask the wrong question—and it all goes to hell in a handbasket."

Smith grunted a reluctant concession as he sat on the truck's running board. "I wish I'd brought my glasses."

I scanned the other books, records, and boards, finding gas receipts, driving assignments, training bulletins, manuals, state and county memos, a calendar still open to last month, and a drawer of assorted junk. I hoped to find a drug inventory for the ambulance, including when and where the drugs were purchased, but found nothing. The record had to exist by law. It must have been aboard the vehicle, or even at Twitchell's home.

I heard a loud voice behind me. In an instant I knew it was not Smith, and it did not take half again so long before I had whirled around, dropped to a crouch, and drew my weapon. The tight spaces were unfamiliar. My knee slammed into the metal cabinet, my wrist bashed painfully against the door frame: I realized I had taken careful aim on the scanner.

"Jumpy?" said Smith dryly.

I holstered the Beretta, gently rubbing my wounds. "Yes."

"A little jumpiness is healthy," consoled Smith. "Don't let it get out of hand."

My wrist hurt badly; I knew I'd soon wear an ugly purple bruise. Tongues of flame seared my knee, traveled up my leg, but despite the pain I knew nothing serious had been done. "There's nothing else in here."

Smith joined me at the door. "Your instincts proved excellent." He pointed at the pages. "The records are quite detailed. Approximately every two weeks the ambulance goes up to Bodwell's for a pickup. This book doesn't detail what it gets. Every incidence of a trip to the druggist occurred on a Monday or a Tuesday, and always in the early afternoon. However, only about a third of the twenty or so trips carried Twitchell aboard." He closed the book, replacing it precisely on the desk. "Legally, I'm not sure what it proves. But it fills in the details."

For the first time in the case, I no longer followed, but led the investigation. Knee and wrist pain dulled out of perception. "So Twitchell has recruited a driver or two. Just like the fishermen who do all the leg work. It fits the pattern. The occasions when he was aboard are more likely coincidence than planning."

"Probably right."

I pointed to the van. "The rest is in there."

He looked over the ambulance the way a climber surveys a cliff face before starting up. "Let's go."

I sidled up the narrow aisle between the trucks. The bumper-to-bumper parking forbade using the rear doors, so I swung open the passenger door. "I'll check the inside. You check outside, okay?"

"Right." Smith squeezed past.

I maneuvered over the seat, around the engine housing, probing for hidden latches. The small glove compartment opened easily, but revealed no secrets. Running my hand under the bottom of the dash, I found nothing but the wiring harness and ventilation hoses. On the driver's side I thought I'd found something as my fingers closed over a recessed catch, but the excitement evaporated as I recognized the fuse box cover. The seats were bolted to framed steel boxes, unable to conceal a pencil. I brought the light low and searched the carpet minutely for anything that might reveal a removable section. Only in one corner where water had rotted the fabric did it show even the slightest yield.

Having certified the cockpit as clean, I moved aft into the work area. The carpet ended behind the front seats, merging into the green rubberized decking beneath a chrome strip. A folding jump seat hung behind the driver. A narrow aisle bisected the van alongside the aluminum-framed stretcher. Along both walls, splints, large bandages, boxes of rubber gloves and tissues, a pair of green oxygen tanks, and a portable radio waited behind low rails. Narrow cabinets lined the van's flanks. The open shelves quickly revealed that they hid no secrets. I checked the cabinets.

The first two were unlocked. Searching them in the dark, cramped compartment proved a difficult task. The first contained electronic equipment, covers all in place, wires neatly stowed. The other contained three plastic trays full of paper-wrapped IV bags, clearly labeled, with needles and tubes wrapped around the middle. The last two were locked behind a steel bar and a brass padlock. I hoped old habits died hard. They did: I found a key taped under the gas pedal, and used it to open the doors. The cabinets were kept locked for good reason: they housed the ambulance pharmaceutical supply and were the most prized theft targets on board. Plastic trays and a tackle box contained a wide assortment of drugs. All were labeled, most factory sealed in small, one-use containers. They looked okay. I replaced the trays, locked the door, and put the key back where I found it.

I meticulously examined the floor, walls, every nook I could think of to hide anything. I found nothing. There were two explanations for this. One, I chased phantoms. I discarded that theory at once. Two, the secret location could be on the outside, for Smith to find. Why hadn't he found it? I reluctantly allowed a third possibility: I had missed it. I went forward to start all over again.

I had only begun to search when I heard Smith call softly. I hopped out the passenger door to the concrete floor to find him kneeling at the back of the ambulance, his hand on the bumper. He waved me closer. "Come here."

My injured knee popped painfully as I knelt. "I couldn't find anything inside."

"I'm not surprised. Look at this."

By "this" he meant the end of the bumper. A quick glance confirmed that it looked pretty much like every other truck bumper I'd ever seen. A steel corner piece joined the main bumper about five inches inside the outer edge. The steel curved ninety degrees around the corner of the truck in a smoothly sculpted turn, the outer edge fastened by a huge chromed rivet. I ran my hand inside, probing what I could not see. "Just a bumper."

"On this side, sure. Come over here." We crossed to the other side of the ambulance. Smith pushed some raincoats out of the way and knelt beside the bumper. "Look at this."

I stared at this mirror image of what I had just seen on the other side. A chromed bumper curved around the corner of the van, held in place. . . . My eyes narrowed. Instead of a nearly flat, round, chromed rivet, an inverted knob with knurled edges held this side of the bumper together. Chromed, round, the same size as its opposite number, from a distance of over four feet it must have looked perfectly authentic. "This isn't right."

"No, it isn't," said Smith. "Try the knob."

"What's inside?"

"I don't know."

"Okay." I gave an experimental turn, with only slight force, but the knob moved. "It's loose."

"It would look damn suspicious if someone came out and hammered the bumper with a pipe wrench every time they made a drop," observed Smith.

I moved closer to get a better grip. After a few turns I held a coarse-threaded nylon bolt with a convincing metallic head. "I think we're onto something."

Smith leaned against the van, peering around the hole more closely. "Try pulling it off."

I set down the bolt. I placed my hands on the top and bottom of the bumper. With barely a tug the corner piece came off. I placed it beside the bolt and looked inside. "Have a look."

Smith emitted a low whistle. "Jackpot."

Inside the bumper a narrow, rectangular channel extended its full length. A fine nylon line fit into a recess on the inside edge. When I pulled it I heard a gentle scraping. I pointed my flashlight inside and pulled again: nothing seemed to happen. I tried again—this time the compartment seemed to get smaller. When I pulled continuously I realized I was pulling a ram closer to my side of the bumper. Clever, I thought: a quick and easy way to unload the bumper. The dimensions were so nearly the same as what we found at sea that there could be no doubt of its use. "You could store about ten of those cocaine bricks in here."

"Maybe an even dozen," said Smith.

I sat back, falling onto the floor. "Jesus. We were right."

Smith patted my shoulder. "Good work, detective."

I examined the bumper cover closely. "This is a professional job."

"You've seen the operation; the size of the planning, the logistics," said Smith. "Would you expect any less?"

I minutely examined the bumper piece in the flashlight beam. "This is identical to the genuine factory part. I'm sure of it."

Smith took the cap when I offered it. He studied it carefully before agreeing. "Probably installed during the customizing." He handed back the fitting. "Which explains not only why Eagle Harbor has a new ambulance, but also why Twitchell so zealously sought it."

Another piece fell into place. "He kept right on top of the whole project, from research, through delivery. He wrote up the specs, found the manufacturer. For a while he went to Pennsylvania a few days every month to make sure nothing went wrong."

Smith ran his hand along the truck side. "He had a lot riding on this vehicle."

I shook my head. At every turn Twitchell revealed himself to be far more clever and duplicitous than I had ever given him credit for. "The town started considering a new ambulance nearly two and a half years ago." I stood up. "If this bumper was the major reason for the whole project, that means Twitchell has been involved in the operation for at least three years."

Smith nodded. "If my memory serves correctly, Frederickson moved to Maine and became Martin about four years ago. Evidently, he didn't waste time before initiating his new network."

I could not believe what I heard, but the evidence of the bumper was clear and irrefutable. Eagle Harbor had needed a new ambulance, but the primary reason for purchasing that vehicle had been to use a small, isolated fishing port to bring cocaine into the United States, far from the ever-watching but overtaxed eyes of the DEA. Any shred of hope that Mike Twitchell could not be involved died. "I'm convinced."

"Maybe. Our case is hardly enough to satisfy a prosecutor."

Walker's orders returned to me. "We have enough to tell Wiley. Let him build his own fortress. We need to make sure Twitchell doesn't go to ground."

"How do you propose to do that?"

"A simple stakeout," I replied. "We'll go—" I froze as a muted but distinct metallic click blew into my ears. My thumb silently rotated the plastic light switch, killing my light. Smith's went a fraction of a second later. In the abrupt darkness, I could only barely make out the shapes of the fire equipment by the dim glow of the radio LEDs. I stayed still, waiting for the sound again, wishing it not to, yet knowing it must come. Long seconds passed, time enough to dampen my entire scalp. Nothing happened. Just as I prepared to relax, the door creaked.

Instantly I dropped to a crouch, set down my flashlight, and withdrew my weapon. Anyone entering the building with legitimate reasons would not have been so quiet and would not keep the lights off. Whoever had entered the fire station clearly did not wish to be detected.

I could not see the intruder, but a faint backshine on the polished concrete floor told me the visitor had elected to check the back room first. I felt Smith approach, leaning closer. "He's out back," I whispered.

"Have you seen anyone?"

"Just lights shining on the floor."

"I'm going to the back of this truck. You've got to reassemble the bumper."

"Right."

"Got your gun?"

"Yeah. But I can't see anything yet."

"Try not to shoot me, okay?" I heard no sound, but I knew he had left.

Praying the visitor remained preoccupied, I shuffled to the brush truck, pulling an axe off the rack. I used the blunt end to push the ram as deeply as I could, then re-coiled the nylon line more or less the way I'd found it. I fumbled for the end cap, angry I had not paid closer attention when I took it off, now that I had to replace it by touch. I felt for ridges or alignment pins; the round piece fitted into a long plastic shaft, coarsely threaded. I felt along the bumper, looking for some protrusion into which the piece would fit. I found a threaded stud just below the top edge, guarding the entrance to the tunnel. I placed the cap over it and violently twisted the knob.

The back door creaked again. I stopped instantly. Our guest headed into the bay, his muffled paces sounding softly on the concrete. Peering underneath the ambulance, I saw a small, round puddle of light emerge from the hall, followed by heavy boots. They stopped just behind the pumper as the light began swinging around the garage.

Fearing he might check beneath the trucks, I retreated behind the tire. Hoping the plastic pieces would mate quietly, I reached out to the bumper and continued to tighten the cap. I twisted until it resisted more than my fingers could overcome, then felt around the edges: the piece did not fit properly. I found a wide gap between the bottom of the bumper and the top of the cap. I tried to tighten the bolt, but it refused to move. I must have cross-threaded it. I had to withdraw the bolt and try again.

I clenched my teeth, cursing myself. In my haste to unscrew the cap, I dropped it: it clattered to the floor. Overhead, the flashlight beam quickly traversed the boots and helmets, flashing from the dispatch office to the main door. The beam dipped lower, illuminating the floor. Though the beam never came close to me, I clearly saw Smith's silhouette.

The beam moved on. I tightened the cap, felt the edge to ensure it had seated correctly, and retreated, Beretta raised. The light beam disappeared from my side of the garage, flitting along the opposite side. It scanned for a moment, stopping outside my field of vision. Footsteps pounded across the slab floor. I knelt down, watching the shadow advance along the side of the pumper. It stopped directly opposite me. I heard a loud metal snap, followed by a dull thud. My teeth set tight. Our visitor had found the open locker door where I had borrowed the flashlights.

I looked toward Smith, but he no longer squatted behind the truck. I hoped that wherever he hid it would serve him well. The boots across the garage aligned with my position: the flashlight beam shrunk, growing brighter. From his present angle the tires would not cover me. I placed one foot on the ambulance bumper, dug my fingers into the roof gutter and hauled myself off the floor just as the beam flashed underneath the trucks, a splash of light appearing where I had just been. The beam swept the area, stopping at the flashlight I had left on the floor.

The beam disappeared. Cautious but quick steps approached from the far side of the pumper. I had few options. I put a foot on the tire, wrapped an arm around a light bar, and jumped onto the roof. The visitor, expecting a trap, slowed as he approached the ambulance. I stayed low, minimizing my profile. The visitor stopped by the bumper.

The rounded chrome back of a spotlight on the ambulance roof provided an excellent mirror: a tall, bearded man knelt by my flashlight. A baseball hat and deep shadows obscured his face, but the beard, height, narrow shoulders, and short legs told me that the sheriff's department had not managed to apprehend Winter. He examined the light, then cast his own light on the bumper: Winter knew about the compartment. I wondered how many other trusted friends would be swept into the net before we reeled it in.

Winter surveyed his surroundings, flashlight in one hand, a heavy black revolver in the other. He advanced along the side of the ambulance, to the hood before returning to the bumper. "Come on, Hoitt," he yelled. I could have heard him across the garage: he clearly had no idea of my location. "I know you're here somewhere. I padlocked the back door, so you can't get out."

He paced along the wall. "Come on, Jimmy, don't make this

hard. We can all get out. No sweat. But you've got to come out now." He stopped beside the driver's door. "You hear me, Hoitt? You hear me?"

"I hear you." Winter turned quickly, the flashlight swinging around to stop on Smith, his hands raised standing behind the utility truck.

Winter moved closer. "Who the hell are you?"

"I, ah, broke in. Thought I could steal something. I need the money."

Winter's eyes narrowed. "Wait a minute," he said. "I know you."

Dumb as he was, Winter was not fooled. I crept toward the edge.

"Yeah, you do," said Smith. "I live up on the hill, behind town."

"I don't think so." He let the flashlight fall to his side, thrusting the gun ahead of him. "Tell me the truth. And do it fast."

"Okay." I could not be certain, not then or in considering it later, but I thought Smith's eyes flicked in my direction. "I guess it's now or never."

I braced against a light, and flung myself over the edge. The waxed surface offered little resistance. I flew through the air, catching Winter at the hips. He grunted, his hands flying skyward as we fell to the floor; when we landed his hands were empty. Winded but quick, he scrambled to his feet. I grabbed his legs and brought him down again. He pounded my shoulders and head, with hard blows. My hands were occupied holding him down. I butted my head into his ribs, as much to protect myself as to attack.

A flashlight beam landed on us. "All right, stop," said Smith. Despite the glare in my eyes, I detected the black revolver in his hand. "Winter, stay right where you are. Hoitt, roll clear."

I did as instructed, slightly surprised that Winter did the same. I got to my feet. "Thanks."

"Got any handcuffs?" he asked.

"No. But there's rope in the truck."

"Get it. Bind him. Then call the sheriff, get him down here first."

I grabbed a light and made my way to the pumper. I removed a length of ⅜-inch nylon rope, returned to Winter and Smith, and trussed Winter's hands and feet. I began to secure him to the bushwhacker on the truck, but Smith stopped me. "No. Gag him, too. We'll leave him in the boneyard. Somebody may be coming down to join him—better there's no evidence we were here."

I tore a piece of polish cloth from a pile in the office and jammed it into his mouth. "That will hold him."

"Good." Smith pocketed the gun. "I'll keep this, if you don't mind. Let's call the cavalry."

"Hang on." I ransacked Winter's pockets. I found keys, a wallet, some spare change. In his shirt pocket I got lucky: a quick-load set of shells for the revolver and a brass key. The shells I gave to Smith.

He pocketed them. "What's the key?"

"Padlock on the door."

I left a brief message with the sheriff's office dispatcher, telling them where they could find Winter. He gave us all the trouble he could, but with enough effort, we hauled him through the shrubs, over the wall, into the graveyard. I used a short piece of rope from my truck to tie him to a granite monument, checked the gag—not too tight, not too loose—and clambered into the truck. "Where are we going?" asked Smith.

"Twitchell's house. We have a score to settle."

"You should keep the sheriff informed," said Smith. "You're going to make him damn mad if you keep up this solo game."

"Walker be damned," I snapped. I hadn't realized I felt so strongly until it blasted out. "This is personal."

"No vendettas, Hoitt," replied Smith. "Keep it professional."

"Twitchell didn't send Winter to stop the sheriff or the DEA," I said. "He sent him after me, Jimmy Hoitt. He deserves the courtesy of a personal reply."

Smith grabbed the suicide strap. "I don't imagine this will be a slow ride."

Mike Twitchell lived east of town, not on the water but up on the side of the ridge. The town line bisects the ridge, so his six acres fall partly in the next town. His house stands on the Eagle Harbor side. Anyone who had meandered the top of the ridge as I have knows that the political boundary fades among the rocks. The whim of a surveyor had placed Twitchell within my town. Part of me wished his house were on the opposite side of the ridge, but I knew separation by so tenuous a barrier would have meant nothing.

As I approached the drive, I had no plan. A wide, well-worn gravel path led to the house, switching back as it climbed the forty feet to the house. From below, we could see only the ridgepole of the peaked roof. We could not tell whether Twitchell was home. Gleaming dully in my headlamps, a piece of quarter-inch steel cable hung between two stout trees, presenting a simple gate. It required only a moment's thought. I backed off, pushing the tailgate deep into the growth alongside the road, shifted into first, raced the engine, and popped the clutch. The rear wheels chirped as the truck hopped across the road. As any freshman physics major can tell you, three thousand pounds moving at even a low speed possess a lot of kinetic energy. Even above the roar of the straining engine, the twang of the stretching cable reached my ears, followed quickly by the explosion as it snapped. I swung the wheel hard, easing up the accelerator to prevent us from skipping right off the drive. As soon as we rounded the hairpin, the house stood out from the background of black sky.

Twitchell's Suburban was parked by the front door. I pulled up directly behind, blocking it. On the front of the house, two rectangles of glass topped by a pair of trapezoidal loft panes exploited the harbor view. They also gave an excellent view of approaching intruders. We were ideal targets for anyone inside. I yanked open my door, took my automatic in hand, and rolled clear of the cab, quickly joined by Smith.

I peeked over the bed. A quick glance took in the four windows and the brightly lit living room beyond, but revealed no one. I rose up to take a more careful look and still saw nothing. I dropped down. "Can't see anyone."

Smith nodded. His eyes scanned the shadows. Though our intrusion had been quick, the biggest danger still came from the rear. "You know the layout?"

"Small house. Five rooms. Huge living room, den and kitchen off the back. Stair goes up the side wall to a pair of bedrooms. Last I knew, he used the room closest to the stairs."

"Any outbuildings?"

"Shed about twenty yards beyond the kitchen door, about eight by ten. Aluminum, like you buy at Sears."

"What's he use it for?"

I shrugged. "How the hell should I know?"

"I take it he lives alone."

"Not for lack of trying."

Smith stared down the drive. "Watch our backs. I want to have a peek."

We switched positions. I covered the rear as Smith peeked over the bed. "I don't see anyone around. Where's the other car?"

"Under a tarp out back." I pointed into the treeline. I knew what I was looking for but even I couldn't see it. "It should be out there."

"You see it?"

"No. Too dark. But where would he go?"

"First things first," said Smith. "We have to find out if he left or not before we go chasing him."

"All right," I said. "The front is too well lit. Let's move around back. We'll use the kitchen door."

"Wait." He pointed at the Suburban. "Let's deflate the tires before we leave."

Staying low to use my truck as cover, we dashed up to his truck. While Smith tended to the rear, I unscrewed the cap from the front tire valve and depressed the stem. A cold micro-hurricane of rapidly expanding air hissed past my fingers. The tire quickly lost its shape. I had no sooner thrown away the cap than Smith joined me. He motioned with the revolver. "Around the front of the truck, then past the house. Stop at the back corner. I'll watch our backs."

"Right." I raised the automatic and stepped around the van, placing my steps carefully until I reached the house. I paused, checked around for any peculiar shadows. I figured anyone expecting me would also expect me to stay glued to the wall, so I kept away from it as I advanced to the far corner. I spared only a second's glance backward. Smith's shadow detached from the Suburban. I concentrated on the darkness ahead.

Smith joined me momentarily. "What's out back?"

I checked around the corner. "Awful dark." I took a slower look, this time examining not just the back of the house but also the lawn, spindly bushes at the edge of the crag behind the house, and the square structure of the shed. On the far side of the house a large shadow merged with the deeper darkness of the woods behind it. Too large for a person; probably a tarp-covered wood pile. It provided good cover that would bear watching.

I pulled back. "A lot of shadows, but I don't see anything unusual. The porch light is off. I think the kitchen light is off."

Smith nodded. Just past his shoulder a window pane reflected stars. He pointed to it. "The den?"

"Yuh."

"He's sure to go there before leaving. The lights could go on at any second. Remember that."

"No problem."

"What's the kitchen door look like?"

I had a quick peek. "Crossbuck wooden bottom, windows in the top, handle on the right."

"Storm door?"

"Nope."

"You sure?"

I glanced again. "Yuh."

He pointed at my gun. "How good are you with that thing?"

"Ninety-four out of a hundred in the black," I said.

"I could never beat eighty, even in my prime." He moved ahead, pulling even with me. "I'll take point and kick the door. Follow me close, cover, when it's clear go inside. I'll be right behind you. Okay?"

I took a deep breath before replying. "Ready."

Sparing one last glance behind us, Smith sprinted around the corner. I followed, circling outward as he advanced on the entrance. I stopped six feet out from the door, planted my feet firmly to brace myself for a shot, or to anchor for the vault through the door if I didn't shoot. I brought up the Beretta, sighting on the center window in the door. I exhaled through tight lips. I nodded at Smith.

In one hand he held the revolver, with the other he experimented with the doorknob. Twitchell could have been proving himself a novice, or he might have been careless; either way, to leave the back door unlocked was a serious mistake. Smith turned the knob, then pushed gently. The door swung inward, unhindered by bolt or chain. He pushed until it cleared the jamb, allowing a ribbon of light to escape. He backed to one side, motioning me closer. I obeyed, taking the opposite side, holding my aim. With the door surrounded, Smith pulled back, pushing on the wooden lower half with his toe. At first it opened silently and smoothly, then the balance must have shifted: the door fell away from Smith's boot. He reached out to stop it, missed it, and got out of the way as we waited it for it to slam against the stop. It never happened: halfway through its arc the edge rubbed against a throw rug. The rug bunched up, stopping the door before it hit the counter. Even to me, as I watched, the gentle bump made no sound.

I pulled in closer to the wall, edging forward, my aim imprecise but ready to instantly lock onto a target. At the door jamb a quick peek revealed nothing. I took a second look to confirm the lay of the kitchen. Countertops, stove, and sink surrounded three sides. An open door into a bathroom finished the square. Two wooden chairs flanked a small, square table directly at the center. I looked across the jamb at Smith, who looked back at me. His clear eyes, now outlined in the glow of the house lights, sparkled. I took that as an affirmation of his readiness. I crouched lower, braced my foot, took one last look around the back yard, then launched myself into the kitchen.

Silence during the approach had been essential. Now, cover and safety mattered more. With little regard for the noise I made, I dove between the table legs, eyes straight ahead, gun in hand, careening across the floor. My left shoulder rammed into the leg, but the pine table moved easily on the slick floor. A water glass rolled off the edge of the table and crashed onto the floor as I skidded to a stop.

I concentrated on the door. I brought up the Beretta, steadying it in both hands, shifting it slowly through a rectangle delineated by the inside of the door. I barely noticed the ghost that flitted through the open back door, drifting over the linoleum before taking refuge in the bathroom. When the revolver peered out through the slatted doors, I knew Smith was ready. A sudden silence gripped the house. Our entry must have been noted. How many were inside? I thought. Just Twitchell? How many of his EMTs were with him? Were they armed? Would they investigate? Or simply leave?

Before I could answer the questions, I froze. When we entered the house, a pair of floor lamps had flooded the living room. Now, with no forewarning, the light died. Only a feeble table lamp in the farthest corner provided illumination. Among the shadows I could only just begin to discern the fuzzy shapes of furniture. My hands felt damp and clammy on the grip as I tried to stop trembling. "Sheriff's department!" I cried. "Drop your gun and come out. Now!"

Nothing happened. No one surrendered, no one started shooting. There was no sound, either. "Come out at once!" I yelled.

Still no response. I wondered what to do next.

Then I heard a soft voice: "Jimmy, listen."

The whisper came from behind. I did not want to look away, fearing I might miss my one chance to defend myself. "Go on."

"On three, roll left to the counter."

"Right."

Quickly, he counted off. "One, two, three!" The blast could not have been louder had he fired battleship cannon. The boom of Smith's revolver completely masked the destruction of the light bulb. On three I rolled sideways, hunching tightly to clear the table legs. I just touched the baseboard when three blasts from the living room seconded the dying echo of Smith's shots. At least one came close, tugging at the back of my shirt. I covered the doorway again waiting for anything to move. As my finger tightened, I forced myself to relax. An unnecessary shot would only betray my position. My chance would come. I could see the living room furniture more distinctly now. I rose to a crouch, advancing to the cover of a corner by the stove.

Still, tense seconds passed. No advantage came from waiting, I thought. I had no idea what Smith planned, but knew I could not wait for him to do everything. I reviewed the kitchen topography, estimated that I was about seven feet from the door, and edged past the stove until my probing hand found the door jamb. I took a quick peek around the corner. Twitchell's taste in furniture ran toward modern: sharp angles, straight lines, muted solid colors. Near the couch, an out-of-place rounded shadow stood out. I made another quick peek: the shape had altered, moving slightly left. I held the scene I had just witnessed in my mind, concentrated on it, focused tightly on the image. I slid a foot forward, braced, reached around the corner and squeezed off two shots. Even as I fired the second shot, I caught the round shadow fleeing farther left, well away from the couch. I knew I had missed. I pulled back.

My breath came in short gasps, my hands remained locked around the grip. Spent gunpowder hung in the air, pungent against the thick, stale night air. Smith's shape detached from the bathroom door, seeming to line up on something. A fraction of a second later, an orange blast and a pair of echoing booms confirmed my suspicions.

I stayed clear of the doorway while he fired. As soon as he finished, I checked around the corner. Only shadows of furniture looked back. Nothing interrupted the pattern. Smith might have been luckier than I had been. I withdrew to listen. A wounded man should make some noise. A dead man and a stalking one sound remarkably similar. Simply by ear, how could I tell the difference? I detected a soft swishing, like rubber soles passing on polished wood. Firing by sound is never easy. I tried to fit the sound into my mental blueprint of the room. Either he hid very close to the left wall, by the baseboards, or along the front wall, near the windows. The first position was too exposed; he had to be by the window. I sighted on my mental target, rose higher off the floor to prevent reappearing in my last firing position, slid around the corner, and fired two pairs of shots.

Those shots initiated an avalanche of sound. One shot missed everything in the room, smashing into the plate glass window by the front door. The glass dissolved into a gray web before exploding with a shattering jingle that rivaled the fall of a great chandelier. Smith added two shots, the booming roar of his revolver clear above my own staccato pistol blasts. The suspect returned fire quickly, firing wide. The muzzle flash betrayed him. I shifted my aim and fired twice. A dull thud coincided with a scream of pain to end the noise.

With the suspect down, I had no time to lose. "I'm going through." I pushed off the door jamb into the living room, firing my last rounds blindly into the couch. Past the den door, I stayed low, crashing into an end table before establishing a new position behind a corner chair. I came to a stop on one knee, gun up and steady,

breathing rapidly through clenched teeth. I ejected the spent magazine, exchanging it for a full one. I watched the shadows, listening.

No movement: no shuffling, no stumbling, no footfalls. As my
own breathing eased, I heard wheezing from beneath the shattered
window, interspersed with authentic groans: irregular, chopped,
strained, not the even, tentative groans of a performance. Nothing
came from the kitchen, the den behind me remained silent as a tomb,
the floorboards upstairs did not squeak. I felt confident the suspect
would not shoot. I half rose, reached out a hand to find the end
table, and felt around for the lamp I knew must be there. I found it
and ran my fingers to the switch. "Smith, stay back," I said. "I'm hitting the lights." I balanced my gun in one hand, took a good bead
on the loft just in case, and flipped the switch.

Shadows instantly fled, replaced by the concrete forms of square
furniture. I looked for any movement, sweeping round the room. If
anything had moved anywhere, I would have fired. I looked up
where the light abruptly ended at the balcony rail, but nothing disturbed the straight line of the beams. I scanned the living room, almost firing at my reflection in the three intact windowpanes. Smith,
still crouched beside the door, methodically swung his revolver to
cover the room, his eyes, arms, all moving robotically behind the
weapon grasped firmly in his hands. His eyes met mine for a second
before he reversed his search. "You all right?"

"Yuh." With the light on, I could see that the hand supporting
the Beretta trembled. I had often fired in practice, distinguished myself as a marksman, but in three years of police work, I had never
fired on duty. A dry, tightness at the back of my mouth and a hollow,
leaden sensation deep in my stomach told me I did not want to make
it a habit. "I'm okay."

"Good." His gun steadied on a point behind me, holding steady
as he came out of the doorway. "Recognize our friend?"

Crumpled against the wall, his face no mask for the pain he felt,
sat a boy. He gasped irregularly, each new breath wracking his face
with agony. He clutched a .32 revolver in his right hand, but the gun
remained immobile, pointing at the basement. His left hand clutched
at his right shoulder; blood oozing between the fingers. A growing
burgundy stain soaked through his shirt, already saturating his shoulder and working toward his chest. He couldn't be more than a couple months older than seventeen. He shared classes with my sister.

"Jesus Christ."

All thoughts of finding Twitchell fled as I set down my gun on
the carpet and crouched beside him. I did not completely forget my

job. First I pried the gun from his hands and kicked it away. "His name's Danny Hodgdon," I said, gently pulling his arm away from the wound to reveal a combination of blood, shredded flesh, and torn shirt. I pushed his left hand firmly against the wound and pressed against the back of his hand. "He goes to MDI with my sister. Shares his father's lobster boat during the summer."

"Nice kid," Smith said from over my shoulder. "I'll have a quick look around."

"There's got to be a crash kit in the kitchen," I replied. "At least get a couple towels."

I returned to the patient. He had no business being involved, I thought. Whatever plans he'd had for a quick buck, he could not have expected this. I wanted to ask him how Twitchell had persuaded him to join the team. Perhaps the lucrative assignment of high school sales? My head burned at the thought that Twitchell could dump cocaine into my own school. Angrily I looked into Danny's eyes, but the anger drained away. It wasn't Danny I was mad at. Terrified, shocked eyes stared back from a face so twisted by pain it had no room for anything else. "Take it easy, Danny," I soothed. "Relax."

His lips trembled as he tried to speak; but all that came forth was a thin trickle of blood. Tears fell down his face, disappearing into his open mouth.

Smith dropped a first-aid kit beside me. I could not tell whether Danny had been hit by my gun or Smith's, but the bullet had passed clean through his shoulder. I suspected that Winter's gun fired common, lead-nosed ammunition, and the injury looked more like the work of my metal-jacketed 9-mm shell. Not that it mattered. The immediate problem was the bleeding: there was blood everywhere. I tried to pull as much of the shirt as I could out of the wound. I ripped open the biggest piece of gauze in the box, folded it into quarters, and slipped it under his hand before pressing it firmly against the pulsing red tide.

Smith returned. "No one else here. Place is clean. Your friend must have been sent to collect a few things. Twitchell must think we're close."

He carried a lot of stuff, but I was too busy to examine his findings. "What do you have?"

"Three packages of a dense white powder," he said. "There's a gym bag in the loft. I found the bags inside. And this." He held something beside my head; I heard a cricketlike rasp, and a soft puff on my cheek. "Money. Right off the truck, in bank bundles of twenties and fifties. Around fifty thousand dollars. Worth sending the kid for."

"But not worth risking his own ass," I said. The blood had already soaked through the gauze and had begun to pool between Danny's fingers. I wiped off what I could with another bandage, then put another piece of gauze under his palm. He was growing paler by the second. His breathing was fast and shallow. I touched his cheek; the skin was already icy cold, clammy. "We need an ambulance up here, Smith."

He looked over Danny. "Whatever he's doing, you can bet Twitchell has one ear glued to his radio," he said pensively. "If we call in an emergency at his house, he's going to know what happened."

The sterile gauze wasn't enough. I ripped a piece of Danny's shirt and jammed it under his hand. "He's going into shock. He needs more help than I can give him. We don't have a choice."

Smith nodded. "If Twitchell has any doubt you're on his trail, this will confirm it. He'll run for certain."

So much happened so quickly—the shooting, Winter at the firehouse, and Twitchell at trail's end—it was hard to think straight. How could I help Danny without letting Twitchell slip away? He needed an ambulance fast. Even just a better-trained EMT with some additional supplies would be better than nothing.

"Call 2427. Ask for Ben Cruickshank. He's a good EMT and carries a crash pack. He lives down at the bottom of the hill. He can tend to Danny until we can nail Twitchell."

"Danny needs a hospital."

"Ben can handle it for a while. I trust him. If we tip off Twitchell now, we'll never see him again."

Smith looked down at the pitiful form on the floor. "Two four two seven?"

"Yuh."

"I'll be right back."

I sighed. I trusted Ben as much as I trusted any of the other ambulance corpsmen. Then I thought of Twitchell, and the role the ambulance played in distribution. Could I truly trust any of them? But what choice did I have? "It's bad enough that one side has no regard for human life," I mumbled softly as I changed dressings again. "We don't all have to act like jackasses."

Danny's right hand touched my wrist. He grimaced at the pain, but held on. Had he been healthier, the touch would have been a grab, but as it was, he held on to me the same way my grandmother did just before she died. I looked up at his face. His mouth moved, but the words were indistinct. He tried again. "He already knows," he croaked.

"What?" I said. "What do you mean?"

His fingers dug deeper into my wrist as he struggled against the onset of shock. "Twitch knows you're after him," he gasped. "He heard about the DEA hitting the pharmacy."

"How the hell could he know so fast?" I said.

"Anyone with a scanner could have figured it out," said Smith as he knelt down. "Cruickshank said he'll be here in five minutes."

"Who told him?" I pressed Danny.

He shook his head, momentarily forgetting that the muscles that moved his head were anchored in his shoulders; he was reminded quickly. "I don't know, Jimmy. I don't know," he pleaded. A steady cascade of tears ran down his cheeks. He grimaced, howling against the pain. "He sent me here for the bag."

"Where is he?" I asked insistently. He did not respond, so I repeated the query. "Where is he, Danny?"

"He said he had stuff to do. He had to keep you away. He thought he'd make it if he could just clear the island. He wanted to buy some time."

"Buy some time?" I replied. My voice came harshly as stress-tightened vocal cords raised the pitch. "How was he going to do that?"

"I don't know, Jimmy. I swear I don't know!"

"You must have a clue, Danny. Come on. You do, don't you? What is it? Tell me!"

Another hand clamped onto my forearm, significantly tighter. "Let go, Jimmy," said Smith. "Let him go."

Smith gently but firmly pried my arm off Danny's shoulder. Once I was disconnected from Danny, my anger flowed away again. I blinked a couple of times and fell against the couch.

Smith changed the dressing, pressing Danny's left hand against it. "Press tightly on this." He turned to me. "Even as desperate as he must be, I can't believe Twitchell would tell Danny anything. He sent him here because he's expendable. You don't tell expendable people your plan."

"What plan can he have?" I asked. "He needs to get to the mainland, simple as that. Once he crosses the bridge, where does he go from there?"

"Anywhere he pleases," answered Smith. "On the island, he's confined. Ashore, he can go in any direction, by any means. As his options increase, the chances of our picking the right one diminish."

"If he's smart, he's already off the island," I grumbled. "We'll never catch him."

"He must need something before he can go. At least he wants

to get the cash." Smith faced Danny. "Once you had the bag, Danny, where were you supposed to take it?"

"He told me to throw it in a dumpster at the Bar Harbor municipal dock."

Smith shook his head. "This guy is crafty. Keeps his options open. He can get there any way, any time, before pick-up day. Or someone else can bring it to him."

"Great," I said. "He's smart, he's clever. What now?"

"You forgot something," he said after a moment.

I shook my head, sighing. The log of my investigation was a series of things forgotten, overlooked, or ignored. "What?"

"He's scared."

I stopped. I had not expected him to say that. "Scared?"

"Yes, scared. For some reason, you make him nervous." He pointed over his shoulder. "If you believe Danny, Twitchell sounds desperate to keep you away from him."

"Why?" I said. "He's got the county sheriff, the DEA, and the state police on his trail. Why should he fear one rookie detective?"

He shrugged. "He must think you know more about him."

"If he's got a scanner, he knows we haven't called the sheriff. We can't have too much."

"If he knows we're after him, he might suspect we're keeping the channels clear to fool him. He might expect us to call in soon, like any good detective. He wants to buy time—he wants to delay you from calling in."

"How can he do that?" I said. "If he wanted me, why didn't he come up here and wait himself? He had to know I'd show up eventually. If he's so damn smart why didn't he—" In an instant every trace of color in my face drained away. In that instant I knew I had grossly underestimated Twitchell. "Oh, God, no," I whispered. "No, he can't."

I rose to my feet, eyes unfocused. Bouncing headlights and the roar of a large truck engine signaled Cruickshank's approach. Smith stood beside me. "What is it?" he said. "What's wrong?"

I had no more time for words, no more time for investigating, gathering evidence, or any of the other banal details of detective work. Walker and Wiley could keep their procedures. I had to do this one now, free of their help or hindrance. Reading the paperwork had failed to convey the ruthlessness that allowed a man to import and sell drugs, to run over a jogger on the highway, or to arm a boy like Danny and send him to fend off the police. A man who could do that would stop at nothing to save his own skin. Twitchell, though I had not noticed it in time, was such a man.

My right hand dropped onto my gun, the joints tightening. Had I looked, I knew the knuckles would have been whiter than my face. One word formed on my lips. "Robyn."

11

Saturday Night

Patrol Area: Mount Desert Narrows area
Warm, muggy, 85–90°F;
wind nil; sky clear

As fast as the realization set, I changed from an EMT, right through a police officer, becoming something dangerously close to a vigilante. I abandoned my patient, hurdling his sprawled legs, and sending a lamp to its noisy demise. "Robyn!" I said again, one hand on the door.

Headlights caught me full as I ran through the door. Cruickshank's pickup came to a stop. Ben turned to me as he stepped out. "Jimmy?" he said hesitantly. "What's the hurry—"

"Victim's inside," I heard Smith call back from just behind me. "Jimmy will explain later." I fumbled with my keys, swearing profusely. I slid the key into the ignition. The engine roared to life, as if eager to engage the enemy.

I rammed the transmission into reverse, looked back through the window, just catching Smith in the corner of my eye as he flung open the passenger door. He had one foot on the running board as I dispatched a spray of gravel to bounce off the side of Ben's truck. Smith held on tightly, one hand on the open door, one hand on the seat back, one foot on the board, one dangling. I could not spare time to see to his safety.

When I cleared Cruickshank's pickup, I swung hard right, barely missing a thick pine. I turned hard left, jammed the gearshift into first, heard the passenger door slam as Smith came inside, set my teeth, and sent a shower of grass and topsoil back against the side of the house. I took the hairpin in the drive too fast: only a rapid, wild slew prevented the rear end from bouncing off a tree trunk. I braked hard, swinging onto the road.

"Don't go faster than you can handle," said Smith. Although I had no time to listen to him, some part of my mind registered his words. "You can't help her if we don't make it."

I eased up on the pedal. A back road along the ridge offered a route significantly shorter than the highway. Potholes, frost heaves, and poorly laid repair patches competed for a chance to annihilate the suspension as we raced down the road. I needed to replace the shocks anyway, I thought. Might as well ensure the old ones are worn out.

"What do you plan to do when you get to Robyn's house?" he said.

I had no answer. "I'll think of something."

"Think about it," he replied. "If we're not already too late, we won't be much help if we just drive up and look stupid."

I turned hard to avoid a washout. "I'm kind of busy, Smith."

"You drive. I'll plan," he said.

Aided as much by a lack of traffic as by my intense anger, I shaved two minutes off my own best time. We bumped our way off the gravel, took one last bone-crunching hit as the rear axle slammed into the asphalt square on, then tore off down the highway.

Though the vibration and the jarring, numbing crashes were gone, the blast of wind and the howl of the engine at near-maximum revolutions remained. I stole a glance at Smith. He clung to the suicide strap over the door with one hand, the other hand locked on the dashboard edge. He saw my glance, replying with a grim smile. "I prefer this road to the last."

Under seven minutes later—another personal best—I swung into the driveway, miscalculating enough to tear up a sizable portion of the lawn. Robyn's Volkswagen gave me a second's hope that died stillborn when I saw the screen door torn off its hinges, the front door left ajar. I jerked up the parking brake, one foot on the ground as the locked wheels skidded over the grass. A cloud of thick dust overtook me as I jumped over the door, up the steps, and came to a stop in the doorway, my hand immobile on the door frame.

I should have gone faster.

Robyn could not have anticipated their coming, but she clearly had resisted. The front door would have been locked: that's why they tore it down. They got inside, but gave her warning. The living room had been hit hardest. The couch feet touched the wall rather than the floor. The armchair balanced on two legs, back against the wall, hung halfway between up and down. The floor lamp sprawled full length on the floor, shade askew against the corner of the coffee table. The table had been split in half, one splintered end on the rug, the other a vertical wall a few feet away. Papers and magazines completely obscured the throw rug beneath the table.

I absorbed it all in a second. I drew my gun, advancing into the kitchen with more speed than caution. It was quite orderly; the primary conflict had clearly been in the living room. I checked the back door, found it locked and bolted from the inside. Twitchell had come to the front door, leaving by the same route.

I left the kitchen, ran through the living room, quickly checking the bedroom, then the bathroom. Nowhere was there any sign of Robyn, any sign of where she might have been taken. My gun arm dropped to my side as I returned to the living room, pushed the armchair flat on the floor, and fell heavily into it.

Smith entered, his eyes roving around the room. He retraced my steps, passing through the other three rooms before returning to the living room. He pushed the couch upright and sat down on one arm. "Looks like he beat us."

I stared emptily at the pile of papers. "Looks like it."

He leaned forward, wringing his hands. "I'm sorry."

I shook my head. "I should have driven faster."

"We went fast enough," he replied. "We were too late to make a difference."

"I should have kept out of it."

"You had to do your job, Jimmy," he said sympathetically. "And you had to do it as best as you could."

"I should have—"

"Just shut up, will you?" he commanded softly. "This is not your fault. You're after a ruthless coward. He would have taken anyone who might have helped him."

Binkley jumped onto the back of the couch and mewed experimentally. His eyes were wide, his back so tense he trembled with each tentative step. He had probably been beside Robyn when it happened, and had taken refuge in his litter box. He moved to Smith, pushing himself closer until Smith picked him up. "Twitchell obviously knew her, knows who you are. He might have taken her even if it hadn't been you after him."

"If he tries anything, I'll . . . ." I let it trail off. Neither for myself nor for Smith did I need to finish.

"I doubt he'll hurt her unless he's backed into a corner." He sat back, absentmindedly stroking the cat, thinking. "He may not even know what to do with her."

For a moment, I considered the prospect of not getting her back alive. I couldn't even think about that: it simply could not be. My life, my future depended on Robyn Cole. I had never thought about her in such a way before. I remembered our discussion on her back porch, when I did not have an answer for her. Twitchell's actions gave my thoughts from that night a voice. "I have to get her back, Smith," I said. "The whole case can go to hell. I'll let him go wherever he wants, with whatever he can carry, but I've got to get her back."

Smith leaned forward. "More than anyone else could, I know what you're going through," he said gently. "I hope this turns out better for you than it did for me."

"I'll never forgive myself."

"Let's hope you don't have to." He sat up straight again. "Because you're absolutely right."

"What next?" I said after a moment. "Wait here? Head for the bridge? Chase around the island? Call the sheriff?"

An insistent electronic buzz sounded under the pile of papers. It came a second time. Smith pushed the cat aside, lunged forward and flung the papers aside. He uncovered the telephone on the third ring. "We answer the phone." He handed it to me.

I picked up the receiver. "Hello?"

"Hello, Jimmy. I thought I'd find you there."

There could be no mistaking that voice, at once familiar and foreign. I did not waste courtesy on him. "Where's Robyn?"

"She's fine, Jimmy."

"Let me talk to her."

"Listen, Jimmy, we don't have time to waste arguing," he said coldly. "Do you want to hear why I called, or would you rather argue and waste the few minutes I can spare?"

"No," I said quickly. "Talk."

"Here's the deal. You haven't called the sheriff yet, for which I am exceedingly grateful."

"How do you know I haven't called?" I said. "How do you know they're not on their way now?"

"For Chrissake, Hoitt, don't treat me like a moron," he snapped, and he was right. I had done so before. As a result, he had Robyn, and I didn't. "I have a radio or two!"

"Go on."

"I don't know why you didn't call before, but we can both use that. Let me off the island, Hoitt. That's all I ask."

"I'm not the only thing stopping you."

"Right now, you are. Keep it that way. Sit tight. Keep your mouth shut. Stay away from the phone."

"Okay," I replied. "What about Robyn?"

"As soon as I cross the bridge, if I don't see anyone but you, I'll let her out, no harm done. Deal?"

I put the phone down, wishing a moment to consider my options. It didn't take much thinking to realize I didn't have any. "Agreed."

"You're smarter than the others, Hoitt," said Twitchell. "Don't disappoint me now."

"Yeah, yeah," I answered. "Just hurry up and get off my island. I'll be waiting." I felt helpless, controlled, manipulated. I seized the only option for control available: I slammed down the receiver.

"Twitchell, I presume."

I recounted the conversation for Smith. He nodded at its conclusion. "Cocky bastard, isn't he?"

"Damn cocky for a guy who's trapped on an island, surrounded by the police."

Smith rose. "With so many people so close to him, I don't think he can disappear fast enough, even if he does reach the mainland."

"I've underestimated him," I said tiredly. "I wouldn't bet we can track him once he clears the island. Too many options. He's had too much time to prepare for this, just in case his operation fell down around him."

"Which is more important?" he asked after a moment. "Stopping him, or sparing Robyn?"

"That's not a fair question."

A grim smile flashed over his face. "Tell me about it."

I put my head in my hands, staring at the floor. "If we let him go, he can kill more people than just one woman. Hundreds of people."

"He can hurt thousands," said Smith.

"Thanks," I replied.

Smith knelt on the floor beside me. "I understand what you're going through, Jimmy. You're torn between an oath and a vow. An oath to protect people and property, and a vow to one woman."

"We're not married."

He shrugged it off. "It's not about a civil ceremony. It's about a private commitment."

I knew he was correct.

"You can't balance the two against each other, then obey the stronger. You have to do what seems right, what seems to be the one you can live with for a week, or a year, from now. That's what I had to do. It's what you have to do now." He stood up. "Whatever happens, you must accept the consequences. It's your call."

He was right. I knew he was right in everything he had said. Underlying it all I knew, too, that he did his best to subtly bias my decision in the light of his own painful lessons. "What would you do?" I asked.

"Another unfair question," he replied.

I crouched forward, running my hand through hair damp with humidity and anger. It wouldn't have mattered what he answered, anyway. "Somewhere on this island is a man I thought I knew," I said sourly. "I worked for him saving people's lives. I have dined and fished with him, I've stood on the dock and talked with him. Yet he fooled me. He kept his second life a deep secret. I don't trust him any further than I could heave him." I took a deep breath, stood up and faced Smith. "Which I would greatly enjoy doing right now."

"I don't see any reason you should trust him," said Smith. "So what?"

"I think he's lying. If he gets over the bridge, he's history. Why should he slow down to let Robyn go? She might be useful again."

"A good businessman doesn't waste his assets," observed Smith. "Bad for business."

"Good businessmen don't harm children, either. He's used the dirtiest tactics all along. He won't change his MO now."

"You intend to call Wiley and the sheriff? Set up an ambush?"

"No," I replied. "That would guarantee bloodshed. We'll keep it small. Just us."

"The sheriff won't approve of this. Wiley won't enjoy being cut out of the climax."

Smith underestimated Walker. He'd have me flogged, keel-hauled, and thrown in irons. Too damn bad, I thought. "The hell with them. When their wives are on the line, then we'll play it their way. Tonight, this is my game."

"All right," said Smith. "You have a plan?"

"No."

Smith crossed his arms, eyeing me curiously. "We're not going to get far just standing here."

"I have two things," I answered. "First, a hunch. He's had ample time since the pharmacy raid to leave the island. Yet he hasn't. He needs something."

"Only cash and some cocaine at his house," said Smith. "Fifty thousand in petty cash. More tied up in the coke, but it's not exactly liquid. Not like traveler's checks."

"We might have interrupted Danny before he reached the big

stash. More important, if he sent Danny out there, who's to say he didn't send out others?"

"So he's either waiting to collect everything, or he plans to get it all himself. Must be pretty important."

I forced myself to think. The money was the only thing Twitchell could use. "Wiley couldn't trace the money because Twitchell is an old-fashioned fisherman. He didn't spend it, he stuffed it away. Literally. That's why there were no bank records. He probably has vast stores of cash, hidden all over the island. He'll be needing all the cash he can get. He can't come back. If he returns to the island, sooner or later he'd be recognized. He leaves, he's gone."

"I'm convinced. What's the other thing?"

I tapped the remains of the coffee table. "We know how he's going to clear the island."

"How?"

"The same way he got everything off the island without raising an eyebrow." Despite the way I felt, I couldn't help but smile. "By ambulance."

"How do you know?"

"He keeps coming back to it, in everything he does. No reason he should change now, at the last minute. I'll bet that's why Winter was there—to get the ambulance ready to go. There's only one place he can easily get his hands on an ambulance."

"He could have it already," said Smith. "He could be on his way while we've been jabbering."

"He needed to buy time," I replied. "That's why he called. That's why he didn't just leave."

Smith looked at his watch. "We may have some time, but I guarantee we don't have much."

"Then we have no time to lose."

Another screaming, bouncing run over the west ridge brought us into Eagle Harbor. I gambled that Twitchell had no lookouts, shut off the lights and drifted, engine off, into the church parking lot. I circled the church, dashed across the lawn, advancing on the fire station from a scraggly, half-dead hedge. Despite the darkness on either side of the door, the reflective orange paint revealed the presence of the ambulance. He hadn't left yet.

Smith joined me, huffing and puffing. "Well?"

"It's still there," I said.

"Maybe it's still there because no one plans to use it."

I shrugged. "Then we have nothing to lose."

Smith laid a hand on my shoulder. "I have to go to my boat. I'll be right back. If he shows up, don't wait for me."

"Don't worry. I won't."

The hand on my shoulder melted away. I barely heard him go as he scrambled over the rocks.

I could do nothing but sit and wait, nothing except pray I hadn't bungled it one final time. If Twitchell escaped Mount Desert Island, evading Wiley's dragnet, I had no one to blame but myself. If he released Robyn as promised, well and good, though I doubted Sheriff Walker would see it that way. If Twitchell kept Robyn, or killed her, he would be gone, and our last chance to catch him would have disappeared because I squatted behind a hedge watching a garage door on the wrong side of the island. I had one chance to get it right, one slim hunch that closed in on me as the time ticked away with no sign of Twitchell.

Smith returned. He'd traded the revolver for the smooth barrel of a .12-gauge shotgun. He held it loosely, professionally in his hands. "Since you're the marksman, I thought I'd trade precision for stopping power."

"Nice piece."

He patted the barrel. "Custom."

"Ever used it before?" I asked.

Starlight glinted off his teeth. "Once or twice." The smile vanished. "Any luck?"

I shook my head. "I'm beginning to wonder whether I have any future as a detective."

Smith craned his neck to peer over the hedge. "You show promise. He's coming up now."

Sure enough, creeping down the street came Twitchell, driving Danny Hodgdon's battered Buick, following a Ford estate wagon at a discreet distance. Dazzled by two sets of headlights, I could not see Robyn—whether he had placed her in the passenger seat, or the back seat, or indeed whether she was visible at all. The hedge ran close enough to the road that even through its tangled underbrush I could see the Buick. I dropped down lower, though I could see no reason Twitchell should expect visitors.

The Ford moved past. Twitchell turned into the driveway. He immediately doused the lights, but his foot lingered on the brake pedal. From my position the brake lights flashed right in my eyes; not only would they make it easier for him to see us, they also made it impossible for me to see past the trunk inside.

Finally the brakes went out. The dome light glowed dull orange as he opened the door. For the first time since I had realized who and what he was, I saw Twitchell. Outwardly, I saw the same tall, narrow-shouldered man in the plaid shirt. Even now, as he attempted to flee forever, the squat fire-call beeper hung on his belt. I wondered if he even felt it, or whether it had become as much a part of him as the thick lenses that hid his eyes. Tension carved deep furrows along his haggard face. When he moved his hands, or especially as he jerked his head in response to sounds, the desperation of his situation heightened his natural jumpiness. He looked like a strung out junkie. I could not help but smile at the irony.

The smile died. His head snapped around, searching all directions as he slammed the driver's door. The unsteady, nervous hand yanked open the rear door, reached in, and hauled out a clearly uncooperative female. Though street lights penetrated the alley between the church and the station house, I didn't recognize the clothes. Yet the figure, the way she moved, left me certain of her identity. An automatic reaction within me tightened my leg muscles, tensed me to vault the hedge as my right hand dropped unbidden to the holster. A firm hand on my shoulder brought me back under control. Not yet.

Twitchell's head bobbed like a feeding gull, constantly trying to see behind him, never seeing quite enough to satisfy him. In the hand that did not hold Robyn, I now saw a compact, blunt shape dully reflecting the light. While a respectable weapon, the snub-nosed .38 could not hope to match either the .12-gauge shotgun or the 9-mm Beretta, let alone both. Yet as long as the distance between that little revolver and Robyn remained significantly smaller than the range from it to me, it held more power than any cannon.

Captive and captor rounded the hood. Twitchell fumbled with the keys, said something to Robyn, then, juggling keys and gun together, he unlocked the door. They passed inside. A resonant slam accompanied the rattle of loose glass as he shut it behind him.

I sat on the grass for a moment, my back to the station. Wonderful, I thought: I had managed to apply what I had learned to successfully predict where he would go, then beat him there. Chances were good I could even guess how he intended to leave the island. Problem was, what did I intend to do about it?

"I presume he's armed," said Smith. "But I didn't see anything."

"A revolver, probably a snub-nosed .38."

"That figures." He touched his pocket, revealing a bulge I hadn't noticed before. He hadn't abandoned the .38 after all. "He seems to like them."

"He'll head for Thompson's Point from here. There's really no place to ambush him, even if we had time to set it up."

"Sure you don't want to call the sheriff?"

"Positive." I got to my feet, turned around, and surveyed the target. It was dark in there. Obviously scared, he wasn't hitting the lights. "We've got to try now. He's going to have to open the door before he can leave. It's electric. When he does that, I'll go through. You go for the back door."

"It's probably locked."

"When the front door goes up—you'll know, it's a cheap, loud motor—I don't care how you do it, but get in."

"You had a key before," he said patiently.

I cursed myself for allowing the excitement to block parts of my brain that I still needed. I handed over the keys. "Noise be damned once the door opens."

"Better hurry."

"Right."

He went left around the hedge; I went right. The L-shaped hedge allowed him to cut directly across the road, heading for the cover offered by the tangle of shrubs by the church. Forced to head first for the water, then double back, I came to a stop as a row of six or seven cars crept past. It seemed to me, as I stood outlined against the dock lights, that any common sea snail could have zoomed past me in the time it took those cars to pass. At least one passenger noticed me crouching beside the hedge, I wondered what they thought of the gun in my hand.

The last car finally passed. I immediately moved out into the road, so close to the last car I nearly hit it. A quick glance to the left, but no sign of Smith. He would have to take care of himself. There had once been a large colonial house between the station and O'Brien's, but now only a low stone foundation marked the spot. I crawled over it, advancing to the corner of the station.

Though a window beckoned only a few feet to my left, I did not bother to peer inside. Racks of fire equipment obscured most of the view. Twitchell would have a better chance to see me peering in than I would of catching a glimpse of him or Robyn. I took a quick peek around the front, but, as expected, the door remained closed. I withdrew, stepped gingerly onto the stones abutting the station house, and waited. Twitchell could not possibly see me. In the last few hours I had been granted explicit evidence that he had other people working for him. Any of his staff covering the outside could not fail to see me. I kept a wary eye roving the perimeter, trying to penetrate the threatening spaces that surrounded me.

A low-pitched rumble inside halted my exterior search. The walls and distance effectively garbled any clear identification, but it sounded like a voice. I heard another—a second, or simply the same person speaking in a different tone? Agitated, perhaps? Twitchell had given Robyn an order, she had failed to comply, and now he raised his voice. Or perhaps he had an accomplice with him? As long as the door remained closed, I could not tell the truth.

Another sound, sharper, more metallic: the ambulance door slamming shut. Driver's, passenger's, or rear door, they were all alike. Whichever door, it would most likely be Robyn. I doubted Twitchell would enter the vehicle first and hope she followed. The specter of an accomplice complicated everything, but I had no evidence that Twitchell was not alone with Robyn. Could I dare to ignore the possibility? If they were not alone, who would most likely—

A ratchety, metallic clanking began. The motor started, the chain jangled against the metal frame, then followed a tired creak as the door moved. No more time for speculation. I assembled a mental image of the layout, noting the position of the door switch, the ambulance, the rear hall through which I hoped Smith would come, where I suspected Twitchell and Robyn to be. I jumped around the corner and took up my post near the center of the door. It was already two feet off the ground, and I dared not wait for it to rise higher. I crouched low, had a quick peek inside, which revealed nothing except the trucks, rolled under and in, and scrambled to my feet.

The door clanked upward. I maintained a defensive crouch, which prevented me from seeing inside the ambulance immediately to my right. The engine had not yet started, though the door must have been nearly high enough. In the dark, cavernous garage, I could discern only large shapes, the radio operating lights, a dim pool of light on the floor from the exit sign over the back door. I looked closely at the last, hoping to see a sign that Smith had made it inside, but I saw nothing.

I began to advance, but a loud click beside my head stopped me. Immediately I swung toward the sound, hoping to line up my gun on the source. Directly in front of me, the handle on the side door of the ambulance moved downward, then the entire door slid back. Despite the deep darkness, I had no difficulty in recognizing Twitchell's face. "Well, well, Jimmy," he said amiably. "I had a feeling you might crash the party."

I steadied the gun on his chest. I wondered for a second how he could have reached the vehicle so quickly after opening the garage—the switch hung on the wall beside the office. "Where's Robyn?"

"Don't you want to arrest me first?"

"Where's Robyn?" I insisted.

"Get the interior light," he said, obviously not to me. The lights inside the ambulance momentarily dazzled me, but it passed instantly. Twitchell had not been so affected: he'd had the foresight to place his palm over his brow. His left palm, an awkward pose, but I quickly saw why as I followed his extended right arm to his hand, locked around the revolver against the back of the driver's neck—Robyn's neck. "Got the picture, Jimmy?"

"Let her go."

"That would hardly be in my best interests." He dropped his left hand; he blinked a couple times, but his eyes never closed long enough for me to act. Not that he needed to see to pull the trigger. "Drop your gun, Hoitt. Now."

I hesitated. I wished I had formed a better plan. I sighted on the center of Twitchell's forehead, but the gun sight wavered before me. I could not hold it steady. My proud reputation as a marksman had abandoned me. I could not guarantee a hit, much less a fatal one. If I dropped the gun, I became the target. If I fired, he might have just the time needed to fire before he died. What the hell was I supposed to do?

"No."

His calm, easy manner disappeared instantly. "It's now or later," he said. "You're outnumbered two to one. That doesn't even consider my obvious advantage. Any second now, someone is going to come up behind you."

I resisted the urge to check my rear. I backed away until I reached the pumper. I preferred not to be jumped. "That's pretty old, Mike."

"Old tricks are often the best. Come on, I don't have all—" Shattered glass, two heavy thuds, and a groan from the back of the station halted his speech. He looked away, his eyes narrowing to see the doorway, but as I tensed to lunge, he looked back. "Don't get smart. You weren't alone."

"One of us is outnumbered." I decided to play bold, even though I did not feel that way. "Care to gamble who it is?"

"I think I'll hedge my bets." He pushed the gun harder into Robyn's neck. She slid forward, but didn't make a sound. "Start the truck."

"Do it yourself," she snapped.

While I admired her spirit, her timing needed improvement. "Robyn, do what he says. Please."

She leaned forward to turn the key. The engine caught at once. "There. Happy now?"

"Soon enough, Robyn, soon enough." His voice was tremulous and strained; the knuckles on the revolver were sickly white. I didn't think he held much faith in his partner anymore, either. "We're leaving, Hoitt. Stay away, and I might consider sticking to my deal. I hope not to see you again." Keeping his eyes on me and the gun on Robyn, he slid the door closed. "Let's go. Turn left."

She obeyed this time, starting to roll outside. He must have goaded her on, for she gave it some gas as the emergency lights ignited. They gained speed and headed north.

I ran into the driveway, the gun limp in my hand. Any concerns I might have had about another suspect inside fled as surely as the ambulance. They slipped around the corner, leaving behind only the smell of gasoline and the flicker of white and red lights.

"Damn it."

"Sorry I missed the party," puffed Smith, materializing beside me. He bent over, his hands on his knees, gasping. "I was unavoidably detained."

"They're heading for Thompson's. Robyn's driving."

"Hoitt, it's time to call the sheriff. He has much better resources for this kind—"

"No!" I shouted. "If they set up a roadblock, she's as good as dead. Whether he shoots her or she's caught in the crossfire, she's dead. I'll handle this."

"You're taking a big chance."

"I'm the one who'll have to live with it. If I have to live with it, we're going to do it my way. You can stay here if you want."

"Don't be stupid."

"If we're going to do anything, we've got to get there first." I ran back to the truck, Smith hot on my heels.

I jumped in, fired it up, and began rolling as he took the right seat. "Oh, God," groaned Smith. "Not another bump and grind over the back roads."

"Last one, I promise." I headed right. Knowing what I intended to do, I buckled my seat belt. "There's an emergency light under your seat. Put it on the dash. It might help."

He reached down. "I hope there's nothing in our way."

I had no idea how hard Twitchell intended to push Robyn, how much whip-cracking he would try to reach the bridge quickly. With an official emergency vehicle, he had an excuse to violate whatever speed limit he encountered. But even a speeding ambulance would eventually draw attention. If he elected for the fastest speed, I couldn't beat him. I had no alternative but to drive as fast as my skill, truck, and nerve would allow.

We raced northward, hoping the flashing light would clear a path. Other traffic was only a momentary distraction. I lost track of time; it seemed only minutes before we crested the hill before the narrows, and the country store guarding the island came into view. I slowed and scanned the bridge for the target. I intended to stop at the store and ask whether the ambulance had screamed past. Another second and I didn't have to ask: the white-and-orange van squealed up Route 3 and sped over the causeway. I downshifted a couple gears to put us in close pursuit. I threw the emergency light on the floor. I did not want to alert Twitchell any sooner than necessary. The red light continued to rotate, beaming its light around the cab. I barely noticed. With any luck, Twitchell's escape route would be just over the bridge, and he would be so intent on searching for it that he would never see us.

That hope died a premature death. My headlights beamed through the van, up to where Twitchell sat on the jump seat, covering Robyn with the revolver. His head whipped around and he stared straight at me. He smashed the rear window and pointed his revolver through the hole. A flash indicated he had fired, but over the roaring engine I heard nothing. I began a violent jinking to foil his aim as he fired again. Flash, no sound, but my windshield starred, collapsing inward.

"Two can play this," said Smith. He opened the door; shotgun in one hand, holding tightly onto the end of the seat belt, he braced and fired. The howling engine and whistling wind could not drown out the report from that cannon. Twitchell ducked, but any hope he had been hit faded fast. He rose, smashed the other window, and took aim on Smith. He fired four more shots, with no results. Smith emptied the shotgun into the ambulance without success. He reloaded, firing again with remarkable speed and precision. His third blast hit the mark: a scatter pattern of black holes perforated the door. Twitchell dove low, but I knew the pellets had no hope of penetrating the steel to do him any harm.

Smith retreated, hauling the door shut and refastening his seat belt. "He's too small a target. I might as easily hit Robyn."

"Smash out the windshield," I yelled. "Then shoot straight ahead. Keep him pinned down so I can get closer."

As Smith pulled and pushed away the remnants of the glass, I stomped on the accelerator. The distance narrowed as we raced over the bridge at ninety miles per hour. I wondered why Robyn wasn't slowing down. I doubted Twitchell had the coordination to both cover her and shoot at us while the van bucked and reared. As long as he kept out of sight, I had no way of knowing what he had on her. Beside me, Smith created a firing port, drew a bead on the ambulance, but held his fire. Twitchell's head popped up once, but dropped instantly as he saw the barrel staring back. "I don't have a clean shot," Smith cried.

With less than fifteen feet separating us, the ambulance brake lights ignited. The chattering squeal of heavy-duty tires skidding over the pavement screamed in my ears as I fought to control the wheel. I stood on the brake, but could not stop fast enough. The bumpers connected, but did little to dampen the inertia of four tons of moving trucks. My seat belt bit sharply, my head flopped forward. An explosive hiss filled the compartment as the airbags inflated, slowing but not stopping my progress. The back doors to the ambulance buckled. The plastic taillight lenses shattered. My hood crumpled upward, and abrupt blackness signaled the destruction of my headlights. As I kept on the brakes, the ambulance began to pull away; I realized Robyn had released the brakes, and punched it. Smith altered his aim, firing both barrels toward the tires as the ambulance headed away.

We slid to a full stop. "You all right?"

"Fine, fine. Hurry up, I think I hit him."

The engine had stalled. It caught reluctantly with a horrid screeching. I figured it had to be the fan rubbing against the radiator. White steam thick with the pungent, sweet scent of coolant drifted into the cab. I knew we had very little time. For now, it still ran. I pushed the air bag out of the way, slammed the gearshift into first, snapped on the roll bar spotlights, and charged into the attack.

Five hundred yards ahead the ambulance bore right, into the dead-end road to the Hancock County Airport. Its lights winking, a small plane climbed into the clear night sky overhead as I turned onto the access road. At last Twitchell's escape plan became clear. Caught for a second in my spotlights, the rear tire smoked as they slid in. A glance at my instruments revealed fatal damage to the cooling system had already raised the coolant temp into the red. The engine, if not the whole truck, was doomed. I figured I might as well get everything out of the truck it had left. I floored it, cutting across the grass to intercept.

We had gone no more than two hundred yards when a loud explosion, a blast of black smoke, and a grinding crunch halted our pursuit: the engine seized. I pushed in the clutch, but that too failed. We bounced over the top of a small hill, and started rolling down the other side toward a car-sized granite boulder. I jumped on the brakes, but there wasn't anything left. The truck skidded uncontrolled down the grass toward the stone. "Brace yourself!"

The truck slammed into the boulder. White steam billowed from beneath the crumpled hood, gushing through the open windshield to fill the cab with dense fog. My chest and hips ached from where the belt had twice bit into them, but I had not hurt anything else. "You all right?"

Smith's belt had not caught so quickly: where his head had hit the frame a spreading spot oozed blood down one side of his face. "No time to waste lamenting our wounds."

I kicked open my door, jumped out, and ran across the grass toward the ambulance a hundred yards off. Twitchell punched out the side windows and opened fire, but the shots did not come close. The ambulance careened into one last corner; Robyn was going far too fast. The top-heavy van leaned far to the left, hanging on two squealing wheels. It seemed about to recover, then tipped toward the outside of the turn. With a surprising absence of sound, the ambulance toppled onto the grass, sliding down the slope to a stop.

I pumped my legs even faster, charging for the wreck. From my angle the cab was hidden. I couldn't tell whether Twitchell had survived—or Robyn. I prayed she had her seat belt on. Worried as I was, I didn't forget my duty: I reached the ambulance with my pistol cocked and ready. The loading door swung wide. Twitchell jumped out, a bulky case in his hand. He fired a wide shot, then bolted toward the hangar. I gave three steps chase, then halted beside the upturned chassis of the ambulance. First things first.

Robyn hung on the edge of the passenger door, pulling herself clear. A wound on her forehead would become an enormous bruise. Blood flowed from a dozen cuts and scratches along her arms. Smith, who had not spared Twitchell a second glance, jumped onto the van side to lend her a hand, while I climbed up to join them. "You all right?" I asked.

"I guess so," she said, dazed. "How did I do?"

I took her hand, holding it tightly. "You did fine."

"He kept wanting to go faster. Your lights blinded me, and I couldn't see him. He kept yelling, 'Faster! Faster, or I'll kill you!' I told him I didn't think I could, and he—"

"Ssh. Don't worry about it," I soothed. "We have to talk."

Through the sweat, the blood, and the pain, she smiled. "Get that asshole, first."

Smith took my hand from hers, grabbing me by the shoulders. "She'll be all right. If Twitchell reaches a plane, he's history. Understand?"

My eyes and thoughts lingered on Robyn only a second before I met his gaze. "I understand."

He handed me his shotgun. "Have some extra firepower."

I took Robyn's hand again. "I'll be back."

"I'll be here," replied Robyn.

"Go!" yelled Smith.

I jumped to the ground and ran toward the planes.

Hancock County Regional isn't much more than a paved cow pasture. Most of the business and traffic come from local private pilots. There are a few scheduled flights via commuter lines, but not enough to warrant a full-time staff. The terminal and hangars were empty, lit only by the automatic night lights. The terminal would be locked. I figured Twitchell would be more likely to be wandering amid the aircraft than trying to break into the terminal. I kept my pistol in my right hand, the shotgun in my left. Out among the planes, I would need precision, not firepower. The blue taxiway lights offered little help; the amber runway lights were too distant. Intermittent light from the beacon—green, then white, then green again—was more a nuisance than a help. The planes cast angular, crisp-edged shadows everywhere. I would be damn lucky to find Twitchell; then again, he'd be lucky to find me.

He got lucky first. I heard the bullet sink into the plane beside me before I heard the double report. I dropped to the ground and rolled under the closest plane, ran to the next and rolled under it before looking back. Nothing. I moved around the nose to get a better look. Three planes down, under the imposing nose of a vintage DC-3, a shape detached from the undercarriage. I crouched, squeezing off two shots. The range was too long: I missed. I had not been shooting at shadows. The shape dove back underneath the bulbous fuselage.

I preferred to risk losing him rather than stay put and offer an easy target. I ran past two more planes beside the hangar, kept low between it and a twin-engine jet, angling toward the terminal. I peeked out from behind the engines. Twenty yards down the line Twitchell advanced plane to plane, searching, hunting, running to the next one. I had a better bead on him than he had on me. I used the beacon, hiding during the white, and searching during the green. During the next cycle I took up a firing stance, and when he appeared I shot twice. He fired back, noisily peppering the aluminum siding. Fearing I was not as invisible as I'd hoped, I dove under the wings of the jet, came out on the other side, and dodged wingtips until I came out at the front of the line. I doubled back to his starting point, and established my position under the DC-3, waiting for any immediate response. None came. In the near distance, I heard sirens. It was about time. Once they arrived, Twitchell had no chance. I couldn't wait for reinforcements, however; I didn't want to lose him now. I headed back under the tail, emerging cautiously into the next row. No shadows, nothing moved. I reached the last row, but still came up with nothing. Where had he gone?

From the far side of the hangar came the whine of an engine start. He had tricked me into going the wrong way, then doubled back. I ran toward the noise as the whine became a cough and a sputter, then a roar as the engine caught. It had barely got its breath before he gunned it. The flat fan howl of the propeller reverberated off the aluminum hangar walls. I had not even reached the near wall when a white nose separated from the line of parked aircraft, dragging a twin-engine Beechcraft after it. The tail had not cleared the line before the plane turned toward me. The right propeller glittered, a silver disk in the beacon. The loud whine and the slowly spinning left prop betrayed his left engine start as he edged onto the taxiway. I drew up short, knelt, took aim, and fired the rest of the clip at the cockpit. The left window starred, but if it accomplished anything else, I couldn't see. As the nose centered on me, I abruptly realized that, while he could not fire his revolver, a spinning propeller makes an excellent weapon. I ran flat out for the shelter of the planes, hoping he wouldn't sacrifice his escape for my sake.

The plane maintained its course right at me. I wondered if I had correctly divined his intentions. Abruptly the plane pivoted, pulling away. The left engine coughed, spluttered, and caught. I stopped, dropped the Beretta onto the concrete, and drew up the shotgun. The plane cruised by unhindered as I fired: black holes peppered the fuselage; a passenger window imploded. I tried for the engine, but too much wing blocked the shot. I pumped and fired again, this time at the wing tank. A ragged hole appeared near the base of the tank, immediately accompanied by the sharp tang of escaping gasoline. I pumped and fired, this time opening holes along the tail. I fired again, but the plane was an insignificant target as it sped away; there was no sense in wasting ammunition.

Beyond the Beech, blue, red, and white flashing lights converged on the airport. They would be right beside me in a half-minute. By then Twitchell would be gone. Before I could explain the situation and get a cruiser to block the runway, Twitchell would be airborne.

I ran. I began to run to where the Beech already revved up its engines, but I soon realized I'd never reach him in time. I cut across the grass median to the runway. I dropped to a crouch and reloaded the shotgun. I braced, ready to fire, but as my finger tightened, I realized I had to wait for my shot. I lowered the shotgun, then brought it up slowly and held it steady. The plane was approaching, gaining speed. Twitchell snapped on the landing lights, blinding me. He was closing, fast. Three hundred yards off and accelerating rapidly, he wasn't going to be brought down by random shots. I took a deep breath and waited. The plane came closer: two hundred yards. The landing lights made it impossible to see much of anything, so I focused on the red-and-green wingtip lights. One hundred yards: Twitchell yanked back on the control wheel too soon; the nose wheel left the runway, but the Beech lacked the speed to lift off. The rise of the nose took the landing lights out of my eyes. About fifty yards away, the plane filling my entire field of vision, I sighted on one engine and fired. The plane kept coming, the propellers seamless silver disks, the engines wailing. I flattened onto the concrete as the prop chopped the air over my head, the landing gear whistling by only a yard above me. I pumped, rolled onto my back, and fired my last shot somewhere over my head as the plane screamed past.

The roar of the engines receded into the night as the echo of the gunshots reverberated off the hangars like distant thunder. The engine notes weren't uniformly smooth anymore: one engine hesitated. It sputtered roughly, backfired, emitting uneven puffs of thick, oily smoke. A quarter-mile down the runway, less than a hundred feet in the air, the landing gear began to retract. The engine note descended into a coughing fit. The plane banked right. With one loud bang and a tongue of orange flame from the exhaust, the spluttering and coughing ceased. The beacon caught the plane just then: the right prop no longer a silver disk but instead a spoked green wheel trailed by billows of green smoke.

The bank steepened. The left engine roared as strongly as ever, but to no avail. The plane rolled up on one wing, falling until the right wingtip scraped the runway amid a shower of white sparks. The tank separated, the wingtip crumpled. The plane cartwheeled across the runway, off the grass ringing the north side of the airport. The last of its momentum carried the wreckage into the first row of trees and tore off the remaining wing stubs. For a second nothing happened, then a searing white flame erupted from the left engine, starkly illuminating everything around. The white turned orange, the detonation growing outward as it encompassed the surrounding trees. It took a few seconds for the sound to reach me, but when it did, the loudest blast I have ever heard ripped at my eardrums. Even at that distance, a formidable shock wave pushed me flat on the ground.

Instinctively reacting to the emergency, I began to run toward the wreck. I had only reached the grass when I stopped, staring at the flames. Let the other paramedics pick up the pieces, I thought. I wondered if the body amid the wreckage was any more recognizable than Frederickson's body nine days before. I turned around, and began jogging toward the ambulance.

12

Tuesday Night

Patrol Area: Mount Desert Island
Hot, humid; skies overcast;
wind 5–8 knots, SE

The annoying drone of my alarm dragged me from a world of exquisite dreams to gray-painted reality. My first reaction was surprise. During my extended week on the Frederickson case, I had grown used to days that began after sunrise and ended late in the night. The ensuing two weeks' vacation ensured a thorough reset of my internal clock to banker's hours. I cherished it. I hadn't expected to get much sleep the afternoon before my return to patrol, but my mind and body knew the routine too well. I hit the button, checking the time: 4:30 P.M., right on schedule. I massaged the back of my neck, indulged in a few moments wishing I could stay in bed, then tossed back the covers. A quick twenty sit-ups got the blood flowing, before I headed for the shower.

It was easy to fall back into the routine. As I shaved, dug out the components of a fresh uniform, and started hooking the buttons, I forgot I hadn't done so for nearly a month. When I bent to reach for my shoes, a shooting pain from my neck through my shoulder reminded me of the grabbing seat belt that had probably saved my life. It simultaneously refreshed the memory of the entire case, from its vague beginning to the desperate, frenetic close. As soon as I remembered, a peculiar comfort swept over me. In the mirror was a reflection at once familiar and new: the old clothes, the same job, but not exactly the same man. I hitched up my gun belt, took my gun out of its case, and dropped it into the holster. The civilian and the detective were gone, while the patrolman had undeniably returned.

I glanced at the kitchen clock on the way out—I didn't really notice the time, only that I wasn't late. Before going to sleep, I had placed my briefcase, clipboard, and bag on the table, expecting to be late. Now they were a convenience. I grabbed them in one easy swoop, hooked the keys on one finger, and slipped out the back door. I had been issued Hancock County's brand-new State Police Special Caprice while my car got a new fender. Just the short trip from Ellsworth had convinced me of its exquisite appointments. A delicate balancing act kept everything in place while I fitted the key into the passenger door lock. The damn thing wouldn't slide into the slot; with all the weight I carried I couldn't properly work it. My gear ended up in a disorderly pile on the grass while I found the key to try again. Even with both hands free, it refused to budge. "Oh, shit," I said as I immediately realized the problem: I'd picked up Robyn's spare keys by mistake. I didn't even step back inside, just reached around the corner of the doorway to exchange key rings. In the brief moment I held the door, Binkley decided he had had enough time outside, and scurried around my feet.

I set the case and the clipboard on the seat, then put the bag in the trunk. The collection was not right: something was missing. I swore as I realized I had left my Mag-Lite in the truck. Beside the cruiser sat my new burgundy-and-black 4x4, the dealer plates still on it. When I opened the door, the overpowering new-car smell of fresh plastic, virgin carpet, and perfumed cleaners assailed my nose. I'd hardly gotten used to the truck yet, but already its power and comfort made me forget my old one. I retrieved the MagnaLite and climbed into the plush, soft seat of the cruiser. The oddest, sharpest reminder that I was not out for a pleasure cruise was my gun: it felt alien to me. I had not been in a cruiser or performed any act as a police officer since firing the gun at the airport. I shook off the distraction, started the cruiser, and headed for the harbor.

Street parking was full as I approached the diner. I had just decided to go down to the wharf when a pair of brake lights alerted me. I slowed, and as a beige Lincoln with Virginia plates pulled away from the curb, I maneuvered into the spot before it could get cold. The Caprice still felt unfamiliar. I ended up farther from the curb than I would have liked, but not so far that I felt a need to try again.

I decided first to check in with my father. I saw the *Janet Kathleen III* tied up at the bait dock. I strolled down the pier, past a pair of noisy and probably inebriated boaters. They turned suddenly very quiet and walked rigidly erect when they saw my uniform. I said nothing. It looked as if they were in for the night. So long as they stayed off the roads, they weren't my concern. My father stood at the break in the rail, guiding a blue plastic bucket with one hand while he worked the hoist controls in the other. I leaned against the rail beside him. "Evening, Dad."

"Hey, Jimmy, how's it goin'?" he said without taking his eyes off the bucket.

"Can't complain."

He pushed the bucket clear of the dock, then began to lower it. Time enough for him to check me over quickly. "Back in uniform, I see."

"Yuh. Back to the old routine."

"Could be a lot worse," he said with an odd cheerfulness. He expertly delivered the bucket onto the deck with barely a sound. He let go of the controls, mounting the ladder to descend to the deck. "You headed up for dinner?" he said on his way down.

"Thought I'd grab a bite before I left."

He abandoned the ladder for the boat, setting it gently rocking, squeaking softly as the gunwale rubbed against the pilings. A jerk on the shackle and a tug on the chain, and the lifting tackle came clear of the bucket. "I'm heading up there later. Just trying to get a head start on tomorrow. It's awful down here in the mornings now."

"I don't doubt it." With the high point of the lobster season, a good run on fishing going on, and the added burden of the tourist trade, the town dock was an extremely busy place in the mornings. It would be like that until August, when the fishing started to slacken. Two more foul-smelling buckets waited on the dock, so I picked up the hoist controls. "You clear?"

He began lugging the bucket back toward the transom. "Hoist away."

I hit the button. The motor whined; without any load, the lifting tackle rapidly came up. I started to grab it, but he stopped me. "Don't bother," he said sharply. He already had the first bucket tied down, and was halfway up the ladder. "No sense messin' up your uniform. Bad enough that you probably picked up the smell."

"Just trying to help."

As his head broached the level of the dock, he looked up at me, grinning. "I know." He had the lift tackle in his hand before he stepped off the ladder, hauling it over to the bucket. "I'll finish this up, put her out on the mooring, and head over for dinner with your mother. Maybe I'll see you up there before you go."

"Okay." I slapped his shoulder. "If I don't see you, take it easy, huh?"

He winked at me. "You too, Jimmy."

As I turned to head up to the diner, a flash of color caught my eye. When I looked up, *Aquila*'s red hull turned into the wind just off her mooring. The now familiar man inside the cabin gave the wheel a sharp turn, hopped onto the deck, gingerly fetched the boat hook, and deftly brought the pick-up buoy onto the bow as the boat drifted to a stop. A few quick turns on the cleat, and Smith had *Aquila* secured down for the night.

Smith waited until the wind pushed the boat back before he let go. He looked up just then. His steady, even gaze fixed on me at once. Simultaneously, we raised our arms in silent greeting. Whenever we met, there was a hesitation, as if we wanted to say something more but couldn't find the words. We'd stare at each other as if unsure we knew one another. The moment passed. He returned to the cabin, and I climbed up to the diner.

Inside, a handful of people spread themselves thin across the floor. At a window table, the swerving couple from the dock contemplated the menu in shrill tones, oblivious to everyone around them. In the corner, four gray-haired diners spoke in constantly changing pairs, dropping one topic for another: a group of people who savored each other's company and were quite clearly having a good time.

By the door sat the Eagle Harbor elders, talking, drinking coffee, watching the world pass by outside their window. As I closed the front door a silence, strange for its sudden arrival, draped over their table. Berman froze, his coffee cup halfway between the saucer and his lips, his dull gray eyes locked on mine. If not for the wisp of smoke drifting out of Killington's pipe, he could have been a statue. Adams, his back to me, seemed to be able to see me reflected in his friends eyes. Even though he didn't turn around, I had the distinct feeling he was staring at me more intently than the others. I became acutely aware that Adams wasn't just looking at me, he was examining my uniform. It was the first time I had appeared in uniform since the investigation ended. What were they thinking? The jingle of the bell jarred me out of my trance. I tipped my hat into my hand. "Evening, gentlemen."

Blank stares and still lips were the only reply. Then, as if on command, they all moved together. Killington switched his pipe to the other side of his mouth as Adams stirred his coffee. "Evening, Jimmy," said Berman. The cup soundlessly nestled back into the saucer. "How you doin'?"

"Pretty good, Ed," I replied, quite honestly. "You?"

"The same," he answered with a nod. The tiniest crack of a smile danced on his lips. It wasn't much, but it was as much pleasure as he'd shown at his daughter Cathy's wedding. I could read an awful lot into that hint of levity; I'm sure I saw things in it that just weren't there. All the same, I knew the deacon had passed judgment on my work. "About the same."

"See you got a new car," said Adams. "Chevy, ain't it?"

"Yuh. Caprice," I told him. "Just a loaner, though."

"Not too bad. How's she ride?"

"Pretty smooth, Sam. Can hardly feel the bumps out on the McKay road."

"Been thinkin' about a new car," he said to no one in particular. "Looks pretty good. How much it cost?"

"It's a police special—loaded to the max. Ran around twenty thousand, I think."

"Ought to be cheaper for a civilian like you," said Killington.

"Still be a big chunk of cash," grumbled Adams. "Lot to spend on a damn car."

"What are you complaining about?" goaded Killington. "It's not like you don't have it. That can't be much more than that brand new truck you buy every year."

"I don't get one every year," he said defensively. "Maybe every other year, but that's because they wear out so damn soon."

I left them to their debate, glad to have the noise back. Two male teenagers took up the counter seats at the far end, talking in low whispers. I recognized them the way I knew most of my sister's friends: familiar faces, unknown names. They tried their best not to look my way, but I could tell they had seen the uniform. I ignored them, taking a seat near the middle. Denise was setting up an order, arranging the tartar sauce, plastic baskets, and red-and-white paper lobster buckets on the tray for optimum balance. She looked up and waved at me. "Janet, Jimmy's here," she yelled into the kitchen.

The double door flipped open; my mother came right behind it, drying her hands on a well-worn towel. "Hi, Jimmy. Didn't know if you were going to make it."

"I told you I'd be down."

"I know, I know." She tossed the towel under the countertop. "I figured first day back, you'd be running late."

"Sorry to disappoint you."

"Oh, shush," she snapped. Without asking she took a cup and saucer from the tray behind her. "What do you want?"

"Who's in the kitchen tonight?"

"Paul and Bob."

Great, I thought. Amateur night. "Who's the fry guy tonight?"

"Paul."

"Is he in a good mood?"

She shrugged. "I guess."

"If he'll give me some of the shrimp that came off the truck this morning, I'll have the shrimp basket."

"He'll have to go out to the walk-in. He owes me a favor, but he'd still better be in a real good mood." She glanced up to check her tables. "You want anything, Sam?"

"I'm fine, Janet," said Adams.

"Let me go see the master chef." Sidestepping Denise and her full tray, she went into the kitchen. An abandoned copy of the *Bangor Daily News* rested on the next stool. I scanned through it. I thought I had been out of touch a long time. Only a few minutes' reading proved that I had not missed much.

The door bell jingled, announcing a young couple's entrance. They'd moved to Eagle Harbor about two years before, taking up residence in one of the older houses along the ridge. They kept to themselves their first year, but since the spring thaw they had begun coming out of their shells. They spent many nights at the diner, became quite active members of the church. He waved to Ed Berman, with whom they chatted briefly. They drifted to a corner table, passing Denise on her way back. She dropped her tray on the pass-through, then stood before my station. "Evening, Jimmy. How you doin'?"

"Pretty good, Denise."

"See Robyn much?"

"More than a little."

With Denise, the urge to pry is never far beneath the surface. "You see her a lot?"

The funny thing about talking to Denise is that sometimes you just want to play her along. "More than a little."

"Your mother said you went away for a while."

"We did."

"Where'd you go?"

I sipped my coffee. "Away."

"You're in one of those moods, huh?"

"Looks like it, Denise."

"I hope you're all recovered and rested up," she smirked.

"Kind of eager to go back, though."

"Go back to what? Policing?"

"Yuh. It's what I do, Denise."

"I know it is, Jimmy. I don't get it, but I know. None of us thought Mike could do anything like that. What a shock."

"I couldn't really believe it either, at first. But when the evidence started to stack up—well, I couldn't deny the truth."

"A drug kingpin right here, living among us. A trusted and respected citizen, of all people. I can't believe it. I mean, I know it's true and all, but I just can't believe it."

I nodded. "I know what you mean."

"Marisa, my friend from Northeast Harbor who works at the hospital, she said they couldn't identify the body. As if he escaped."

"It wasn't easy to identify, but we managed. I'm convinced that was Mike Twitchell laid out up to Eastern Maine Medical Center." I involuntarily shivered. The whole grisly event at the morgue was seared into my memory. I hadn't wanted to be present for the autopsy, yet, at the same time, I had to know, firsthand, that it was finally over. I wouldn't be able to accept the results if I had not been at least a mute party to the examination. This was no monster who had taken over the village; it was a man, a mortal man, and I had killed him. I didn't want to be there, but I couldn't have passed it up: the clinical choreography; stark, bare illumination; the novel and horrible stench; the businesslike voices and the dry, scratchy rasp whenever the body was moved, or prodded, or cut; the state police detectives taking exhaustive notes while Dr. Gibbs analyzed the body in a detached, even bored manner; Wiley, gowned and masked, pointing at marks on and items embedded in the body on the stainless steel table; Dickinson's strong grip on my arm ushering me out of the room before I passed out.

"Twitchell won't be back."

"How's Robyn handling it all?"

"She's okay."

"All healed up?"

"Physically. She's still feeling the shock mentally after being taken hostage, being caught in the middle of the crossfire. She'll be fine."

"I know." She sighed mightily. "Thank God that's over."

"For now."

"What do you mean?"

"You're kidding yourself if you think it can't happen again."

She looked at me quizzically, trying to gauge my sincerity. I must have convinced her: she shuddered from head to toe. "At least it's over for now."

"That's what I said, Denise."

"It's a good thing you cracked the case."

"I hardly broke the case, Denise. I just did my part."

"You did a hell of a lot, Jimmy. It wouldn't have gone the same if it had been somebody else. But it was you, you know? People are going to be talking about this for a long, long time."

I sipped my coffee. "Maybe we should talk more around here and whisper a little less."

"I heard some people talking." She nodded with pretentious subtlety to indicate the men by the door. "Some people are wondering what you're going to do next."

"I just want to get back to work."

"Well, you were always funny that way." Elbows splayed wide, she reached behind her to adjust her hair. "Me, I'd rather stay on vacation than go back to work."

"Find another job."

"Around here? Are you crazy? Besides, I love it here."

The contradiction so obvious to me would no doubt be lost on her. I saw no reason to bother pursuing it. "Whatever works for you, Denise."

"I like working with people," she said simply. She slid forward, jamming herself hard against the counter. "See them over there?" she uttered softly, tilting her head toward the windows.

"Who? That loud foursome by the window?"

"No. The couple, you dope."

"You mean the Knights."

"Oh, you know them?"

"I know of them, is more like it."

"Knight is his name, you know," she said. "Her name is Toscetti."

I nursed my coffee. It might have to last a long time. "So?"

"They're not married."

"It's not a crime."

"She's pregnant."

"Not a crime, either."

"Oh, come off it. You know what I mean. They're living together. They must have had a little accident."

I shrugged. "Maybe they planned it that way. Not everyone gets married anymore, Denise."

"Well, maybe not," she said haughtily. "But it still isn't right."

"Come on, Denise. It happens all the time."

"That doesn't justify anything."

"You know, Denise, sometimes you just flat-out amaze me."

She screwed up her eyes to look me over very closely. "I'm going to assume that was a compliment, even if it was a backhanded one. Now, you owe me one."

"I don't owe you anything."

"Quid pro quo, Jimmy," she answered sharply. Ever since she rented *Silence of the Lambs,* it's the same thing when you talk to her. "I told you about Toscetti. Quid pro quo."

"I didn't ask about Toscetti," I protested.

"That's not the point. It's your turn. Did they go, or didn't they?"

You have to pay close attention to stay with Denise and her sudden, unpredictable tacks. The way she checked to see if my mother was close at hand before she told me who "they" were. "I really don't know, Denise."

"You must know something. She's your sister."

"Before I went away, she asked to borrow some of my hiking gear. She took mostly cooking and camp gear." I hadn't given the matter any thought since she had asked. Now, with Denise's questions, I wondered why. I wasn't accusing her of anything—it was her life to lead—but I was a little curious. "She might have stayed out a few nights, but I don't know when, or where, or with whom. For all I know she set up camp in my mother's back yard with three of her basketball friends."

"You don't know what she did with it?"

" 'Fraid not."

"Well, that's not much help," she said sourly.

I shrugged. "Sorry. I don't know anything else."

Denise pursed her lips. "I can't believe you don't even know what your own sister is doing. She's your sister, Jimmy!"

"What can I say? We don't see much of each other during the summer. It's been that way as long as I can remember."

"That's awful."

The lack of sincere sympathy told me the only reason she thought it was awful concerned the fact that her best source was a dead end. "That's life."

I thought I might escape with that, but when she set her elbows on the counter, checking both ways, I knew I had only postponed my fate. "I heard they reopened the murder investigation."

"I don't think so," I said, sipping the coffee. "I think the conclusion was thorough and final."

"You've been off for two weeks," she shot back. "Things may have changed up there since you left. You know how mad Walker was with you. Maybe he reopened the case behind your back."

"Walker isn't mad at me." I sipped my coffee. "Just concerned."

"That's not what I heard."

"Don't believe everything you hear, Denise."

"I have my sources. One of those female trooper friends of yours was by last week."

Denise made no distinction between patrolmen and state troopers. "Sarah Pendleton?"

"No. She's the one with a single eyebrow, isn't she?"

Not flattering, but accurate. "Yuh, that's her."

"No, the other one. You know, the petite one with auburn hair and a tiny little waist."

"Rae Greene?"

"That's the one. She stopped by on patrol last week, and told me all about you and the sheriff."

"I can imagine."

"She said you were lucky you still had a job."

"It's not luck, Denise."

"Well, with you on the sheriff's shit list, if they—"

"I'm not on anybody's shit list."

"Whatever you want to call it, if they—"

"Walker and I had a very long talk. We reached complete agreement. He's glad to have me back on patrol, and I'm glad to be doing it."

"Look, Jimmy, whatever. All I'm saying is that with your track record on this case and all, if they decided to look into the case again, they might not tell you."

"If they had reopened my case, then they would have called me for my notes," I replied coolly. "Unless. . . ."

I had dangled too tantalizing a lure for Denise to ignore. She leaned closer, her eyes wide with excitement, a feral grin on her glossy lips. "What? Unless what?"

"Unless, of course, I'm one of the suspects."

It took a moment to register, then she blinked. A puzzled looked washed over her face, then she narrowed her gaze and snapped my wrist with her washcloth. "Oh, very funny, Jimmy. Very, very funny."

She turned on her heel and lunged for the kitchen door, nearly knocking over my mother. A wise veteran of diner service, my mother did a graceful half-turn, raising the tray over her head as she spun before lowering it down to the counter before me, setting it down delicately without a drop spilled. "Take it easy, Denise," she warned the empty door. "What's the hurry?"

"Just wants to get away from me, I guess," I offered.

She set out a napkin-wrapped flatware set beside the dinner basket. "What did you say to her?"

"It's what I didn't say. She wanted me to—" I chopped my words abruptly, remembering the topic. "She wanted to know about the investigation."

"I thought it was over."

"It is. She heard somebody say it was open again, that's all."

My mother took out her check pad and began tallying. "Probably one of the Greer boys. They've been hanging around her a lot lately. The older one—what's his name?"

"Kurt," I supplied.

"Yes, Kurt. I think they're dating. At least one of them thinks so, anyway." She forgot what she was doing and stared off into space. "Kurt's a very impressionable young man, and not too long on brains. He's very active in the ambulance corps, you know."

"Really?" I had been toying with my shrimp and I didn't like what I was seeing. "I didn't know that."

"I think he'd really latched onto Mike Twitchell. Now there's a void in his life and he doesn't quite know how to fill it."

"Enter Denise."

"Something like that." She remembered what she was doing, completed the tally, then put away the checks. "I suppose he's telling all kinds of stories. Everybody is, after the fact. They knew this, they knew that. Never trusted him, they'll say, or they saw it coming. And, of course, they weren't all that close to him."

"Of course."

"I suppose it's some form of denial. Maybe they need it. I guess we were just never that close to him in the first place."

"Uh-huh." How conveniently she had forgotten all the times she'd waited on Twitchell, or worked beside him at functions. It's not like he had never been over to the house. She completely forgot how, when he first moved back, she'd been one of the mother hens clucking over him regularly while they tried unsuccessfully to set him up with one of her friends' eligible daughters. "Everybody has to cope, somehow."

"Yuh. And poor Denise," she said, hooking her thumb over her shoulder. "I think Kurt's muckled onto her and she's getting all she can handle. I'm sure he talks about little else right now. That's where she's getting those ideas. I'm sure of it."

"She's just mad at me because I won't confirm them."

"You know Denise—it's always some little thing. She's been like this all day. Asking everybody about everything. Just doesn't know when to quit. She's been pushing me to tell her about Jenny and her camping trip with Matt."

I nearly gagged. "Her what?"

"Your sister and her new boyfriend, Matt. They went camping a week ago," she said matter-of-factly. "I thought you knew."

"I did," I replied, trying quickly to sort everything out. "I didn't know *you* knew."

"Oh, please, Jimmy, I'm not stupid." She checked over her shoulder, then lowered her voice and leaned closer. "Denise seems to think it's a big scandal. I really don't know why. I suppose she's been talking with Steve's mother again. Their breakup wasn't exactly friendly, you know what I mean."

"Jen's always had a rough time with that part of it."

"Anyway, something—I don't know, something playful, something silly, something evil in me—just felt Denise coming on, and I decided to play her for a while. Now she's mad and I feel so guilty. I don't know how to calm her down again. Oh, Jimmy," she said, slapping a hand against her face. "The trouble I bring on myself sometimes."

"I know what you mean."

Her waitress radar picked up a subtle signal from the far table. "Got to go. Do you want any pie, or anything?"

"No, thanks."

"Good. Take your time." She took out her checks, ripped off the top one and jammed it on the spike beside the register. "First night back, so this one's on me."

"Thanks, Mom."

She pulled me closer, kissing me quickly on the forehead. "You be careful tonight, Jimmy. Take it easy while you get back into the routine." With an economy of motion that had to be seen to be believed, she swept up the coffee pot in one hand, dropped a handful of creamers into her apron, and slipped through the counter to tend to her party.

I was just about done with dinner. Paul was not the most experienced or patient fry cook. His effort tonight proved that not just *anyone* could run a Fryolater. I picked at the tastier morsels, ate the least soggy of the french fries, and was glad the coleslaw had been made during the afternoon by someone who knew what they were doing. I had probably eaten just barely more than half, but that was plenty. I pushed aside the remnants, taking a few minutes to finish my coffee. My mother returned with a new order, which she tagged to the spindle over the pass-through. Paul and Bob studied it as if it held some cosmic truth, then they went to work. Denise brought a tray out to the floor. She looked at me as she passed, smiling as if nothing had been wrong before. "Have a good night, Jimmy."

I took a last swallow of the cold coffee, wedged a couple dollars under the basket, and headed for the door. I waved to Berman, Killington, and Adams. Ed waved back, but the heated argument—about tires?—at the table took far too much from Murray and Sam to elicit any response. The doorknob twisted in my hand as I touched it. I pulled it back to stand toe-to-toe with my father. "Too late to share a bite, I guess."

"Wish I could stay, but I have to get to work," I said sincerely.

"I know." He clapped my shoulder, and winked. "See you in the morning. We'll try to pass each other around breakfast, okay?"

"Right, Dad."

"Take it easy." He slipped around me as I went outside. I took a quick step to the road, but one look at the white Cabriolet buzzing into the space behind me brought me up short. Robyn parked hastily, yanking up on the brake so hard, so early, that the nose pitched down. She ran around the VW onto the sidewalk, not stopping until we were in each other's arms. We stood together, silently rocking. Anyone passing by would have thought we'd been apart for weeks instead of a few hours. It wasn't easy for either of us; my return to work marked a transition back to a world forever changed. No, the world hadn't changed much at all, I thought: it was me.

She pulled her head back, though her arms remained tightly around my waist. "I knew I was going to be late."

"For what?"

"I'd wanted to have dinner with you before you went on duty, but I got tied up."

"Don't sweat it," I soothed. "It's only been a couple weeks. We've been on separate schedules all our lives. It'll take some time for us to get in sync."

"I wanted to be here tonight."

"It's all right."

"No, it's not all right," she said, putting her head back down again. "But it's what happened."

"Don't worry about it," I said.

"It's not dinner I'm worried about," she said sharply.

"I know," I said. I didn't know what else to say. "How'd things go this afternoon?"

"Fine," she answered, picking up her head. "The doctor said everything looks fine. It's healing up nicely. She recommended I go to therapy again."

"Couldn't hurt."

"I don't feel like talking through my feelings again," she said angrily. "It's a waste of my time and money, thank you very much."

"Hey, I didn't say you should go."

"I know." Her head fell once more to my chest. "I have my own therapy."

"Whatever works." We stood again, embracing silently. I didn't want to let go, but patrol duty called strongly. I checked my watch. I had used up just about all the extra time I'd earned by waking a little early. "Robyn, I have to go. I don't want to be late my first day back."

She didn't respond for a while. Then, in a delicate, fragile, but insistent voice, "Try to stay out of trouble tonight, huh?"

"Don't I always?"

"I suppose." She held me tighter. "Look out for the trouble that's out for you, too, okay?"

"Okay."

I am sure neither of us wanted to break off the embrace. I know I didn't. But work called and I knew she had things to do. We couldn't very well hold each other forever, standing in front of the Eagle Diner. Reluctantly, gently, I pushed her away. "Have a good dinner. You'd better stay away from the shrimp."

"Visit me at rehearsal."

"I will if I can. Otherwise, I'll see you back home."

"Take it easy, Jimmy." We kissed one more time, with an intensity that denied its brevity. Our hands lingered in each other's before she walked up the curb. Without looking back, I headed around the front of the cruiser, hopped inside, and fired it up. Unexpectedly, the magnitude of what I was doing overtook me. I felt as if I had opened a door and walked into a hurricane. The moment passed. It was time to get to work.

I took a good look around the interior. It had been so long since I had done patrol, it took a moment to remember where everything belonged. I had to turn on this radio, reset that computer, check the gas—there were so many things to do, I decided I might as well get rolling. I pulled away from the curb, careful to watch the road as I focused more attention than I should have on getting everything secured. I was passing through Manset before I got everything squared away. I pulled the mike off the bracket and keyed the transmitter. "County nineteen to Hancock Dispatch."

The reply came back pretty quick. "Dispatch. Go nineteen."

"County nineteen is ten-eight, patrolling on Route 102 North."

"Ten-four, county nineteen. Logged in at 18:57. Have a good one."

It felt paradoxically unfamiliar, yet comfortable, to be back at work, uniformed, driving a marked county car. It didn't take long before I felt I had settled into the old routine again. Tuesday nights are notoriously dull: a monotonous evening of idle patrolling, checking out backyard noises, running license plates that yield nothing. When I think back to the nights I have explored new side roads into the blueberry fields or parked on the pier—ostensibly compiling reports, but in fact watching the harbor seals—it seems, often as not, it's a Tuesday. Don't get the idea I'm shirking my duty, because I'm not. Hancock County is safe and secure as ever. It's just that there isn't a whole lot to do.

What seemed to be a normal amount of traffic slowly cruised along the road. Most of the plates were from out of state and most of the cars, full. When, after a few minutes, I drove past Echo Lake, I happened to notice a couple cars parked by the loading ramp, surrounded by a large group of teenagers. They didn't strike me as doing anything illegal, but I thought it might be a good idea to check it out anyway. I leisurely stopped the car, did a quick 180, and headed down to join them.

As you might expect, every bit of conversation ceased and all attention turned on me as I pulled into the parking lot. There were eight of them, three girls and five boys. The youngest looked to be about fifteen. Most were seventeen or eighteen, except for one guy with a scruffy beard who appeared three or four years older. One bare-legged girl stood shivering, her arms tightly wrapped around herself. It didn't take a genius to figure out they'd just been swimming. None of them looked the least bit threatening. With deliberate slowness, I opened my door and made my way across the lot to the cluster. I went directly for the oldest one. "Hey, guys. What's up?"

"Nothing," answered a tall, athletic blond male. An instinctive reaction from a teenager.

"We were just swimming," explained the bearded one. Up close, I realized he was probably not any older than his friends. "No big deal."

"Good," I replied amiably. "Been here long?"

"No," he replied quickly. "Half an hour maybe."

"Okay. What's your name?"

"Paul."

"Paul what?"

"Paul O'Toole."

I had unobtrusively noticed that one of the cars had an ordinary New York registration; the other, a commercial Connecticut.

Sounded like a good bet to me, so I decided to find out if O'Toole was inclined to tell the truth. "You live around here, Mr. O'Toole?"

He shook his head. "No, I'm from Connecticut. My stepfather has a summer home up here."

"Bar Harbor?"

"No, Northeast."

He seemed quite willing to talk: no hesitation, nothing to hide. "Are you all together?"

"Yeah. That's my cousin, up for the week," said O'Toole, pointing to the tall blond male. "We've just been killing time all day, you know? It's hot, so we figured we'd cool off before we found a place to eat."

Finding his courage, the cousin boldly stepped forward. "We weren't doing anything wrong. What's the problem?"

There was nothing here. Two of them, both fair-skinned, had the lobster-red of fresh sunburns on their faces. Upon closer inspection, I realized water darkened the light shirt of the shivering girl just where you'd expect her wet bathing suit to touch the fabric. Three others had hair that had obviously been wet within the last hour. O'Toole seemed completely lucid, unafraid to let me get close enough to smell his breath. I saw no evidence any of them had been drinking. As a group, they looked far more scared than suspicious. I had every reason to think I had heard the truth from Mr. O'Toole. "No problem," I said. "You know what time it is?"

"No." O'Toole shrugged, pasting a broad smile on his face. "It's summer. Who needs to know what time it is?"

"Well, it turns out you do," I explained. "It's about 7:30, you see. This area closes at 6:00. In fact, you're kind of lucky that the attendant didn't come down and lock the gate on you. Otherwise, you'd have to walk out, and I would have had to come get you out of here."

The smile faded fast. "Jeez, we didn't know. I mean, we looked for a sign, but we figured most of the things around here close at sunset, and the gate was open so—"

I stopped him with an upraised hand. "Don't sweat it. No harm done. But I think you'd better get yourselves squared away and clear out of here as soon as you can."

"Right," said O'Toole. "Right. We'll get out of here right away." He started pointing at people, telling them what to do. He sent the girls to get the towels off the beach, told the blond guy to go get a friend out of the outhouse, then issued car assignments. He had things well in hand. I sauntered back to the cruiser, and got in, leaving the door open.

In about two minutes, with the trunks jam-packed and the back seats full, they began to move, careful not to hurry as they bounced out of the lot and up the drive. After a moment's hesitation at the top, they headed south with careful precision. That was not the way to Northeast Harbor, but O'Toole had never said they were going home for supper. They were just kids, I thought. I secured my seat belt, closed the door, and resumed my patrol.

The kids at the ramp absorbed my mind completely. I can recall more than one summer evening spent doing more or less the same thing. I rounded the corner by the north end of Echo Lake, thinking about Mr. O'Toole and his friends—when suddenly I found myself at the scene of the murder that had changed my life. Inadvertently I slowed. In the faint moonlight, the road surface reflected a dull shine where tires had worn the pavement smooth. The tire marks still cut the pavement, ending abruptly at the road edge where the gravel tracks had long since been erased by rain and passing traffic. Maybe there remained marks in the grass; but driving by at night I couldn't see anything. Part of me wanted to stop and just walk around for a while. There was no compelling reason for me to do so; I kept on going.

For a few moments I drove in a disconnected daze, the cruiser following the road by autopilot as my mind drifted over the events of my last week at work. I wondered how much I would remember in a month, or a year, or ten years. Right then I was startled at the acute clarity with which some of the images dominated my memory: the mangled remains of the body heaped beside the road; Smith pointing a gun at me; floating in Eagle Harbor and watching bullets rip apart the dory; the nighttime pursuit; Twitchell's plane exploding. It had been one hell of a week.

A disembodied voice over the radio broke the spell. "Dispatch to county nineteen."

My hand, as usual, was right next to the microphone. "County nineteen. Go."

"What's your ten-twenty?"

The prospect of something besides driving around loomed suddenly ahead of me. A strange and unfamiliar feeling came over me: something like the plunge you sense as a roller coaster reaches the bottom of the track, just before it starts to climb again. I suppose it was part of the job, but maybe it was just me. Either way, I don't remember ever feeling that way before. "About two miles north of Somesville, northbound on 102."

"Stand by, county nineteen." The voice sounded tight, stressed.

It's hard to identify some people's voices over the radio. We have two dispatchers—Barbara Beecham and Jaime Ganem—whose voices are virtually indistinguishable. It made a difference, since nothing short of a disaster could rouse Barbara from her professional detachment, while Jaime could work herself into a frenzy over a vehicle with a flat tire. I noticed I had started to drum my fingers on the seat. I forced myself to stop. "Dispatch to county twelve."

"County twelve. Go." The voice of Jay Gibbon, a thirteen-year veteran, echoed hollowly; he was probably using his portable radio inside a building.

"County twelve, what's your ten-twenty?"

"Uhh, dispatch, I'm at the gatehouse at Lamoine beach."

A pause from the office: no doubt a moment of discussion between the dispatcher and the duty sergeant. "Disregard, county twelve. County nineteen, do you copy?"

"County nineteen. Standing by."

"County nineteen, respond to the Acadia Waterpark in Trenton to aid a motorist locked out of her car."

The feeling in my stomach fluttered away. "Ten-four dispatch. ETA around ten–fifteen minutes."

"Ten-four, nineteen. We will contact the Waterpark." When I listened carefully, I could easily tell—now—that it was Jaime working dispatch. I should have known. "We're trying to call Lamprey's; we will advise if we get him."

Lamprey's Service not only offered twenty-four-hour towing, but they also had the best man to get into locked cars. Before working at his father's gas station, Owen Lamprey had done time in the Maine Youth Center for his habit of stealing cars. "Send him down if you get him."

"Ten-four, county nineteen. Dispatch clear."

I put away the microphone. There was no point in hitting the blues; it wasn't an emergency. I'd save them to pass any cars that I couldn't legally pass otherwise. If the stranded car owner waited long enough, maybe next time she'd remember the wait—and her keys. I sighed, feeling my shoulders slump. An inauspicious beginning to what I expected was going to be another monotonous, dull evening.

I think I prefer them that way.